Bertha von Suttner

Lay down your arms

The autobiography of Martha von Tilling ... [Microform]

Bertha von Suttner

Lay down your arms
The autobiography of Martha von Tilling ... [Microform]

ISBN/EAN: 9783741154720

Manufactured in Europe, USA, Canada, Australia, Japa

Cover: Foto ©Andreas Hilbeck / pixelio.de

Manufactured and distributed by brebook publishing software
(www.brebook.com)

Bertha von Suttner

Lay down your arms

LAY DOWN YOUR ARMS

THE AUTOBIOGRAPHY OF

MARTHA VON TILLING

BY

BERTHA VON SUTTNER

AUTHORISED TRANSLATION BY

T. HOLMES

REVISED BY THE AUTHORESS

SECOND EDITION

" I'o vo gridando, Pace, Pace, Pace'
—PETRARCA

LONDON

LONGMANS, GREEN AND CO.

AND NEW YORK: 15 EAST 16th STREET

1894

TRANSLATOR'S PREFACE TO THE FIRST EDITION.

WHEN I was requested by the Committee of the International Arbitration and Peace Association, of which I have the honour to be a Member, to undertake the translation of the novel entitled *Die Waffen Nieder*, I considered it my duty to consent; and I have found the labour truly a delight. Baroness Suttner's striking tale has had so great a success on the Continent of Europe that it seems singular that no complete translation into English should yet have appeared. An incomplete version was published some time since in the United States, without the sanction of the authoress; but it gives no just idea of the work.

Apart from its value as a work of fiction—great as that is—the book has a transcendent interest for the Society with which I am connected from its bearing on the question of war in general and of the present state of Europe in particular. We English-speaking people, whether in England, in the Colonies, or in the United States, being ourselves in no immediate danger of seeing our homes invaded, and our cities laid under contribution by hostile armies, are apt to forget how terribly the remembrance of such calamities, and the constant threat of their recurrence, haunt the lives of our Continental brethren. Madame Suttner's vivid pages will enable those of us who have not seen anything of

the ravages of war, or felt the griefs and anxieties of
non-combatants, to realise the state in which people
live on the Continent of Europe, under the grim
"shadow of the sword," with constantly increasing
demands on the treasure accumulated by their labour,
and on their still dearer treasure—their children—drawn
into the ravenous maw of the Conscription, to meet
the ever-increasing demands of war, which seems daily
drawing nearer and nearer, in spite of the protestations
made by every Government of its anxiety for peace.

What can we expect to change this terrible condition
except the formation of a healthy public opinion? And
what can more powerfully contribute to its formation
than a clear conception both of the horrors and sufferings that have attended the great wars waged in our
times, and also of the inadequacy of the reasons, at
least the ostensible reasons, for their commencement,
and the ease with which they might have been avoided,
if their reasons had been indeed their causes? This work
appears to me of especial value, as setting this forth
more plainly than a formal treatise could do, and it is
towards the formation of such a public opinion that we
hope it may contribute. The dawn of a better day in
respect of war is plain enough in our country. We
have advanced far indeed from the state of things that
existed a century ago, when Coleridge could indignantly
say of England :—

> 'Mid thy herds and thy cornfields secure thou hast stood
> And joined the wild yelling of famine and blood !

England since then has given and is giving many
gratifying proofs of her sincere desire for peace, and
her readiness to submit her claims to peaceful arbitra-

tion. Is it too much to hope that we may see our country joining in some well-considered scheme for general treaties of Arbitration and for the institution of an International Court? And may we not hope that our influence, as that of a nation not implicated in the mad race of armaments, and yet not removed from the area of European war, may avail to bring the question of disarmament before an International Conference and thus introduce the twentieth century into a world in which there will be some brighter prospect than that

War shall endless war still breed ?

Let us trust that this may not be found quite an idle dream, and that we may without self-delusion look forward to a more happy era, and join the cry of Baroness Suttner's Rudolf—" Es lebe die Zukunft ".

HAIL TO THE FUTURE!

PREFACE TO THE SECOND EDITION.

THE rapid sale of the first edition of this translation has encouraged the Association at whose request it was made to endeavour to make it more widely known to the various English-speaking populations, by printing a larger edition at a lower price. It is hoped, also, that the enlarged circulation of a work so graphic, and written by one who has so thoroughly studied the real aspects of war, as seen by those on the spot, may lead not so much to sentimental emotions and vague protests, as to a business-like discussion of the means by which the resort to war may be at any rate rendered more and more infrequent. The English Government has lately given repeated and practical proofs of its sincere desire to substitute the peaceful and rational method of arbitration for the rough, cruel, and uncertain decision of force; and the conspicuous success of that method hitherto—though tried under circumstances not altogether favourable—must have prepared thinking men for the question: "Why cannot some scheme for the formation of an International Tribunal of Arbitration be formed and debated among the Powers who, by taking part in the Congress at Paris after the Crimean War, formally admitted the principle, and who have already seen it successfully applied in practice"? To this question, which has been frequently asked, no satisfactory answer has yet been given, nor to the further question why our Government should not introduce the subject to the great Powers, after showing so unmistakably its adherence to the principle. People differ, and, probably, will always differ, as to the light in which they regard war. A very small and rapidly diminishing minority regard it as a good thing in itself—most as an evil which in our present stage of civilisation cannot always be avoided; some as a crime formally prohibited by the moral law and the Christian religion. All of the two latter classes ought to join in any practical steps for diminishing the occasions of war; and of these the one which is most within the scope of politicians is the promotion of International Arbitration. The Association to which I belong has published this work in the confident hope that its circulation will aid in hastening this much-needed reform.

THE TRANSLATOR.

CONTENTS.

LAY DOWN YOUR ARMS.

CHAPTER I.

Girlish days and girlish fancies.—Youthful enthusiasm for war.—Education.—" Coming out."—An important visit to Marienbad.—Love at first sight.—Marriage.—A first child.—The baby-soldier.—Threatenings of war.—Declaration of war with Sardinia.—My husband is to see active service.

AT seventeen I was a thoroughly overwrought creature. This perhaps I should no longer be aware of to-day, if it were not that my diaries have been preserved. But in them the enthusiasms long since fled, the thoughts which have never been thought again, the feelings never again felt have immortalised themselves, and thus I can judge at this present time what exalted notions had stuck in my silly, pretty head. Even this prettiness, of which my glass has now little left to say, is revealed to me by the portraits of long ago. I can figure to myself what an envied person the Countess Martha Althaus —youthful, thought beautiful, and surrounded by all kinds of luxury—must have been. These remarkable diaries, however, bound in their red covers, point more to melancholy than to joy in life. The question I now ask myself is, Was I really so silly as not to recognise the advantages of my position or was I only so enthusiastic as to believe that only melancholy feelings

1

were elevated and worthy of being expressed in poetical form
and as such enrolled in the red volumes? My lot seems not
to have contented me—for thus is it written :—

"O Joan of Arc! heroic virgin favoured of heaven! could
I be like to thee—to wave the oriflamme, to crown my king,
and then die—for the fatherland, the beloved!"

No opportunity offered itself to me of realising these modest
views of life. Again, to be torn to pieces in the circus by a lion
as a Christian martyr, another vocation for which I longed—
see entry of September 19, 1853—was not to be compassed by
me, and so I had plainly to suffer under the consciousness
that the great deeds after which my soul thirsted must remain
ever unaccomplished, that my life, considered fundamentally,
was a failure. Ah! why had I not come into the world as a
boy? (another fruitless reproach against destiny which often
found expression in the red volumes); in that case I would
have been able to strive after and to achieve "the exalted".
Of female heroism history affords but few examples. How
seldom do we succeed in having the Gracchi for our sons, or
in carrying our husbands out to the Weinsberg Gates, or in
being saluted by sabre-brandishing Magyars with the shout,
"Hurrah for Maria Theresa our king". But when one is a
man, then one need only gird on the sword and start off to
win fame and laurels—win for oneself a throne like Cromwell,
or the empire of the world, like Bonaparte. I recollect that the
highest conception of human greatness seemed to me to be
embodied in warlike heroism. For scholars, poets, explorers,
I had indeed a sort of respect, but only the winners of battles
inspired me with real *admiration*. These were indeed the chief
pillars of history, the rulers of the fate of countries; these
were in importance and in elevation near to the Divinity,
as elevated above all other folk as the peaks of the
Alps and Himalayas above the turf and flowers of the
valley.

From all which I need not conclude that I possessed a
heroic nature. The fact was simply that I was capable of

enthusiasm and impassioned, and so I was of course passionately enthusiastic for that which was most highly accounted of
by my school-books and my *entourage*.

My father was a general in the Austrian army, and had
fought at Custozza under "Father Radetzky," whom he venerated to superstition. What eternal campaigning stories had I to
listen to! Dear papa was so proud of his warlike experiences,
and spoke with such satisfaction of the campaigns in which he
had fought, that I felt an involuntary pity for every man who
possessed no such reminiscences. But what a drawback for
the female sex to be excluded from this most magnificent
display of the manly feeling of honour and duty! If anything
came to my ears about the efforts of women after equality—
and of this in my youth but little was heard, and then usually
in a tone of contempt and condemnation—I conceived the
wish for emancipation only in one direction, *viz.*, that women
also should have the right to carry arms and take the
field. Ah, how beautiful was it to read in history about a
Semiramis or a Catherine II. "She carried on war with
this or that neighbouring state—she conquered this or that
country!"

Speaking generally it is history which, as our youth are
instructed, is the chief source of the admiration of war. From
thence it is stamped on the childish mind that the Lord of
armies is constantly decreeing battles, that these are, as it were,
the vehicle upon which the destiny of nations is carried on
through the ages; that they are the fulfilment of an inevitable
law of nature and must always occur from time to time like
storms at sea or earthquakes; that terror and woe are indeed
connected with them; but the latter is fully counterpoised, for
the commonwealth by the importance of the results, for individuals by the blaze of glory which may be won in them, or
even by the consciousness of the fulfilment of the most elevated
duty. Can there be a more glorious death than that on the
field of honour, a nobler immortality than that of the hero?
All this comes out clear and unanimous in all school-books or

"readings for the use of schools," where, besides the formal history, which is only represented as a concatenation of military events, even the separate tales and poems always manage to tell only of heroic deeds of arms. This is a part of the patriotic system of education. Since out of every scholar a defender of his country has to be formed, therefore the enthusiasm even of the child must be aroused for this its first duty as a citizen; his spirit must be hardened against the natural horror which the terrors of war might awaken, by passing over as quickly as possible the story of the most fearful massacres and butcheries as of something quite common and necessary, and laying meanwhile all possible stress on the ideal side of this ancient national custom; and it is in this way they have succeeded in forming a race eager for battle and delighting in war.

The girls—who indeed are not to take the field—are educated out of the same books as are prepared for the military training of the boys, and so in the female youth arises the same conception which exhausts itself in envy that they have nothing to do with war and in admiration for the military class. What pictures of horror out of all the battles on earth, from the Biblical and Macedonian and Punic Wars down to the Thirty Years' War and the wars of Napoleon, were brought before us tender maidens, who in all other things were formed to be gentle and mild; how we saw there cities burnt and the inhabitants put to the sword and the conquered trodden down—and all this was a real enjoyment; and of course through this heaping up and repetition of the horrors the perception that they were horrors becomes blunted, everything which belongs to the category of war comes no longer to be regarded from the point of view of humanity, and receives a perfectly peculiar mystico-historico-political consecration. War must be—it is the source of the highest dignities and honours—*that* the girls see very well, and they have had also to learn by heart the poems and tirades in which war is magnified. And thus originate the Spartan mothers, and the "mothers of the colours," and the frequent invitations to the cotillon which are given to a corps of officers when it is the turn of the ladies

to choose partners.[1] I was not like so many of my companions
in rank educated in a convent, but under the direction of
governesses and masters in my father's house. My mother I
lost early. Our aunt, an old canoness, filled the place of a
mother to us children—for there were three younger children.
We spent the winter months in Vienna, the summer on a family
estate in Lower Austria.

I can remember that I gave my governesses and masters much
satisfaction, for I was an industrious and ambitious scholar,
gifted with an accurate memory. When I could not, as I have
remarked, satisfy my ambition by winning battles like a heroine,
I contented myself with passing judgments on them in my
lessons, and extorting admiration by my zeal for learning. In
the French and English languages I was nearly perfect. In
geology and astronomy I made as much progress as was ordinarily accessible in the programme of the education of a girl, but
in the subject of history I learned more than was required of
me. Out of the library of my father I fetched the ponderous
works of history, in which I studied in my leisure hours. I
always thought myself a little bit cleverer when I could enrich
my memory with an event, a name, or a date out of past times.
Against pianoforte-playing—which was put down in the plan of
education—I made a resolute resistance. I possessed neither
talent nor desire for music, and felt that in it, for me, no satisfaction of my ambition would be found. I begged so long and
so pressingly that my precious time, which I might spend on
my other studies, should not be shortened by this meaningless
strumming, that my good father let me off this musical servitude,

[1] About the "Damenwahl" Bishop Ch. Wordsworth in his *Annals of
my Early Life*, p. 141, thus speaks, describing a ball at Greifswald:
"As I was standing among others looking on at a party of dancers, a
fair Greifswaldese, who had been one of them, came up to me and offered
me her hand. Not knowing who she was or what she said (for she spoke
in German), I could only make to her a low bow and look abashed. It
was explained to me afterwards that the cotillon, which was the dance
going on, allows any lady to offer herself as a partner to any gentleman
whom she chooses, and that I had declined a very pretty compliment."

to the great grief of my aunt, whose opinion was that without pianoforte-playing there could be no proper education.

On March 10, 1857, I celebrated my seventeenth birthday. "Seventeen already!" runs the entry of that date in my diary. This "already" is in itself a poem. There is no commentary added, but probably I meant by it "and as yet nothing done for immortality". These red volumes do me excellent service now, when I want to recall the recollections of a life. They render it possible for me to depict even down to their minutest details the feelings of the past, which would have remained in my memory only as faded outlines, and to reproduce whole trains of thought long forgotten, and long-silent speeches.

In the following carnival I was to be "brought out". This prospect delighted me, but not to such an extraordinary degree as is usually the case with young girls. My spirit yearned for something higher than the triumphs of the ballroom. What was it I yearned for? A question that I could have hardly answered to myself. Probably for love, though I was not aware of it. All those glowing dreams of aspiration and ambition which swell the hearts of young men and women, and which long to work themselves out all sorts of ways—as thirst for knowledge, love of travel or adventure—are in reality for the most part only the unrecognised activity of the growing instinct of love.

This summer my aunt was ordered a course of the waters at Marienbad. She was pleased to take me with her. Though my official introduction into the so-called "world" was not to take place till the following winter, I was yet allowed to take part in some little dances at the Kurhaus, with an idea also of exercising me in dancing and conversation, so that I might not be altogether too shy and awkward in entering on my first carnival season.

But what happened at the first party which I visited? A serious, vital love affair. It was of course a lieutenant of hussars. The civilians in the hall appeared to me like cockchafers to butterflies compared to the soldiers. And of the wearers of uniforms present the hussars were every way the most splendid; and, finally, of all the hussars Count Arno Dotzky was the most dazzling. Over six feet high, with black curly hair, twisted moustaches, glittering white teeth, dark eyes, with such a penetrating and tender expression—in fine, at his question, "Have you the cotillon free, countess?" I felt that there might be other triumphs as exciting as the banner-waving of the Maid of Orleans, or the sceptre-waving of the great Catherine. And he at the age of twenty-two felt something very similar as he flew round the room in the waltz with the prettiest girl in the hall (for one may say so thirty years afterwards)—at any rate he was probably thinking, "To possess thee, thou sweet creature, would outweigh a field-marshal's baton".

"Why, Martha, Martha," remonstrated my aunt, as I sank breathless on the seat at her side, covering her head-dress with the floating muslins of my robe.

"Oh, I beg your pardon, auntie," said I, and sat more upright. "I could not help it."

"I was not finding fault with you for that. My blame was for your behaviour with that hussar. You ought not to cling so in dancing, and who would ever look so close into a gentleman's eyes?"

I blushed deep. Had I committed some unmaidenly offence, and might the Incomparable have conceived a bad idea of me?

I was relieved of this anxious doubt before the ball was over, for in the course of the supper waltz the Incomparable whispered to me: "Listen to me. I cannot help it—you must know it even to-day—I love you."

This sounded a little more sweet than Joan's famous "voices". However, while the dance was going on I could not give him any reply. He must have seen this, for he came to a stop. We were standing in an empty corner of the room, and could continue the conversation without being overheard.

"Speak, countess; what have I to hope?"

"I do not understand you," was my insincere reply.

" Perhaps you do not believe in love at first sight? I myself held it a fable till now, but to-day I have experienced the truth of it."

How my heart beat! but I was silent.

" I have leapt head over heels into my fate," he continued. "You or no one! Decide then for my bliss or my death, for without you I neither can nor will live. Will you be mine?"

To so direct a question I was obliged to give some reply. I sought for some extremely diplomatic phrase which without cutting off all hope would sacrifice nothing of my dignity, but I got out nothing more than a tremulous whispered " yes ".

" Then may I to-morrow propose for your hand to your aunt, and write to Count Althaus?"

" Yes " again, this time a little firmer.

"Oh, what happiness! So at first sight you love me too?"

This time I only answered with my eyes, but they, I fancy, spoke the plainest " yes ".

On my eighteenth birthday I was married, after having been first introduced into society, and presented to the empress on my engagement. After our wedding we went for a tour in Italy. For this purpose Arno had got a long leave of absence; of retirement from the military service nothing was ever said. It is true we both possessed a tolerable property, but my husband loved his profession, and I agreed with him. I was proud of my handsome hussar officer, and looked forward with satisfaction to the time when he would rise to the rank of major, colonel, even general. Who knows? Perhaps he might even be called to a higher fortune; perhaps he might shine in the glorious history of his country as a great military commander!

That the red volumes exhibit a break just during the happy wedding time and the honeymoon is now to me a great grief. The joys of those days would indeed have been evaporated, dispersed, scattered to the winds, even if I had entered them there, but at any rate a reflection of them would have been kept bound tight between the leaves. But no! for my grief and my pain I could not find complaints enough—enough dashes and notes of exclamation. All grievous things had to be cried over carefully before the world, present and to come, but the happy hours I enjoyed in silence. I was not proud of my happiness, and so gave no one, not even myself, in my diary, any information about it, but sufferings and longings I looked on as a kind of merit, and so made much of them. But how true a mirror these red volumes present of my sad experiences, while in the happy times the leaves are quite blank! It is too silly! It is as if during a walk a man were to make a collection to bring home with him, and to collect of all the things he found by the way only those that were ugly, as if he filled his botanic case with nothing but thorns, thistles, worms and toads, and left the flowers and butterflies behind.

Still I recollect that it was a grand time, a kind of fairy dream. I had indeed everything that the heart of a young woman could wish : love, wealth, rank, fortune, and most of it so new, so surprising, so incredible ! We loved each other—my Arno and I—devotedly, with all the fire of our youth, abounding as it was in life and scenes of beauty. And it so happened that my darling hussar was besides a worthy, good-hearted, noble-minded young gentleman, with the education of a man of the world and a cheerful temper—it happened so ; for he might as well, for anything that the ball at Marienbad could testify to the contrary, have been a vicious, rough man—and as it happened also I was a moderately sensible, good-hearted creature ; for he might just as well at the said ball have fallen in love with a pretty capricious, little goose. And so it came about that we were completely happy, and that as a consequence the red-bound book of lamentation remained empty for a long while.

Stop; here I do find a joyous entry—Raptures over the new dignity of motherhood. On the 1st of January, 1859 (was not *that* a new-year's gift ?), a little son was born to us. Of course this event awakened in us as much astonishment and pride as if we were the first pair to which anything of the kind had happened ; and this accounts also for the resumption of the diary. Of this wonder, and of this dignity of mine, the world of the future had to be informed. Besides, the theme "youthful motherhood" is so extremely well adapted for art and literature. It belongs to the class of the best sung and most carefully painted subjects; besides, it may be treated mystically and sacredly, touchingly and pathetically, simply and affectionately— in short, immensely poetically. To nurse this disposition all possible collections of poems, illustrated journals, picture galleries, and current phrases of rapture, such as "mother's love," "mother's happiness," "mother's pride," contribute their power, just as the school-books do to nurse the admiration for war. The highest pitch of deification which has been reached next to the adoration of heroes (see Carlyle's *Hero Worship*) is reached by the multitude in "baby worship"; and of course in this also I was not left behind. My little charming Ruru was to me the mightiest wonder of the world. Ah, my son! my grown-up, stately Rudolf, what I feel for you is such that against it that childish baby-wonder loses colour, against it that blind, apish, devouring love of the young mother is as insignificant as the child himself in swaddling clothes is insignificant by the side of the grown man.

The young father was not less proud of his successor, and built on him the fairest schemes for the future. "What will he be?" This question, not as yet a very pressing one, was nevertheless often discussed over Ruru's cradle and always decided unanimously—a soldier. Sometimes it awoke a weak protest on the mother's part. "But suppose he should meet with any accident in a war?" "Ah, bah!" was the answer to this objection, "every one must die when and where it is appointed him." Ruru was also not to remain the only son; of the following sons one might, please God, be brought up as a diplomatist, another as a country gentleman, a third as a priest; but the eldest, he must choose his father's and grandfather's profession—the noblest profession of all. He must be a soldier.

And so it was settled. Ruru, as soon as he was two months old, was promoted by us to be lance-corporal.[1] Well, as all

[1] "Gefreite"—a soldier exempted from sentinal duty.

crown princes immediately they are born are named "proprietors" of some regiment, why should not we also decorate our little one with an imaginary rank? It was only a regular joke this playing at soldiers with our baby.

On April 1, as the third monthly recurrence of his birthday (for to keep only the anniversaries would have given too few opportunities for festivity), Ruru was promoted from lance-corporal to corporal. But on the same day there happened also something more mournful—something that made my heart heavy, and obliged me to relieve it into the red volumes.

There had been now for a long time a certain black point visible on the political horizon, about the possible increase of which the liveliest commentaries were made in all journals and at all private parties. I had up to that time thought nothing about it. My husband and my father and their military friends might have often said in my hearing, "There will soon be something to settle with Italy," but it glanced off my understanding. I had little time or inclination to trouble myself about politics. So that however eagerly people about me might debate about the relations between Sardinia and Austria, or the behaviour of Napoleon III., of whose help Cavour had assured himself by taking part in the Crimean War, or however constantly they might talk about the tension which this alliance had called forth between us and our Italian neighbours, I took no notice of it.

But on April 1 my husband said to me very seriously :—

"Do you know, dear, that it will soon break out?"

"What will break out, darling?"

"The war with Sardinia."

I was terrified. "My God! that would be terrible! And will you have to go?"

"I hope so."

"How can you say such a thing? Hope to leave your wife and child!"

"If duty calls."

"One might reconcile oneself to it; but to hope—which means wish—that such a bitter duty should arise!"

"Bitter! A rattling jolly war like that must be something glorious! You are a soldier's wife; don't forget that."

I fell on his neck. "O my dear husband, be content. I also can be brave! How often have I sympathised with the heroes and heroines of history! What an elevating feeling it must be to go into battle! If I only might fight, fall, or conquer at your side!"

"Bravely spoken, little wife, but nonsense! Your place is here, by the cradle of the little one, who also is to become a defender of his country when he is grown up. Your place is at our household hearth. It is to protect this, and guard it from any hostile attack, to preserve peace for our homes and our wives, that we men have to go to battle."

I don't know why, but these words, which, or something of the same sort, I had often before heard and read with assent, this time seemed to me to be in a sense mere "phrases". There was certainly no hearth menaced, no horde of barbarians at the gate, merely a political tension between two cabinets. So, if my husband was all on fire to rush into the war, it was not so much from the pressing need of defending his wife, child, and country, but much rather his delight in the march out, which promised change and adventure—his seeking for distinction and promotion. "Oh, yes," was my conclusion from this train of thought, "it is ambition—a noble, honourable ambition —delight in the brave discharge of duty."

It was good of him that he was rejoicing in the *chance* of being obliged to take the field—for as yet there was assuredly no certainty. Perhaps the war might not break out at all, and even in case they came to blows, who knows whether it would be Arno's fate to be sent off?—the whole army does not always see the enemy. No, this splendid, perfect happiness which fate had just built as a snug house for me, it was impossible that the same fate should roughly shatter it to pieces! "O Arno, my dearly-loved husband! it would be horrible to know

that you are in danger!" These and similar outpourings fill
the leaves of the diary which were written in those days.

From this period the red volumes are full for some time
of political stuff. Louis Napoleon is an intriguer; Austria
cannot long be only a spectator. It is coming to war. Sardinia will be frightened at our superior power, and give in.
Peace is going to be maintained. My wishes, despite of all
theoretical admiration of the battles of the past, were, of course,
secretly directed to the preservation of peace, but the wish of
my spouse called openly for the other alternative. He did not
say anything out plainly, but he always communicated any
news about the increase of "the black spot" with sparkling
eyes; while, on the contrary, he always took note of such
peaceful prospects as occurred now and then (but, alas! they
became always rarer) with a kind of dejection.

My father, also, was all on fire for the war. To conquer the
Piedmontese would be only child's play; and, in support of
this assertion, the Radetzky anecdotes were poured out again.
I heard the impending campaign talked about always from the
strategic point of view—*i.e.*, a balancing of the chances on the
two sides; how and where the enemy would be routed, and
the advantages which would thereby accrue to "us". The
humane point of view, *vis.*, that whether lost or won every
battle demands innumerable sacrifices of blood and tears, was
quite left out of sight. The interests which were here in
question were represented as raised to such a height above any
private destiny, that I felt ashamed of the meanness of my way
of thinking, if at times the thought occurred to me: "Ah!
what joy do the poor slain men, the poor cripples, the poor
widows, get out of the victory?" However, very soon the old
school-book dithyrambs came in again for an answer to all
these despairing questionings: "Glory offers recompense for
all". Still—suppose the enemy wins? This question I pro-
pounded in the circle of my military friends, but was igno-
miniously hissed down. The mere mention of the possibility
of a shadow of a doubt is in itself unpatriotic. To be certain

beforehand of one's invincibility is a part of a soldier's duties;
and, therefore, in her degree, of those of a loyal wife of a
lieutenant.

My husband's regiment was quartered in Vienna. From our
house there was a view over the Prater, and from the window
there was such a lovely promise of summer over everything.
It was a wonderful spring. The air was warm and redolent
of violets, and the fresh foliage sprouted out more early than
in other years. I was amusing myself without any anxiety
over the great processions in the Prater which were planned
for the following month. We had, for this purpose, procured
a tasty little equipage—a brake with a four-in-hand team of
Hungarian horses. Even already, in this splendid April
weather, we kept driving almost daily in the alleys of the
Prater—but that was only a foretaste of the pleasure peculiar
to May. Ah! if the war had not broken in on all
that!

"Now, thank God, at last this uncertainty is at an end,"
cried my husband one morning—April 19—on coming home
from parade. "The ultimatum has been sent."

I shrieked out: "Eh, what? What does that mean?"

"It means that the last word of the diplomatic formalities,
the one which precedes the declaration of war, has been spoken.
Our ultimatum to Sardinia calls on Sardinia to disarm. She,
of course, will take no notice of it, and we march across the
frontier."

"Good God! But perhaps they may disarm?"

"Well, then, the quarrel would be at an end, and peace
would continue."

I fell on my knees. I could not help it. Silently, but
still as earnestly as if with a cry, there rose the prayer from my
soul to heaven for "Peace! peace!"

Arno raised me up.

"My silly child, what are you doing?"

I threw my arms round his neck and began to weep. It was
no burst of pain, for the misfortune was certainly as yet not

decided on ; but the news had so shaken me that my nerves
quivered, and that caused this flood of tears.

"Martha, Martha, you will make me angry." said Arno,
reproachfully. "Is this being my brave little soldier's wife?
Do you forget that you are a general's daughter, wife of a
first lieutenant, and," he concluded with a smile, "mother
of a corporal?"

"No, no, Arno. I do not comprehend myself. It was only
a kind of seizure. I am really myself ardent for military glory.
But—I do not know how it is—a little while ago everything was
hanging on a single word, which must by this time have been
spoken—'yes' or 'no'—in answer to this ultimatum as it is
called, and this 'yes' or 'no' is to decide whether thousands
must bleed and die—die in these sunny happy days of spring—
and so it came over me that the word of peace *must* come,
and I could not help falling on my knees in prayer."

"To inform the Almighty of the position of affairs, you dear
little goose!"

The house bell rang. I dried my eyes at once. Who
could it be so early?

It was my father. He rushed in all in a hurry.

"Now, children," he cried, all out of breath, throwing himself into an arm-chair. "Have you heard the great news? The
ultimatum ——"

"I have just told my wife."

"Tell me, dear papa, what you think," I asked anxiously.
"Will that prevent the war?"

"I am not aware that an ultimatum ever prevented a war.
It would indeed be only prudent of this wretched rabble of
Italians to give in and not expose themselves to a second
Novara. Ah! if good Father Radetzky had not died last year
I believe he would, in spite of his ninety years, have put
himself again at the head of his army, and, by God! I would
have marched along with him. We two have, I think, shown
already how to manage these foreign scum. But it seems they
have not yet had enough of it, the puppies! They want a

second lesson.   All right.   Our Lombardo-Venetian kingdom
will get a handsome addition in the Piedmontese territory, and
I already look forward to the entry of our troops into Turin."

"But, papa, you speak just as if war were already declared,
and you were glad of it!   But how if Arno has to go too?"
And the tears were already in my eyes again.

"That he will too—the enviable young fellow!"

"But my terror!   The danger ——"

"Eh!   what?   Danger!   'A man may fight and not be
slain,' as the saying goes.   I have gone through more than
one campaign, thank God, and been wounded more than once
—and yet I am all alive, just because it was ordained that I
should live through it."

The old fatalist way of talking! the same as prevailed to
settle Ruru's choice of a profession—and which even now
appeared to me again as quite philosophical.

"Even if it should chance that my regiment is not ordered
out ——" Arno began.

"Ah, yes!" I joyfully broke in, "there is still that
hope."

"In that case I would get exchanged, if possible."

"Oh, it will be quite possible," my father assured him.
"Hess is to receive the command-in-chief and he is a good
friend of mine."   My heart trembled, and yet I could not help
admiring both the men.   With what a joyful equanimity they
spoke of a coming campaign, as if it were only a question of
some pleasure trip that had been arranged.   My brave Arno
was desirous, even if his duty did not summon him, to go and
meet the foe, and my magnanimous father thought that quite
simple and natural.   I collected myself.   Away with childish,
womanish fear!   Now was the time to show myself worthy of
this my love, to raise my heart above all egotistic fears and
find room for nothing but the noble reflection—"my husband
is a hero".

I sprang up and stretched out both my hands to him:
"Arno, I am proud of you!"

He put my hands to his lips, then turned to papa and said, with a face radiant with joy:—

"You have brought the girl up well, father-in-law!"

Rejected! The ultimatum rejected! This took place at Turin, April 26. The die is cast! War has broken out.

CHAPTER II.

Last hours with the beloved one.—Public feeling in the prospect of war.—The parting.—Employments of the women at home.—Anxieties over the news from the seat of war.—Ill-success of Austria.—Friends in trouble.—The Patriotic Aid Association.—Visit to a friend.—Dreadful news.

FOR a week I had been prepared for the catastrophe, and yet its occurrence gave me a bitter blow. I threw myself sobbing on the sofa, and hid my face in the cushion when Arno brought me the news.

He sat down by me, and began gently to comfort me.

"My darling! Courage! Compose yourself! It is not so bad after all. In a short time we shall return as conquerors. Then we two shall be doubly happy. Do not weep so—it breaks my heart. I am almost sorry that I have engaged to go in any case. But, no; just think, if my comrades are forced to go, with what right could I remain at home? You yourself would feel ashamed of me. No. I must experience the baptism of fire some time, and till that has happened I do not feel myself truly a man or a soldier. Only think how delightful if I come back with a third star on my collar—perhaps with the cross on my breast."

I rested my head on his shoulder, and kept on weeping the more. But I reflected how small such things were. Stars and crosses seemed to be at that moment only empty spangles. Not ten grand crosses on that dear breast could offer me any recompense for the terrible possibility that a ball might shatter it.

Arno kissed me on the forehead, put me softly aside, and stood up.

(18)

"I must go out now, my dear, to my colonel. Have your cry out. When I come back I hope to find you firm and cheerful. That is what I have need of, and not to be shaken with sad anticipations. At such a decisive moment as this my own dear little wife surely will do nothing to take the heart out of me or damp my ardour for exploits? Good-bye, my treasure." And he departed.

I collected myself. His last words were still ringing in my ears. Yes, plainly my duty now was not merely not to damp, but as far as possible to increase, his spirit and his ardour for exploits. That is the only way in which we women can exercise our patriotism, in which we can take any share in the glory our husbands bring from the battlefields. "Battlefields"—it is surprising how this word suddenly presented itself to my mind in two radically different meanings. Partly in the accustomed historical signification, so pathetic, and so calculated to awake the highest admiration; partly in the loathsomeness of the bloody, brutal syllable "fight". Yes, those poor men who were being hurried out had to lie stricken down on the field, with their gaping, bleeding wounds, and among them perhaps—and a loud shriek escaped me as the thought passed through my mind.

My maid Betty came running in all in a fright. "For God's sake, my lady, what has happened?" she asked trembling.

I looked at the girl. Her eyes also were red with weeping. I guessed; she knew the tidings already, and her lover was a soldier. I felt as if I could press my sister in misfortune to my heart.

"It is nothing, my child," I said softly. "Those who go away will surely return."

"Ah, my gracious lady, not all," she replied, breaking out anew into tears.

My aunt now came in, and Betty withdrew.

"I am come, Martha, to speak comfort to you," said the old lady as she embraced me, "and to preach to you resignation in this trial."

"So you know it?"

"The whole city knows it, and great joy prevails, for this war is very popular."

"Joy, Aunt Mary?"

"Oh, yes, among those who see no beloved member of their families ordered out.   I could easily understand that you must be sad, and so I hastened here.   Your papa will also come directly, but not to comfort, only to congratulate.   He is quite beside himself with joy that it is to go on, and looks on it as a noble chance for Arno to take part in it.   And he is right in the main.   For a soldier there is nothing better than a war. And that is the way you must look at it, my dear child.   To fulfil the duty of your calling is before everything.   What must be — —"

"Yes, you are right, aunt; what must be, what is inevitable — —"

"What is the will of God — —" put in Aunt Mary in corroboration.

"Must be borne with composure and resignation."

"Bravo, Martha.   It is certain that everything happens as is before determined by a wise and all-merciful Providence in His immutable counsels.   Every one's death-hour is fixed and written down at the hour of his birth.   And for our dear warriors we will pray so much and so earnestly!"

I did not stop to debate more closely the contradiction that lay between the two assumptions that a fatal event was at the same time ordained and also could be turned aside by prayer. I was myself not clear on the point, and had from my whole education a vague impression that in such sacred matters one ought not to embark on reasonings.   And, indeed, if I had given voice to such scruples before my aunt it would have grievously shocked her.   Nothing could hurt her more than for people to express rational doubt on certain points.   "Not to argue about it" is the conventional commandment in matters mysterious.   As etiquette forbids to address questions to a king, so it is a kind of impious breach of etiquette to want to make inquiries or criticise about a dogma.   "Not to argue

about it" is also a commandment easily obeyed, and on this
occasion I followed it very willingly; and so I did not enter
into any contention with my aunt, but on the contrary clung to
the consolation that lay in the resort to prayer. Yes, during
the whole time my lord was absent, I determined to beg
so earnestly for the protection of Heaven, that it should turn
aside every bullet in the volley from Arno. Turn them aside!
Whither? To the breast of another, for whom, nevertheless,
prayers were also being made? . . . And, besides, what had
been demonstrated to me in my course of physics about the
accurately computable and infallible effects of matter and its
motion? . . . What, another doubt? Away with it.

"Yes, aunt," I said aloud, in order to break short these contradictions that kept crossing each other in my mind. "Yes,
we will pray continually and God will hear us. Arno will keep
unhurt."

"You see—you see, dear child, how in heavy times the soul
still flies to religion. . . . Perhaps the Almighty sends you
this trial in order that you may lay aside your former lukewarmness."

This again did not strike me as correct. That the whole
misunderstanding between Austria and Sardinia, dating even
from the Crimean War, all the negotiations, the despatch of the
ultimatum and its rejection, could have been ordained by God,
in order to warm up my lukewarm spirit!

But to express this doubt would also have been a breach of
propriety. As soon as any one introduces the name of the
Almighty, the claims connected with that name give him a
kind of spiritual immunity. But with regard to the charge of
lukewarmness, it had some foundation. My aunt's religious
feeling came from the depths of her heart, while my piety was
more external. My father was in this respect quite indifferent,
and so was my husband; and so I had had no stimulus from
either the one or the other to any particular zeal of belief. I
had never had any means either of plunging deeply into
ecclesiastical learning, since I had always been able to leave

such things unattacked on the "not-argue-about-them" principle.
True, I went every week to mass and every year to confession,
and attended these services with much reverence and devotion;
but the whole thing was still more or less an observance of the
etiquette becoming to my position : I fulfilled my religious
duties with the same correctness as I went through the figures
of the Lancers at the state ball and made the state courtesy
when the empress came into the room.   Our chaplain at the
château in Lower Austria and the nuntio in Vienna could have
nothing to say against me—yet the charge which my aunt
brought against me was perfectly justified.

"Yes, my child," she went on, "in prosperity and happiness
people easily forget their home above ; but if sickness or fear
of death breaks in on us—or, still more, on those we love—if we
are stricken down or in sorrow ——"

She would have gone on in this style for a long time, but the
door burst open, and my father rushed in.

"Hurrah, it's begun now," was his joyful greeting to us.
"They wanted a whipping, these puppies, did they?   And a
whipping they shall have—that they shall ! "

.   .   .   .

It was a time of excitement.   The war "has broken out".
People forget that it is really two masses of men who are rushing to fight each other, and conceive of the event as if it was
some exalted overruling third power, whose outbreak compels
these two masses into the fight.   The whole responsibility falls
on this power, lying beyond the wills of individuals, and which
on its side merely produces the fulfilment of the destined fate
of the nations.   Such is the dark and awful conception which
the majority of mankind have of war, and which was mine too.
There was no question of my feeling any revolt against making
war in general.   What I suffered from was only that my
beloved husband had to go out into the danger and I to stay
behind in anxiety and solitude.   I rummaged up all my old
impressions from the days of my historical studies, in order to
strengthen and inspire me with the conviction that it was the

highest of human duties which called my dear one away, and
that thereby the possibility was offered to him of covering himself with glory and honour. Now at any rate I was living in
the midst of an epoch of history, and this again was a peculiarly
elevating thought. Since from Herodotus and Tacitus, down
to the historians of modern times, wars have always been represented as the events of most importance and of weightiest
consequence, I concluded that at the present time also a war
of this sort would pass with future historians as an event to
serve for the title of a chapter.

This elevated tone, overpowering in its impressiveness, was
that which prevailed everywhere else. Nothing else was spoken
of in rooms or streets, nothing else read in the newspapers,
nothing else prayed about in the churches. Wherever one went
one found everywhere the same excited faces, the same eager
talk about the possibilities of the war. Everything else which
engaged the people's interest at other times—the theatre, business, art—was now looked on as perfectly insignificant. It
seemed to one as if it were not right to think of anything else
whilst the opening scene in this great drama of the destiny of
the world was being played out. And the different orders to
the army with the well-known phrases of the certainty of victory and promise of glory; and the troops marching out with
clanging music and waving banners; and the leading articles
and public speeches conceived in the most glowing tone of
loyalty and patriotism; the eternal appeal to virtue, honour,
duty, courage, self-sacrifice; the assurances made on both sides
that their nation was known to be the most invincible, most
courageous, most certainly destined to a higher extension of
power, the best and the noblest—all this spread around an
atmosphere of heroism, which filled the whole population with
pride and called out in each individual the belief that he was a
great citizen in a great state.

Such bad qualities, however, as these—lust of conquest, love
of fighting, hatred, cruelty, guile, were also certainly to be
found, and were admitted to be shown in war, but always by

"the enemy". To him, his being in the wrong was quite clear. Quite apart from the political necessity of the campaign just commenced, apart also from the patriotic advantages which undoubtedly grew out of it, the conquest over one's adversary was a moral work, a discipline carried out by the genius of cul- ture. These Italians! what a foul, false, sensual, light-minded, conceited people! And this Louis Napoleon! what a mixture of ambition and the spirit of intrigue! When his proclamation of war, published on April 29, appeared with its motto, "Italy free to the Adriatic Sea," it called out amongst us a storm of indignation. I did allow myself a feeble remark that this was at least an un- selfish and noble idea, which must have an inspiriting influence on Italian patriots, but I was soon put to silence. The dogma that "Louis Napoleon is a scoundrel" was not to be shaken as long as he was "the enemy". Everything proceeding from him was *ab initio* "scoundrelly".

Another slight doubt arose in me. In all the battle-stories of history I had found that the sympathy and admiration of the relaters were always expressed for the party who wanted to free themselves from a foreign yoke and who fought for freedom. It is true that I was not capable of giving any distinct idea of the meaning of the word "yoke," or of that of "freedom," though so abundantly sung about; but one thing seemed to me perfectly clear, *viz.*, that "the shaking off of the yoke" and "the struggle for freedom" lay this time on the side, not of Austria, but of Italy. But even for these scruples, timidly conceived as they were, and still more timidly ex- pressed, I was thundered down. For, here I was so unlucky as again to trench on a sacred principle—namely, that our government—*i.e.*, the government under which one happened to have been born—could never result in a yoke, but only in a blessing; that any who wished to tear themselves loose from "us" could not be warriors of freedom but only simple rebels; and that generally and in all circumstances "we" were always and everywhere wholly in the right.

In the early days of May—they were luckily cold and rainy

days—sunny spring weather would have made too painful a contrast — the regiment into which Arno had exchanged marched. At seven in the morning ——

Ah, the preceding night! what a terrible night it was! If the dear one had only been going on a journey of business, free from any danger, the parting would have made me unspeakably sorrowful—parting is indeed so sad! but to the war! to meet the fiery shower of the enemy's bullets! Why could I no longer on that night apprehend at all in that word "war" its elevated historical signification, but only its terror and threatening of death?

Arno had fallen asleep. He lay there breathing quietly, with a cheerful expression on his features. I had lighted a fresh candle and put it behind a screen; I could not be in the dark that night. Of sleep there was no question whatever for me in that, the *last*, night. I felt that I must spend the whole time in gazing at least into the beloved face. I lay on our bed wrapped in a dressing-gown, and, with my elbow on the pillow, and my chin resting on the palm of my hand, looked down on the sleeper and wept silently. "How I love you, how I love you, my own one—and you are going away from me! Why is fate so cruel? How shall I live without you? O that you may soon come back to me! O God! my good God! my merciful Father above! let him come back soon—him and all. Let there soon be peace! Why then cannot there be peace always? We were so happy—perhaps too happy—for there cannot be any perfect happiness on earth. Oh, rapture! if he comes home unhurt, and then lies at my side as he is doing now, and no parting threatened for the morrow! How quietly you are sleeping, O my dear, brave husband! But how shall you sleep there? There there is no soft bed for you hung with silk and lace; there you must lie on the hard wet earth—perhaps in some ditch—helpless—wounded!" And with this thought I could not help picturing a gaping sabre-cut on his forehead with the blood trickling from it, or a bullet-wound in his breast—and a hot pang of compassion seized me. How I should have liked to throw my arms round him and kiss him—but I dared not wake him, he wanted this invigorating sleep. Not six o'clock yet !—tick-tack, tick-tack, unpityingly swift and sure time marches on to every mark. This indifferent tick-tack distressed me. The light, too, burned just as indifferently behind its screen as this clock ticked with its silly, motionless Cupid. . . . Can it be that all these things have no perception that it is our *last* night ? My tearful lids fell together, my consciousness gradually went away, and letting my head sink on the pillow, I fell asleep at last myself. But only for a short time. Hardly had I lost my sense in the fog of some formless dream, when my heart suddenly contracted painfully, and I awoke with a violent palpitation, and the same feeling of fear as when one is awakened by a cry for help or an alarm of fire. "Parting, parting !" was the alarm cry. When I had started so out of sleep for the tenth or twelfth time it was day, and the candle was flickering out. A knock came at the door.

"Six o'clock, lieutenant," said the orderly, who had been ordered to wake him in good time.

Arno rose up. So now the hour was come—now was to be spoken this sad, sad word—" Farewell ".

It had been settled that I was not to go to the railway with him. The one quarter of an hour more or less together—that was not worth much. And the pain of tearing ourselves asunder at last ! That I did not wish to show to strangers. I wanted to be alone in my room when we exchanged the parting kiss, that I might be able to throw myself on the floor and shriek—shriek out loud.

Arno put on his clothes quickly. As he was doing so he made me all kinds of comforting speeches.

"Courage, Martha ! In two months at the most the affair will be over, and I shall be back again at cuckoo-time; only one in a thousand bullets hits, and that one must not hit me. Others before me have come back from the wars—look at your papa. It must happen sometime or other. You did not marry an officer of hussars with the notion that his business was to grow hyacinths. I will write to you as often as possible, and tell you how pleasantly and livelily the whole campaign is going on. If anything bad were destined for me I could not feel so cheerful. I am going only to win an order, nothing else. Take great care here of yourself and our Ruru; and if I get promotion he shall have another step too. Kiss him for me; I will not repeat the parting of last night. The time will come when it will be a treat for him to have his father tell him how in the year '59 he was present at the great victory over Italy."

I listened to him greedily. This confident chatter did me good. He was going away all pleased and in good spirits, and so my suffering must be egotistic and therefore wrong; this thought ought to give me strength to conquer it.

Another knock at the door.

"Time now, lieutenant."

"I am quite ready; coming directly." He spread out his arms. "Now then, Martha—my wife—my love."

I lay at once on his breast. I could not speak a word. The word "farewell" would not pass my lips. I felt that in saying that word I should give way, and I did not dare to poison the peace, the cheerfulness of his departure. I reserved the outbreak of my pain as a kind of reward for my solitude.

But now he spoke the heartbreaking word.

"Good-bye, my all, good-bye," and pressed his lips closely to mine.

We could not tear ourselves out of this embrace—as though it were our last. Then on a sudden I felt how his lips were trembling, how convulsively his bosom heaved, and then releasing me, he covered his face and sobbed aloud.

That was too much for me. I thought I was going out of my mind.

"Arno, Arno!" I cried out, throwing my arms round him, "stay, stay!" I knew I was asking what was impossible; still I cried out persistently: "Stay, stay!"

"Lieutenant," we heard from outside, "it is now quite time."

One more kiss—the last of all—and he rushed out.

.   .   .   .

To tear charpie, to read the news in the papers, to stick pins with flags into our maps in order to follow the movements of the two armies, and try to solve the chess problems that followed from them in the sense that "Austria attacks and gives mate at the fourth move"; to pray continually in the churches for the protection of our loved ones and the victory of our country's arms; to talk of nothing except the news that came in from the theatre of war; such was what filled up my existence now and that of my relatives and acquaintance. Life with all its other interests appeared suspended as it were during the term of the campaign. Everything except the question "How and when will this war end?" was bereft of importance—nay, almost of reality. One ate, drank, read, saw after one's affairs, but all this had no real concern for us; one thing only concerned us thoroughly—the telegrams from Italy.

My chief gleams of light were, of course, the news that I received from Arno himself. They were in a curt style—letter-writing had never been his strong point—but they brought me the most cheering testimony that he was still alive and unwounded. These letters and despatches could not indeed arrive with much regularity, for the communications were often interrupted, or when an action was impending the field-post was suspended.

If a few days had passed thus, without my hearing from Arno, and a list of killed and wounded was published, with what terror did I not read over the names! It is as great a strain as for the holder of a lottery ticket to look through the winning numbers in the list of a drawing—but in the opposite sense; what one seeks in this case, well knowing, thank God, that the chance is against one, is the chief prize in misery.

The first time that I read the names of the slain—and I had been four days without news—and saw that the name of Arno Dotzky was not among them, I folded my hands and cried aloud: "My God, I thank Thee!" But the words were hardly out of my mouth when it seemed to me like a shrill discord. I took the paper in my hand again and looked at the list of names once more. So I thank God because Adolf Schmidt and Carl Müller and many others were slain, but not Arno Dotzky. Then the same thanksgiving would have been appropriate if it had risen to heaven from the hearts of those who trembled for Schmidt and Müller, if they had read "Dotzky" instead of those names. And why should my thanks in particular be more pleasing to Heaven than theirs? Yes, this was the shrill discord of my ejaculation, the presumption and the self-seeking which lay in it, in believing that Arno had been spared in love for me, and thanking God that not I but Schmidt's mother and Müller's affianced and fifty others had to burst out in tears over that list.

On the same day I received from Arno another letter :—

"Yesterday we had another stout fight. Unfortunately—unfortunately a defeat. But comfort yourself, my beloved Martha, the next battle will bring us victory. It was my first great affair. I was standing in the midst of a heavy storm of bullets—a peculiar feeling. I will tell you by word of mouth—but it is frightful. The poor fellows whom one sees falling around one, and must leave there in spite of their sad cries—*c'est la guerre!* Hope to see you soon again, my dear. If we can once dictate terms of peace at Turin, you shall travel after to meet me. Aunt Mary will be kind enough to take care of our little corporal."

But if the receipt of letters like these constituted the sunshine of my life, its darkest shadows were my nights. If I woke out of some dream of blessed forgetfulness, and the horrible reality with its horrible possibilities came before my consciousness, I was seized with an almost intolerable pain, and could not sleep again for hours. I could not get rid of the idea that Arno was perhaps at that moment lying in a ditch groaning and dying—thirsting after a drop of water, and calling longingly for me. The only way that I could gradually compose myself was by bringing, with all my force, the scene of his return

before my imagination. This was, at any rate, as probable—
nay, perhaps more probable than his lonely death; and so I
pictured him to myself as bursting into the room, and how I
should fling myself on his bosom, and how I should then lead
him to Ruru's cradle, and how happy and how joyful we might
then once more be.

My father was much cast down. One bad news came upon
another. First Montebello, then Magenta. And not he
alone, but all Vienna was cast down. We had at the beginning so confidently hoped that uninterrupted messages of
victory would give occasion for mounting flags on our houses
and singing *Te Deums*, but instead of this the flags were
waving and the priests singing at Turin. There the word now
was: "Lord God, we praise Thee that Thou hast helped us
to strike down the wicked 'Tedeschi'".

"Do not you think, papa," I began, "that if another defeat
was to happen to us, peace would then be made? In that
case I should wish that ——."

"Are you not ashamed to say anything of the kind? I
had rather it should be a seven years'—aye, a thirty years'
war, so that our arms should conquer at last, and we dictate
the terms of peace! What do men go to war for? I suppose
not to get out of it again as quickly as possible; if so, they
might as well remain at home!"

"And that would be by far the best," sighed L

"What a cowardly lot you women folk are! Even you—
you, who have been so well grounded in the principles of love
of country and feelings of honour, are yet quite out of heart
already, and prize your personal quiet more than the welfare
and fame of your country."

"Ah! if I did not love my Arno so dearly."

"Love of your husband, love of your family—all that is very
good; but it ought only to occupy the second place."

"*Ought* it?"

.   .   .   .

The list of killed had already brought the names of several

officers whom I had known personally. Among others, that
of the son—her only one—of an old lady for whom I had
conceived a great feeling of respect.

That day I determined to visit the poor lady. It was,
for me, a painful, heavy journey. I could certainly give her
no consolation—could only weep with her. But it was the
duty of affection, and so I set out.

When I got to Frau v. Ullmann's dwelling, I long hesitated
before pulling the bell. The last time I had been there was
to a cheerful little dance. The dear old mistress of the house
was herself then full of joy. "Martha," she said to me in the
course of the evening, "we are the two most enviable women in
Vienna. You have the handsomest of husbands, and I the
most excellent of sons." And to-day? I still, indeed, had
my husband. But who knows? The shells and grape-shot
were flying there still without ceasing. The minute just past
might have made me a widow: and I began to weep before
the door. That was the proper temper for so mournful a visit.
I rang. No one came. I rang a second time. Again no
answer. Then some one put his head out of the door of
one of the other floors.

"It is no good ringing, miss. The dwelling is empty."

"What! Has Frau v. Ullmann gone?"

"She was taken to a lunatic asylum three days since." And
the head disappeared again as the door shut.

I remained for a minute or two motionless, rooted to the
spot, and the scenes which must have been going on here
passed before my eyes. To what a height must the poor
lady's sufferings have risen before her agony broke out in
madness!

"And there is my father wishing that the war might last
thirty years for the welfare of the country! How many more
such mothers in the country would have been driven to
desperation!"

I went down the stairs shaken to my inmost depth. I
determined that I would pay another visit to a young lady, a

friend of mine, whose husband, like mine, was at the theatre of war.

My way led me through the Herrengasse, past the building called the Landhaus, where the "Patriotic Aid Association" had established its offices. At that time there was not as yet any "Convention of Geneva," any "Red Cross," and this aid association had been formed as a forerunner of these humane institutions, its task being to receive alms of all kinds, in money, linen, charpie, bandages, etc., for the poor wounded, and forward them to the seat of war. The gifts came flowing in abundantly from all sides; it was necessary to have whole shops to receive them, and scarcely were the different articles packed up and sent off when new ones were piled up again in their place.

I went in. I was in distress till I could hand over to the committee all that I had in my purse. Perhaps that might bring health and deliverance to some suffering soldier, and save *his* mother from madness.

I knew the president. "Is Prince C—— here?" I asked the porter.

"Not just now. But the vice-president, Baron S——, is upstairs." He showed me the way to the room where the alms in money were paid. I had to pass through several halls, where on long tables were the packets lying in rows. Parcels of linen, cigars, tobacco, and especially mountains of charpie. It made me shudder. How many wounds must be bleeding there, to be covered with all this torn linen? "And there was my father," I thought again, "wishing that for the country's good the war might last another thirty years! How many of the country's sons must in that case sink under their wounds!"

Baron S—— received my contribution with thanks, and gave me the most ready information about the working of the association in reply to my numerous questions. It was joyful and comforting to hear how much good was thus done. Just as the time came the postman with some letters that had newly arrived, and announced that two barrows of offerings had to delivered from the country. I placed myself on a sofa which was in the lower part of the room to watch the reception of the packets. They were, however, delivered in another room. A very old gentleman now came in, who by his bearing was evidently an old soldier.

"Permit me, baron," he said, as he drew out his purse and sat down on a stool by the table, "permit me to add my little mite too to your noble work." And he gave him a note for a hundred florins. "I look on all this organisation of yours as really angelic; you see I am an old soldier myself," and he gave his name as General ——, "and I can judge what an enormous blessing it is to the poor fellows who are fighting out there. I served in the campaigns of the years '9 and '13— at that time there was no 'Patriotic Aid Association'—at that time no one sent chests of bandages and charpie after the wounded. How many must then have bled to death in misery when the resources of the army surgeons were exhausted, who might have been saved by sending such things as I see here! Ah! yours is a blessed work. You good noble men, you do not know—no, you do not know—how much good you are doing there." And two great tears fell on the old man's white moustache.

A noise of steps and voices arose outside. Both leaves of the entrance door were thrown open and a guardsman announced "Her Majesty the Empress".

The vice-president hurried out to the gate to receive his exalted visitor, as beseemed, at the foot of the stairs, but she had already got into the ante-room.

I, from my concealed position, looked with admiration on the young sovereign who in common walking dress appeared to me almost lovelier than in her state robes at the court ball.

"I am come," she said to Baron S——, "because I received a letter to-day from the emperor from the seat of war, in which he writes to tell me how useful and acceptable the gifts of the Patriotic Aid Association have proved, and so I wished to look

3

into the matter myself, and put the committee in receipt of the emperor's acknowledgment."

On this she made them give her information about all the details of the working of the association, and examined as she went along the various objects from their stores. "Just look, countess," she said to the mistress of the robes, who was with her, taking an article of underclothing in her hand, "how good this linen is, and how beautifully sewn." Then she begged the vice-president to conduct her into another of the rooms, and left the hall by his side. She spoke to him with visible contentment, and I heard her say besides: "It is a fine patriotic undertaking, and to the poor soldiers ——"

I could not catch any more. "Poor soldiers," the word kept coming back to me for a long time, she had pronounced it with so much pity. Yes, "poor" indeed, and the more one could do to send them help and comfort the better. But it ran through my head: "If they had not sent these poor people into this misery at all, would not that have been much better?"

I tried to scare away the thought. It must be so! It must be so! There is no other excuse for the cruelty of making war except what is contained in the little word "must".

Now I went on my way again. The friend whom I was going to visit lived quite close to the Landhaus on the Kohlmarkt. As I walked along I went into a book and print shop to buy myself a new map of Upper Italy—ours had become quite riddled with sticking in the little flags on pins. Besides me there were many other customers in the place. All were asking for maps, diagrams, and so forth. Now came my turn.

"Do you want the theatre of war, too, please?" asked the bookseller.

"You have guessed it."

"No difficulty in that. There is hardly anything else bought."

He went to get what I wanted, and while he wrapped up the roll in paper for me, he said to a gentleman standing next to me: "You see, professor, just now things go badly for those who write or publish books on *belles lettres* or science. No one asks for such things. As long as the war lasts no interest is taken by any one in intellectual matters. It is a bad time for writers and booksellers."

"And a bad time for the nation," replied the professor, "since a loss of interest in such things is naturally followed by its decline in the intellectual scale."

"And there is my father wishing," thought I for the third time, "that for the good of the country a thirty years' war ——"

I now took part audibly in the conversation.

"So your business is doing badly?"

"Mine only? No, almost all, your ladyship," answered the bookseller. "Except the providers for the army there are no tradesmen to whom the war has not brought untold loss. Everything is at a standstill; work in the factories; work in the fields; men without number are without places and without bread. Our paper is falling; the exchange rising; all desire for enterprise is decaying; many firms must go bankrupt—in short, it is a misery! a misery!"

"And there is my father wishing ——" I repeated in silence as I left the shop.

.   .   .   .

My friend was at home.

Countess Lori Griesbach was in more than one respect the sharer of my lot. A general's daughter, like me—married for only a short time to an officer, like me—and, like me, a "grass widow". In one thing she went beyond me: she had not only a husband, but two brothers also at the war. But Lori was not of an apprehensive nature; she was fully persuaded that her dear ones were under the peculiar protection of a saint whom she highly venerated, and she counted confidently on their return.

She received me with open arms.

"Ah! God bless you, Martha; it is indeed good of you to come and see me. But how pale and worn you are looking; you have not had any bad news from the seat of war?"

"No, thank God! But the whole thing is so sad."

"Ah, yes! You mean the defeat. But you must not think too much of that, the next news may announce a victory."

"Whether we conquer or are conquered, war is in itself dreadful altogether. Would it not be better if there could be nothing of the kind?"

"Then what would be the good of soldiers?"

"What, indeed!" I assented; "then there would be none ——"

"What nonsense you are talking. That would be a nice state of things; nothing but civilians! It makes me shudder. Happily that is impossible."

"Impossible? Yes, you must be right. I *will* believe so, or else I could not conceive that it would not long since have happened."

"What happened?"

"The abolition of war. But, no; I might as well talk of the abolition of earthquakes."

"I don't know what you mean. As far as I am concerned I am glad this war has broken out, because I hope that my Louis will distinguish himself. And for my brothers, too, it is a good thing. Promotion has been going on so slowly; now they have at least a chance."

"Have you had any news lately?" I interrupted. "Are your relatives all well?"

"No, not for a pretty long time now. But, you know, the postal service is often interrupted, and when people are tired out with a hot march or a battle, they have not much taste for writing. I am quite easy. Both Louis and my brothers wear blessed amulets. Mamma hung them on herself."

"What would you expect to happen, Lori, in a war in which every man in both armies wore an amulet? If the bullets were flying on both sides, would they retire back into the clouds and do no harm?"

"I do not understand you. You are so lukewarm in faith. Your Aunt Mary often laments about it to me."

"Why do you not answer my question?"

"Because it involves a sneer at a thing which to me is sacred."

"Sneer; oh, no! only a reasonable reflection."

"But you must know that it is a sin to entrust your own reason with the power of judging in things which are above us."

"Well, I have done, Lori. You may be right. Reflection and research are of no use. For sometime all kinds of doubts have risen within me about my most ancient convictions, and I find only pain from them. If I were to lose the conviction that it was a necessity and a good thing to begin this war, I should never be able to forgive him who ——"

"You mean Louis Napoleon. What an intriguer he is!"

"Whether he or another, I should like to remain in the undisturbed belief that there are no men at all who have caused the war, but that it 'broke out' of itself—broke out, like a nervous fever, like the eruption of Vesuvius."

"How excited you get, my love. But let us speak reasonably; so listen to me. In a short time the war will be over and our husbands will come back captains. I will then try to get mine to obtain four or six weeks' leave, and take a trip with me to a watering-place. It will do him good after all the fatigues he will have undergone; and me also, after the heat, and the ennui, and the anxiety I have undergone. For you must not think that I have no fear at all. It may be God's will after all that one of my dear ones should meet with a soldier's death—and even though it is a noble, enviable death, on the field of honour, for emperor and fatherland ——"

"Why, you are speaking just like one of the proclamations to the army!"

"Yet it would be frightful—poor mamma!—if anything was to happen to Gustave or Karl. Don't let us talk about it! And so, to refresh us after all our terror, it would be good to have a gay season at a watering-place. I should prefer Carlsbad, and I went there when I was a girl, and amused myself amazingly."

"I too went to Marienbad. It was there I made Arno's

acquaintance. But why are we sitting here idle like this?
Have you no linen at hand that we could tear into charpie?
I was at the Patriotic Aid Association to-day, and there came
in, who do you think?"

Here I was interrupted. A footman brought in a letter.

"From Gustave," cried Lori joyfully, as she broke the seal.

When she had read two lines she gave a shriek, the paper
fell out of her hand and she threw herself on my neck.

"Lori, my poor dear, what is it?" I cried, deeply moved;
"your husband?"

"O God, O God!" she groaned. "Read for yourself."

I took the letter from the floor and began to read. I can
reproduce the phraseology exactly, because afterwards I begged
the letter from Lori to copy it into my diary.

"Read out loud," she said; "I was not able to read it
through."

I did as she wished.

"Dear Sister,—Yesterday we had a hot combat; there must
be a long list of casualties. In order that you, and in order
that our poor mother may not hear in that way of the misfortune, that you may be able to prepare her for it gradually
(tell her he is severely wounded), I write at once, my dear,
to tell you that our brave brother Karl is of the number of the
warriors who have died for their country."

I interrupted my reading to embrace my friend.

"I had got so far," she said gently.

With tearful voice I read on.

"Your husband is untouched, and so am I. Would that
the enemy's bullet had hit me instead! I envy Karl his
hero's death. He fell at the beginning of the battle, and did
not know that this one again was lost. It is really too bitter.
I saw him fall, for we were riding near each other. I jumped
down at once to pick him up. Only one look and he was
dead. The bullet must have passed through his lungs or
heart. It was a quick painless death. How many others
had to suffer for hours, and to lie helpless on the field in

the heat of the battle, till death released them! It was a murderous day—more than a thousand corpses, friend and enemy, covered the battlefield. I recognised among the dead the faces of so many dear friends; and, amongst others, there is poor"—here I had to turn the page—"poor Arno Dotzky."

I fell unconscious on the floor.

CHAPTER III.

First years of widowhood.—Solitude, study, enlarged views.—
I return into society.—Renewed enjoyment of life.—Thoughts
of second marriage.—I chaperon my younger sisters.—I am
introduced to Baron Tilling.—He brings me an account of
the manner of Arno's death.

"Now, Martha, it is all over. Solferino was decisive—we are
beaten."

My father came hastily one morning on to the terrace, with
these words, where I was sitting under the shadow of a clump
of lime trees.

I had gone back home, to the house of my girlhood, with
my little Ruru. A week after the great battle, which had
struck me down, my family moved to Grumitz, our country
house in Lower Austria, and I with them. I should have
been in despair alone. Now all were again around me, just
as before my marriage—papa, Aunt Mary, my little brother,
and my two growing sisters. All of them did what they possibly
could to mitigate my grief, and treated me with a certain consideration which did me good. Evidently they found in my sad
fate a sort of consecration, a something which raised me above
those around me, even a kind of merit. Next to the blood
which soldiers pour out on the altar of their country, the tears
which the bereaved mothers, wives, and sweethearts of the
soldiers pour on the same altar become a libation hardly less
sacred. And thus it was a slight feeling of pride, a consciousness that to have lost a beloved husband on the field of
honour conferred a kind of military merit, which helped me

(40)

most to bear my pain ; and I was far from being the only one. How many, ah ! how many women in the whole of the country were then mourning over their loved ones sleeping in Italian earth !

At that time no further particulars were known to me of Arno's end. He had been found dead, recognised, and buried. That was all I knew. His last thought doubtless had flown towards me and our little darling, and his consolation in the last moment must have been : " I have done my duty, and more than my duty ".

" We are beaten," repeated my father gloomily, as he sat down by me on the garden seat.

" So those who have been sacrificed were sacrificed in vain." I sighed.

" Those who have been sacrificed are to be envied, for they know nothing of the shame which has befallen us. But we will soon pick up again for all that, even if at present peace, as they say, must be concluded."

" Ah, God grant it," I interrupted. " Too late, indeed, for my poor Arno, but still thousands of others will be spared."

" You are always thinking of yourself and of individuals. But in this matter it is Austria which is in question."

" Well, but does not she consist entirely of individuals ? "

" My dear, a kingdom, a state, lives a longer and more important life than individuals do. They disappear, generation after generation, while the state expands still farther, grows into glory, greatness and power, or sinks and crumples up and disappears, if it allows itself to be overcome by other kingdoms. Therefore the most important and the highest aim for which any individual has to struggle, and for which he ought to be glad to die, is the existence, the greatness and the well-being of the kingdom."

I impressed these words on my mind in order to put them down the same day in the red volume. They seemed to me to express so clearly and strongly the feeling which I had derived in my student days from the books of history, a feeling which in these last times, after Arno's departure, had been driven out of my mind by fear and pity. I wanted to cleave to it again as close as possible, in order to find consolation and support in the idea that my darling had fallen in a great cause, and that my misfortune itself was only one element in this great cause.

Aunt Mary had, on the other hand, a different source of consolation ready.

" Do not weep, dear child," she used to say, when I was sunk in profound grief. " Do not be so selfish as to bewail him who is now so happy. He is among the blessed, and is looking down on you with blessing. After a few quickly passing years on earth you will find him again in the fulness of his glory. For those who have fallen on the field of battle Heaven reserves its fairest dwellings. Happy those who were called away just at the moment when they were fulfilling a holy duty. The dying soldier stands next in merit to the dying martyr."

" 'Then I am to be glad that Arno —— "

" No, not to be glad, that would be asking too much, but to bear your lot with humble resignation. It is a probation that Heaven sends you, and from which you should emerge purified and strengthened in faith."

" So, in order that I might be tried and purified, Arno had to —— "

" No, not on that account. But who dare seek to sound the hidden ways of Providence? Not I at least."

Although such objections always would rise in me against Aunt Mary's consolations, yet in the depths of my heart I readily fell in with the mystical assumption that my glorified one was now enjoying in Heaven the reward of his death of sacrifice, and that his memory on earth was adorned with the eternal glory of sainthood.

How exalting, though painful at the same time, was the effect on me of the great mourning celebration at which I was present in the cathedral of St. Stephen's on the day of our departure! It was the *De Profundis* for our warriors who had fallen on foreign soil and were buried there. In the centre of the church a high catafalque had been erected, surrounded by a hundred lighted candles and decorated with military emblems, flags and arms. From the choir came down the moving strains of the requiem, and those present, chiefly women in mourning, were almost all weeping aloud. And each one was weeping not only for him whom she had lost, but for the rest who had met with the same death, for all of them together, all the poor brave brothers-in-arms, who had given their young lives for us all —that is, for the country, the honour of the nation. And the living soldiers who attended this ceremony—all the generals and officers who had remained behind in Vienna were there, and several companies of soldiers filled the background—all were waiting and ready to follow their fallen comrades without delay, without murmur, without fear. Yes, with the clouds of incense, with the pealing bells, and the voice of the organ, with the tears poured out in a common woe, there must surely have risen a well-pleasing sacrifice to Heaven, and the Lord of armies must shower His blessing down on those to whom this catafalque was erected.

So I thought at that time. At least these were the words with which the red book describes this mourning ceremony.

About fourteen days later than the news of the defeat of Solferino came the news of the signing of the preliminaries of peace at Villafranca. My father took all the pains possible to explain to me that for political reasons it was a matter of pressing necessity to conclude this peace, on which I assured him that it seemed to me joyful news anyhow that this fighting and dying should come to an end. But my good papa would not be hindered from setting forth at length all his exculpatory statements.

"You must not think that we are afraid. Even if it has a look as if we had made concessions, yet we forego nothing of our dignity, and know perfectly what we are about. If it concerned ourselves only we should never have given up the game on account of this little check at Solferino. Oh, no! far from it. We should only have had to send down another *corps d'armée*, and the enemy would have been obliged to evacuate Milan again in quick time. But you know, Martha, that other things are concerned—general interests and principles. We renounced the further prosecution of the war for this reason : in order to secure the other principalities in Italy which are menaced—those that the captain of the Sardinian robbers, with his French hangman-ally, would be glad to fall upon also. They want to advance against Modena, Tuscany—where, as you know, dynasties are in power related to our own imperial family— nay, even against Rome, against the Pope, the Vandals. If we do provisionally give up Lombardy, yet we keep Venetia all the time, and are able to assure the south Italian states and the Holy See of our support. So you perceive that it is merely for political reasons, and in the interest of the balance of power in Europe ——"

"Oh, yes, father," I broke in; "I perceive it. But oh that these reasons had prevailed before Magenta!" I continued, sighing bitterly. Then, to change the subject, I pointed to a parcel of books that had come in that day from Vienna.

"See here! the bookseller has sent us several things on approval. Amongst them there is the work of an English natural philosopher—one Darwin—*The Origin of Species*, and he calls our attention to it as being of special interest, and likely to be of epoch-making importance."

"My worthy friend must excuse me. Who, in such a momentous time as this, could take an interest in these tomfooleries? What can a book about the kinds of beasts and plants contain of epoch-making importance for us men? The confederation of the Italian states, the hegemony of Austria in the German Bund—these are matters of far-stretching influence; these will long keep their place in history, when no living man shall any longer know anything about that English book there. Mark my words."

I did mark them.

. . . . .

Four years later, my two sisters, now seventeen and eighteen years old, were to be presented at court. On this occasion I determined that I would also again "go into society".

The time which had elapsed had done its work, and gradually mitigated my pain. Despair changed into mourning, mourning into sorrow, sorrow into indifference, and even this at last into renewed pleasure in life. I woke one fine morning to the conviction that I really was in an enviable condition, and one that promised happiness. Twenty-three years old, beautiful, rich, high-born, free, the mother of a darling child, a member of an affectionate family—was not all this enough to make my life pleasant?

The short year of my married life lay behind me like a dream. No doubt I had been desperately in love with my handsome hussar—no doubt my loving husband had made me very happy—no doubt the parting had caused me grievous pain and his loss wild agony! but that was all over—over! My love had assuredly never grown so closely into the whole existence of my soul that I could never have survived its uprooting, never have lost the pain of it; our life together had been too short for that. We had adored each other like a pair of ardent lovers; but to have entered into each other, heart to heart, soul to soul, to be fast bound to each other in mutual reverence and friendship, to have shared for long years our joys and our sorrows—this, which is the lot of some married people, had not been given to us two. Even I was assuredly not his highest object, not something indispensable, otherwise he could not so cheerfully and with no compulsion of duty (for his own regiment was never ordered out) have left me. Besides, in these four years I had gradually become another creature, my spiritual horizon had enlarged in many respects, I had come into possession of acquirements and views of which I had no notion when I married, and of which Arno also—as I could now perceive—had no idea either, and so—if he could have risen again—he would have stood in the position of a stranger towards many parts of my present spiritual life. How had this change come about with me? This is how it happened.

One year of my widowhood had passed. The first phase—despair—had given place to mourning. But it was very deep mourning, and my heart was bleeding. Of any renewal of the intercourse of society I would not hear. I thought that from this time my life must be occupied only with the education of my son Rudolf. I called the child no longer Ruru, or corporal. The baby-jokes of the pair of married lovers were over. The little one turned into "my son Rudolf"—the sacred centre of all my effort, hope, and love. In order to be one day a good teacher for him, or rather in order to follow his studies, and be able to become his intellectual companion, I wanted to acquire myself all the knowledge that I could, and with this view reading was the only amusement I allowed myself; and so I plunged anew into the treasures of the library of our château. I was especially impelled to take up again the study which was my peculiar favourite—history. Latterly, when the war had demanded such heavy sacrifices from my contemporaries and myself, my former enthusiasm had become much cooled, and I now wished to light it up again by appropriate reading. And, in fact, it brought me sometimes a kind of consolation, if I had been reading a few pages of accounts of battles with the praises of the heroes which are the natural continuation of those accounts, to think that the death of my poor husband and my own widowed grief were comprised as items in a similar grand historical process. I say "sometimes"—not always. I could not get myself back entirely and absolutely into the feelings of my girlhood, when I wanted to rival the Maid of Orleans. Much, very much, in the over-wrought tirades of glory, which accompanied the accounts of the battles, sounded to me false and hollow, if at the same time I set before me the terrors of the fight—as false and hollow as a sham coin paid as the price for a genuine pearl. The pearl, life—can it be fairly paid for with the tinsel phrases of historical glory?

I had soon exhausted the provision of historical works to be

found in our library. I begged our bookseller to send me some
new historical work to look at. He sent Thomas Buckle's
History of Civilisation in England. "The work is not
finished," wrote the bookseller, "but the accompanying two
volumes, which form the introduction, compose by themselves
a complete whole, and their appearance has excited, not only
in England, but in the rest of the educated world, the greatest
attention. The author, it is said, has in this work laid the
foundation for a new conception of history."

Yes, indeed, quite a new one. When I had read these two
volumes, and then read them again, I felt like a man who had
dwelt all his life in the bottom of a narrow valley, and then, for
the first time, had been taken up to one of the mountain tops
around, from which a long stretch of country was to be seen,
covered with buildings and gardens and ending in the boundless
ocean. I will not assert that I—only twenty years old and who
had received only the well-known superficial "young lady's"
education—understood the book in all the extent of its bearings,
or, to keep to the former metaphor, that I appreciated the
loftiness of the monumental buildings and the immensity of
the ocean which lay before my astonished gaze; but I was
dazzled, overcome; I saw that beyond the narrow valley in
which I was born there lay a wide, wide world, of which, up to
this time, I had never heard. It is not till now that, after
fifteen or twenty years I have read the book again and have
studied other works conceived in the same spirit, I may,
perhaps, take it on myself to say that I understand it. One
thing, however, was clear to me even then : that the history of
mankind was not decided by, as the old theory taught, kings
and statesmen, nor by the wars and treaties that were created
by the greed of the former or the cunning of the latter, but by
the gradual development of the intellect. The chronicles of
courts and battles which are strung together in the history
books represent isolated phenomena of the condition of culture
at those epochs, not the causes which produce those conditions.
Of the old-fashioned admiration with which other historical

writers are accustomed to relate the lives of mighty conquerors
and devastators of countries I could find absolutely nothing in
Buckle. On the contrary, he brings proof that the estimation
in which the warrior class is held is in inverse ratio to the height
of culture which the nation has reached; the lower you go in
the barbaric past, the more frequent are the wars of the time,
the narrower the limits of peace, province against province,
city against city, family against family. He lays stress on the
fact that, as society progresses, not only war itself, but the love
of war will be found to diminish. That word spoke to my
innermost heart. Even in my short spiritual experience this
diminution had been going on, and though I had often repressed
this movement as something cowardly or unworthy, believing
that I alone was the cause of such a fault within me, now, on
the contrary, I perceived that this feeling in me was only the
faint echo of the spirit of the age, that learned men and thinkers,
like this English historian, and innumerable men along with
him, had lost the old idolatry for war, which, just as it had been
a phase of my childhood, was represented in this book as being
also a phase of the childhood of society.

And so in Buckle's *History of Civilisation* I had found just
the opposite of what I sought. And yet I counted what I found
as all pure gain. I felt myself elevated by it, enlightened,
pacified. Once I tried to talk with my father about this
point of view that I had just attained, but in vain. He would
not follow me up the mountain, *i.e.*, he would not read the
book, and so it was to no purpose to talk with him of things
which one could only see from the top of it.

Now followed the year—my second phase—in which mourning turned into melancholy. I now read and studied with
even greater assiduity. This first work of Buckle had given
me an appetite for reflection, and given me an inkling of an
enlarged view of the world. I wanted now to enjoy this yet
more and more; and therefore I followed this book up with
a great many more conceived in the same spirit. And the
interest, the enjoyment, which I found in these studies helped

me to pass into the third phase, *i.e.*, to cause the disappearance of
my melancholy. But when the last change was wrought in me,
i.e., when my joy in life awoke again, then all at once books
contented me no longer, then I saw all at once that ethno-
graphy and anthropology, comparative mythology, and all the
other 'ologies and 'graphies were insufficient to set my longings
at rest, that for a young woman in my position, life had other
flowers of bliss all ready, and for which I had only to stretch
my hand out. And so it came about that in the winter of 1863
I offered myself to introduce my younger sisters into the world
and opened my saloons to Vienna society.

.   .   .   .

"Martha, Countess Dotzky, a rich young widow." It was
under this promising title that I had to play my part in the
comedy of the "great world". And I must say that the character suited me. It is no slight pleasure to get greetings from
all sides, to be *fêted*, spoiled, on all hands, and overwhelmed
with distinctions. It is no slight enjoyment, after nearly four
years' separation from the world, to come all at once into a
whirlpool of all sorts of pleasures, to make the acquaintance
of interesting and influential persons, to be present at some
splendid entertainment almost every day, and when there to
feel yourself the centre of universal attention.

We three sisters had got the nickname of the "three goddesses
of Mount Ida"; and the "Apples of Discord," which the several
young Parises distributed amongst us, were innumerable. I, of
course, in the dignity of my description in the list of *dramatis
personæ* as "rich young widow," was the one generally preferred. Besides it was taken as a settled thing in our family,
and even ever so little in my own inward consciousness, that I
was to marry again. Aunt Mary was no longer in the habit in
her homilies of dwelling on the blessed one who "was waiting
for me above," for if I, in my few short years on earth that
separated me from the grave, united myself to a second husband, an event desired by Aunt Mary herself, the pleasantness

4

of the meeting again in Heaven would be a good deal spoiled
thereby.

Every one around me seemed to have forgotten Arno's existence. I was the only one who did not. Though time had relieved
my pain about him, his image had not been extinguished. One
may cease to mourn for one's dead; mourning does not
depend quite on the will, but one ought not to forget them.
I looked on this dead silence about the dead, which was preserved by my *entourage,* as a second and additional slaughter,
and shrank from killing the poor fellow in my thoughts. I had
made it my duty to speak every day to little Rudolf of his
father, and the child had always to say in his prayers at night:
"God make me good and brave as my dear father Arno
would have me!"

My sisters and I "amused" ourselves extremely, and
certainly I not less than they. It was, so to speak, my *début*
also in society. The first time I was introduced as an engaged
girl, and a newly-married woman; and so all admirers had of
course held aloof from me; and what is a higher enjoyment
in society than the admirers? But, strange to say, however
much I was pleased to be surrounded by a crowd of wor-
shippers, none of them made any deep impression on me.
There was a bar between them and me which was quite
impassable. And this bar was what I had been erecting during
my three years of lonely study and thought. All these brilliant young gentlemen, whose interests in life culminated in
sport, the ballet, the chatter of the court, or (with those who
soared highest) in professional ambition (for most were soldiers),
had not the faintest idea of the things which I had looked at
from afar in my books, and on which my soul's life depended.
That language, of which I grant I had only as yet learned the
elements—but as to which I was assured that it was in it that
men of science would debate and ultimately decide the highest
questions—that language was to them not Greek merely, but
Patagonian.

From this category of young folks I was not going to select

a husband ; that was quite settled. Besides, I was in no hurry to give up once more my freedom, which was very pleasant to me. I managed to keep my would-be suitors sufficiently at a distance to prevent any from making an offer, and at the same time to prevent anybody in society from putting about concerning me the compromising rumour that I was laying myself out for lovers. My son Rudolf should hereafter be able to feel proud of his mother, no breath of suspicion should sully the pure mirror of her reputation. But if the case should occur that my heart should glow once more with love—and that could only be for one worthy of it—then I was fully disposed to realise the claim which my youth still had to happiness in this world, and enter into a second marriage.

Meanwhile, apart from love or happiness, I thoroughly enjoyed myself. The dance, the theatre, dress—I found the liveliest pleasure in all of them. But I did not for them neglect either my little Rudolf or my own education. It was not that I plunged into special studies, but I always kept *au courant* with the movement of the intellectual world, by procuring all the most prominent new productions in the literature of the age, and regularly reading attentively all the articles, even the most scientific, in the *Revue des deux Mondes* and similar magazines. These occupations had indeed the result that the bar I have just spoken of, which cut off my inward life from the surrounding world of young men of fashion, became constantly higher—but it was right that it should be so. I would gladly have drawn into my saloons a few persons from the world of literature and scholarship, but that could hardly be done in the society in which I moved. Bourgeois elements could not be mixed with what was called "the circles" of Vienna. Especially at that period—since then this exclusive spirit has somewhat changed, and it has become the fashion to open one's saloons to individual representatives of art and science. At the time of which I speak this was not the case yet ; any one not "Hof-fähig," *i.e.*, who could not count sixteen ancestors, was excluded thence. Our ordinary society would

have been most unpleasantly surprised to have met at my house
people not ennobled, and could not have hit on the right tone
to converse with them.   And these persons themselves would
certainly have found my drawing-room, full of countesses and
sportsmen, old generals and old canonesses, intolerably dull.
What part could men of intellect and science, writers and artists,
take in the eternally same conversation—who had given a dance
yesterday and who would give one to-morrow—whether Schwar-
zenberg, or Pallavicini, or the Court—what love affairs Baroness
Pacher was causing—which party Countess Palffy was opposing
—how many estates Prince Croy possessed—what right the young
Lady Almasy possessed to the title of a lady of rank, whether
as a Festetics or a Wentheim, and if a Wentheim whether by
that Wentheim whose mother became a Khevenhöller, etc.?
That was indeed the matter of most of the conversations that
went on around me.   Even the intellectual and educated
people, some of whom were really to be found in our circle,
statesmen and so forth, thought themselves bound when they
associated with us, the young folks who danced, to adopt the
same frivolous and meaningless tone.   How gladly would I
often have gone to some dinner in a quiet corner at which one
or two of our travelled diplomatists or eloquent parliamen-
tarians, or other men of mark might express their opinions on
weighty questions!—but that was not feasible.   I had to keep
along with the other young ladies, and talk of the toilettes
that we were getting ready for the next great ball.   And even
if I had squeezed into such a company the conversations that
might have been just begun about the economy of nations,
about Byron's poetry, about the theories of Strauss and Renan,
would have been hushed, and the talk would have been: " Ah,
Countess Dotzky, how charming you looked yesterday at the
ladies' pic-nic ; and are you going to-morrow to the reception
at the Russian embassy?"

   "Allow me, dear Martha," said my cousin Conrad Althaus,
"to introduce to you Lieutenant-Colonel Baron Tilling."

   I bowed.   The introducer went away, and the one introduced did not speak. I took this for an invitation to dance, and rose from my seat with my left arm raised and bent, ready to lay it on Baron Tilling's shoulder.

"Forgive me, countess," he said, with a slight smile, which showed his dazzlingly white teeth, "I do not dance."

"Indeed! so much the better," I answered, sitting down again. "I had just retreated here to get a little repose."

"And I had requested the honour of being introduced to you, countess, as I had a communication to make to you."

I looked up in amazement. The baron put on a very serious face. He was altogether a man who looked very serious, no longer young, somewhere about forty, with a few streaks of grey on the temples—on the whole, a prepossessing sympathetic look. I had accustomed myself to look sharply on each new introduction with the question: "Are you a suitor? and should I take you?" Both questions I answered in this case with a prompt negative. The person before me had not that expression of intimate adoration which all those are in the habit of assuming who approach ladies with "views," as the saying is, and the other question was resolved in the negative at once by his uniform. I would give my hand to no soldier a second time, that I had absolutely fixed with myself, not alone because I would not be again exposed to the horrible pain of seeing my husband depart to the campaign, but because since that time I had arrived at views about war in which it would be impossible for me to agree with a soldier.

Lieutenant-Colonel v. Tilling did not avail himself of my invitation to sit beside me.

"I will not intrude on you long, countess. What I have to communicate to you is not suited for a ballroom. I only wanted to ask you for permission to present myself in your house; could you be so very kind as to fix a day and hour in which I may speak to you?"

"I receive on Saturdays between two and four."

"Then your house between two and four on Saturday most

likely resembles a bee-hive, where the honey bees are flying in
and out."

"And I sit in the middle as queen you would say, a very
pretty compliment."

"I never make compliments, no more than I make honey,
so the hour of swarming on Saturday does not suit me at all.
I must speak to you alone."

"You awaken my curiosity.   Let us say then to-morrow,
Tuesday, at the same hour.   I will be at home to you and no
one else."

He thanked me, bowed, and went away.   A little later my
cousin Conrad came by.   I called him to me, got him to sit
by my side, and asked for information about Baron Tilling.

"Does he please you?   Has he made a deep impression on you that you ask after him so eagerly?   He is to
be had, *i.e.*, he is not yet married.   Still he may not be free
for all that.   It is whispered that a very great lady (Althaus
named a princess of the royal family) holds him to herself by
tender bonds, and therefore he does not marry.   His regiment
has only recently been moved hither, and so he has not been
much seen in society as yet; and he is also it seems an enemy of
balls and things of that sort.   I made his acquaintance in the
Nobles' Club, where he passes an hour or two every day, but
generally over the papers in the reading-room, or absorbed in a
game of chess with some of our best players.   I was astonished
to meet him here; however, as the lady of the house is his
cousin, that explains his short appearance at the ball; he is off
again already.   As soon as he had taken leave of you, I saw
him go out."

"Have you introduced him to many other ladies besides?"

"No, only to you.   But you must not imagine from that that
you have brought him down at a long shot, and that therefore
he is anxious to know you.   He asked me: ' Could you tell me
whether a certain Countess Dotzky, *née* Althaus, probably a
relation of yours, is here at present?   I want to speak to her.'
' Yes,' I answered, pointing to you, ' sitting in that corner on

the sofa, in a blue dress.' 'Oh, that is she! Will you be so kind as to introduce me?' That I did with much pleasure, without any idea that I might be ruining your peace of mind thereby.''

"Don't talk such nonsense, Conrad. My peace is not so easily disturbed. Tilling? Of what family is he? I have never heard the name before."

"Aha! you will not confess! Perhaps he is the favoured one! I have tried by the exercise of all my power of witchery to penetrate into your heart for the last three months, but in vain! And now this cold lieutenant-colonel—for, let me tell you, he is cold and without feeling—came, saw, and conquered. Of what family is Tilling, do you say? I believe of Hanoverian origin. But his father before him was in the Austrian service. His mother is a Prussian. You must surely have noticed his North German accent."

"Yes, he speaks most beautiful German."

"Of course. Everything about him is most beautiful." Althaus got up. "Well, I have had quite enough now. Permit me to leave you to your dreams. I will try to entertain myself with ladies who ——"

" May appear most beautiful in your eyes. There are plenty such."

I left the hall early. My sisters could remain behind under Aunt Mary's guard, and there was nothing to detain me. The desire for dancing had left me. I felt tired, and longed for solitude. Why? Surely not to have the opportunity for thinking about Tilling without interruption? Still it seemed so. For it was about midnight that I enriched the red book by transferring into it the conversation above set down, and added the following observations : "An interesting man this Tilling. The great lady who is in love with him is thinking probably about him now, or perhaps at this moment he is kneeling at her feet, and she is not so lonely—so lonely as I am. Ah, to love any one so entirely and inwardly! Not Tilling, of course—I do not know him even. I envy the princess, not on account of Tilling, but on account of her being beloved. And the more passionately, the more warmly she is attached to him, so much the more I envy her."

My first thought on waking was once more—Tilling. And naturally, for he had made an appointment with me for to-day, on account of some important communication. Not for a long time had I felt so excited as I was about this visit.

At the appointed hour I gave orders that no one should be admitted except the gentleman expected. My sisters were not at home. Aunt Mary, that indefatigable chaperon, had gone with them to the skating rink.

I placed myself in my little drawing-room, in a pretty house dress of violet velvet (violet, it is allowed, suits blonde complexions), took a book in my hand and waited. I had not to wait long. At ten minutes past two Freiherr v. Tilling entered.

"You see, countess, I have punctually availed myself of your permission," he said, kissing my hand.[1]

"Luckily so," I answered laughingly, as I showed him a chair, "otherwise I should have died of impatience; for really you have thrown me into a state of great suspense."

"Then I will say what I have got to say at once, without any long introduction. The reason I did not do so yesterday was in order not to disturb your serenity."

"You frighten me."

"In one word, I was present at the battle of Magenta."

"And you saw Arno die?" I shrieked.

"Yes. I am in a position to give you information about his last moments."

"Speak," I said shuddering.

"Do not tremble, countess. If those last moments had been as horrible as those of so many other of my comrades, I would assuredly have said nothing about it to you; for there

---

[1] This an Austrian fashion, and does not imply any extraordinary attachment or freedom.

is nothing sadder than to hear of a dear one dead that he died
in agony: but that is not the case here."

"You take a weight off my heart. Go on with your
narrative."

"I will not repeat to you the empty phrase with which the
survivors of soldiers are usually comforted, 'He died like
a hero,' for I do not quite know what that means. But I
can offer you the substantial consolation that he died without
thinking about death. He was convinced from the beginning
that nothing would happen to him. We were much together,
and he often told me of his domestic happiness, showed me
the picture of his beautiful young wife, and of his child; he
invited me, 'as soon as ever the campaign was over,' to visit
him in his home. In the massacre of Magenta I found myself,
by accident, at his side. I spare you the sketch of the scenes
that were going on—one cannot relate such things. Men, who
have the warrior spirit, are seized in the midst of the powder-
fog and bullet-rain with such an intoxication that they do not
know exactly what is going on. Dotzky was a man of this kind.
His eyes sparkled. He laid about him with a firm hand.
He was in the full intoxication of war. I who was sober could
see it. Then came a shell, and fell a few steps from where we
were. When the monster burst ten men were blown to pieces,
Dotzky among them. There rose a shriek of anguish from
the injured men, but Dotzky gave no cry—he was dead. I
and a few comrades stooped down to see to the wounded, and
give them aid if possible. But it was not possible. They
were all writhing in death, terribly torn and dismembered—
the prey of horrible tortures. But Dotzky, at whose side I
first knelt on the ground, breathed no more; his heart had
stopped beating, and out of his torn side the blood was flowing
in such a stream that if even his state was only faintness and
not death, there was no fear that he would come to again."

"Fear?" said I weeping.

"Yes, for we had to leave him lying there helpless. Before
us the murderous 'Hurrah!' burst out again, and behind us

mounted squadrons were coming on, who must charge over these dying men. Lucky those who had lost consciousness! His face had a perfectly placid, painless look, and when after the battle was over we picked up our dead and wounded, I found him on the same spot, in the same position, and with the same peaceful look. That is what I had to say to you, countess. I might indeed have done so years since, or, even if I had not met you, have written it to you, but the idea only came into my head yesterday when my cousin said she was expecting among her guests the beautiful widow of Arno Dotzky. Forgive me if I have recalled painful memories. I think, however, I have discharged a duty and freed you from torturing doubts."

He stood up. I gave him my hand.

"I thank you, Baron Tilling," I said, drying my tears. "You have indeed conferred a precious gift on me—the tranquillity of knowing that the end of my dear husband was free from pain or torment. But stay a little, I beg you. I should like to hear you speak more. You struck a note in your way of expressing yourself before which made a certain chord vibrate in my feelings. Without beating about the bush, you abhor war?"

Tilling's visage clouded.

"Forgive me, countess," he said, "if I cannot stop to talk with you on this subject. I am sorry, too, that I cannot prolong our interview. I am expected elsewhere."

It was now my countenance which assumed a cold expression. The princess, I suppose, was expecting him, and the thought was unpleasant to me.

"Then I will not detain you, colonel," I said coldly.

Without any request to be allowed to come again, he bowed, and left the room.

CHAPTER IV.

Progress of my friendship for Tilling.—The toy soldiers.—A dinner at my father's.—The brave Hupfauf.—Darwin.— A charming tête-à-tête, ending in a misunderstanding.— Growing attachment.—A call on Countess Griesbach.— Jealousy dispelled.—Absence of the loved one.—A touching letter from Tilling on his mother's death.

THE carnival was over. Rosa and Lilly, my sisters, had "amused themselves immensely". Each had a list of half-a-dozen conquests. Still there was no desirable *partie* among them, and "the right person" had not shown himself for either. So much the better. They would gladly enjoy a few years more of maidenhood before taking on themselves the married yoke.

And as to me? I noted my impression of the carnival in the red volume as follows: "I am glad that this dancing is over. It has already begun to be monotonous. Always the same rounds, and the same conversation, and the same dancers, for whether it happens to be X——, lieutenant of hussars, or Y-——, brevet-captain of dragoons, or Z——, captain of uhlans, there are always the same bows, the same remarks, the same sighs and glances. Not an interesting man amongst them—not one. And the only one who in any case—we will say nothing about him. He belongs, I know, to his princess. She is a beautiful woman truly, I admit it, but I think her very disagreeable."

Though the carnival with its great balls was over, yet the enjoyment of society had not stopped. Soirees, dinners, concerts—the whirl went on. There was also a great amateur

theatrical performance projected, but not till after Easter.
During the fasting season a certain moderation in our pleasures
was enjoined on us. In Aunt Mary's opinion we were far
from being as moderate as we ought. She could not quite forgive me for not going regularly to the Lenten sermons, and
indemnified herself for my lukewarmness by dragging Rosa and
Lilly to hear all the preachers at the Chapel Royal. The girls
submitted to this easily. Occasionally they found their whole
coterie assembled at church. Father Klinkowström was as
much the fashion at the Jesuits' Church as Mdlle. Murska
at the opera, and so they were tolerably gay—in a mild way.

Not only from the sermons, however, but from the soirees
too, I held myself a good deal aloof during this season. I had
all at once lost my taste for society parties, and delighted in
staying at home to play with my son, and when the little fellow
was taken to bed, to sit by the fire with a good book and read.
Sometimes my father visited me at these times, and chatted
away for an hour or two with me. Of course the campaigning
reminiscences came to the front then continually. I had communicated to him Tilling's account of Arno's death, but he
received the story rather coolly. Whether a man's death was
painful or painless seemed to him a secondary consideration.
To be "left on the field"—as death in battle is called—
appeared to him an end so glorious, bestowed by such an
elevated destiny, that the details of the bodily suffering which
might possibly have occurred were not worth taking into
account. In his mouth to be "left on the field" always
sounded like the grudging admission of an especial distinction,
and next to "being left" what was most pleasant evidently was
to be severely wounded. The style and manner in which he
proudly showed his respect for himself or any one else in saying that he had been wounded at a fight named after this or
that place made one quite forget that the thing in itself could
have given anybody pain. What a difference from Tilling's
short recital! in his sketch of the ten poor creatures who were
shattered by the bursting shell, and broke out in loud shrieks!

What a different tone of shuddering pity in it! I did not repeat Tilling's words to my father, because I felt instinctively that they would have seemed to him unsoldierly, and would have diminished his respect for the speaker, which would have hurt me, for it was just the horror—unsoldierly it might be, but certainly nobly humane—with which he saw and told of the terrible end of his comrades that had penetrated into my heart.

How gladly would I have spoken further on this theme with Tilling, but he seemed not to wish to cultivate my acquaintance. Fourteen days had elapsed since his visit, and he had neither repeated the visit, nor had I met him in society. Only two or three times had I seen him in the Ringsstrasse,[1] and once at the Burg Theatre. He bowed respectfully, and I acknowledged his greeting in a friendly manner, but nothing more. Nothing more? Why did my heart beat at these accidental meetings? Why could I not for hours get his gesture as he greeted me out of my mind?

"My dear child, I have something to beg of you." My father came into my house one morning with these words. He held in his hand a parcel wrapped in paper, and added, "Here is something I am bringing for you," as he laid the thing on the table.

"What, a request and a present together?" I said laughing. "That is bribery indeed!"

"Then hear my request before you unpack my gift, and are blinded by its magnificence. I have to-day a tedious dinner."

"Yes, I know. Three old generals and their wives."

"And two Ministers and their wives—in short, a solemn, stiff, sleepy business."

"But you do not expect that I ——"

"Yes, I expect you there, because, as ladies are pleased to honour me with their company, I must at least have a lady to do the honours."

"But Aunt Mary has always undertaken that office."

---

[1] One of the chief streets of Vienna.

" She is again attacked to-day by her usual headache, and so I have nothing else left ——"

" But to offer up your daughter, as other fathers did in ancient times; for example, King Agamemnon with Iphigenia? Well, I submit."

" Besides, there are among the guests a pair of younger elements: Dr. Bresser, who treated me in my last illness so excellently that I wished to show him the attention of an invitation; and also Lieutenant-Colonel Tilling. Why, you are getting as red as fire ! What is the matter with you ?"

" Me ? It is curiosity. Now, I really must look at what you have brought me."   And I began to take the parcel out of its paper wrapping.

" Oh, that is nothing for you. Don't expect a pearl necklace. That belongs to Rudi."

" Yes, I see, a plaything.   Ah ! a box of lead soldiers! But, father, a little child of four cannot ——"

" I used to play at soldiers when I was only three years old. You can't begin too early. My very earliest impressions were of drums, sabres, manœuvres, words of command : that's the way to awaken the love for the trade, that's the way."

" My son Rudolf shall never join the army," I interrupted.

" Martha ! I know at least it was his father's wish."

" Poor Arno is no more. Rudolf is all I have, and I do not choose ——"

" That he should join the noblest and most honourable of professions ? "

" The life of my only child shall not be gambled for in a war."

" I was an only son also and became a soldier. Arno had no brothers, as far as I know, and your brother Otto is also an only son, yet I have sent him to the Military Academy. The tradition of our family requires that the offspring of a Dotzky and an Althaus should devote his services to his country."

" His country will not want him as much as I."

" If all mothers thought so ——"

"Then there would be no more parades and reviews, no walls of men to batter down, no 'food for powder,' as the common expression for them goes. And that would be far from a misfortune."

My father made a very wry face; but then he shrugged his shoulders.

"Oh, you women," he said contemptuously. "Luckily the young one will not ask your permission. The blood of soldiers is running in his veins. Nay, and he will surely not remain your only son. You must marry again, Martha. At your age it is not good to be alone. Tell me, is there none of your suitors that finds grace in your sight? For instance, there is Captain Olensky, who is desperately in love with you; he has been just now pouring out his sighs to me again. He would suit me thoroughly as a son-in-law."

"But not me as a husband."

"Then there is Major Millersdorf."

"No; if you run down the whole military gamut to me, it is in vain. At what time does your dinner take place? when shall I come?" I said to turn the subject.

"At five. But come half-an-hour earlier; and now, adieu—I must go. Kiss Rudi for me—the future commander-in-chief of the Imperial and Royal Army."

.   .   .   .

A solemn, stiff, sleepy business, that is how my father qualified his proposed dinner, and that is how I should have looked on the ceremony also if it had not been for the one guest whose presence moved me in a singular way.

Baron Tilling came the instant before the meat—so when he saluted me in the drawing-room I had no time for more than the briefest exchange of words; and at table, where I sat between two snow-white generals, the baron was removed so far from me that it was impossible for me to draw him into the conversation carried on at our end of the table. I was pleased at the return into the drawing-room; there I meant to call Tilling to me and question him still further about that battle-scene: I

longed to hear again that tone of voice which had at first
sounded so sympathetically in my ears.

But no opportunity offered itself to me at first to carry out
this intention; the two old generals kept constant to me after
dinner too, and sat down at my side when I took my place in
the drawing-room to pour out *café noir*. To them joined themselves in a semicircle my father, the Minister, Dr. Bresser, and,
finally, Tilling, but the conversation which arose was on general
topics. The rest of the guests—all the ladies among them—
had got together in another corner of the drawing-room where
smoking was not going on; whilst in our corner smoking was
allowed, and even I myself had lighted a cigarette.

"Suppose it should soon break out again?" suggested one
of the old generals.

"Hum," said the other, "I think the next war we shall have
will be with Russia."

"Must there always be a 'next war'?" I interposed, but no
one took any notice.

"With Italy first," my father persisted; "we must at all
events get back our Lombardy. Just such a march into Milan
as we had in '49 with Father Radetzky at our head. I should
like to live to see that. It was on a sunny morning——"

"Oh," I interrupted, "we all know the story of the entry
into Milan."

"And do you know also that of the brave Hupfauf?"

"I do; and I think it very revolting."

"What do you understand of such things?"

"Let us hear it, Althaus; we do not know the story."

My father did not wait to be asked twice.

"Well, this Hupfauf, of the regiment of Tyrolese Jaegers,
he was a Tyrolese himself; he did a famous piece of work. He
was the best shot that can be imagined; he was always king
at all the shooting matches; he hit the mark almost always.
What did he do when the Milanese revolted? Why, he begged
for permission to go on the roof of the cathedral with four
comrades, and fire down from thence on the rebels. He got

permission and carried out his plan. The four others, each of whom carried a rifle, did nothing else but load their weapons without intermission and hand them to Hupfauf, so that he might lose no time. And in this way he shot ninety Italians dead, one after the other."

"Horrible!" I cried out. "Each of these slaughtered Italians on whom that man fired down from his safe position above had a mother and a sweetheart at home, and was himself no doubt reckoning on his opening life."

"My dear, all of them were enemies, and that alters the whole point of view."

"Very true," said Dr. Bresser; "as long as the idea of a state of enmity between men is sanctioned, so long the precepts of humanity cannot be of universal application."

"What say you, Baron Tilling?" I asked.

"I should have wished for the man a decoration to adorn his valiant breast, and a bullet to pierce his hard heart. Both would have been well deserved."

I threw the speaker a warm, thankful glance; but the others, except the doctor, seemed affected unpleasantly by the words they had just heard. A little pause ensued. As the French say: "*Cela avait jeté un froid*".

"Have you ever heard, excellency, of a book by an English natural philosopher named Darwin?" said the doctor, turning to my father.

"No, never."

"Oh yes, papa, just recollect. It is now four years ago since our bookseller sent us the book, just after its appearance, and you then said it would soon be forgotten by the whole world."

"Well, as far as I am concerned, I have quite forgotten it."

"The world in general, on the contrary, seems in a pretty state of excitement about it," said the doctor. "There is a fight going on for or against the new theory of origin in every place."

"Ah, you mean the ape theory?" asked the general on my right. "There was a talk about that yesterday in the casino.

5

These scientific gentlemen hit on strange notions sometimes
—that a man should have been an ourang-outang to begin
with!"

"To be sure," said the Minister nodding (and when Minister
——— said "to be sure" it was always a sign that he was making
himself up for a long talk), "the thing sounds rather funny, and
yet it is capable of being taken seriously. It is a scientific
theory built up not without talent, and with the apparatus of
an industrious collection of facts; and though, to be sure, these
have been satisfactorily controverted by the specialists, yet like
all adventurous notions, however extravagant they may be, it
has produced a certain effect, and finds its defenders. It has
become a fashion to discuss Darwin; but this will not last long
—though the word Darwinism has been invented—and then,
to be sure, the so-called theory will itself cease to be taken
seriously. It is a pity that people get so hot fighting over this
eccentric Englishman; his theory thus acquires an importance
to which it has no claim. It is, of course, the clergy who
especially set themselves in array against the imputation, which,
to be sure, is a degrading one, that man, created in the
image of God, should now all of a sudden be thought to be
derived from the race of brutes—an assumption which, to be
sure, is very shocking from a religions point of view. Still it
is notorious that ecclesiastical condemnation of a theory which
introduces itself in the garb of science is not capable of stop-
ping its dissemination. Such a theory does not become harmless till it has been reduced *ad absurdum* by the representatives
of science, and that in respect of Darwinism, to be sure ———"

"But what nonsense!" broke in my father, fearful, as it
seemed, that another long string of "to be sures" might weary
the rest of his guests, "what nonsense! From apes to men!
Surely what is called the ordinary healthy common-sense is
enough to refute all such mad notions—scientific refutation
is hardly wanted."

"Well, I can scarcely regard these refutations as so perfectly
and demonstrably certain," said the doctor. "They have,

it is true, awakened reasonable doubts of it; but, still, the theory has much probability in its favour, and it will take some little time to bring men of learning to unanimity about it."

"I think these gentry will never be unanimous," said the general on my left, who spoke with a harsh accent, and generally used the Viennese dialect; "why, they live by disputing. I have also heard something of this ape business. But it was too stupid, to my mind, to suit me. Why, if one bothered oneself about all the chatter that the star-gazers and grass-collectors and frog-dissectors use to make us believe that X is Y, one should lose one's ears and eyes. Besides, a little while ago, in an illustrated paper, I saw the visage of this Darwin, and that is itself so apish that I can well believe his grandfather was a chimpanzee."

This joke, which pleased the speaker mightily, was followed by a burst of laughter, in which my father joined with the affability of a host.

"Ridicule is, to be sure, a weapon," said the Minister seriously, "but it does not prove anything. It is possible, however, to meet Darwinism—I may use this new term—and conquer it, with serious arguments resting on a scientific basis. If one can oppose to an author of no authority such names as Linnæus, Cuvier, Agassiz, Quatrefages, his system must fall in pieces. On the other hand, to be sure, it cannot be denied that between men and apes there is a great similarity of structure and that ——"

"In spite of this similarity, however, the cleft is miles wide," broke in the quieter general. "Can you imagine an ape capable of inventing the telegraph? Speech alone raises men so far above beasts ——"

"I beg your excellency's pardon," said Dr. Bresser, "speech and artistic inventions were not originally congenital in mankind. Even to-day a savage could not construct any sort of telegraphic apparatus. All this is the fruit of slow improvement and development."

"Yes, yes, my dear doctor," replied the general. "I know

'development' is the cant word of the new theory. Still you cannot develop a camel out of a kangaroo, and why does not one at this time see an ape turning into a man?"

I turned to Baron Tilling.

"And what say you? have you heard of Darwin, and do you reckon yourself among his followers or opponents?"

"I have heard a good deal about the matter, countess, but I have formed no judgment on it; for as to the work under discussion, *The Origin of Species*, I have not read it."

"I must confess," said the doctor, "that I have not either."

"*Read* it? Well, to be sure, I have not either," said the Minister.

"Nor I—nor I—nor I," came from the rest.

"But," the Minister proceeded, "the subject has been so much spoken of, the cant words of the system 'fight for existence,' 'natural selection,' 'evolution,' etc., are in everybody's mouth, so that one can form a clear conception of the whole matter and select a side decidedly with its supporters or opponents, to which first class, to be sure, belong only some Hotspurs who love violent changes and are always grasping after effect, while the cool, strictly critical people, who demand proof positive, cannot possibly choose any other than the position of opponents—shared by so many specialists of consideration—a position which, to be sure ——"

"That can hardly be positively asserted," said Tilling, reviewing the whole matter, "unless one knows the position of its supporters. In order to know what the strength of the opposing arguments is, which, as soon as a new idea comes up, are heard shouting in chorus all round it, one must oneself have penetrated into the idea. It is generally the worst and weakest reasons which are repeated by the masses with such unanimity; and on such grounds I do not choose to pass a judgment. When the theory of Copernicus came up, only those who had gone through the labour of following the calculations of Copernicus could see that they were correct: the others, who

guided their judgment by the anathemas which were thundered
against the new system from Rome ——"

"In our century," interrupted the Minister, "as I observed
before, scientific hypotheses, if incorrect, are no longer rejected
on the grounds of orthodoxy but of science."

"Not only if incorrect," answered Tilling, "but even when
they are going afterwards to be established, new hypotheses are
always at first controverted by the old fogeys of science. This
set does not like even in our day to be shaken in their long-
accustomed views and dogmas—just as at that time it was not
only the fathers of the Church but the astronomers also who
were zealous in attacking Copernicus."

"Do you mean by this," broke in the rough-speaking general,
"that this ape-notion of our eccentric Englishman is as correct
as that the earth goes round the sun?"

"I will make no assertion at all about it, because, as I said, I do
not know the book. But I will make a point of reading it.
Perhaps (but only perhaps, for my knowledge of such matters
is only slight) I shall then be able to form a judgment. Up
to the present time I must confine myself to supporting my
opinion on the fact that this theory meets with widespread
and passionate opposition—a fact, 'to be sure,' which, to my
mind, speaks rather for than against its truth."

"You brave, straightforward, clear spirit," said I to myself,
apostrophising the speaker.

About eight o'clock the guests in general broke up. My
father wanted to detain them all longer, and I also murmured
mechanically a few hospitable phrases, e.g., "At least you will
stay for a cup of tea"—but in vain. Each produced some
excuse: one had an engagement at the casino; another at a
party; one of the ladies had her box at the opera and wanted to
see the fourth act of the "Huguenots"; another expected some
friends at her house; in short, we were obliged to let them go,
and not so unwillingly as we pretended. Tilling and Dr.
Bresser, who had risen at the same time as the others, were the
last to take their leave.

"And what have you two so important to do?" asked my father.

"I myself, nothing," answered Tilling smiling; "but as the other guests are going, it would be indiscreet ——"

"That is my case too," said the doctor.

"Well, then, I will not let either of you go."

A few minutes later my father and the doctor had seated themselves at a card table, and were deep in a game of piquet, while Baron Tilling kept close to the fire by my side. "A sleepy business," this dinner? "No, truly no evening could have passed in a more pleasant and more awakening manner," was the thought that passed through my mind. Then I said aloud :—

"Really, I have to scold you, Baron Tilling. Why, after your first visit, have you forgotten the way to my house?"

"You did not ask me to come again."

"But I told you that on Saturdays ——"

"Oh, yes; between two and four. But, frankly, you must not expect that from me, countess. Honestly, I know of nothing more horrible than these official reception days. To enter a drawing-room full of strangers, bow to the hostess, take your seat on the outer edge of a semicircle, listen to remarks about the weather—and if one manages to sit next to an acquaintance, venture on a remark of one's own; to be distinguished by the lady of the house, in spite of every difficulty, with a question which you answer in all possible haste, in the hope that it may originate a conversation with her whom you came to see; but in vain. At that moment comes in another guest, who has to be received, and who then takes the nearest empty place in the semicircle, and, under the impression that the subject has not yet been touched, propounds a new observation about the weather; and then, ten minutes after, perhaps a new reinforcement of visitors comes—say a mamma with four marriageable daughters, for whom there are not chairs enough—and so you have to get up along with some others, take leave of the lady of the house, and go. No, countess, that sort of thing passes my talents for company, which are only weak at the best."

" You seem, as a general rule, to keep yourself apart from society. One sees you nowhere. Are you a misanthrope? But, no ; I withdraw the question. From a good deal you have said I drew the conclusion that you love all men."

" I love humanity ; but as to all men, no. There are too many among them worthless, *bornés*, self-seeking, cold-blooded, cruel. Those I cannot love, though I may pity them, because their education and circumstances have not allowed them to be worthy of love."

"Circumstances and education? But character depends chiefly on one's inborn disposition. Do you not think so?"

" What you call ' inborn disposition ' is, however, nothing more than circumstances—ancestral circumstances."

" Then, are you of the opinion that a bad man is not blamable for his badness, and, therefore, not to be abominated?" .

" The consequent is not determined by the antecedent ; he may be not blamable and still to be abominated. You also are not responsible for your beauty, still you are to be admired ——"

" Baron Tilling ! we began to talk about serious matters like two reasonable persons. Do I deserve then all of a sudden to be treated like a compliment-hunting society lady?"

" I beg your pardon, I did not so intend it. I only used the nearest argument I could find."

A short pause followed. Tilling's look rested with an ad_miring, almost tender, expression on my eyes, and I did not drop them. I am quite aware that I ought to have looked away; but I did not. I felt my cheeks glow, and knew that, if he had thought me pretty before, I must at that moment be looking still more pretty—it was a pleasant, "mischievous," confusing sensation, and lasted half-a-minute. It could not continue longer. I put my fan before my face and changed my position ; then in an indifferent tone I said :—

" You gave Minister ' To-be-sure ' a capital answer just now ".

Tilling shook his head as if he were rousing himself out of a dream.

"I? Just now? I don't recollect. On the contrary, I fancy that I gave offence by my remark about Springauf—or Hupsauf was it?—or whatever the name of the brave sharpshooter was."

"Hupfauf."

"You were the only one who liked what I said. Their excellencies, on the other hand, I offended, of course, by an expression so unbecoming to an imperial and royal lieutenant-colonel as 'hard heart,' applied to one who had given the enemy so grand a sample of his shooting. Blasphemy! Soldiers, as is well known, are the more agreeable company the more coolly they deal out death, while there is no more sentimental character to move the feelings in the melodramatic repertory than the warrior grey in battle, but soft of heart—a wooden-legged veteran who could not hurt a fly."

"Why did you become a soldier?"

"You put the question in a way which shows you have looked into my heart. It was not I, nor Frederick Tilling, thirty-nine years old, who had seen three campaigns, who chose the profession, but little Freddy, ten or twelve years old, who had grown up among wooden war-horses and regiments of leaden soldiers, and to whom his father, the decorated general, and his uncle, the lady-killing lieutenant, would put the question cheeringly: 'Now, my boy, what are you going to be?' What else except a real soldier, with a real sabre, and a live horse?"

"I had a box of leaden soldiers given me to-day for my son Rudolf, but I am not going to give them to him. But why, now that Freddy has grown into Frederick, why have you not quitted a condition which has become hateful to you?"

"Hateful? That is saying too much. I hate the position of affairs which lays on us men such cruel duties as making war; but as this position does exist, and exists inevitably, why, I cannot hate the people who take on themselves the duties arising from it, and fulfil them conscientiously with the expenditure of their best powers. Suppose I left the service of the army, would there be any the less warfare? Truly not. It would only be that some one else would hazard his life in my place, and I can do that myself."

"Could not you render better service to your fellow-men in another condition?"

"I do not know. I have learned nothing thoroughly except soldiering. A man can always do something good and useful in his surroundings. I have plenty of opportunity of lightening the lot of those around me. And as far as concerns myself—for I may regard myself also as a fellow-man—I enjoy the respect which the world pays to my profession. I have passed a tolerably distinguished career, am beloved by my comrades, and am pleased at what I have attained. I have no estate, and, as a private person, I should not have the means to assist any one else, nor even myself. So on what grounds should I abandon my way of life?"

"Because killing people is repulsive to you."

"If it is a question of defending one's life against another man attacking it, one's personal responsibility for causing death ceases. War is often, and justly, styled murder on a large scale; still, no individual feels himself to be a murderer. However, that fighting is repulsive to me, that the sad entry on to a field of battle causes me pain and disgust, that is true enough. I suffer from it, suffer intensely, but so must many a seaman suffer during a storm from sea-sickness; still, if he is anything of a brave man, he holds out on deck, and always, if needs must, ventures to sea again."

"Yes, if needs must. But must there then be war?"

"That is a different question. But individuals *must* do their share in it, and that gives them, if not pleasure, at least strength to do their duty."

And so we went on speaking for a time in a low tone, so as not to disturb the piquet-players, and perhaps, too, in order not to be overheard by them, for the views we exchanged, as Tilling sketched a few more episodes of war and the horror he had experienced from them, and I communicated to him the observations made by Buckle about the diminution of the war-spirit with the advance of civilisation—such conversation would have decidedly not suited the ears of General Althaus. I felt that it was a sign of great confidence on Tilling's part to display his inward feeling to me on this matter so unreservedly, and assuredly a stream of sympathy passed from one soul to another between us.

"Why, how deep you are plunged in your eager whispers there," cried my father to us once while the cards were being shuffled; "what are you two plotting about?"

"I am telling the countess campaigning tales."

"Oh, well, she is accustomed to that from her childhood. I tell her some too occasionally. Six cards, doctor, and a quart-major."

We resumed our whispered talk.

Suddenly, as Tilling spoke—and he had again fastened his gaze on mine, and such intimate sympathy spoke in his voice— I thought of the princess.

It gave me a stab, and I turned my head away. Tilling stopped in the middle of a sentence.

"Why do you change countenance so, countess?" he asked in alarm. "Have I said anything to displease you?"

"Oh no! it was only a painful thought: pray go on."

"I have forgotten what I was talking about. I would rather you would confide your painful thought to me. I have been the whole time pouring my heart out to you so openly. Now repay it to me."

"It is quite impossible for me to confide to you what I was thinking about just now."

"Impossible! May I guess? Was it about yourself?"

"No."

"Me?"

I nodded.

"Something painful about me, and something you cannot tell me. Is it ——?"

"Do not trouble your head about it : I refuse any more information." Then I rose and looked at the clock. "Why, it is half-past nine ! I am going to say good-bye to you now, papa."

My father looked up from his cards.

"What ! are you too going to a party ? "

"No ; I am going home. I went to bed very late yesterday."

"And so you are sleepy ? Tilling, that is not very complimentary to you ! "

"No, no," I protested laughingly, "it is no fault of the baron ; we have been talking very livelily."

I took leave of my father and the doctor—Tilling begged to be permitted to see me into my carriage. It was he who put my cloak on in the ante-room and gave me his arm down the steps. As we went down he stopped for a moment and asked me seriously :—

"Once more, countess, have I anyhow offended you ? "

"No ; on my honour."

"Then I am pacified."

When he put me into the carriage he pressed my hand hard and put it to his lips.

"When may I wait on you ? "

"On Saturday I am ——"

"At home —I understand—not at all then."

He bowed and stepped back.

I wanted to call after him, but the servant shut the carriage door.

I threw myself back in the corner, and should have liked to cry—tears of spite like a naughty child. I was in a rage with myself ; how could I ever have been so cold, so impolite, so rough almost to a man with whom I feel such warm sympathy ? It was the fault of the princess. How I hated her ! What was this ? Jealousy ? Then the explanation of what was moving me burst on me—I was in love with Tilling. "In love, love, love ! " rattled out the wheels on the pavement. "You are in love with him ! " was what the street lamps as they flew

past darted on to me. "You love him !" was breathed to me
out of my glove, which I pressed to my lips on the place that
he had kissed.

Next day I wrote the following lines in the red book:
" What the carriage wheels and the street lamps were saying to
me yesterday is not true—or at least much exaggerated. A
sympathetic attraction to a noble and clever man. True; but
passion ? Ha ! I am not going to throw my heart away on any
man who belongs to another woman. He also feels sympathy
for me. We understand each other in many things. Perhaps
he is the only man who shares my views about war; but he is
not on that account anywhere near falling in love with me, and I
ought to be just as far from falling in love with him. That I did
not ask him to visit me on another day than the regular reception day, which he hates so, might indeed have looked a little
unkind, after the intimate conversation we had been having. But
perhaps it is better so. After the interval or a week or two,
after yesterday's impressions, which have shaken me so, I shall
be able to meet Tilling again quite calmly, relying on the idea
that he is in love with another lady, and shall be able to refresh
myself with his friendly and suggestive conversation. For it is
indeed a pleasure to converse with him; it is so different, so
totally different, from all others. I am truly glad that I am
able to-day to sum up this so calmly. Yesterday I might for an
instant have even apprehended that my peace was gone, that I
might become the prey of torturing jealousy. This fear has
to-day disappeared."

The same day I paid a visit to my friend Lori Griesbach—
the same at whose house I heard of the death of my poor
Arno. She was the one among the young ladies of my acquaintance with whom I associated most, and most intimately.
Not that we agreed in many of our views, or that we understood
each other completely—though this is no doubt the foundation
of a real friendship--but we had been playmates as children, we
had shared the same position as young married women, had then
seen each other almost daily; and so a certain habitual familiarity

had sprung up between us, which, in spite of so much difference in the principles of our nature, made our conversation together quite pleasant and comfortable. The province on which we met each other was limited and narrow, but in it we were perfectly happy together. Whole pages of my spiritual life were quite closed to her. Of the views and judgments which I had reached in my quiet hours of study I had never told her a word, nor did I feel any desire to do so. How rarely can one give oneself *entirely* to any one! I have often experienced this in life, that I could lay open to one person only one side, to another only another, of my spiritual personality; that, as often as I conversed with one or the other, a certain part, so to say, of the register was opened; while all the rest of the notes remained mute.

Between Lori and me there were plenty of circumstances which gave us material for hours of chat—our childish recollections, our children, the events and incidents in the circle of our acquaintance, dress, English novels, and the like.

Lori's boy Xavier was of the same age as my son Rudolf and his favourite playmate, and Lori's little daughter Beatrix, who was then ten months old, was playfully destined by us to become one day Countess Rudolf Dotzky.

"So here you are again at last," was Lori's greeting to me. "Lately you have become quite a hermit! Even my future son-in-law I have not had the honour of seeing for ever so long! Beatrix will be quite offended. Now tell us, dear, what are you about? and how are Rosa and Lilly? Besides, I have some interesting news for Lilly, which my husband brought me yesterday from the café. There is some one deeply in love with her, one that I thought was making up to you; but I will tell you all about it later. What a lovely gown that is that you have on! It is from Francine's I know. I could tell that at once. She has such a peculiar style of her own. And your bonnet is from Gindreau? It suits you completely. He makes dresses too, now, not bonnets only, and with immense taste too. Yesterday evening at the Dietrichsteins (why were

you not there?) Nini Chotek was there with an Gindreau dress,
and looked almost pretty."

So she went on for some time, and I answered in the same
style. After I had dexterously led the talk to the gossip which
was current in society, I put this question in the most unconcerned tone possible :—

"Have you heard that Princess —— has a *liaison* with a
certain Baron Tilling?"

"I have heard something of it, but, anyhow, that is *de
l'histoire ancienne.* To-day it is a perfectly well-known thing
that the princess is mad after a low comedian. What, have
you any interest in this Baron Tilling? Why, you are blushing! Ah! it is no good shaking your head! Better confess!
But for this, it would be an unheard-of thing that you should
remain so long cold and unfeeling. It would be a true satisfaction for me to know you were in love at last. It is true
that Tilling would be no match for you; for you have more
brilliant suitors—and he must have absolutely nothing. To
be sure, you are rich enough yourself, but then, besides, he is
too old for you. How old would poor Arno have been now?
Oh! that moment, it was too sad, when you read my
brother's letter out to me. I shall never forget it. Ah! war
is certainly a sad business, for some. For others it is an
excellent business. My husband wishes for nothing more
ardently than that something should occur, he so longs to distinguish himself. I can understand it. If I were a soldier I
should also wish, myself, to do some great exploit; or, at least,
to get on in my profession."

"Or to be crippled or shot dead?"

"I should never think of that. One should not think of
that, and besides it only happens to those whose destiny it is.
Your destiny, my love, was to be a young widow."

"And the war with Italy had to break out to bring it about?"

"And suppose it is my destiny to be the wife of a relatively
young general."

"Well then, must there be a general war in order that

Griesbach may get quick promotion? You prescribe a very simple course for the government of the world. But what were you going to tell me in reference to Lilly?"

"That your cousin, Conrad, raves about her. I expect he will very soon make an offer for her."

"I doubt that. Conrad Althaus is too flighty a madcap to think of marrying."

"Oh! they are all madcaps and flighty—still they do get married when they get foolishly fond of a girl. Do you think Lilly likes him?"

"I have not observed at all."

"It would be a very good match. On the death of his uncle Drontheim he inherits the Selavetz estate. Talking of Drontheim, do you know that Ferdy Drontheim—the same that broke off his connection with Grilli the *danseuse*—is now to marry a rich banker's daughter? However, no one will receive her. Are you going to the English embassy to-night? What, again no? Well, really you are right. In these embassy routs one feels after all not quite at home, there are such a lot of funny people there, of whom one never can be certain whether they are *comme il faut*. Every English tourist who can get an introduction to the ambassador is invited—if he is only a commercial man turned landowner, or even a mere tradesman. I like Englishmen only in the Tauchnitz editions. Have you yet read *Jane Eyre*? Is it not really wonderfully pretty? As soon as Beatrix begins to talk I shall hire an English nurse. About Xavier, I am not at all pleased with his French maid. A little while ago I met her in the street, as she was walking out with the boy, and a young man, who looked like a shopman, was walking with her, and seemed in intimate conversation. All at once I stood before them—you should have seen their confusion! One has always some trouble with one's people. There is my own maid, who has given me warning, because she is going to get married just now when I had got used to her! There is nothing more intolerable than new faces among one's servants. What! do you want to go?"

"Yes, my love. I must pay some calls now that cannot be put off. Adieu."

And I would not be moved to stay "only for five minutes more," though the calls that could not be put off were a fiction. At another time I might no doubt have entertained myself for hours in hearing such meaningless tittle-tattle and tattling back again, but to-day it displeased me. One longing had seized me—for a talk like yesterday evening! Ah, Tilling! Frederick Tilling! The carriage wheels were right then in their refrain! A change had happened in me, I had been raised into another world of feeling; these petty matters in which my friend was so deeply interested—dresses, nursemaids, stories about marriages and estates—all that was too pitiful, too insignificant, too stifling. Away from it—above it—into a different atmosphere of life! And Tilling was really free; the princess "is mad after a low comedian". He could not surely have ever been in love with her! some transitory, yes, *transitory* adventure, nothing more.

.   .   .   .

Several days passed without my seeing Tilling again. Every evening I went to the theatre, and from thence to a party, expecting and hoping to meet him, but in vain.

My reception day brought me many visitors, but, of course, not him. But I did not expect him. It was not like him after his decisive "That you really must not expect from me, countess," and his saying at the carriage door in so hurt a manner "I understand—then not at all," to present himself after all at my house on a day of the kind. I had offended him that evening—that was certain; and he avoided meeting me again—that was clear. Only, what could I do? I was all on fire to see him again, to make amends for my rudeness on the former occasion, and get another hour of a talk such as I had had at my father's—an hour's talk the delight of which would now be increased to me an hundredfold by the consciousness, which had now become plain to me, of my love.

In default of Tilling, the following Saturday brought me at least

Tilling's cousin, the lady at whose ball I had made his acquaintance. On her entrance my heart began to beat. Now I could at least learn something about the man who gave me so much to think about. Still I could not bring myself to put a direct question to this effect. I felt that I was not in a condition to speak out his very name without blushing so as to betray myself; and therefore I talked to my visitor about a hundred different things—even the weather amongst the rest—but avoided that very topic which lay at my heart.

" Oh, Martha," said she, without any preparation, " I have a message to give you. My cousin Frederick begs to be remembered to you. He went away the day before yesterday."

I felt the blood desert my cheeks. " Went away? Where? Is his regiment moved? "

" No; but he has taken a short leave of absence, to hurry off to Berlin, where his mother is on her deathbed. Poor fellow, I am sorry for him, for I know how he adores his mother."

Two days afterwards I received a letter in a hand I did not know, with the postmark of Berlin. Even before I saw the signature, I knew that the letter was Tilling's. It ran thus :—

"8 FRIEDRICH ST., *Mar.* 30, 1863, 1 A.M.

" Dear Countess,—I *must* tell my grief to some one, but why to you? Have I any right to do so? No; but I have an irresistible impulse. You will feel with me. I know you will.

" If you had known her who is dying you would have loved her. That soft heart, that clear intellect, that joyous temper—all her dignity and worth—all is now destined for the grave. No hope! I have spent the whole day at her bedside, and am going to spend the night also up here—her last night. She has suffered much, poor thing. Now she is quiet. Her powers are failing. Her pulse is already almost stopped. Besides me there are watching in her room her sister and a physician.

6

"Ah! this terrible separation! Death! One knows, it is true, that it must happen to every one; and yet one can never rightly take in that it may reach those whom we love also. What this mother of mine was to me I cannot tell you. She knows that she is dying. When I arrived this morning she received me with an exclamation of joy. 'So that is you! I see you once more, my Fritz. I did so fear you would come too late.' 'You will get well again, mother,' I cried. 'No! No! There is nothing to say about that, my dear boy. Do not profane our last time together with the usual sick-bed consolations. Let us bid each other good-bye.'

"I fell sobbing on my knees at the bedside.

"'You are crying, Fritz. Look! I am not going to say to you the usual "Do not weep". I am glad that your parting from your best and oldest friend gives you pain. That assures me that I shall long live in your remembrance. Remember that you have given me much joy. Except the anxiety which the illnesses of your childhood caused, and the torture when you were on campaign, you have given me none but happy feelings, and have helped me to bear every sadness which my lot has laid on me. I bless you for it, my child.' And now another attack of her pain came on. It was heartrending to see how she cried and groaned, how her features were distorted. Yes! Death is a fearful, a cruel enemy; and the sight of this agony called back to my recollection all the agonies which I had witnessed on battlefields and in the hospitals. When I think that we men sometimes hound each other on to death gratuitously and cheerfully, that we expect youth in the fulness of its strength to offer itself willingly to this enemy, against whom even weary and broken old age yet fights desperately— it is revolting!

"This night is fearfully long. If the poor sufferer could only sleep! but she lies there with her eyes open. I pass constantly the space of half-an-hour motionless by her bedside; and then I slip off to this sheet of paper, and write a few words, and then back again to her. In this way it has come to four o'clock. I have just heard the four strokes pealing from all the clock towers—it strikes one as so cold, so unfeeling, that time is striding on steadily and unerringly through all eternity, while at this very moment for one warmly-loved being time must stop— for all eternity. But by how much the colder, the more unfeeling, the universe seems to our pain, by so much the more longingly do we fly back to another human heart which we believe is beating in unison with our feelings. And therefore it is that this white sheet of paper, which the physician left lying on the table when he wrote his prescription, attracted me, and therefore it is that I send you this letter.

"Seven o'clock. It is over.

"'Farewell, my dear boy.' Those were her last words. Then she closed her eyes and slept. Sleep soundly, my dear mother. In tears I kiss your dear hands.

"Yours in deadly sorrow,

"FRIEDRICH TILLING."

I still keep this letter. How frayed and discoloured the sheet looks now! It is not only the twenty-five years that have elapsed which have caused this decay, but also the tears and kisses with which I covered the beloved writing : " In deadly sorrow ". Yes, but "shouting for joy" was what I felt also when I read it. Though there was no word of love in it, yet no letter could give plainer proof that the writer loved the recipient, and no one else. That at such a moment, at the deathbed of his mother, he longed to pour out his grief into the heart, not of the princess, but into mine, must surely stifle every jealous doubt.

I sent on the same day a funeral wreath of a hundred large white camelias, with a single half-blown red rose in it. Would he understand that the pale scentless flowers belonged to the departed as a symbol of mourning, and the little rose—to himself?

CHAPTER V.

THREE weeks had passed.

Conrad Althaus had proposed for my sister Lilly, and met with a refusal. But he did not take the matter much to heart, and remained a zealous visitor at our house, and hovered about us in the drawing-rooms of our society. I expressed to him once my admiration for his unshaken fidelity to his slavery.

"I am very glad," I said, "that you are not angry; but it is a proof to me that your feeling for Lilly was not so ardent after all as you pretend, for rejected love is wont to be angry and resentful."

"You are mistaken, my respected Mrs. Cousin; I love Lilly to distraction. At first I believed that my heart belonged to you, but you held yourself so aloof and were so cold that I stifled my budding passion in good time; and then for a time I was interested in Rosa; but at last I fixed my affection on Lilly, and to this affection I will now remain true to the end of my life."

"Oh, that is very like you!"

"Lilly or no one!"

"But as she will not have you, my poor Conrad?"

"Do you think I am the first who has been met by a refusal, and has gone back to the same lady a second and a third time, and has been accepted at the fourth offer, just to stop his importunity? Lilly has not fallen in love with me, which is a matter not easily to be accounted for, but is still a fact. That under these circumstances she should have resisted the temptation, which for so many maidens is irresistible, to become a wife, and would not accept an offer which in a worldly point of view would be a desirable one, that seems to me most good in her, and I am more in love with her than ever. Gradually my devotion will touch her and awaken a return of love, and then, dearest Martha, you will become my sister-in-law. I hope you will not go against me?"

"I? Oh no! On the contrary, your system of perseverance pleases me. With time and the exhibition of tenderness one can always succeed in 'wooing and winning,' as the English call it. But as to *minnen und gewinnen*,[1] our young gentlemen seem hardly disposed to take the necessary trouble. They want not to strive after and gain their happiness, but to pluck it without any trouble, like some wayside flower."

In a fortnight Tilling was back in Vienna, as I heard, and yet he did not come to my house. I could not, of course, expect to meet him in people's drawing-rooms, since his bereavement kept him away from all society. Still I had hoped that he would have come, or at least written to me; but one day after another passed and did not bring the expected visit or letter.

"I cannot think, Martha, what has come to you," said Aunt Mary to me one morning. "For some time you have been so out of humour, so *distraite*, so—I don't know what to call it. You are very wrong not to lend an ear to any of your suitors. This solitary existence, as I have said from the very first, is not good for you. The consequence of it is these low spirits which distinguish you just now. Have you quite forgotten your Easter devotions? They would help to do you good."

[1] The German words for "woo and win".

" I think that both things—I mean both marrying and going
to confession—should be done for love of the thing itself, not as
a remedy for low spirits.   None of my suitors please me ; and
as for confession ——."

" Well, it is high time for that ; to-morrow is Maundy
Thursday.   Have you tickets for the foot-washing ? "

" Yes, papa has sent me some, but I really do not know
whether I shall go."

" Oh ! but you must.   There is nothing more beautiful and
more elevating than this ceremony.   The triumph of Christian
humility.   The emperor and empress prostrating themselves
to the earth to wash the feet of poor men and women in
their service.   Does not that symbolise well how small and
insignificant is earthly majesty before the heavenly ? "

" In order to represent humility symbolically by kneeling
down one must feel oneself to be really a very exalted personage.
It means—'What God's Son was in comparison with the
apostles, I, the emperor, am in comparison with these poor
folks'.   This fundamental motive of the ceremony does not
strike me as peculiarly humble."

" What curious notions you have, Martha.   In these three
years that you have passed in solitude in the country, and
in the perusal of wicked books, your ideas have become so
perverted."

" *Wicked* books ? "

" Yes, wicked.   I maintain that the word is correct.   The
other day when in my innocence I spoke to the archbishop
about a book I had seen on your table, and which from its title
I took for a religious work, *The Life of Jesus*, by one Strauss,
why, he smote his hands together above his head, and cried
out : ' Merciful Heaven, how came you by such a profligate
work ? '   I turned as red as fire, and assured him that I had not
read the book myself, but had only seen it at a relation's.
' Then demand of your relation, as she values her salvation, to
throw this book into the fire.'   And that I do now Martha.
Will you burn the book ? "

"If we were two or three centuries earlier we might have watched, not the book, but the author, going to the flames. That would have been more effectual—more effectual for the time, though not for long."

"You give me no answer. Will you burn this book?"

"No."

"What! nothing but no?"

"Why should we have any long talk about it? We do not yet understand each other in these matters, dear auntie. Let me rather tell you what little Rudolf yesterday ——"

And thus the conversation was happily led off to another and a fruitful subject, in which no difference of opinion came in between us; for we were both agreed on this matter, that Rudolf Dotzky was the dearest, the most original, and, for his age, the most advanced child in the world.

Next day I resolved nevertheless to attend the foot-washing. A little after ten, in black clothes, as beseems Passion week, my sister Rosa and I presented ourselves in the great hall of state in the Burg. On a scaffold there places were reserved for members of the aristocracy and of the diplomatic corps. Thus one was again in one's own set, and greetings were exchanged left and right. The gallery too was closely packed, also with persons selected, and who had got cards of admission, but still a little "mixed," not belonging only to the *crème*, as we were on our scaffold. In short, the old caste separations and privileges, to correspond with this *fête* of symbolical humility. I do not know whether the others were in a mood of religious devotion, but I awaited what was coming with just the same feeling with which one looks forward in the theatre to a promised "spectacle". Just as there, after exchanging salutations from box to box, one looks with excitement for the rise of the curtain, so I was looking in the direction in which the chorus and soloists in the show before me were to appear. The whole scene was already set, especially the long table at which the twelve old men and twelve old women had to seat themselves.

Still I was glad I had come, for I felt excited, and this is always a pleasant feeling, and one which delivers one from troublous thoughts for the moment. My trouble was constantly "Why does not Tilling show himself?" Just now this fixed idea had left me. What I was expecting and wishing to see was the imperial and the humble actors in the *fête* before me. And exactly at that moment, when I was not thinking of him, my eyes fell on Tilling.

The mass was just over, the dignitaries of the Court had just entered the hall, followed by the general staff and the corps of officers, and I was letting my gaze wander unconcernedly over all these persons in uniform, who were not the chief actors, but only intended to fill the stage—when suddenly I recognised Tilling, who had taken his position just opposite our seat. It ran through me like an electric shock. He was not looking our way. His look showed traces of the suffering he had gone through during the last few weeks—an expression of deep sorrow rested on his features. How gladly would I have shown my sympathy with him by a silent warm pressure of the hand! I kept my gaze firmly fixed on him, hoping that by this magnetic power I might compel him to look in my way too—but in vain.

"They are coming! they are coming!" cried Rosa, nudging me. "Only look! How beautiful—what a picture!"

It was the old men and women, clothed in the old German costume, who were now introduced. The youngest of the women—so said the newspapers—was eighty-eight years old, the youngest of the men eighty-five. Wrinkled, toothless, bowed—I could not see really the point of Rosa's "How beautiful!" What pleased me, however, was the costume. This was peculiarly and excellently suited to the whole ceremony, so penetrated with the spirit of the Middle Ages. The anachronism, in this respect, was ourselves—in our modern clothes and with our modern notions we did not harmonise with the picture.

After the twenty-four old people had taken their seats at the table, a number of gentlemen, mostly elderly, bedizened with gold-sticks and orders, came into the hall ; the privy councillors and chamberlains, many countenances of our acquaintance, Minister "To-be-sure" among the rest, were there. Lastly followed the priests, who had to officiate in the solemn rite. So now the march of the supernumeraries into the hall was over, and the expectation of the public rose to the highest pitch of excitement.

My eyes, however, were not so closely fixed as those of the other spectators in that direction from which the court was to come, but kept always turning back to Tilling. The latter had at last looked my way, and recognised me. He saluted me.

Rosa's hand was again laid on my arm.

"Martha, are you ill ? You have turned pale and red all at once ! Look ! Now ! Now !"

In fact, the chapel master—I should have said the chief master of the ceremonies—raised his staff and gave the signal of the approach of the imperial couple. This promised at any rate a sight worth seeing, for, apart from their being the highest, they were certainly one of the most beautiful couples in the land. At the same time as the emperor and empress several archdukes and archduchesses had entered, and now the ceremony was to begin. Stewards and pages brought in the dishes, full of food, and the emperor and empress placed them before the old people as they sat at table. This afforded more *tableaux* than ever. The utensils, the meats, and the way in which the pages carried them, reminded one of many famous pictures of banquets in the Renaissance style.

Scarcely, however, had the dishes been put on, when the table was taken away again, a labour which again, as a sign of humility, was done by the archdukes. And when the table had been carried away, the special climax-scene of the piece (what the French call *le clou de la pièce*)—the foot-washing— began. This was indeed only a sham washing, as the meal had been only a sham meal. Kneeling on the floor, the emperor stroked down the feet of the old men with a towel, while the assisting priest made a show of pouring water out of a can over them ; and so he glided from the first to the twelfth old man, whilst the empress—whom one was accustomed to see only majestically seated on high—in the same humble attitude, in which she did not however lose anything of her accustomed grace, went through the same proceeding with the twelve old women. The accompanying music, or, if you like, the explanatory chorus, was formed by the reading of the gospel of the day.

I should have been glad for a few moments to have been able to feel what was passing in the minds of these old people while they were sitting in this strange costume stared at by a glittering crowd, and with the country's father, the country's mother—their majesties — at their feet. Probably, if the momentary exchange of consciousness I wished for could have been granted me, it would have been no definite feeling I should have experienced, but only a confused, dazzled half dream, a sensation at once glad and painful, confused and solemn, a complete suspension of thought in those poor heads, already so ignorant and weak with age. All that was real and comprehensible in the matter for the good old folks might have been the prospect of the red silk purses with the thirty silver pieces in them which were hung about each neck by their majesties' own hands, and of the basket of food which was given to each on their departure home.

The whole ceremony was soon over, and the hall then began to empty at once. First the Court went out, then all the others who had taken parts withdrew, and the public out of the scaffold and gallery at the same time.

" It *was* beautiful ! It *was* beautiful ! " whispered Rosa with a deep breath.

I answered nothing. I had, in fact, no cause to pity the confusion and incapacity of thought of the old folks in the ceremony, for my own conception of what had been going on was just as confused, and I had only one thought in my mind—" Will some one be waiting for us outside ? "

However, we did not get to the exit so quickly as I should

have liked. First there was shaking hands and exchanging a few words with nearly all the spectators on the scaffold, who had left their places at the same time as ourselves. They kept standing in a great group on the stairway, and it became a regular morning party.

"Good-day, Tini!"

"*Bon-jour*, Martha."

"Ah! are you there too, countess?"

"Are you engaged for Easter Sunday?"

"Good-day, your highness, don't forget that we are expecting you to a little dance on Monday evening."

"Were you at the sermon at the Dominicans' yesterday?"

"No; I was at the Sacred Heart, where my daughters are in retreat."

"The next rehearsal for our charity performance is on Tuesday, at twelve, dear baron; pray be punctual."

"The empress looked superb again."

"Did you notice, Lori, how the Archduke Ludwig Victor kept sidling off to the divine Fanny?"

"*Madame, j'ai l'honneur de vous présenter mes hommages.*"

"*Ah! c'est vous, marquis, charmée!*"

"I wish you good-morning, Lord Chesterfield!"

"Oh! how are you? awfully fine woman, your empress."

"Have you yet secured a box for Adelina Patti's performance? A wonderfully rising star."

"So the news of Ferdy Drontheim's engagement with the banker's daughter is quite confirmed. It *is* a scandal!"

And so the chatter went on from all sides. An unimpassioned listener would hardly have concluded from these speeches that they sprang out of the impressions of a scene of humble devotion just concluded.

At last we got out of the gate, where our carriages were in waiting, and a crowd of people were collected. These folks wanted at least to see those who had been so lucky as to have seen the gentry who had been spectators of the Court; and then,

on their side, they could pass themselves off as people only a
little less distinguished, as having seen the spectators.

We had scarcely got out when Tilling stood before me. He
made me a bow.

"I have to thank you again, Countess Dotzky, for the
beautiful wreath."

I gave him my hand, but could not speak a word.

Our carriage had come up; I was obliged to get in, and
Rosa was pressing me forward. Tilling raised his hand to his
cap, and was retiring. Then I made a great effort, and said,
in a tone which sounded quite strange in my own ears :—

"On Sunday, between two and three, I shall be at home".

He bowed in silence, and we got in.

"You must have taken cold, Martha," remarked my sister as
we drove away. "Your invitation sounded quite hoarse; and
why did not you introduce that melancholy staff-officer to me?
I have seldom seen a less cheerful visage."

On the day appointed, and at the hour named, Tilling was
announced. Before that I had made the following entry in
the red book :—

"I expect that this day will be decisive of my fate. I feel
such a solemnity, such an anxiety, so sweet an expectation. I
must fix this frame of mind on these pages, so that, if I turn
back to them again after long years, I may be able to recall
quite vividly the hours which I am now looking forward to with
so much emotion. Perhaps it will turn out quite differently
from what I expect—perhaps exactly the same. At any rate
it will be interesting to me to see how far anticipation and
reality correspond. The expected guest loves me; the letter
he wrote from his mother's deathbed proves that. He is loved
in return; the rosebud in the funeral wreath must have shown
him that. And now we are to meet without witnesses, moved to
our hearts' core—he in need of comfort, I penetrated with the
desire to console him. I expect there will not be many words
pass. Tears in both our eyes, hands clasped tremblingly, and
we shall have understood one another. Two loving, two happy
mortals. earnest, devoted, passionate, devoutly happy ; while

in society the thing will be announced indifferently and drily, somewhat in this fashion: 'Have you heard? Martha Dotzky is engaged to Tilling—a poor match!' It is five minutes past two. He may come now any minute. There is a ring! This palpitation, this trembling: I feel that ——— "

This is as far as I got. The last line is scrawled in letters which are almost illegible—a sign that "this palpitation, this trembling" was not a mere figure of rhetoric.

Anticipation and reality did not correspond. During his half-hour's call Tilling behaved very reservedly and very coldly. He begged my forgiveness for the liberty he had taken in writing to me, and hoped I would attribute this breach of etiquette to the loss of control which a man in such sorrowful moments may well experience. Then he told me something more of the last days and of the life of his mother; but of what I was looking for, not a word. And so I also became every moment more reserved and cold. When he rose to go I made no effort to detain him, and I did not ask him to come again.

When he had gone I rushed again to the red book, which was lying there open, and went on with the interrupted topic.

" I feel that all is over—that I have shamefully deceived myself, that he does not love me, and will even think now that he is as indifferent to me as I to him. I received him in an almost repellent way. I feel that he will never come again. And yet the world holds for me no second man. There is no one else so good, so noble, so intellectual—and there is no other woman, Frederick, who has loved you as I have loved you— assuredly not your princess, to whom, as it seems, you have turned back again. Son Rudolf, you must now be my consolation and my stay. From this time I will have no more to do with woman's love—it is mother's love alone which must now fill my heart and my life. If I can succeed in forming you into such a man as *he* is—if some day I may be wept by you, as he weeps for his mother— I shall have gained my end."

It is surely a foolish habit—this diary-writing. These wishes, plans, and views, always changing, vanishing and

coming anew, which form the current of our soul's life—to strive
to immortalise them by writing them down is a mistake to start
with, and brings before oneself, when one peruses it in after
years, the constant shame of having to recognise one's own
fickleness. Here are recorded now on the same page, and
under the same date, two such different humours—first the
most confident hope, and by its side the most complete
despair, and the pages next it may give proof of something
quite different again.

The Easter Monday was favoured by the most splendid
spring weather, and the ride in the Prater, which takes place,
according to custom, on that day, a kind of holiday preparatory
to the great Corso of May Day, went off with especial lustre.
I cannot say how much this lustre, this delight in holiday
and spring which was all around me, contrasted with the sorrow
which filled my spirit. And yet I would not have given up my
sorrow, would not have had again the same light, and therefore also empty heart, as two months before—when I had
not made Tilling's acquaintance. For, though my love was,
according to all appearance, an unhappy one, yet it was love—
and this implies a raising of the intensity of life—that warm,
tender feeling which expanded my heart as often as the dear
image passed before my inward eye. I could not have lived
without it.

I had never thought it likely that the subject of my dreams
would come before my eyes here in the Prater, in the midst of
this whirl of worldly pleasure. And yet when, without thinking, I happened once to let my gaze wander towards the ride,
I saw far off galloping down the promenade in our direction an
officer, in whom—though my short sight could not distinguish
him clearly—I at once recognised Tilling. As soon as he came
near, and crossed our carriage, with a salute in passing, I
returned his greeting, not with a mere bow, but with warm
gestures. At the same moment I was aware that I had done
what was unbecoming and improper.

"Who is that you were making those signs to?" asked my

sister Lilly. "Ah, I see," she added, "there is the inevitable Conrad walking—you were waving your hand to him?"

This timely appearance of the "inevitable Conrad" came very *apropos* for me. I was thankful to my trusty cousin for it, and proceeded at once to give effect to my gratitude.

"Look here, Lilly," I said, "he is, I am sure, a good man, and, no doubt, is here only on your account again. You should take pity on him—you should be good to him. Oh, if you knew how sweet it is to have any one dear to you, you would not shut your heart so. Go make him happy, the good fellow."

Lilly stared at me in astonishment.

"But suppose he is indifferent to me, Martha?"

"Perhaps you are in love with some one else?"

She shook her head: "No, no one".

"Oh, poor thing!"

We made two or three more turns up and down the promenade. But the one whom my eyes were searching after all about I did not see a second time. He had quitted the Prater again.

. . . .

A few days later, in the afternoon, Tilling was announced. He did not, however, find me alone, for my father and Aunt Mary had come to call, and besides these Rosa and Lilly, Conrad Althaus and Minister "To-be-sure" were in my drawing-room.

I almost uttered a cry of astonishment—this visit came upon me with such a surprise and at the same time so delighted and excited me. But the delight was soon over, when Tilling, after exchanging salutations with the company, and taking a seat opposite to me, at my invitation, said in an unconcerned tone:—

"I am come *pour prendre congé*, countess. I am leaving Vienna in a few days."

"For long?" "Where are you going?" "What is the

reason?" "What is it about?" asked the others, all at once, and with interest, while I remained dumb.

"Perhaps for good." "To Hungary." "Exchanging into another regiment." "For love of the Magyars," explained Tilling, in answer to his different questioners.

Meanwhile I had collected myself.

"It was a sudden resolution," I said, as calmly as I could. "What harm has our Vienna done to you that you quit it in such a violent hurry?"

"It is too lively and too gay for me. I am in a mood which makes one long to mope in solitude."

"Oh, well!" said Conrad, "the gloomier one's mood, the more one ought to seek amusement. An evening in the Karls theatre has a much more refreshing effect than passing all day musing alone."

"The best thing, my dear Tilling, to give you a shake up," said my father, "would, I am certain, be a jolly rattling war, but unluckily there is no prospect of that before us. The peace threatens to last as long as one can see."

"Well," I could not help remarking, "that is an extraordinary collocation of words, ' war ' and ' jolly,' ' peace ' and ' threatening '."

"To be sure," assented the Minister, "the political horizon at the moment does not show any black point, still storm-clouds sometimes rise quite unexpectedly all of a sudden, and the chance can never be excluded that a difference—even unimportant in itself—may cause the outbreak of war. I say that for your comfort, colonel. As for myself, since I, in virtue of my office, have to manage the home affairs of the country, my wishes must, to be sure, be directed exclusively to the maintenance of peace as long as possible—for it is this alone which is naturally adapted to further the interests lying in my domain. Still this does not prevent me from taking note of the just desires of those who from a military point of view are, to be sure —— "

"Permit me, your excellence," interrupted Tilling, "as far

as I am myself concerned, to protest against the assumption that I wish for a war, and also to protest against the underlying principle that the military point of view ought to be different from the human. We exist in order to protect the country should an enemy threaten it, just as a fire engine exists in order to put out a fire if it breaks out, but that gives the soldier no right to desire war any more than a fireman to wish for a fire. Both involve misfortune—heavy misfortune—and no one, as a man, ought to rejoice over the misfortunes of his fellow-men."

"You good, you dear man," I said, in silence, to the speaker.

The latter continued :—

" I am quite aware that the opportunity for personal distinction comes to the one only from conflagrations and to the other only from campaigns ; but how poor of heart and narrow of mind must a man be before his selfish interests can seem to him so gigantic as to blot out the sight of the universal misery ! Peace is the greatest blessing, or rather the absence of the greatest curse. It is, as you said yourself, the only condition in which the interests of the population can be furthered, and yet you would give to a large fragment of this population, the army, the right to wish for the cessation of the condition of growth and to long for that of destruction? To nourish this 'just' wish till it grows into a demand, and then, perhaps, obtains its fulfilment? To make war that the army may anyhow be occupied and satisfied is just as if we set fire to houses that the fire brigade may distinguish itself and earn renown."

"Your comparison, dear colonel, is a lame one," replied my father, giving Tilling, contrary to his habit, his military title, perhaps to remind him that his opinions were not consistent with his calling. "Conflagrations do nothing but damage, while wars may get power and greatness for the country. How else have states been formed and extended except by victorious campaigns? Personal ambition is surely not the only thing that makes soldiers delight in war. It is above all things,

7

pride in one's race, in one's country, that finds its dearest nourishment there—in a word, patriotism."

"Especially love of home?" replied Tilling. "I do not really understand why it is we soldiers in particular who make as if we had a monopoly of this feeling, which is natural to the majority of mankind. Every one loves the soil on which he grows up; every one wishes the elevation and the good of his own countrymen. But happiness and renown are to be reached by quite other means than war; pride can be excited by quite other exploits than deeds of arms. I, for instance, am much prouder of Anastatius Grün than of any of our field-marshals"

"Well, but can anybody even compare a poet with a commander?" cried my father.

"That is my question too. The bloodless laurel is by far the more lovely."

"But, my dear baron," said my aunt at this point, "I have never heard a soldier speak so. What becomes, then, of the ardour of battle, of the warlike fire?"

"Dear lady, those are feelings not at all unknown to me. It was by them that I was animated when as a youngster of nineteen I took the field for the first time. But when I had seen the realities of butchery, when I had been a witness of the bestialities which are connected with it, my enthusiasm evaporated, and I went into my subsequent battles, not with pleasure, but with resignation."

"Listen to me, Tilling. I have been present at more campaigns than you, and have also seen plenty of scenes of horror; but my zeal has not yet cooled. When in the year '49 I followed Radetzky, though a middle-aged man, I felt all the same delight as on the first occasion."

"Excuse me, your excellence. But you belong to an older generation—a generation in which the warlike spirit is much more lively than in ours, and in which the feeling for humanity, which is zealous for the abolition of all misery, and which is at this time extending in ever-widening circles, was still totally unknown."

"What is the good? Misery there must always be : it can no more be abolished than war."

"Pray observe, Count Althaus, that in these words you are defining the only point of view (one now much shaken) from which the past used to regard all social evils—*i.e.*, the point of view of resignation—as one looks at what is inevitable, what is a natural necessity. But if ever, at the sight of a great evil, the doubtful question has forced itself on one's heart, 'Must this be so?' then the heart can no longer remain cold ; and, besides pity, a kind of repentance springs up. Not a personal repentance indeed, but—how shall I express it?—a *protest from the conscience of the age.*"

My father shrugged his shoulders. "That is above me," said he. "I can only assure you that it is not only we old grandfathers who think with pride and joy on our old campaigns, but also that most of the young men and boys, if asked whether they would like to go out to a war, would answer at once : 'Yes, with pleasure, all possible pleasure '."

"The boys, surely. They have still in their hearts the enthusiasm which is implanted at school. And of the others, many answer, as you say, 'With pleasure' because that answer is looked on, according to the popular conception, as manly and courageous ; and the honest 'Not willingly' might easily be interpreted as a proof of cowardice."

"Oh !" said Lilly, with a little shudder, "I should be a coward too. Oh, how horrible it must be with bullets flying on all sides, and death threatening every instant !"

"That is a sentiment which is natural in your mouth as a young girl," replied Tilling. "But we men have to repress the instinct of self-preservation. Soldiers have also to repress the compassion, the sympathy for the gigantic trouble which invades both friend and foe ; for, next to cowardice, what is most disgraceful to us is all sentimentality, all that is emotional."

"Only in war, my dear Tilling," said my father, "only in war. In private life, thank God, we too have soft hearts."

"Oh yes! I know it. It is a kind of magic. Immediately on the declaration of war one says all at once of any horror: 'Oh! that goes for nothing'. Children sometimes make the same agreement in their games. 'If I do this or that it goes for nothing,' you may hear them say. And in the game of war the same conventions, though unspoken, apply. Manslaughter is no longer to count as manslaughter; robbery counts no longer as robbery; theft is not thieving but 'requisition'; villages burnt represent, not conflagrations, but 'positions taken', To all the precepts of the statute book, of the catechism, of the moral law, as long as the game lasts, the same applies—'It goes for nothing'. But if ever occasionally the gambling fervour slackens, if the convention that 'it goes for nothing' disappears from one's conscience for one moment, and one comprehends the scenes around one in their reality, and conceives of this depth of misery, this wholesale crime as meaning something, then one would wish for one thing only to deliver one out of the intolerable woe of such a sight—namely, to be dead."

"Well, really!" remarked Aunt Mary meditatively, "sentences like 'Thou shalt not murder,' 'Thou shalt not steal,' Love thy neighbour as thyself,' 'Forgive thine enemies' ——"

"Go for nothing," repeated Tilling; "and those, whose calling it is to teach these sentences, are the first to bless our arms and call down Heaven's blessing on our murderous work."

"And rightly so," said my father. "The God of the Bible was of old time the God of battles, the Lord of armies. He it is who commands us to draw the sword. He it is ——"

"Men always," interrupted Tilling, "decree that what they themselves want to see done is His will; and they attribute to Him the enactment of eternal laws of love, which, whenever His children begin the great game of hatred, He suspends by His divine 'Goes for nothing'. Just as rough, just as inconsistent, just as childish as man is the God whom man has set before us. And now, countess," he added, getting up, "forgive me for having inflicted such a tedious discussion on you, and allow me to take leave."

Stormy feelings were thrilling through me. All that he had just said had rendered the beloved man yet dearer to me. And must I now part from him, perhaps never to see him again? To exchange thus a cold farewell with him before other people and let all end so? It was not possible. I should have been obliged, if the door had closed on him, to burst out in sobs. That must not be: I rose up.

"One moment, Baron Tilling," I said; "I must at any rate show you that photograph I spoke to you about a little while ago."

He looked at me in amazement, for no talk about a photograph had ever passed between us. However he followed me to the other corner of the drawing-room, where some albums were lying on a table, and where we were out of hearing of the others.

I opened an album, and Tilling stooped over it. Meanwhile I spoke to him in a low voice and all in a tremble.

"I cannot let you go in this way. I will, I must speak to you."

"As you will, countess; I am listening."

"No, not now; you must come again—to-morrow, at this hour."

He seemed to hesitate.

"I command it. By the memory of your mother, for whom I wept with you!"

"Oh, Martha!"

My name so pronounced thrilled through me like a flash of joy.

"To-morrow then," I repeated, and looked into his eyes, "at the same hour."

We had settled it. I returned back to the others, and Tilling, after he had put my hand to his lips again and saluted the others with a bow, went out of the door.

"A singular person," remarked my father, shaking his head. "What he has been saying just now would find little favour in the higher circles."

When the appointed hour struck next day I gave orders, as on the occasion of his first visit, to admit no one else except Tilling.

I looked forward to the coming visit with a mixture of feelings—passionate anxiety, sweet impatience, and some degree of embarrassment. I did not quite know the precise things I should say to him; on that subject I would not reflect at all. If Tilling asked me some such question as "Now then, countess, what have you to communicate to me—what do you wish with me?" I could not surely answer him with the truth: "I have to communicate to you that I love you; my wish is that you should stay here". But he would not surely cross-examine me in so bald a way, and we should readily understand each other without such categoric questions and answers. The main point was to see him once more; and not to part, if parting must come, without having spoken one heartfelt word and exchanged one fervent farewell. But even in *thinking* the word "farewell" my eyes filled with tears.

At this moment the appointed visitor came.

"I obey your command, countess, and—but what is the matter with you?" said he, interrupting himself. "You have been weeping? You are weeping still?"

"I? No, it was the smoke, the chimney in the next room. Sit down, Tilling. I am glad you have come."

"And I happy that you ordered me to come, do you recollect, in the name of my mother. On that I determined to tell you all that is in my heart. I ——"

"Well, why do you stop?"

"To speak is even harder to me than I thought."

"You showed so much confidence in me on that night of pain when you were watching by the deathbed. How comes it that you have now lost all confidence again?"

"In those solemn hours I had gone out of myself: since then my usual shyness has again seized me. I perceive that on that occasion I had overstepped my right, and I have avoided your neighbourhood that I might not overstep it again."

"Yes, indeed, you seem to avoid me—why?"

"Why? Because—because I adore you!"

I answered nothing, and to hide my emotion I turned my head away. Tilling also was struck dumb. At last I collected myself and broke the silence.

"And why did you wish to leave Vienna?" I asked.

"For the same reason."

"Could not you recall the determination?"

"Yes, I certainly could; the exchange is not yet settled."

"Then remain."

He seized my hand.

"Martha!"

It was the second time he had called me by my name. These two syllables had an intoxicating sound for me. I was compelled to answer what would sound as sweet to him—another two syllables, in which lay all that was bursting my heart—so, lifting my eyes to his, I said softly :—

"Frederick".

At this instant the door opened and my father came in.

"Ah! you are there. The footman said you were not at home, but I replied I would wait for you. Good-day, Tilling! I am much surprised to find you here after your adieu of yesterday."

"My departure is put off again, your excellence, and so I came ——"

"To pay my daughter an arrival-call—all right. And now to tell you what brought me here, Martha. There is a family event ——"

Tilling got up.

"Then I am perhaps in the way."

"Oh, my communication is not so very pressing."

I wished papa and his family event at the Antipodes. No interruption could have come more inopportunely. Tilling could do nothing now but go. But after what had passed between us going did not mean parting. Our thoughts, our hearts remained united.

"When shall I see you again?" he asked in a low voice,
as he kissed my hand on leaving.

"To-morrow, at nine o'clock, in the Prater, on horseback,"
I answered rapidly in the same tone.

My father took a rather cold leave of him as he went out,
and when the door was shut behind him—

"What is the meaning of this?" he asked, with a stern
countenance. "You tell them to deny you—and I find you
tête-à-tête with this gentleman?" I turned red, half in anger,
half in embarrassment.

"What is the family event which you —— "

" *This* is it—I wanted to get your lover out of the way, so
that I might tell you what I think of it. And I regard it as a
very important event for our family that you, Countess Dotzky,
née Althaus, should trifle with your reputation in this way."

"My dear father, the most secure guard of my reputation
and my honour has been given me in the person of little
Rudolf Dotzky—and, as to what concerns the authority of the
Count Althaus, allow me to remind you with all possible
respect that, in my capacity as an independent widow, I have
outgrown it. I have no intention at all of taking a lover, if
that is what your conjecture points at, as it seems to be—but,
if I choose to decide on marrying again, I reserve myself the
right of choosing quite freely according to my own heart."

"Marry Tilling? What are you thinking about? That
would be a real calamity in the family. I should almost like
better—but, no—I won't say that; but, seriously, you have no
such notion, I hope."

"What is there to say against it? It is only a little while
since you came offering me a brevet-captain, a captain, and
a major—Tilling has already risen to the rank of lieutenant-
colonel —— "

"That is the worst thing about him. If he were a civilian,
he might be pardoned for such views as he expressed yesterday—but in a soldier they come near the bounds of treason.
. . . No doubt, he would like to get his discharge, so as not

to be exposed to the danger of having to make another campaign, the fatigues and sufferings of which he evidently dreads.
And, as he has no fortune, it is a very good idea of his to want
to make a rich marriage. But I hope to God that he will not
find a woman to carry this idea out who is the daughter of an
old soldier, that has fought in four wars, and would be ready
to-day to turn out with all possible pleasure, and the widow of
a brave young warrior, who found a glorious death on the field
of honour."

My father, who had been pacing up and down the room with
great strides as he spoke thus, had become as red as fire, and
his voice trembled with excitement. I also was moved to my
heart's core. The set of the phrases, the contemptuous words
in which the attack on the man of my heart was clothed
annoyed me. But I did not care to make any rejoinder. I
quite felt that my defence could not remove the unfounded
injustice here done to Tilling. That my father considered the
views expressed yesterday as so completely false depended
merely on a total failure to understand them. My father
was utterly blind to the point of view which Tilling had
reached. I could not make him see. I could not teach him
to apply a different ethical standard than the military (which
indeed was, in General Althaus's eyes, the highest standard)
to the thoughts which Tilling cherished as a man and as a
philosopher. But while I remained so completely dumb in
presence of the outbreak that I had had to listen to, that my
father might well believe he had made me ashamed of myself,
and stifled my project in the bud, I felt myself drawn with
redoubled longing towards the man so misunderstood, and
strengthened in my resolve to be his. By good luck, I was
really free. My father's disapproval might, to be sure, trouble
me ; but, as to restraining me from following my heart's impulse,
that it could not do. And, besides, there was no room in
my soul for any great trouble. The wonderful, the mighty
happiness which had opened before me in the last quarter of
an hour was too lively to allow any vexation to mingle with it.

.   .   .   .

Next morning I woke with a feeling like the one I always had as a child on Christmas Eve, and once on the morning of my marriage with Arno—the same inexpressible expectation, the same excited anxiousness, that to day something joyful, something great was at hand. The remembrance of the words which my father spoke the day before did, to be sure, cause a little trouble, but I quickly chased this thought away again.

It had not struck nine when I left my carriage at the entry to the Prater Promenade and mounted my horse which had been sent forward with the groom. The weather was spring-like and mild—sunless, indeed, but only the milder for that; and, besides, I carried the sunshine in my heart. It had rained in the night; the leaves were adorned in their freshest green, and a smell of moist earth rose up out of the soil.

I had hardly ridden a hundred paces down the promenade when I was aware of the tread behind me of a horse coming on at a round trot.

"Ah, how are you, Martha? I am pleased to meet you here."

It was Conrad—the inevitable. I was not at all pleased at this meeting. However, the Prater was certainly not my private park, and on such a beautiful spring morning the ride is always full. How could I have been so foolish as to reckon on an undisturbed rendezvous here? Althaus had made his horse follow the pace of mine, and settled himself evidently to be my faithful attendant in my ride. At this time I perceived Frederick v. Tilling at a distance, who was galloping down the ride in our direction.

"Cousin! you are my good ally, are you not? You know that I take all possible trouble to dispose Lilly in your favour?"

" Yes, my noblest of cousins."

"Only yesterday evening I was again vaunting your good qualities, for you are really a grand young fellow—pleasant, discreet —— "

" Whatever do you want with me?"

" Just to give your horse the spur and ride off."

Tilling was by this time quite near. Conrad looked first at him, then at me, and, without speaking a word, nodded at me with a smile, and went off as if he was flying for his life.

"'This Althaus again" were Tilling's first words after he had turned round, so as to ride on by my side. In his tone and his manner jealousy was plainly expressed.

I was pleased at it.

" Is he so out of patience at seeing me? or has his horse run away?"

" I sent him away, because —— "

" Countess Martha, odd that I should meet you with this Althaus, of all people! Do you know that the world says he is in love with his cousin?"

" It is true."

" And is trying to win her favour?"

" That is true also."

" And not without hope?"

" Not quite without hope."

Tilling was silent. I looked into his face with a happy smile.

" Your look contradicts your last words," he said, after a pause. " For your look seems to me to say 'Althaus loves me without hope'."

" He is not in love with me at all. The object of his suit is my sister Lilly."

" You take a weight off my heart. This man was one of the reasons for my wishing to leave Vienna. I could not have borne to be obliged to look on."

" And what other reasons had you besides?" I interposed.

" The fear that my passion was increasing; that I should not be able to conceal it longer; that it would make me ridiculous and miserable at the same time."

" Are you miserable to-day?"

" Oh, Martha! Since yesterday I have been living in such

a tumult of feeling that I am almost beside myself. But not without the fear, as when one has too sweet a dream, that I may suddenly awake to a painful reality. I have no right to expect any return for my love. What can I offer you? To-day your favour smiles on me, and lifts me into the seventh Heaven. To-morrow, or a little later, you will withdraw from me again this undeserved favour, and plunge me into an abyss of despair. I know myself no longer. How hyperbolically I am speaking—I who was formerly such a calm, circumspect man, an enemy of all extravagance. But in your presence nothing seems to me extravagant. In your power it lies to make me happy or wretched."

" Let me speak of my doubts too. The princess —— "

"Oh, has that chatter come to your ears too? There is nothing in it, nothing at all."

" Of course you deny; that is your duty."

" The lady in question, whose heart is now imprisoned, as is well known, in the Burg theatre, and how long will that last?— for it is a heart which gives itself away pretty often—this lady is one about whom the most circumspect gentleman need hardly observe the silence of death. So you are doubly bound to believe me. And, besides, should I have wished to leave Vienna if that rumour had had any foundation ?"

" Jealousy does not draw reasonable inferences. Should I have ordered you to remain here if I had been near making up a match with my cousin Althaus ?"

" It is hard for me, Martha, to be riding so quietly by your side. I should like to fall at your feet, to kiss at least your beloved hand."

" Dear Frederick," said I tenderly, "such outward acts are not needed. One can embrace with words too, and caress all the same as —— "

" If we kissed," he said, concluding the sentence.

At this last word, which thrilled through us both like an electric shock, we looked for some time into each other's eyes and found that one can kiss even with looks.

He spoke first. "Since when?" I understood the unfinished question well enough.

"Since that dinner at my father's," I replied. "And you?"

"You? That *you*[1] does not suit, Martha. If I am to answer the question it must be put in a different form."

"Well? and *thou*?"

"I? Just since the same evening. But it was not so clear and decided to me till at the deathbed of my poor mother. With what longing did my thoughts turn to you!"

"Yes, that I understood. But you, on the contrary, did not understand what the red rose meant which was wound in among the white flowers of death, or else, when you came here, you would not have so avoided me. I do not yet comprehend the reason of this holding off, and why you wanted to go away!"

"Because my thoughts never rose to the hope that I could win you. It was not till you ordered me, by the memory of my mother—ordered me to come to you, and to remain near you—that I understood that you were favourably disposed to me, that I might dedicate my life to you."

"So if I had not myself 'thrown myself at your head,' as the French say, you would not have troubled yourself about me?"

"You have a great many admirers. I could not mix myself up among these swarms."

"Oh, they do not count for anything. Most of them have no other object except as to the rich widow."

"Don't you see? That word describes the bar which kept me from paying my court—a rich widow, and I quite without fortune. Better perish of unrequited love than be despised by the world, and especially by the woman I adore, for the very thing which you have just imputed to the crowd of your suitors ——"

---

[1] *Sie*, "you," is used in German to strangers; *Du*, "thou," to intimates. But as no such habit prevails in England, *Du* is translated into the ordinary "you" throughout the book.

"O you proud, noble, dear fellow! I should never have been capable of attributing one low thought to you."

"Whence this confidence? You really know me so little as yet."

And now we began questioning each other further. On the question "Since when" had we loved each other, followed now the discussion "Why?" What had first attracted me was the way in which he had spoken of war. What I had thought and felt in silence—believing that no soldier could think any such thing, much less utter it—he had thought more clearly than I, felt it more strongly, and uttered it with perfect freedom. Then I saw how his heart towered above the interests of his profession and his intellect above the views of the period. It was that which, so to speak, laid the foundation of my devoted love for him; and besides that there were innumerable other "becauses" in reply to the "why". Because he had so handsome and distinguished a presence; because in his voice there thrilled a soft yet firm tone of its own; because he had been such a loving son; because . . .

"And you—why do you love me?" I asked, interrupting myself in thus rendering my account.

"For a thousand reasons and one."

"Let us hear. First the thousand."

"The great heart; the little foot; the lovely eyes; the brilliant mind; the soft smile; the lively wit; the white hand; the womanly dignity; the wonderful ——"

"Stop! stop! Are you going through the whole thousand? Better tell me the one reason."

"That is no doubt simpler, since the one in its power and irresistibleness embraces all the others. I love you, Martha, because I love you. That is why."

.   .   .   .

From the Prater I drove direct to my father's. The communication which I had to make to him would, I foresaw, give rise to unpleasant discussions. Still I wanted to get over these inevitable unpleasantnesses as quickly as possible—and I preferred to face them at once under the first impression of the happiness I had just won. My father, who was a late riser, was still sitting over his breakfast, with the morning papers, when I ran into his study. Aunt Mary was present also, and likewise busy over the paper.

On my rather hasty entrance my father looked up in surprise from the *Presse*, and Aunt Mary laid down the *Fremdenblatt*.

"Martha! so early, and in riding dress! What does that mean?"

I embraced them both, and then said, as I threw myself into an arm-chair:—

"It means that I am come from a ride in the Prater, where something has taken place which I wanted to tell you about without delay. So I did not even take the time to drive home and change my dress."

"And what is this thing so important and so pressing?" asked my father, lighting a cigar. "Tell us, we are all anxiety."

Should I beat about the bush? Should I make introductions and preparations? No, better leap in head over heels, as people leap from a spring-board into the water.

"I have engaged myself ——"

Aunt Mary flung her hands over her head and my father wrinkled his brow.

"I hope, however, not ——" he began, but I did not let him finish.

"Engaged myself to a man, whom I love from my heart, and reverence, and of whom I believe that he will make me completely happy—Baron Fried. v. Tilling."

My father jumped up!

"What do you say? After all I said to you yesterday."

Aunt Mary shook her head.

"I would sooner have heard a different name," she said. "In the first place, Baron Tilling is not a match for you, he cannot have anything; and, in the second, his principles and his views seem to me ——"

"His principles and views coincide entirely with mine; and as to looking for 'a match,' as it is called, I am not disposed to do so. Father, dearest father of mine, do not look so cruelly at me, do not spoil the great happiness which I feel at this moment! my good, dear, beloved papa!"

"Well, but, my child," he replied, in a somewhat softened tone, for a little coaxing used always to disarm him, "it is nothing but your happiness which I have in view. I could not feel happy with any soldier who is not a soldier from his heart and soul."

"But really you have not to marry Tilling," remarked Aunt Mary, in a very judicious way. "The soldiership is the least matter in question," she added; "but I could not be happy with a man who speaks in a tone of such little reverence of the God of the Bible, as the other day ——"

"Allow me, dearest Aunt Mary, to call your attention to the fact that you also have not to marry Tilling."

"Well, what a man chooses is a heaven to him," said my father with a sigh, sitting down again. "Tilling will quit the service, I suppose?"

"We have not mentioned the subject as yet. I own I should prefer it, but I fear he will not do so."

"To think," sighed Aunt Mary, "that you should have refused a prince; and now, instead of raising yourself, you will come down in the social scale."

"How unkind you are, both of you, and yet you say you love me. Here I come to you, the first time since poor Arno's death, with the news that I feel perfectly happy, and instead of being glad of it, you try to embitter it with all kinds of matters —militarism, Jehovah, the social scale!"

Still, after half-an-hour or so, I had succeeded somehow or other in talking the old folks round. After the conversation he had held with me the day before, I had expected my father's opposition to be much more violent. Possibly if I had only spoken of projects and inclinations he would have still striven hard to quench such projects and inclinations; but in presence of the *fait accompli* he saw that resistance could not be of any further use. Or, possibly, it was the effect of the overflowing feeling of bliss which must have been sparkling in my eyes and quivering in my voice which chased away his annoyance and in which he was obliged against his will to take a sympathising part—in fine, when I stood up to go he pressed my cheek with a hearty kiss, and made me a promise that he would come to my house the same evening, and there salute his future son-in-law in that capacity.

How the rest of the day and the evening passed I am sorry to find not described in the red book. The details have escaped my recollection after so long a time. I only know they were delightful hours.

At tea I had the whole family circle assembled round me, and I presented my Freid. v. Tilling to them as my future husband.

Rosa and Lilly were delighted. Conrad Althaus cried "Bravo, Martha! And now, Lilly, you take a lesson!" My father had either overcome his old antipathy, or he managed to conceal it for my sake; and Aunt Mary was softened and touched.

"Marriages are made in Heaven," she said, "and every one's lot is according to His will. You will be happy if you have God's blessing, and I will pray continually that you may have it."

The "new papa" was presented to son Rudolf too, and it was to me a moment of peculiar delight and joyful anticipation when the dear man took up my dear child in his arms, kissed him warmly, and said: "Of you, little fellow, we two will make a perfect man".

In the course of the evening my father put his idea about quitting the service into words.

"You will give up your profession, Tilling, I suppose? As you are already not in love with war."

Tilling threw his head back with a gesture of surprise.

"Give up my profession! Why, I have no other! And

8

a man need not be in love with war to perform his military
duty, any more than ——— "

"Yes, yes," my father interposed, "that is what you said the
other day—any more than a fireman need be an admirer of
conflagrations."

"I could bring forward more instances.   No more than a
physician need love cancer or typhus, or a judge be an especial
admirer of burglaries.   But to give up my way of life?   What
motive is there for that?"

"The motive," said Aunt Mary, "would be to spare your
wife the life of a garrison town, and to spare her anxiety in
case of a war breaking out—though such anxiety is, to be
sure, nonsense, for if it is decreed to any one to live to be old,
he lives so, in spite of all dangers."

"The reasons you have named would no doubt be weighty.
To keep the lady who is to be my wife from all the unpleasantnesses of life, as far as possible, will certainly be my most
earnest endeavour ; but the unpleasantness of having a husband
who would be without any profession or business would, I am
sure, be even greater than those of garrison life.   And the
danger that my retirement might be charged against me by any
one as laziness or cowardice would be even more terrible than
those of a campaign.   The idea really never occurred to me for
a moment ; and I hope not to you either, Martha ? "

"But suppose I made a condition of it ? "

"You would not do so.   For otherwise I should have to
renounce the height of bliss.   You are rich.   I have nothing
except my military standing, and the outlook to a higher rank
in the future ; and that is a possession I will not give up.   It
would be against all dignity, against my ideas of honour."

"Bravo, my son !   Now I am reconciled.   It would be a
sin and an outrage against your profession.   You have not
much farther to go to be colonel, and will certainly rise to
general's rank—may at last become commandant of a fortress, governor, or minister of war.   That gives your wife also
a desirable position."

I remained quite silent. The prospect of being a com-mandant's lady had no charms for me. It would have better suited me to have spent my life with the man of my choice in retirement in the country; but, still, the resolution he had just expressed was dear to me, for it protected him from any stain of the suspicion which my father nourished against him, and which would certainly have clung to him in the eyes of the world.

"Yes, quite reconciled," my father went on, "and rightly too: for I believed it was chiefly for that purpose ——- Now, now, you need not look in such a rage—I mean *partly*, for the purpose of withdrawing into private life; and that would have been very unfair of you. Unfair too towards my Martha—for she is the child of a soldier, the widow of a soldier; and I don't believe that she could love a man in civilian's costume for a continuance."

Tilling was now obliged to smile. He threw me a look which said plainly "I know you better," and answered aloud: "I think so too; she really only fell in love with my uniform ".

CHAPTER VI.

Marriage and visit to Berlin.—Lady Cornelia von Tessow and her son.—A wedding tour.—Life in garrison at Olmütz.—Christmas at Vienna.—Rumours of war.—A new-year's party.—Back at Olmütz.—War imminent.— Outbreak of the Schleswig-Holstein War.—History of the quarrel.

In September of this year our marriage took place.

My bridegroom had got two months leave for the wedding-tour. Our first stage was Berlin. I had expressed a wish to lay a wreath on the grave of Frederick's mother, and begin our tour with that pilgrimage.

We stopped eight days in the Prussian capital. Frederick introduced me to his relatives who were living there, and all seemed to me the most amiable people in the world. And, really, everything we met was pleasant and beautiful—wearing as we did the rose-coloured glasses through which one looks at the outside world during the honeymoon. Besides, the newly-married pair were greeted on all sides with cheerful and kindly politeness; every one seemed to find it a duty to strew new roses on a path already so sunny.

What pleased me particularly in North Germany was the dialect. Not only because it was marked by my husband's accent—one of his qualities which had excited my love at first —but also because in comparison with the way of speaking used in Austria it seemed to announce a higher level of education, or rather did not *seem*, but was really its result. Grammatical solecisms such as deform the common speech of the best circles in Vienna do not occur in good society at Berlin. The Prussian substitution of the accusative for the dative, "Gib mich einen Federhut," is confined to the lower classes, while in Vienna the ordinary confusions of cases, such as "Ohne dir," "Mit die kinder," are heard commonly enough in the best drawing-rooms. We may for all that call our way of speaking kindly, and get foreigners to take it as being so, but it shows some inferiority nevertheless. . If one measures human worth by the scale of education—and what more correct standard can one have?—then the North German is a little bit more of a man than the South German—an assertion that would sound very arrogant in the mouth of a Prussian, and may seem very "unpatriotic" from the pen of an Austrian authoress; but how seldom is there any outspoken truth which does not give offence, somewhere or somehow?

Our first visit in Berlin, after the churchyard, was to the sister of the deceased. From the amiability and intellectual accomplishments of this lady I could infer how amiable and accomplished his mother must have been if she was like Frau Cornelia v. Tessow. The latter was the widow of a Prussian general, and had an only son, who had just then become a lieutenant.

I never met with a handsomer young man in my whole life than this Godfrey v. Tessow. It was touching to see the affection between mother and son; and in this also Frau Cornelia seemed to have a resemblance to her deceased sister. When I saw the pride which she visibly had in Godfrey, and the tenderness with which he treated his mother, I was already delighting myself with imagining the time when my son Rudolf should be grown up. One thing only I could not understand, and this I expressed to my husband, thus:—

"How can a mother allow her only child, her treasure, to embrace so dangerous a profession as the army?"

"My dear, there are simple reflections which no one ever makes," Frederick answered, "considerations which lie so near one that no one ever heeds them. Such a reflection is the danger of the

military profession. People do not allow themselves to take
that into consideration; it is thought a kind of impropriety or
cowardice to allow that to weigh with one. And so it is
assumed as a matter of course and inevitable that such danger
must be survived, and indeed is nearly always survived by
good luck (the percentages of killed are distributed over other
people), and so the chance of being killed is not thought of.
To be sure, it exists; but so it does for every one born into
the world, and yet no one thinks about death. The mind
can do a great deal to chase away troublesome thoughts. And,
lastly, what more pleasant and more respected position can a
Prussian nobleman occupy than that of a cavalry officer?"

Aunt Cornelia appeared also pleased with me.

"Ah!" she sighed on one occasion, "how I wish that my
poor sister could have lived to feel the joy of having such a
daughter-in-law and seeing her Frederick so happy as he is
now with you. It was always her warmest wish to see him
married. But he demanded so much from marriage ——"

"That it did not seem likely he would fall in love with me,
aunty."

"That is what the English call 'fishing for a compliment'.
I only wish my Godfrey could get such a prize. I have been
long impatient to know the joy of being a grandmother. But
I shall have long to wait for that, my son is only twenty-one."

"He may turn many young ladies' heads," I said, "break
many hearts."

"That would not be like him; a better, more straightforward
young man does not exist. One day he will make a wife very
happy ——"

"As Frederick makes his."

"You cannot tell that quite yet, my dear. We must talk
about that ten years hence. In the first few weeks almost
every one is happy. Not that I would express any doubt of
my nephew or of you; I believe quite that your happiness will
be lasting."

This prophecy of Aunt Cornelia I wrote down in my diary,

and wrote underneath it : " Did it come true? The answer to
be written ten years hence." And then I left a line blank.
How I filled up that line in the year 1873—well, that must not
be set down in this place as yet.

After leaving Berlin we went to the German watering-places.
If my short tour in Italy with Arno were left out of account—
and of this I had besides only a dreamy recollection—I had
never been away from home. To make acquaintance in this
way with new places, new people, new ways of life, put me into
a most elevated state of mind. The world appeared to me to
have become all at once so beautiful, and thrice as interesting.
If it had not been for my little Rudolf that I had left behind,
I should have pressed Frederick : " Let us travel about like
this for years. We will visit the whole of Europe and then
the other quarters of the globe. Let us enjoy this wandering
life, this unfettered roving to and fro, let us collect the treasures
of new impressions and experiences. Anywhere that we come
to, however strange may be the people or the country, we
shall be sure, in virtue of our companionship, to bring a sufficient portion of home along with us." What would Frederick
have answered to such a proposition? Probably, that a man
cannot make it his business to spend his life in a wedding-tour,
that his leave only lasted for two months, and many more such
reasonable matters.

We visited Baden-Baden, Homburg, and Wiesbaden. Everywhere the same cheerful, elegant way of living ; everywhere so
many interesting people from all the chief countries of the
world. It was in intercourse with these foreigners that I first
became aware that Frederick was a perfect master of the
French and English languages—a thing which made him rise
to a still higher place in my admiration. I was always dis-
covering new qualities in him—gentleness, liveliness, the most
quick feeling for everything beautiful. A voyage on the Rhine
threw him into raptures, and in the theatre or concert-room,
when the artists performed anything peculiarly excellent, his
enjoyment shone out of his eyes. This made the Rhine and

its castles seem to me doubly romantic; this redoubled my admiration of the performances of celebrated musicians.

These two months passed over only too swiftly. Frederick applied for an extension of his leave, but it was decided against him. It was my first unpleasant moment since my marriage when this official paper arrived, which, in curt style, ordered' our return home.

"And men call that freedom!" I cried, throwing the offending document down on the table.

Tilling smiled. "Oh! I never looked on myself as free in the least, my mistress," he replied.

"If I were your mistress I could find it in my heart to command you to bid adieu to military service, and live only to serve me in the future."

"On this question we had agreed ——"

"Yes, I know. I am obliged to submit; but that proves that you are not my slave; and at bottom I feel that that is right, my dear, proud husband!"

.   .   .   .

On our return from our tour, we went to a small Moravian city, the fortress of Olmütz, where Frederick's regiment lay in garrison. There was no opportunity for social intercourse in the neighbourhood, so we two lived in complete retirement, with the exception of the hours given up to duty—he as lieutenant-colonel with his dragoons, I as a mother with my Rudolf. We gave ourselves up to each other only. The necessary ceremonial calls and return calls had been exchanged with the ladies of the regiment; but I could not lend myself to any intimate acquaintance; it did not amuse me in the least to go to afternoon tea parties and hear stories about servant-maids and the gossip of the town, and Frederick held off quite as far from the gambling parties of the colonel and the drinking bouts of the officers. We had something better to do. The world in which we moved, when we sat in the evening by the boiling tea-kettle, was worlds away from the world of Olmütz society. "Worlds away" often in a literal sense; for some of the favourite excursions of our spirit were directed towards the firmament. For we often read together scientific works and instructed ourselves in the wonders of the formation of the world. In this way we penetrated into the depths of the earth's centre, and the heights of the heavenly spaces. In this way we explored the secrets of the infinite minuteness revealed by the microscope, and the infinite distances of the telescope ; and by how much the wider the universe expanded before our gaze, by so much did the affairs of the Olmütz circle shrink into narrower dimensions. Our readings did not confine themselves to the natural sciences, but embraced many other branches of inquiry and thought. Thus I took up, among other things, my favourite Buckle, for the third time, to make Frederick acquainted with that author, whom he admired quite as much as I did ; and, at the same time, we did not neglect the poets or novelists. And so our evening readings together became real feasts of the mind, while the rest of our existence besides was a continual feast of the heart. Every day we became more fond of each other. As passion cooled in its flame, affection increased in its intimacy and respect in its steadfastness. The relations between Frederick and Rudolf were a source of delight to me. The two were the best friends in the world, and to see them playing together was charming. Frederick was, if anything, the more childish of the two. Of course I joined in the game at once, and all the nonsense that we acted and said at these times we hoped the wise and learned men would forgive us, whose works we read when Rudolf had been put to bed. Frederick, it is true, maintained that apart from him he was not very fond of children ; but, in the first place, the little boy was the son of his Martha, and in the next, he was really such a dear good little fellow, and suited his stepfather so wonderfully. We often laid plans for the boy's future. A soldier ? No. He should have no aptitude for it, since in our scheme of education there would be no drilling him into a love for military glory. A diplomatist? Perhaps. But most likely a country gentleman. As heir, presently, to the Dotzky estate,

which must come to him on the death of Arno's uncle, now
sixty-six years old, he would have sufficient business in managing his possessions properly.   Then he might take his little
bride Beatrix to himself and live happily.   We ourselves were
so happy that we would gladly have seen all the world—aye, and
future generations too—assured of the treasures of all life's
joys.   Yet we did not shut our eyes to the misery in which the
greater part of mankind was groaning, and in which, for some
generations at any rate, they must continue to groan—poverty,
ignorance, want of freedom, exposed to so many dangers
and ills ; and among these ills the most dreadful of all—War.
" Ah, could one contribute anything towards warding it off ? "
This wish often sprang with groans from our hearts; but
the contemplation of the prevailing circumstances and
views was enough to discourage us and make us feel that it
was impossible.   Alas ! the beautiful dream that for every
one it might " be well with them, and they might live long
upon the earth " could not be fulfilled, at least not at present.
The pessimist theory, however, that life itself is an evil,
that it would have been better for every one if he had never
been born—that was radically refuted by our own lot.

At Christmas we undertook an excursion to Vienna, in order
to spend the holidays in the circle of my family.   My father
was now fully reconciled to Frederick.   The fact that the
latter had not quitted the army had chased away his former
doubts and suspicions.   That I had made "a bad match"
remained indeed the conviction both of my father and Aunt
Mary ; but, on the other hand, they could not help perceiving
the fact that my husband made me very happy, and that they
reckoned in his favour.

Rosa and Lilly were sorry that they would have to go into
"the world" next carnival not under my supervision but the
much more severe one of their aunt.   Conrad Althaus was
still, as before, a constant visitor at the house ; and I could see,
I thought, that he had made progress in Lilly's graces.

Christmas Eve turned out very gay.   A great Christmas

tree was lighted up and all kinds of presents were exchanged between one and the other. The king of the feast and the one who had most presents was, of course, my son Rudolf, but all the others were thought of. Amongst the rest Frederick got one from me, at the sight of which he could not repress a cry of joy. It was a silver letter-weight in the form of a stork. In its bill it held a slip of paper on which in my writing were the words: "I am bringing you something in the summer of 1864". Frederick embraced me warmly. If the others had not been there he would certainly have waltzed round the room with me.

On Boxing Day the whole family gathered together again at dinner at my father's. There were no strangers except the Right Honourable "To-be-sure" and Dr. Bresser. As we were sitting at table in the familiar dining-room I could not help having a lively remembrance of that evening when we two first plainly recognised our love. Dr. Bresser had the same thought.

"Have you forgotten the game of piquet which I was playing with your father, while you chatted over the fire with Baron Tilling?" he asked me. "I seemed, it is true, quite absorbed in my play, but nevertheless I had my ear cocked in your direction, and heard from the sound of the voices—for I could not catch the words — something which awoke in me the conviction, 'Those two will come together'. And now that I observe you together a new conviction arises in me, 'Those two are and will remain happy together'."

"I admire your penetration, doctor. Yes, we *are* happy. Shall we remain so? That, unfortunately, depends not on ourselves but on Fate. . . . Over every happiness there hangs a danger, and the more heartfelt is the former so much the more terrible the latter."

"What have *you* to fear?"

"Death."

"Ah, yes! That did not occur to me. As a physician, it is true, I have frequent opportunities of meeting the gentleman, but I do not think of him. And, indeed, for young and healthy people, like the happy pair we are speaking of, he lies so far in the distance ——"

'What is a soldier better for youth and health?"

"Chase away such ideas, dear baroness. There is really no war in prospect. Is it not true, your excellency," he said, turning to the Minister, "that at present the dark point so often spoken of is not visible?"

"'Point' is far too little to say," he replied. "It is rather a black, heavy cloud."

I trembled to my heart's core.

"What," I cried out sharply, "what do you mean?"

"Denmark is going altogether too far ——"

"Oh, Denmark?" I said, much relieved. "Then the cloud is not threatening us? It is indeed to me a sad thing, under any circumstances, to hear that there is to be fighting anywhere; but if it is to be the Danes and not the Austrians, I feel pity indeed, but no fear."

"Well, you have no need for fear either," my father broke in hastily; "even if Austria were to protect her own interests. If we have to defend the rights of Schleswig-Holstein against the supremacy of Denmark, we are not risking anything in doing so. There is no question of any Austrian territory, the loss of which might be involved in an unsuccessful campaign."

"Do you think then, father, that if our troops should have to march out I should be thinking of such things as Austrian territory, Schleswig-Holstein's rights, or Danish supremacy? I should see one thing only—the danger of our dear ones. And that would remain just as great, whether the war were waged for one cause or another."

"My dear child, the fate of individuals does not come into consideration in cases where the events of the world's history are being decided. If a war breaks out, the question whether one or another will fall in it or not is silenced in the presence of the one mighty question whether one's own country will gain or lose in it. And, as I said, if we fight with the Danes we have nothing to lose in the war, and may improve our power and position in the German Bund. I am always dreaming that the Hapsburgs may yet one day get back the dignity of German emperor, which is their birthright. It would indeed be only proper. We are the most considerable state in the Bund —the Hegemony is secured to us, but that is not enough. I should welcome the war with Denmark as a very happy event, not only to wipe out the stain of '59, but also so to improve our position in the German Bund that we should get a rich compensation for the loss of Lombardy, and—who knows?— gain in power to such an extent that the reconquest of that province will be an easy task."

I looked across to Frederick. He had taken no part in the conversation, but had engaged in a lively laughing prattle with Lilly. A stab of pain shot through my soul, a pain which united into one twenty different fancies: war; and he, my All, would have to go, would be crippled, shot dead; the child in my bosom, whose coming he had greeted with such joy yesterday, would be born into the world an orphan; all destroyed, all destroyed, our happiness yet scarcely full-blown, but bearing the promise of such rich fruit! This danger in the one scale— and in the other ——? Austria's consideration in the German Bund, the liberation of Schleswig-Holstein, "fresh laurels in the army's crown of glory "—*i.e.*, a lot of phrases for school themes and army proclamations—and even that only dubious, for defeat is always just as possible as victory. And this supposed benefit to the country is to be set against not one individual's suffering—mine—but thousands and thousands of individuals in our own and in the enemy's country must be exposed to the same pain as was now quivering through me. Oh! could not this be prevented? Could it not be warded off? If all were to unite, all learned, good, and just men to avert the threatened evil!

" But tell me," I said aloud, turning to the Minister, " are affairs really in so bad a condition? You ministers and diplomatists, have you no means of hindering this conflict? Do you know of no way of preventing it from breaking out?"

"Do you think then, baroness, that it is our office to maintain perpetual peace? That would, to be sure, be a grand mission, only not practicable. We exist only to watch over the interests of our respective states and dynasties, to work against anything that may threaten the diminution of their power, and strive to conquer for them every supremacy possible, jealously to guard the honour of the country, to avenge any insult cast on it —— "

"In short," I interrupted, "to act on the principle of war —to do the enemy, i.e., every other state, all the harm possible, and if a dispute begins, to persist as long as possible in asserting that you are in the right, even if you see you are in the wrong. Eh?"

"To be sure."

"Till the patience of the two disputants gives way, and they have to begin hacking away at each other. It is horrible."

"But that is the only way out. How else can a dispute between nations be decided?"

"How then are trials between civilised individuals decided?"

"By the tribunals. But nations have no such over them."

"No more have savages," said Dr. Bresser, coming to my help. "Ergo, nations in their intercourse with each other are still uncivilised, and it will take a good long time yet before we come to the point of establishing an international tribunal of arbitration."

"We shall never get to that," said my father. "There are things which can only be fought out, and cannot be settled by law. Even if one chose to try to establish such an arbitration court, the stronger governments would as little submit to it as two men of honour, one of whom has been insulted, would carry their difference into a court of law. They simply send their seconds and fight to set themselves right."

" But the duel is a barbarous, uncivilised custom."

" You won't alter it, doctor."

"Still, your excellency, I would not defend it."

"What say you, then, Frederick?" said my father, turning to his son-in-law. "Is it your opinion that a man who has received a slap on the face should take the matter before a court of law and get five florins' damages?"

" I should not do so."

" You would challenge the man who insulted you?"

"Of course."

"Aha, doctor—aha, Martha," said my father in triumph. " Do you hear? Even Tilling, who is no friend of war, submits to, and is a friend of, duelling."

"A friend? I have never said so. I only said that in a given case I would, as a matter of course, have recourse to the duel, as indeed I have actually done once or twice: just as, equally as a matter of course, I have several times taken part in a war; and will do so again on the next occasion. I guide myself by the rules of honour; but I by no means imply thereby that those rules, as they now exist amongst us, correspond to my own moral ideal. By degrees, as this ideal gains the sovereignty, the conception of honour will also experience a change. Some day an insult one may have experienced, and which is unprovoked, will redound as a disgrace, not on the receiver, but on the savage inflicter; and when this is the case, self-revenge in matters of honour also will fall as much out of use as in civilised society it has become practically out of the question to right oneself in other matters. Till that time comes ——"

" Well, we shall have some time to wait for that," my father broke in. "As long as there are persons of quality anywhere ——"

"But that too may not perhaps be for ever," hinted the doctor.

"Holloa! you would not get rid of rank, Mr. Radical?" cried my father.

"Well, I would, of feudal rank. The future has no need for 'nobility'."

"So much the more need for noble men," said Frederick in confirmation.

"And this new race will put up with their slaps on the face?"

"First of all they will give none ——"

"And will not defend themselves if a neighbouring state makes a hostile attack on them?"

"There will be no attacks from neighbouring states, no more than our country seats now are besieged by neighbouring citizens. As the nobleman no longer needs armed squires to defend his castle ——"

"So the state of the future will dispense with its armed hosts? What will become then of you lieutenant-colonels?"

"What has become of the squires?"

And so the old dispute began again, and was prolonged for some time longer. I hung with delight on Frederick's lips. It did me more good than I can say to see the cause of noble humanity so firmly and so confidently defended; and in spirit I applied to himself the name he had just used—"noble man".

. . . .

We stayed a fortnight longer in Vienna. But it was by no means a pleasant holiday to me. This fatal "prospect of war," which now filled all newspapers and all conversations, robbed me of all pleasure in my life. As often as I thought of any of the things of which my happiness was made up, and especially my possession of a husband who was becoming daily dearer to me, so often was I reminded also of the uncertainty, of the imminent danger which hung over all my happiness, in view of the war which was looming in sight. And so I could not, as the saying is, "feel myself comfortable". Of the accidents of sickness and death, conflagrations, inundations, in short, all the menaces of Nature and the elements, there are sufficient; but one has habituated oneself not to think about them, and one lives in a certain sense of security in spite of these dangers. But how is it that men have created for themselves other dangers arbitrarily devised by themselves, and thus of their own will and in pure wantonness thrown into artificial eruption the volcanic soil on which the happiness of this life is founded? It is true that people have also accustomed themselves to think of war too as a natural phenomenon, and to speak of it as eluding calculation in the same category with the earthquake or drought—and therefore to think of it as little as possible. But I could no longer bring myself to this way of looking at it. The question, of which Frederick had once spoken: "Must it then be so?" I had often answered with a negative in the case of war—and at this time instead of resignation I felt pain and vexation—I should have liked to shout out to them all: "Do not do it; do not do it". This business of Schleswig-Holstein and the Danish constitution, what did it matter to us? Whether the "Protocol-Prince" abolished the fundamental law of November 13, 1863, or confirmed it, what did it matter to us? Yet all the journals and speeches at that time were full of discussions on this matter, as if it were the most important, most decisive, most universally comprehensive question in the world, so that in comparison with it the query "Are our husbands and sons to be shot dead?" ought not even to be considered. Only at intervals could I myself for a moment feel anyhow reconciled to this state of things, i.e., when the conception of "duty" came directly before my soul. It was true, no doubt, we belonged to the German Bund, and, in common with our brothers of Germany combined in that society, we were bound to fight for the rights of German brothers who were being oppressed. The principle of nationality was no doubt a thing that with elemental force demanded its field of action, and therefore from this point of view the thing *must* be. By sticking to this idea the painful indignation of my soul subsided a little. Had I been able to foresee how, two years later, the whole of this German band of brothers would be broken up by the bitterest enmity, that then the hatred of Prussia would have become far more burning in Austria than

9

the hatred of Denmark now was, I should have recognised even so early what I learned to know later on, that the motives which are adduced in order to justify hostilities are nothing but phrases—phrases and pretexts.

New-Year's eve we again spent in my father's house. As it struck twelve he raised his glass.

"May the campaign which is before us in this new year be a glorious one for our arms," he said solemnly; and at these words I put my glass, which I had just lifted up, down on the table again. "And," he concluded, "may our dear ones be spared to us!"

In that I concurred.

"Why did you not drink to the first half of my toast, Martha?"

"Because I can have no wish about a campaign, except that it may never occur."

When we had got back into the hotel, and into our bedroom, I threw myself on Frederick's neck.

"My own one! Frederick! Frederick!"

"What is the matter with you, Martha? You are weeping; and to-day—on New-Year's night! Why then salute the New Year with tears? Are you not happy? Have I given you any offence?"

"You? Oh no! no! You make me only too happy—much too happy—and that makes me anxious ——"

"Superstitious, Martha? Do you then conjure up for yourself envious gods, who destroy men's happiness when it is too great?"

"Not gods; it is senseless men who call misery down on themselves."

"You are hinting at this possible war. But it is certainly not settled as yet. Why then this premature grief? Who knows whether it will come to blows? and who knows, if so, whether I shall be called out? Come here, my darling, and let us sit down," and he drew me to the sofa by his side. "Do not spend your tears on a bare possibility."

"Even the possibility is terrible to me. If it were a certainty, Frederick, I should not be crying so softly and quietly on your shoulder. I should have to shriek and wail out loud. But the possibility, nay, the probability, that in the year which is opening you may be torn from my arms by a marching order. That is quite enough to transport me with anxiety and grief."

"Bethink you, Martha. You are yourself going to meet a peril, as this Christmas box of yours so charmingly informed me, and yet we two do not think of the cruel possibility which threatens every woman in childbed about as much as every man on the battlefield. Let us enjoy our life, and not think of the death which is impending over the heads of all of us."

"You are talking just like Aunt Mary, dearest, as if our lot depended on 'Providence,' and not on the thoughtlessness, cruelty, excesses, and follies of our fellow-men. Wherein lies the inevitable necessity of this war with Denmark?"

"It has not yet broken out, and there may still —— "

"I know, I know; accidents may still happen to avert the evil. But it is not accident, not political intrigues and humours which ought to decide such questions of destiny; but the firm, righteous *will* of mankind. But what is the good of my 'ought' or 'ought not'? I cannot alter the order of things. I can only complain of it. But do help me so far, Frederick! Do not try to console me with hollow conventional evasions! You do not believe in them yourself! You yourself are shuddering with noble repugnance! The only consolation I find is in thinking that you condemn and bewail as I do what will make me and numberless others so unhappy."

"Yes, my dear; if this fatality should come to pass, then I will say you are right. Then I will not hide from you the shuddering and the hate which the national slaughter ordained on us awakes in me. But to-day let us still enjoy our life. We surely have each other—nothing separates us. There is not the slightest bar between our souls! Let us enjoy this happiness as long as we have it; enjoy it to the full. Let us not think of the threatened destruction of it. No joy assuredly can last for

ever. In a hundred years it will be all the same whether our
life has been long or short. The number of beautiful days is
not the question, but the degree of their beauty. Let the
future bring what it pleases, my dearly-loved wife; our present is so beautiful, so very beautiful, that I cannot now feel
anything but a blessed delight."

As he said this, he threw his arm around me, and kissed my
head, which rested on his breast. And then the threatening
future disappeared for me also, and I too let myself sink into
the sweet transport of the moment.

.   .   .   .

On 10th January we returned to Olmütz.

No one any longer doubted about the outbreak of war. I
had heard a few individuals in Vienna hope that the Schleswig-
Holstein dispute could even yet be capable of diplomatic
settlement; but in the military circles of our garrison town
all possibility of peace was held to be out of the question.
Among the officers and their wives there prevailed an excited,
but on the whole joyfully excited, temper. Opportunities for
distinction and advancement were in prospect, for the satisfaction of the love of adventure in one, the ambition of another,
the thirst for promotion of a third.

"This is a famous war which is in prospect," said the
colonel, to whose house, with several other officers and their
wives, we were invited to dinner; "a famous war, and one that
must be immensely popular. No danger to our territory; and
even the population of our country will suffer no diminution,
since the scene of war lies on foreign soil."

"What inspires me in the matter," said a young first lieutenant, "is the noble motive, to defend the rights of our
brethren under oppression. The fact that the Prussians are
marching with us—or rather we with them—assures us in the
first place of victory, and in the next place it will bind still
closer the bonds of nationality. The national idea —— "

"I had rather you would not talk about that," interposed the
colonel rather sternly. "That humbug does not sit well on

an Austrian. It was that that raised up the Italian war against us; for it was on this hobby-horse, 'Italy for the Italians,' that Louis Napoleon kept always mounting, and the whole principle is specially unsuitable for Austria. Bohemians, Hungarians, Germans, Croats—where is the bond of nationality? We know one principle only which unites us, and that is a loyal love of our reigning family. Therefore, what ought to put spirit into us when we take the field is not the circumstance that we are Germans, and have Germans as allies, but that we can render loyal service to our exalted and beloved commander-in-chief. The emperor's health!"

All stood up to drink the toast. A spark of animation even reached my heart, inflaming it for a moment and filling it with a warmth that did me good. That thousands should love one and the same cause, one and the same person, is a thing which produces a peculiar, a thousandfold impulse of devotion. And that is the feeling which swells the heart under the name of loyalty, patriotism, or *esprit-de-corps*. It is in reality nothing but love; and this has such a mighty working that a man regards the work of hatred ordained in its name, even the most horrible work of the deadliest hatred—War—as the fulfilment of the duty of his love.

But this glow only lasted in my heart for one instant, for a love stronger than that for any earthly fatherland or father of the country filled its depths—the love of my husband. *His* life was to me in all cases the dearest of my possessions, and if *it* was to be the stake I could do nothing but abhor the game, whether it was to be played for Schleswig-Holstein or Japan.

The time which now followed I passed in unspeakable anxiety. On 16th January the powers of the Bund addressed a demand to Denmark calling on her to abrogate a certain law, against which the Convocation of Estates and the nobles of Holstein had invoked the protection of the Bund, and to do this in twenty-four hours. Denmark refused. Who would consent to be commanded in that fashion? This refusal had been foreseen, of course, for Austrian and Prussian troops stood ready posted on the frontier; and on 1st February they crossed the Eider.

So the bloody die was cast again—the game had begun. This gave occasion to my father to send us a letter of congratulation.

"Rejoice, my children," he wrote. "Now we have at length an opportunity to repair the losses we got in '59, by inflicting losses on the Danes. When we have come back from the north as conquerors, we shall be able to turn our faces south-wards again. The Prussians will remain our constant allies; and in that case these shabby Italians and their intriguing Louis Napoleon cannot again stand up against us."

Frederick's regiment, to the great disappointment of the colonel and the corps of officers, was not despatched to the frontier. This fact brought us a paternal letter of condolence:—

"I am heartily sorry that Tilling has the ill-luck to be serv-ing in just one of the regiments which are not called on to open the campaign which has such glorious prospects, but there remains always the possibility that he will be marked out to follow in support. Martha, indeed, will look on the best side of the business, and be glad that the fear for her beloved hus-band is spared her, and Frederick also is confessedly no friend of war; but I think he is only against it in principle, that is to say, he would rather, on grounds of so-called 'humanity,' that it should never come to fighting, but when it has so come, then he would, I know, rather have a part in it, for then I know his manly love of battle would awake. In truth it ought to be the *whole* army that should always be sent to meet the foe; at such a time to be forced to stay at home is surely something altogether too hard on a soldier."

"Does it strike you as hard, my Frederick, to remain with me?" I asked, after reading the letter.

He pressed me to his heart. The dumb reply contented me.

But what was the good of it? My peace was gone. The order to march might come any day. If the unhappy war could only be brought to an end quickly! With the greatest

eagerness did I read in the newspapers the news from the seat
of war, and warmly did I wish that the allies might win speedy
and decisive victories. I confess that the wish had no patriotism
at all in it. I should indeed have preferred that the victory
should be on our side ; but what I hoped from it was the termination of the wár, before my "all on earth" was out there ;
and then only in the second degree the triumph of my countrymen, and quite in the last the "sea-surrounded" patch of
country. Whether, however, Schleswig was to belong to Denmark or no, what in the world could that matter to me ? And
finally, what matter could it make to the Danes and Schleswig-
Holsteiners themselves ? Could not then the two nations
themselves see that it was only their rulers who were quarrelling
about the possession of territory and power, and that in the present case, for example, the question was not their good or their
suffering, but the wishes of the so-called Prince "Protocol"
and of the Augustenburgs? If a number of dogs are
fighting over some bones, it is still only the dogs themselves
who tear each other ; but in the history of nations it is chiefly
the poor silly bones themselves that rush at each other and knock
each other to pieces on the two sides, in fighting for the rights of
the combatants who covet them. "Lion wants me," or "Towser
has a claim on me". "I protest against Caro's fangs," or "I
reckon it an honour to be swallowed by Growler," cry the bones.
"Denmark up to the Eider," shouted the Danish patriots.
"We will have Frederick of Augustenburg for our duke,"
shouted the loyalists of Holstein. The articles in our papers
and the talk of our quidnuncs were all of course permeated by
the principle that the cause for which "we" had entered into the
war was the right one, the only one which was "historically
developed"—the only one necessary for the maintenance of
"the balance of power in Europe". And of course the opposite
principle was maintained with equal emphasis in the leading
articles and the political speeches in Copenhagen. Why not on
both sides weigh the rival claims, in order to come to an
understanding: and if this should fail, make a third power

arbitrator? Why go on always shouting on both sides, " I, I am in the right "—and even shouting it out against one's own conviction, till one has shouted oneself hoarse, and finishes by leaving the decision to *Force!* Is not that savagery? And even should a third power mix in the strife, it also does so, not with a balancing of rights or a judicial sentence, but equally with downright blows! And that is what people call "'foreign politics". Foreign and domestic savagery it is—statesman-like tomfoolery—international barbarism!

. . . .

It is true that I did not at that time look at what was going on in this light with such certainty as this. It was only for a few moments that doubts of this sort woke up in me, and then I took all possible pains to chase them away. I attempted to persuade myself that the mysterious thing called " reasons of state," a thing elevated above all private reason, and particularly my own poor faculties, was a principle on which the life of states depends, and I began a zealous study of the history of Schleswig-Holstein, in order to arrive at a conception of the " historic rights " which it was the object of the present proceedings to maintain.

And then I discovered that the strip of land in dispute had, as early as the year 1027, been ceded to Denmark. So, in reality, the Danes are in the right. They are the legitimate kings of the country.

But then, 200 years later, the district was made over to a younger branch of the royal house, and then ranked rather as a fief of the Danish crown. In 1326 Schleswig was given over to Count Gerhard of Holstein, and "the Constitution of Waldemar" provides that " it should never again be so far united with Denmark that there should be but one lord". Oh! then the right is still on the side of the allies. We are fighting for the Constitution of Waldemar. That is quite correct, for what is the use of these securities on paper if they are not to be upheld?

In the year 1448 the Constitution of Waldemar was again

confirmed by King Christian I. So there can be no doubt that there must and shall never again be "one lord". What has the Protocol-Prince to do in the matter?

Twelve years later, the ruler of Schleswig dies without issue, and the Estates of the country meet at Ripen (it would be well if we always knew with such exactness when and where the Estates met—well, it was in 1460 at Ripen), and they proclaim the King of Denmark Duke of Schleswig, in return for which he promises them that the countries "shall remain together for ever, undivided". This makes me again a little confused. The only point to hold by is that they "shall remain together for ever".

But the confusion goes on constantly increasing, as this historical study takes a wider circuit; for now in spite of the formula "for ever undivided" (the word "for ever" plays an exquisite part generally in political business), there commences an everlasting cutting up and division of the territory amongst the king's sons and a reunion of these under a succeeding king, and the founding of new families, Holstein-Gottorp and Schleswig-Sonderburg, which with reciprocal shuffling and cessions of their shares, again separate themselves into the families of Sonderburg - Augustenburg, Beck - Glücksburg, Sonderburg-Glücksburg, Holstein-Glückstadt. In short, I no longer knew where I was.

But there is more to come. Perhaps the "historical claim" for which the sons of our country have to bleed to-day may not have been established till later.

Christian IV. mixed himself up in the Thirty Years' War, and the Imperialists and Swedes invaded the duchies. Now was made (at Copenhagen, 1658) another treaty, by which the lordship over the Schleswig portion was secured to the house of Holstein Gottorp, and so at last we have got done with the Danish feudal lordship. Done with it for ever. Thank God. Now I find myself again all right.

But what happened by the Patent of 22nd August, 1721? Simply this: the Gottorps' dominion of Schleswig was incorporated into the kingdom· of Denmark. In January, 1773, Holstein also was ceded to the royal house of Denmark ; the whole ranked now as a Danish province.

That changes the affair, the Danes are in the right.

Yet not entirely so. The Congress of Vienna, in 1815, declares Holstein to be a part of the German Bund. This, however, vexes the Danes. They invent the cry: "Denmark up to the Eider," and struggle for the complete possession of Schleswig—called by them "South Jutland," against which the "hereditary right of Augustenburg" was employed as a watchword and used in German national proclamations. In the year 1846 King Christian writes a public letter in which he proposes the integrity of the entire state as his object, and against this "the German countries" protest. Two years later the complete union is announced from the Throne, no longer as an object, but as a *fait accompli*, and then the uprising occurs in the "German countries". And now the fighting begins. At first the Danes gain the victory in one fight, next the Schleswig-Holsteiners in a second. Then the German Bund intervenes. The Prussians "occupy" the heights of Düppel, but that does not terminate the strife. Prussia and Denmark make peace. Schleswig-Holstein has now to fight the Danes single-handed, and is struck down at Idstedt.

The Bund now calls on the "revolters" to discontinue the war, which they proceed to do. Austrian troops take possession of Holstein, and the two duchies are *separated*. So what has become of the paper-stipulation "to be for ever united"?

Still the situation is not made completely secure. Now I find a Protocol of London, 8th May, 1852 (it is a good thing that we always know so exactly the date when these fragile treaties are made), which secures the succession of Schleswig to Prince Christian of Glücksburg ("secures" is good). And now I know at any rate the origin of the name "Protocol-Prince".

In the year 1854, after each duchy had received a constitution of its own, both were "Danised". But in 1858 the Danisation of Holstein had to be revoked again. And now this historical sketch is coming quite close to the present time ; and yet it is not so clear to me to whom the two countries "rightly belong," or what was the precise cause of the outbreak of the present war.

On 18th November, 1858, the famous "Fundamental law for the mutual relations between Denmark and Schleswig" was passed by the Reichsrath. Two days afterwards the king died. With him again was extinguished a family—that of Holstein-Glückstadt—and when the successor of the monarch presented himself on the scene, in reliance on the two-days-old law, Frederick of Augustenburg (a family I had nearly for-gotten) raised his claim, and together with his nobility turned for support to the German Bund.

The latter at once occupied Holstein with Saxon and Hano-verian troops, and proclaimed Augustenburg duke. Why ? But Prussia and Austria were not of accord in this proceeding. Why ? That I do not to this day understand.

It is said the London Protocol had to be respected. Why ? Are these Protocols about things which concern us absolutely nothing so exceedingly to be respected, that we must defend them at the price of the blood of our own sons ? If so, there must lie in the background some mysterious "reason of state" for it. It must be firmly held as a dogma that what the gentle-men round the green table of diplomacy may decide is the highest wisdom, and has for its aim the greatest possible advance of the power of one's country. The London Protocol of 8th May, 1852, had to be maintained intact ; but the Fundamental Law of Copenhagen, of 13th January, 1863, had to be abolished, and that within twenty-four hours. On that hung Austria's honour and welfare. The dogma was a little hard to believe, but in political matters, almost more willingly than in religious, the masses allow themselves to be led by the principle of the "*quia absurdum*"—they have renounced beforehand the attempt to reason and understand. When the sword is once drawn nothing more is necessary than to shout "Hurrah," and press hotly on to victory. Besides that, all that is necessary is to invoke the

blessing of heaven on the war.   For so much is certain, that it
must be the business of the Almighty to see that the Protocol
of the 8th May is maintained, and the Law of 5th November
repealed.   He must conduct the matter so that the precise
number of men bleed to death and villages are set on fire, that
are necessary in order that the family of Glückstadt. or that of
Augustenburg should rule over a particular spot of earth.
What a foolish world—still in leading strings—cruel, unthinking !   Such was the result of my historical studies.

CHAPTER VII.

The course of the Danish war.—Suspension of hostilities.—War renewed.—My husband ordered off just on the eve of my confinement.—The parting.—My confinement occurs simultaneously with my husband's departure.—A dead child.— The mother in deadly peril.—Frederick's letters from the seat of war.—Cousin Godfrey and the alliance between Austria and Prussia.—My recovery.—Anxiety and relapse. —Return of my husband.

FROM the theatre of war came good tidings. The allies won battle after battle. Immediately after the first combats the Danes were forced to abandon the entire Danewerk. Schleswig and Jutland up to Limfjord were occupied by our troops, and the enemy only maintained himself in the lines at Düppel and at Alsen.

I knew all this so accurately, because on the tables were again laid the maps stuck about with pins on which were marked the movements and positions of the troops as each despatch arrived. "If we could now only take the lines at Düppel, or if we could even conquer Alsen," said the citizens of Olmütz (for no one is so fond of speaking of deeds of war with the "we" as those who were never present at them), "then we should be at an end of it. Now our Austrians are showing again what they can do. The brave Prussians too are fighting splendidly. Both together are of course invincible. The end will be that all Denmark will be overrun and will be annexed to the German Bund—a glorious, beneficent war."

I too wished for nothing so anxiously as the storming of

(141)

Düppel—the sooner, the better—for this action would at any rate be decisive and put an end to the butchery. Put an end to it, I hoped, before Frederick's regiment got marching orders.

Oh, this Damocles' sword! Every day when I woke the fear came on me that the news would be brought "We are to march". Frederick was calm about it. He did not wish it, but saw it coming.

"Accustom yourself, dear, to the thought of it," he said to me. "Against inexorable necessity no striving is of any avail. I do not believe that even if Düppel falls the war will thereby terminate. · The allied army which has been despatched is far too small to force the Danes to a conclusion; we shall be obliged to send considerable reinforcements besides, and then my regiment will not be spared."

In fact, this campaign had lasted more than two months, and yet no result. If the cruel game could have been settled in one fight like a duel! But no; if one battle is lost, another is offered; if one position has to be given up, another is taken, and so on till one or the other army is annihilated, or both are exhausted.

At last, on 14th April, the lines of Düppel were stormed.

The news was received with such a shout of joy as if the recovered paradise had lain behind these lines. People embraced each other in the streets. "Don't you know? Düppel —Oh, our brave army! An unheard-of exploit. Now let all join in thanking God!" And there was singing of *Te Deums* in all the churches, and among the military choirmasters an industrious composition of "The Lines of Düppel March,' "Storm of Düppel Galop," and so forth.

My husband's comrades and their wives had, it is true, a drop of bitterness in their cup of joy, not to have been there, to have been obliged to miss such a triumph; what bad luck!

This victory gave me one great joy, for immediately after it a peace conference assembled in London and occasioned a suspension of hostilities. What a recovery of free breath even that word "suspension of hostilities" caused.

How the world would at last breathe again, thought I then for the first time, if on all hands could be heard: "Lay down your arms," down with them for ever! I put the words into my red book, but beside them I wrote despondingly in brackets "Utopia".

That the London Congress would make an end of the Schleswig-Holstein War I made no doubt at all. The allies had won, the lines of Düppel were carried, these lines had played so great a part in recent times that their capture seemed to me to be finally decisive: how could Denmark hold out longer? The negotiations dragged on for an incredible length of time. This would have been torture to me if I had not from the very beginning had the conviction that their result must be peaceful. If the plenipotentiaries of great states, who therefore must be reasonable, well-meaning persons, unite together to attain so desirable an end as the conclusion of peace, how could it fail? So much the more horribly was I undeceived when after debates continued for two months the news came that the congress had dissolved without accomplishing anything.

And two days later came marching orders for Frederick!

For preparations and for leave-taking he had twenty-four hours given him. And I was on the point of my confinement. In the heavy death-menacing hours, when a woman's only comfort lies in having her dear husband by her, I had to remain alone, alone with that consciousness awful beyond everything that this dear husband was gone to the war—knowing too that it must be just as painful to him to leave his poor wife at such a moment as it would be painful to me to be without him.

It was in the morning of 20th June. All the details of this memorable day remain impressed on my memory. Oppressive heat prevailed outside, and to shut this out the Venetian blinds had been let down in my room. Covered with light, loose clothing, I was lying exhausted on the sofa. I had passed an almost sleepless night, and had now shut my eyes in a dreamy half-doze. Near me on my table was standing a vase with some powerfully smelling roses. Through the open window the sound of a distant exercise in trumpet-playing came in.

Everything was provocative of slumber, yet consciousness had not quite left me. Only one half of it—I mean that of care—had departed. I had forgotten the danger of war and the danger that stood before myself. I knew only that I was alive—that the roses, along with the rhythm of the *reveillé* which the trumpeter was playing, were giving out sweet soothing influences—that my beloved husband might come in at any minute, and if he saw me asleep would only tread in the lightest manner so as not to awaken me. I was right; next minute the door opposite to me opened. Without raising my lids I could see through a tiny cleft between the eyelashes that it was he whom I was expecting. I made no attempt to rouse myself from my half-slumber, for by doing so I might chase away the whole picture; for it might be that the appearance at the door was only the continuation of a dream, and it might be that I was only dreaming that I had opened my eyelids ever so little. So now I shut them entirely and took pains to continue the dream—that the dear one came closer, that he bent over me and kissed my forehead.

And so indeed it was. Then he knelt down by my couch and remained motionless for a while. The roses were still breathing and the distant horn playing its tra-ra-ra.

" Martha, are you asleep?" I heard him ask softly.

Then I opened my eyes.

" For God's sake, what is it?" I cried out, frightened to death, for the countenance of my husband as he knelt by me was so deeply overclouded by sorrow that I guessed at once that some misfortune had happened. Instead of replying he laid his head on my breast.

I understood all. He had to go. I had thrown my arm round his neck, and we remained both in the same position for some time without speaking.

" When?" I asked at length.

" Early to-morrow morning."

" Oh, my God! my God!"

" Calm yourself, my poor Martha."

"No, no, let me weep. My misfortune is too great, and I know—I see it in your face—so is yours. Never did I see so much pain in any human face as I have just read in your features."

"Yes, my wife. I am unfortunate to have to leave you in such a moment ——"

"Frederick, Frederick; we shall never see each other again. I shall die ——"

"Or I shall fall. Yes, I believe it, too; we shall never see each other again!"

It was a heart-breaking parting that occupied these last twenty-four hours. This was now the second time in my life that I had seen a dear husband depart to the war. But this second tearing ourselves apart was incomparably worse than the first. Then my way of taking it and still more Arno's was quite different and more primitive. I looked on the departure as a natural necessity which overbalanced all personal feelings, and he looked at it even as a joyous expedition in search of glory. He went with cheerfulness. I remained without a murmur. There still clung to me something of the admiration for war which I had imbibed from my youthful education. I still shared to some extent with the departing soldier in the pride which he visibly felt in the "great emprise". But now I knew that he who was going went to the work of death with horror rather than with exultation, I knew that he loved the life which he had to set on the hazard—that to him one thing was dearer than everything, yes, everything, even the claims of the Augustenburgs—his wife—his wife who in a few days was to be a mother. Whilst in Arno's case I had the conviction that he departed with feelings for which he was surely to be envied, I discerned that in this second separation both of us were deserving of equal pity. Yes, we suffered in equal measure, and we confessed it and bewailed it to each other. No hypocrisies, no empty phrases of consolation, no swagger; we were one in all things, and neither sought to deceive the other. It was still our best consolation that each could fully understand the other's inconsolability. We did not seek to conceal the magnitude of the misfortune that had burst on us by any conventional cloaks or masks of patriotism or heroism. No, the prospect of being allowed to shoot and hack at the Danes was to him no compensation for the anguish of having to leave me—on the contrary, rather an aggravation—for killing and destroying is repulsive to every "noble man". And to me it was no recompense—absolutely none—for *my* suffering to think that my dear one might perhaps gain a step in rank. And should the misfortune of this perilous separation rise to the still greater misfortune of parting for ever—should Frederick fall—the reasons of state on account of which this war had to be waged were not in the faintest degree elevated or holy enough to my mind to balance such a sacrifice. "Defender of his Country," that is the fair-sounding title with which the soldier is decorated. And in fact what nobler duty can there be for the members of a commonwealth than to defend their state when menaced? But then why does his military oath bind the soldier to a hundred other warlike duties, besides the defensive? Why is he obliged to go and attack? Why must he, in cases where there is not the slightest menace of any invasion of his country, hazard the same possessions—his life and his hearth—in the quarrels of certain foreign princes for territory or ambition, as if it were a question, as it surely ought to be to justify war, of the defence of endangered life and hearth? Why, for example, in the present instance, must the Austrian army march out to set the Augustenburgs on a foreign throne? Why? Why? The question is one which to address to an emperor or pope is in itself treasonable and blasphemous, which in the latter case passes for irreligion and in the former for want of loyalty, and which never deserves an answer.

The regiment was to march at 10 A.M. We stayed up the whole night. Not a minute of the time still left to us to spend together would we lose.

There was so much that we had still to say to each other, and yet we spoke little. It was mainly kisses and tears, which said more plainly than any words: "I love you, and I have to leave you". From time to time there dropped in a hopeful word, "When you come back again". It was certainly possible. Surely there are so many that come back; yet it was strange I repeated "When you come back" and tried to put before myself the delights of this event; but in vain. My imagination could form no other picture than that of my husband's corpse on the field of battle, or myself on the bier, with a dead child in my arms.

Frederick was filled with similar gloomy forebodings, for his "When I come back" did not sound natural; and more often he spoke of what might happen, "If I should fall".

"Do not marry a third time, Martha! Do not wash out, by the impressions of a new love, the recollections of this glorious year! Has it not been a happy time?"

We now recalled a hundred little details which had impressed themselves on our minds, from our first meeting to the present hour, and passed them through our remembrance.

"And my little one, my poor little one, whom perhaps I may never press to my heart, what is its name to be?"

"Frederick or Frederica."

"No; Martha is prettier. If it is a girl call it by the name which its dying father at the last moment ——"

"Frederick, why do you talk always about dying? If you come back ——"

"Ah! *if I!*" he repeated with a sigh.

As the day was beginning to dawn, my eyes, weary with weeping, closed, a light slumber fell on both of us. We lay there with our arms linked together, but without losing the consciousness that this was our parting hour.

Suddenly I started up and broke out into loud groans. Frederick got up at once.

"In God's name, Martha, what is the matter with you? It is not yet come? Oh speak! Is it ——"

I nodded affirmatively.

Was it a cry, or a curse, or an ejaculation of prayer, that escaped his lips? He clutched the bell and gave the alarm.

"Run at once for the doctor—for the nurse," he shouted to the maid who had hurried in. Then he threw himself down on his knees beside me, and kissed my hand as it hung down.

"My wife! my all! and *now, now* I have to go."

I could not speak. The most violent physical pain that one can conceive was racking and wringing my body; and besides this, the agony of my soul was yet more horrible, that he "had to go *now, now*"; and that he was so wretched about it. Those who had been summoned came quickly, and at once made themselves busy about me. At the same time Frederick had to make his last preparations for the march. After he had done this: "Doctor, doctor," he cried, seizing the physician by both hands, "you promise me, do you not, that you will bring her through? And you will telegraph to me to-day, and afterwards there and there," naming the stations which he had to pass on the march. "And if there is any danger —— Ah! but what good is it?" he interrupted himself. "If even the danger were ever so great, could I come back then?"

"It is hard, baron," the physician replied; "but do not be too anxious, the patient is young and strong. This evening it will be all over, and you will receive a tranquillising despatch."

"Oh yes! You mean to send good news in any case, because the opposite would do no good! But I *will* have the truth! Listen, doctor! I must have your most sacred word of honour on it. The *whole* truth. Only on this condition could a tranquillising account really give me tranquillity. Otherwise I should think it all a lie. So swear to do this."

The physician gave the promise required.

"O my poor, poor husband"—the thought cut me to the soul—"even if you receive the news to-day that your Martha is lying on her deathbed, you cannot turn back to close her eyes! You have something more important on hand—the claims of the Augustenburgs to a throne."

"Frederick!" I cried out loud.

He flew to my side. At this moment the clock struck. He had now only a minute or two. But we were cheated out of even this last respite, for another attack seized me, and instead of the words of adieu, I could only utter groans of anguish.

"Go, baron—finish this scene," said the physician, "for the patient such excitement is dangerous."

One more kiss, and he rushed out. My cries and the doctor's last word, "dangerous," gave him his dismissal.

In what frame of mind must he have been when he departed? The local newspapers of Olmütz gave this report next day :—

"Yesterday the —th Regiment left our town with music playing and banners waving, to gain fresh laurels for themselves in the sea-surrounded brotherland. Cheerful courage filled the ranks ; one could see the joy of battle glowing in the men's eyes ——" and so on, and so on.

Frederick had already telegraphed to Aunt Mary before his departure that I was in want of her help, and she came a few hours later to me. She found me senseless and in great danger.

For several weeks I hovered between life and death. My child died the day of its birth. The mental pain, which parting from my beloved husband had caused me, just at the time when I wanted all my strength to master the bodily pain, had rendered me incapable of bearing up against it, and I was near succumbing altogether.

The physician was obliged by his plighted word to send my poor husband the sorrowful news that the child was dead, and the mother in danger of death.

As to the news which came from him, they could not be communicated to me. I knew no one and was delirious day and night. A strange delirium. I brought back with me a

feeble reminiscence of it into the period of recovered consciousness, but to reproduce this in reasonable words would be
impossible for me.   In the abnormal whirl of the fevered brain,
conceptions and images form themselves for which there is no
expression in language suitable to our normal thoughts.   Only
so much can I set down—and I have attempted to fix the
fantastic sketch in the red volumes—that I confused the two
events—the war and my confinement—together.   I fancied
that cannon and naked weapons (I distinctly felt the bayonet
thrusts) were the instruments of delivery, and that I was lying
there the prize of contention between two armies rushing on
each other.   That my husband had marched out I knew, but
I saw him still in the form of the dead Arno, while by my side
Frederick dressed as a sick nurse was stroking the silver stork.
Every moment I was awaiting the bursting shell which was to
shatter us all three—Arno, Frederick, and me—to pieces, in
order that the child could come into the world, who was
destined to rule over " Denstein, Schlesmark, and Holwig." . . .
And all this gave me such unspeakable pain and was so unnecessary. . . . There must, however, be some one somewhere
who could change it and remove it all, who could lift off this
mountain from my heart and that of all humanity by some
word of power; and I was devoured with a longing to cast
myself at this somebody's feet and pray to him : " Help us ! for
the sake of mercy and justice help us !   Lay down your arms !
down !"   With this cry on my lips I woke one day to consciousness.   My father and Aunt Mary were standing at the foot of
the bed, and the former said to me to hush me :—

" Yes, yes, child, be quiet.   All arms down."

This recovery of the sense of personality after a long suspension of the intellect is certainly a strange thing.   First the
joyful astonished discovery that one is alive, and then the
anxious questioning with oneself who one really is . . .

But the sudden answer to that question, which burst in with
full light upon me, changed the just awakened pleasure of
existence into violent pain.   I was the sick Martha Tilling,

whose new-born child was dead, and whose husband was gone
to battle. . . . How long ago? That I knew not.

"Is he alive?—have you letters there?—messages?" were my
first questions. Yes; there was quite a little heap of letters
and telegrams piled up which had come during my illness.
Most of them were merely inquiries after *my* condition, requests
for daily, and as far as possible, hourly information. This, of
course, was so long as the writer was at places where the telegraph could reach him.

I was not permitted to read Frederick's letters at once; they
thought it would excite me too much and disturb me; and now
that I was hardly awake out of my delirium I must, before all
things, have repose. They could tell me as much as this:
" Frederick was unhurt up to the present time ". He had
already been through several successful engagements. The
war must now soon be over. The enemy maintained themselves
at Alsen only; and if this position once were taken our troops
would return, crowned with glory. This was what my father
said for my comfort, and Aunt Mary gave me the history of
my illness. Several weeks had now passed since her arrival,
which was the very day on which Frederick departed, and my
child was born and died. Of that I had preserved a recollection, but what passed in the interval—my father's arrival—the
news that had come from Frederick—the course of my illness—
of all that I knew nothing. Now I heard for the first time
that my condition had become so much worse that the medical
men had quite given me up, and my father had been called to
see me "for the last time". The bad news must certainly
have been sent to Frederick; but the better news also—for
the doctors had given hope again some days ago—must by this
time have reached him.

" If he himself is still alive," I struck in, with a deep sigh.

" Do not commit a sin, Martha," my aunt admonished me;
" the good God and His saints would not have preserved you, in
answer to our prayers, in order afterwards to send such a visi-
tation upon you. Your husband also will be preserved to you,

for whom I—you may believe me when I say so—have prayed
as fervently as for you. I have even sent him a scapulary.
Oh yes ! Do not shrug your shoulders ; you have no trust in
such things, but they can do no harm anyhow, can they ? And
how many proofs there are of their good effect ! You yourself are again another proof what effect the intervention of the
saints has ; for you were, believe me, on the edge of the grave,
when I addressed myself to your patron and protectress, St.
Martha —— "

"And I," interrupted my father, who was very clerical
indeed in his politics, but in the practical way did not at all
sympathise with his sister, "I wrote to Vienna for Dr. Braun,
and he saved your life."

Next day, on my urgent prayer, I was permitted to read
through all the messages that had come from Frederick. Mostly
they were only questions in a single line, or news equally laconic.
"An engagement yesterday. I am unhurt." "We march
again to-day. Send messages to ——" A longer letter bore
this direction on the envelope : "To be delivered only if all
danger is over ". This I read last :—

"My all ! Will you ever read this ? The last news which
reached me from your physician ran : 'Patient in high fever ;
condition grave '. 'Grave !' He used the expression perhaps
out of consideration, so as not to say 'Hopeless'. If you have
this put into your hands you will know by that that you have
escaped the danger ; but you may think, in addition, what my
feelings were, as, on the eve of a battle, I pictured to myself
that my adored wife was lying on her deathbed ; that she was
calling for me, stretching out her arms for me. We did not
even say any regular adieu to each other ; and our child, about
whom I had had such joy, dead ! And to-morrow, I myself—
suppose a bullet find me ? If I knew beforehand that you were
no more, the mortal shot would be the dearest thing to me ;
but if you are preserved—no ! then I do not wish to know anything more of death. The 'joy of dying,' that unnatural feeling
which the field preachers are always pressing on us, is one no

happy man can know; and if you are alive, and I reach home, I have still untold treasures of bliss to gather. Oh, the joy of living with which we two will enjoy the future, if any such is to be our lot.

"To-day we met the enemy for the first time. Up to that our way had been through conquered territory, from which the Danes had retreated. Smoking ruins of villages, ravaged corn-fields, weapons and knapsacks lying about, spots where the land was ploughed up by the shells, blood stains, bodies of horses, trenches filled with the slain—such are the features of the scenes through which we have been moving in the rear of the victors, in order, if possible, to add more victories to the account—*i.e.*, to burn more villages, and so forth. . . . And that we have done to-day. We have carried the position. Behind us lies a village in flames. The inhabitants had the good luck to have quitted it beforehand; but in the stable a horse had been forgotten. I heard the beast in despair stamping and shrieking. Do you know what I did? It will procure me no decoration most certainly; for, instead of bringing down a Dane or two, I rushed to the stable to set the poor horse free. Impossible; the manger had already caught fire, then the straw under his hoofs, then his mane. So I put two revolver bullets through his head. He fell down dead, and was saved from the pain of being burned to death. Then, back into the fight, the deathly smell of the powder, the wild alarm of the whistling bullets, falling buildings, savage war-cries. Most of those around me, friends and foes, were, it is true, seized by the delirium of battle; but I remained in unblessed sobriety. I could not get myself up to hate the Danes. They are brave men, and what did they do but their duty in attacking us? My thoughts were with you, Martha! I saw you laid out on your bier, and what I wished for myself was that the bullet might strike me. But at intervals, nevertheless, a ray of longing and of hope would shine again. ' What if she is alive? What if I should get home again?'

"The butchery lasted more than two hours, and we remained

as I said, in possession of the field. The routed enemy fled.
We did not pursue. We had work enough to do on the field.
A hundred paces distant from the village stood a large farm
house, with many empty dwelling-rooms and stables; here we
were to rest for the night and hither we have brought our
wounded. The burial of the dead is to be done to-morrow
morning. Some of the living will, of course, be shovelled in
with them, for the 'stiff cramp' after a severe wound is a common phenomenon. Many who have remained out, whether
dead or wounded, or even unwounded, we are obliged to
abandon entirely, especially those who are lying under the ruins
of the fallen houses. There they may, if dead, moulder slowly
where they are; if wounded, bleed slowly to death; if unwounded, die slowly of famine. And we, hurrah! may go on
with our jolly, joyous war!

"The next engagement will probably be a general action.
According to all appearance there will be two entire *corps
d'armée* opposed to each other. The number of the killed and
wounded may in that case easily rise to 10,000; for when the
cannons begin their work of vomiting out death the front ranks
on both sides are soon wiped out. It is certainly a wonderful
contrivance. But still better would it be if the science of artillery could progress to such a point that any army could fire a
shot which would smash the whole army of the enemy at one
blow. Then, perhaps, all waging of war would be entirely
given up. Force would then, provided the total power of the
two combatants were equally great, no longer be looked to for
the solution of questions of right.

"Why am I writing all this to you? Why do I not break out,
as a warrior should, into exalted hymns of triumph over our
warlike work? Why? Because I thirst after truth, and after
its expression without any reserve; because at all times I hate
lying phrases; but at this moment, when I am so near death
myself, and am speaking to you who, perhaps, are yourself
lying in the death-agony, it presses on me doubly to speak what
is in my heart. Even though a thousand others should think

differently, or should hold themselves bound at least to speak differently, I will, nay, I *must* say it once more before I fall a sacrifice to war—I hate war. If only every man who feels the same would dare to proclaim it aloud, what a threatening protest would be shouted out to heaven! All the hurrahs which are now resounding, and all the cannon-thunder that accompanies them, would then be drowned by the battle-cry of humanity panting after humanity, by the victorious cry denouncing 'war on war'.

"Half-past three in the morning. I wrote the above last night. Then I lay down on a sack of straw and slept for an hour or two. We shall break up in half-an-hour, and then I shall be able to give this to the field-post. All is stirring now and getting ready for the march. Poor fellows! they have got little rest since the bloody work accomplished yesterday : little refreshment for that which is to be accomplished to-day. I began with a turn round our improvised field-hospital, which is to remain here. There I saw among the wounded and dying a pair for whom I would gladly have done the same as for the horse in the fire—put a bullet as a *coup de grâce* through their heads. One was a man who had had his whole lower jaw shot away, and the other—but enough. I cannot help him. Nothing can but Death. Unfortunately he is often so slow. If a man calls in despair for him he stands deaf before him. On the other hand, he is far too busy in snatching those away who with all their heart are hoping to recover, and calling on him beseechingly : 'Oh, spare me, for I have a beloved wife pining for me at home!' My horse is saddled, so now I must close these lines. Farewell, Martha, if you are still here!"

.   .   .   .   .

Luckily there were tidings of a later date in the packet than the letter above quoted. After the great battle predicted in the last Frederick had been able to tell me :—

"'The day is ours. I am unhurt. These are two pieces of

good news, the first for your papa, the second for you. But I
cannot overlook the fact that the same day has brought numberless griefs to numberless others. . . ."

In another letter Frederick related how he had met with his
cousin Godfrey.

"Picture to yourself my astonishment. Whom should I see
riding before me at the head of a detachment, but Aunt Cornelia's only son! How the poor woman must be trembling for
him. . . . The young man himself is all eagerness and love of
battle. I saw it in his proud, joyful bearing, and he has also
told me so. We were in camp together the same evening and
I invited him into my tent. 'It is indeed splendid,' he cried
out in rapture, 'that we are fighting in the same cause, cousin,
and together. Am not I in luck, that war should have broken
out in the first year of my lieutenancy? I shall gain the Cross
of Merit.' 'And my aunt, how did she take your departure?'
'Oh! in the mother's way, with tears—which she did all she
could to hide, so as not to damp my spirit—with blessings,
with grief, and with pride.' 'And what were your feelings
when you first got into the *melée*?' 'Oh, delightful! ennobling!'
'You need not use falsehood to me, my dear boy. It is
not the staff officer who is asking about your feelings as a
lieutenant bound to duty, but a man and a friend.' 'I
can only repeat, delightful and ennobling. Awful, I grant,
but so magnificent. And the consciousness that I am fulfilling, with God's help, the highest duty of a man to king
and country! And further, that I see Death, the spectre
elsewhere so feared and shunned, so close and busy all round
me, his very breath breathing over me—the thought raises me
to a mood of mind so elevated above the common, so epic that
I feel the muse of history hovering over our heads and lending
our swords the might of victory. A noble rage glows in me
against the presumptuous foe, who would have trampled on the
rights of the German countries, and it is to me an enthusiasm
to have the power of gratifying this hatred. It is a curious,
mysterious thing, this power of killing—nay, this compulsion to

kill—without being a murderer—with a fearless exposure of
one's own life.'

"So the boy chattered on. I let him talk. I had similar
feelings when my first battle was raging round me. 'Epic!'—
yes, there you hit on the right word. The heroic poems and
the heroic histories by whose means our schools bring us up to
be warriors, these are what are set vibrating in our brains by
the thunders of the cannonade, the flash of naked weapons,
and the shouts of the combatants. And the freedom from
ordinary circumstances, the inexplicable freedom from law in
which one finds oneself all of a sudden, makes one feel as if
transported into another world—it is like an outlook beyond
this trumpery earthly existence, with its peaceful domestic quiet,
into a titanic struggle of infernal spirits. But this giddiness
soon passed over with me, and it is only with an effort that I
can bring back to my mind the sensations which young Tessow
sketched to me. I recognised too soon that the desire for
battle was not a *super*-human but an *infra*-human feeling, no
mystic revelation from the realms of the morning, but a reminiscence of the realm of the animal, a re-awakening of the brutal.
And a man who can intoxicate himself into a savage lust for
blood, who—as I have seen several of our men do—can cut
down with uplifted sabre an unarmed enemy, who can sink into
a Berserker, or lower still, a blood-thirsty tiger—that is the
man who, for the moment, revels in the 'joy of battle'. I
never did this. Believe me, my wife ; I never did.

"Godfrey is delighted that we Austrians are united in fighting for the 'right cause' (how does he know that? As if every
cause is not always represented as the 'right' one by its own
side!) with the Prussians: 'Yes, we Germans are all one
united people of brothers!' 'That was seen long ago in the'
Thirty Years' War, and also in the Seven Years' War,' I struck
in half-aloud. Godfrey missed what I said, and went on : 'For
each other and with each other we can conquer every foe'.

What will you say then, my young friend, if to-day or to-
morrow the Prussians and Austrians quarrel, and we two shall

be ranged as foes, one against each other ? '   ' Not conceivable,
now, after the blood of both of us has flowed for the same
cause.   Now surely we can never more ——'   ' Never more ?
I would warn you not to use the expressions "never" or "for
ever" in political matters.   What ephemerides are in the scale
of living beings, such are the friendships and enmities of nations
in the scale of historical phenomena.'

"I write all this down, Martha, not that I think it can interest
you, poor sufferer, nor because I want to make reflections to you
upon it, but I have an idea that I shall fall, and in that case I
do not wish my sentiments to sink into the grave with me
unuttered.   My letter may even be found and read by others, if
not by you.   That which is coming up in the minds of soldiers
who think freely, and feel like men, shall not remain for ever
unspoken and concealed.   'I have dared it' was Ulrich v.
Hutten's motto.   'I have spoken it,' and with this to quiet my
conscience, I can depart this life."

The most recent news that had reached me had been sent
off five days, and arrived two days previously.   What was to
show that in five days—five days of war—anything might not
have taken place?   Anxiety and fear seized me.   Why had no
line come yesterday?   Why none to-day?   Oh, this longing
for a letter—or, better, a telegram!   I believe no one in the
tortures of fever can so long for water as I then was longing
for news.   I was saved; he would have the great joy of
finding me alive, if—always this "if" which nips every hope
for the future in the bud.

My father was obliged to depart.   He could now leave me
with a quiet mind.   The danger was over, and he had now
pressing business at Grumitz.   As soon as I had got the
needful strength, I was to follow him there with my little
Rudolf.   A stay in the fresh country air would in the first
place restore me entirely, and would also do good to the little
boy.   Aunt Mary stayed behind.   She was to keep on nursing
me and then to travel with us to Grumitz where Rosa and
Lilly had already gone on before.   I let them talk and make

plans for me. Without saying anything I had made up my mind, as soon as I was even half able to do so, to set off for Schleswig-Holstein.

Where Frederick's regiment might be at this moment, we knew not. It was impossible to get any despatch forwarded to him, or I should have liked to telegraph to him every hour, and to ask: "Are you alive?"

"You must not excite yourself so," my father preached to me, as he took leave of me, "or else you are sure to get a relapse again. Two days without news—what is there in that? There is really no reason at all for anxiety. There are not letter-boxes or telegraph stations all over the field of battle: leaving out of the question that a man during the march and the battle and the bivouac is in no condition to write. The field post does not always act regularly, and so one may easily remain a fortnight without news, and still that signify nothing bad. In my time I have often been even longer without writing home; but no one was anxious about me on that account."

"How do you know that, papa? I am sure that your relations trembled for you just as much as I am trembling for Frederick. Did you not, aunt?"

"We had more trust in God than you have," she replied. "We knew that a merciful Providence would so order it, that, whether we got any news or none, your father would come back to us."

"And if I had never come back, but had got smashed to bits, you would have had enough love for your country to allow that so small a thing as the life of an individual soldier quite vanishes in the great cause for which he has parted with it. You, my daughter, have not for a long time been patriotic enough. But I will not scold you now. The main point is that you should get well again, and preserve yourself for your Rudi, to make a brave man of him, and bring him up to be a defender of his country."

.   ,   .   .   .

I did not get well so quickly as was hoped at first. The continued absence of news threw me into such excitement and misery that I never really got out of a feverish condition. My nights were filled with horrible phantoms and my days passed in weary longing or troubled stupor, so that it was difficult to get my strength up again.

Once, after a night in which I had had peculiarly terrifying visions—Frederick, alive, but buried under a heap of corpses of men and horses—a relapse actually set in which again brought me in danger of my life. My poor Aunt Mary had a hard time of it. She thought it a duty to preach comfort and resignation to me unceasingly, and her reason for it, the "destiny" which was constantly coming in again, had the effect of irritating me to the extreme, and instead of letting her quietly prose away I set myself to contradict her passionately, to complain of my fate in defiance of her, and to assure her in plain terms that her "destiny" seemed to me folly. All this, of course, sounded blasphemous, and my good aunt not only felt herself personally insulted, but she trembled also for my rebellious soul, so soon, perhaps, to appear before the judgment seat. There was only one means to quiet me for a few minutes. That was to bring little Rudolf into my bed-room. "You beloved child of mine! You are my comfort, my stay, my future!" This is what I cried out in my inward soul to the boy whenever I saw him. But he did not like staying long in the darkened sick-room. It struck him as uncanny to see his mamma who used to be so gay now lying constantly in bed, pale and exhausted with weeping. He became himself quite out of spirits, and so I only kept him with me for a few minutes at a time.

Frequent inquiries and news came from my father. He had written to Frederick's colonel and to several other people besides, but "had no answer as yet". When any list of killed and wounded came in he would send me a telegram: "Frederick not there". "Oh! perhaps you are deceiving me," I once asked my aunt, "perhaps the news of his death has arrived long ago and you are concealing it from me·——"

"I swear to you ——."

"On your honour, on your soul?"

"On my soul."

Such an assurance as this did me more good than I can tell; for I clung with all my might to my hope; every hour I was expecting the arrival of a letter—of a telegram. At every noise in the next room I fancied that it was the postman, almost continually my eyes were turning towards the door with the constant picture of some one coming in with the blessed message in his hand. When I look back on those days they seem to present themselves to my memory as a whole year filled with torture. The next gleam of light for me was the news that a suspension of arms had again been agreed on; this must surely this time be the presage of peace. On the day after the receipt of this intelligence I sat up for a little while for the first time. Peace! what a sweet, what a happy thought! Perhaps too late for me. No matter. I felt myself anyhow unspeakably calmed; at any rate I had no need to fancy every day, every hour, the raging battle going on in which Frederick might at that moment be killed.

"Thank God! now you will soon be well," said my aunt one day after helping me to seat myself on a couch which had been moved to the open window for me. "And then we can go to Grumitz."

"As soon as I have strength for it, I am going to Alsen."

"To Alsen? My dear child, what are you thinking about?"

"I want to find the place there where Frederick was either wounded or ——" I could not finish the sentence.

"Shall I fetch little Rudolf?" said my aunt after a pause. She knew that this was the best way to chase away my troubled thoughts for a time.

"No, not yet, I want to be quite quiet and alone. It would be doing me a kindness, aunt, if even you would go into the next room. Perhaps I may sleep a little, I feel so weak!"

11

"Very well, my dear, I will leave you quiet. There is a bell here on the table by you. If you want anything, some one will be ready at once."

"Has the letter-carrier been here?"

"No, it is not post time yet."

"If he comes, call me."

I lay down and shut my eyes. My aunt went out softly. All the people in the house had lately adopted this inaudible walk.

I did not want to sleep, but to be alone with my thoughts. I was in the same room, on the same couch as on that afternoon when Frederick came to tell me "we have got marching orders". It was just as sultry again as on that day, and again there were roses breathing in a vase near me, and again the trumpet exercise was sounding from the barracks. I could return entirely into the frame of mind of that day. I wished I could go to sleep again in the same way and dream as I then fancied I dreamt—that the door opened gently and my beloved husband entered. The roses were smelling even more powerfully, and through the open window the distant tra-ra-ra was sounding. By degrees my consciousness of present things vanished. I found myself ever more and more transported into that hour; all was forgotten that had happened since, and only the one fixed idea became ever more intense that at any moment the door might open and give my dear one admission. But to this end I had to dream that I was keeping my eyes only half open. It was an effort to force myself to this, but it succeeded. I opened my eyelids ever so little and ——

And there it was, the entrancing vision! Frederick, my beloved Frederick, on the threshold. With a loud sob and covering my face with both hands, I roused myself from my dreamy state. It was clear to me at a stroke that this was only a hallucination, and the heavenly ray of happiness that had been poured round me by this delusion made the hellish night of my misery seem all the blacker to me.

"Oh, my Frederick, my lost one!" I groaned.

"Martha, my wife!"

What was that? A real voice, his own, and real arms that were thrown eagerly round me ——

It was no dream. I was lying on my husband's breast.

CHAPTER VIII.

The joy of re-union.—Summer at Grumitz.—Recollections of the war.—My husband resolves to quit the service.—Education of my little son.—Cousin Conrad's love affair.—The end of the Danish war and the conditions of peace.—New troubles. —I lose my fortune, and my husband is obliged to remain in the service.—Lori Griesbach's flirtation with my husband. —Jealousy.—An April fool.

As in the last hours of his departure our pain had expressed itself in tears and kisses more than in words, so it was in this hour of our seeing each other again. That one can become mad with joy, I plainly felt, as I held fast him whom I had believed to be lost, as sobbing and laughing and trembling with excitement, I kept clasping the dear head again between both my hands, and kissing him on the forehead and eyes and mouth, while I stammered out unmeaning words.

On my first cry of joy Aunt Mary hurried in from the next room. She also had had no idea of Frederick's return, and at his sight she sank on the nearest chair with a loud cry of " Jesus, Maria, and Joseph !"

It was a long time before the first tumult of joy had sufficiently subsided to allow space for questions and counter-questions on both sides, confidences and news. Then we found that Frederick had been left lying in a peasant's house, while his regiment marched on. The wound was not a severe one; but he lay for several days in a fever, unconscious. During this period no letters reached him, nor was it possible for him to send any. When he recovered, the suspension of arms

(164)

had been proclaimed, and the war was virtually at an end.
Nothing prevented his hastening home. At that time he did
not write or telegraph any more, but travelled night and day
in order to get home as soon as possible. Whether I was still
alive, whether I was out of danger, he knew not. He would
not even make any inquiry about it, only get there, get there,
without losing an hour, and without cutting off the hope from
his homeward journey of finding his dearest again. And this
hope was not frustrated; he had now found his dearest again,
saved and happy, happy above all measure.

In a little while we all removed to my father's country-seat.
Frederick had obtained a long leave for the restoration of his
health, and the means prescribed by his physician—rest and
good air—he could best find at our house at Grumitz.

It was a happy time, that late summer. I do not recollect
any period in my life which was more fair. Union at last with
a loved one long sighed for may well be held infinitely sweet;
but to me the re-union with one half given up for lost necessarily seemed almost sweeter still. When I only for an instant
brought back to my own memory the fearful feelings that had
filled my heart before Frederick's return, or called up before
myself again the pictures which had tormented my feverish
nights, of Frederick's suffering all kinds of death-agonies, and
then satiated myself with his sight, my heart leapt for joy. I
now loved him more, a hundred times more, my *regained*
husband, and I regarded the possession of him as ever-increasing riches. A little while ago I looked on myself as a beggar,
now I had drawn the grand prize!

The whole family was assembled at Grumitz. Otto, too,
my brother, was spending his holidays with us. He was now
fifteen years old, and had three years to pass at the Neustadt
Military Academy at Vienna. A fine fellow my brother, and
my father's darling and pride. He as well as Lilly and Rosa
filled the house with their merriment. It was a constant
laughing and romping and playing ball and rackets and all
sorts of mad antics. Cousin Conrad, whose regiment lay not

far from Grumitz in garrison, came as often as possible, riding
over, and took his part gallantly in all these youthful sports. The
old folks formed a second party, namely, Aunt Mary, my father,
and a few of his comrades who were staying as guests in the
house.   Among them there was serious card-playing, quiet
walks in the park, a devoted cultivation of the pleasures of the
table, and immeasurable talks about politics.   The military
events that had just taken place, and the Schleswig-Holstein
question, which the latter had by no means set at rest, offered
a rich field for these talks.   Frederick and I lived practically
separate, or nearly so, from the rest—we only met them at
meals, and not always then—we were allowed to do as we liked.
It was taken as a settled thing that we were going through a
second edition of our honeymoon, and that solitude suited us.
And indeed we were best pleased to be alone.   Not at all, as
the others perhaps thought, to play and caress in honeymoon
fashion, we were not "newly married" enough for that, but
because we found most satisfaction in mutual conversation.
After the heavy sorrows we had just passed through, we could
not share the naïve gaiety of the youthful party, and still less
did we sympathise with the interests and the conversations of
the dignified personages, and so we preferred to secure for ourselves a good deal of retirement, under the privilege of a pair of
lovers, which was tacitly granted to us. We undertook long walks
together—sometimes excursions in the neighbourhood, in which
we stayed away the whole day—we spent whole hours alone
together in the book-room, and in the evening, when the various
card parties were being made up, we retired into our rooms
where over tea and cigarettes we resumed our familiar chat.
We always found an infinity of things to say to each other.
We liked best to tell each other of the feelings of woe and
horror which we experienced during our separation, for this
always awakened again the joy of our re-union.   We agreed that
presentiments of death and such like things are nothing but
superstition, since both of us, from the hour of our leave-taking.
had been penetrated with the conviction that one or the other

must necessarily die, yet here we had each other back ! Frederick had to recount to me in detail all the dangers and sufferings which he had just gone through, and to describe the pictures of horror from the battlefield and hospital which he had absorbed lately into his shuddering soul. I loved the tone of repugnance and pain which quivered in his voice during such recitals. From the way in which he spoke of the cruelties he had witnessed during the confusion of the war, I gathered the promise of an elevation of humanity, the result of which would be, first in individuals, then in the many, and finally in all to overcome the old barbarity.

My father also and Otto often called upon Frederick to interest them with episodes from the late campaign. This indeed was done in quite a different spirit from that in which I begged for such stories, and Frederick's relation was given in quite a different spirit. He contented himself with describing the tactical movements of the forces, the events of the battles, the names of the places taken or defended, recounting single camp-scenes, repeating speeches which had been made by the generals, and such like *miscellanea* of the war. His audience was delighted with it. My father listened with satisfaction, Otto with admiration, the generals with the solemnity of experts. I alone could not find any relish in this dry style of narrative. I knew that this covered a whole world of feelings and thoughts which the matters related had awakened in the depths of the speaker's soul. When I once reproached him with this when we were alone, he replied :—

"Falsehood? Dishonesty? Want of enthusiasm? No, my dear; you are mistaken. It is mere decorum. Do you remember our wedding-tour, our departure from Vienna, the first time we were alone in the carriage, the night in the hotel at Prague? Did you ever repeat the details of those hours, or ever sketch to your friends and relations the feelings and emotions of that happy time?"

"No; of course not. Every woman must surely be silent about such things."

"'Then don't you see that there are things also which every man is silent about? You could not tell of your joys in love; nor could we of our sufferings in war. The former might lay bare your chief virtue, modesty; the latter ours, courage. The delights of the honeymoon, and the terrors of the battlefield, no 'womanly' woman can speak of the one, nor any 'manly' man of the other. What? You may, in the rapture of love, have poured out sweet tears! and I may have in the imminence of the death-agony uttered a cry. How could you acknowledge such a sensibility; how could I such a cowardice?"

"But did you cry out, Frederick, did you tremble? You may surely say it to me. I do not, you know, conceal the joys of my love from you, and you may to me —— "

"Confess to you the fears of death which seize us soldiers on the field of battle? How can it be otherwise? Phrases and poetry tell lies about it. The inspiration artificially caused in this way by phrases and poetry is, I grant, capable for an instant of overcoming the natural instinct towards self-preservation; but only for an instant. In cruel men the pleasure of killing and destroying may also sometimes chase away their fear for their own lives. In men tenacious of honour pride is capable of suppressing the outward manifestation of this fear; but how many of the poor young fellows have I not heard groaning and whimpering? What looks of despair, what faces agonised with the fear of death have I not seen? What wild wailings, and curses, and beseeching prayers have I not heard?"

"And that gave you pain, my good, gentle husband."

"Such pain often that I cried out, Martha. And yet too little to express properly my power of sympathy. . . . One might think that if, at the sight of a single suffering, a man is seized with pity, a suffering multiplied a thousandfold would therefore excite a thousand times stronger pity. But the contrary occurs; the magnitude stupefies one. One cannot be so tenderly grieved for an individual when one sees, all round him, 999 others just as miserable. But even if one has not the

capacity to *feel* beyond a certain level of compassion, yet one
may be capable of thinking and computing that one has an
inconceivable quantity of woe before one."

"You, and one or two others may be capable, but the
majority of men neither think nor compute."

I succeeded in moving Frederick to the resolve of quitting
the service. The circumstance that he had, after his marriage,
served now more than a year, and taken a distinguished part
in a campaign, would defend him from the suspicion which
had occurred to my father during our engagement, that the
whole marriage had for its object only to enable him to give up
his career. Now, when peace should once be made, the preliminaries of which were in train, and when to all probability
there were long years of peace in prospect, retirement from
the army would now not involve anything dishonourable. It
was, indeed, still, to some extent, repugnant to Frederick's
pride to give up his rank and income, and, as he said, " to do
nothing, to be nothing, and to have nothing," but his love
for me was with him an even more powerful feeling than his
pride, and he could not resist my entreaties. I declared that
I could not go through a second time the anguish of mind
which his last parting caused me; and he himself might well
shrink from again calling down on us both such pain. The
feeling of delicacy, which, before his marriage with me, made
him shrink from the idea of living on the fortune of a rich
woman, no longer came into play, for we had become so
completely *one* that there was no longer any perceptible
difference between "mine" and "yours," and we understood
each other so well that no misjudgment of his character
on my part was any longer to be feared. The last campaign
had besides so greatly increased his aversion to the
murderous duties of war, and his unqualified expression of
that aversion had so rooted it in him, that his retirement
got to appear not like a concession made to our domestic
happiness so much as the putting into action of his own
intention, as a tribute to his convictions, and so he promised

me in the coming autumn, if the negotiations for peace were then concluded, to take his discharge.

We planned buying an estate with my fortune, which was then in the hands of Schmidt & Sons, the bankers, and Frederick was to find employment in managing it. In this way the first part of his trouble, "doing nothing, being nothing, and having nothing," would be removed. As to "being" and "having," we could also find a remedy.

"To be a retired colonel in the imperial and royal service, and a happy man, is not that enough?" I asked. "And to have? You have us—me and Rudi—and those who are coming. Is not that enough, too?"

He smiled, and took me in his arms.

We did not choose just at first to communicate anything of our plans to my father and the rest. They would certainly raise objections, give pieces of advice, express disapprobation, and all that was quite superfluous as yet. Later on we should know how to put ourselves above all that, for, when two people are all in all to each other, all foreign opinion falls off them without making any impression. The certainty for the future thus obtained increased still more the enjoyment of the present, which, even without that, was so heightened and enlarged by the delirium of the bitter past which we had gone through. I can only repeat it was a happy time. My son Rudolf, now a little fellow of seven, was beginning at this time to learn reading and writing, and his instructress was myself. I had never given my *bonne* the delight—which, besides, would, I daresay, have been none for her—of seeing this little soul slowly expand, and of bringing to it the first surprises of knowledge. The boy was often the companion of our walks, and we were never tired of answering the questions which his growing appetite for knowledge made him address to us. To answer, that is, as well and as far as we could. We never permitted ourselves to tell a falsehood. We never avoided answering such questions as we could not decide—such as no man can decide—with a plain "*that* no one knows, Rudi". At

first it would happen that Rudolf, not satisfied with such an
answer, took his question sometimes to Aunt Mary, or to his
grandfather, or to the nurse, and then he always got unhesi-
tating solutions.   Then he would come back to us in triumph :
"You don't know how old the moon is? I know now. It's
six thousand years—you remember." Frederick and I exchanged a silent glance. A whole volume full of pedagogic
fault-finding and opinions was contained in that glance and
that silence.

Above all things unbearable to me were the soldiers' games
which not only my father but my brother carried on with the
boy. The idea of "enemy" and "cutting down" were thus
instilled into him, I know not how. One day Frederick and
I came up as Rudolf was mercilessly beating two whimpering
young dogs with a riding-switch.

"That is a lying Italian," he said, laying on to one of the
poor beasts, "and that," on to the other, "an impudent
Dane."

Frederick snatched the switch out of the hand of this
national corrector.

"And that is a cruel Austrian," he said, letting one or two
good blows fall on Rudolf's shoulders. The Italian and the
Dane gladly ran off, and the whimpering was now done by our
little countryman.

"You are not angry with me, Martha, for striking your son?
I am not, it is true, in favour generally of corporal punishment,
but cruelty to animals provokes me."

"You did right," I said.

"Then is it only to men . . . that one may . . . be cruel?"
asked the boy between his sobs.

"Oh, no; still less."

"But you, yourself, have hit Italians and Danes."

"They were enemies."

"Then one *may* hate them?"

"And to-day or to-morrow," said Frederick, aside to me,
"the priest will be telling him that one ought to love one's

enemies. What logic!" Then, aloud to Rudolf: "No; it is not because we hate them that we may strike our foes, but because they want to strike us."

"And what do they want to strike us for?"

"Because we wanted to—No, no," he interrupted himself. "I find no way out of the circle. Go and play, Rudi; we forgive you, but don't do so any more."

Cousin Conrad was, as I thought, making progress in Lilly's favour. There is nothing like perseverance. I should have been very glad to see this match now made up, and I observed with pleasure how my sister's countenance lighted up with joy when the tread of Conrad's horse was heard in the distance, and how she sighed when he rode off again. He no longer courted her, i.e., he spoke no more of his love, and did not bring his suit forward, but his proceedings constituted a regular siege.

"As there are different ways of taking a fortress," he explained to me one day, "by storm or by famine, so there are many ways of making a lady capitulate. One of the most effectual of these is custom; sympathy. It must touch her at length that I am so constant in loving, and so constant in keeping silence about it, and always coming again. If I should stay away, it would make a great gap in her way of life; and if I go on in this way some time longer, she will not be able to do without me at all."

"And how many times seven years do you mean to serve for your chosen one?"

"I have not counted that up. Till she takes me."

"I do admire you. Are there then no other girls in the world?"

"Not for me. I have got Lilly into my head. She has something in the corners of her mouth, in her gait, her way of speaking, that no other woman can equal, for me. You, for example, Martha, are ten times as pretty, and a hundred times as clever."

"Thank you."

"But I would not have you for a wife."

"Thank you."

"Just because you are too clever. You would be sure to look down on me from a higher level. The star on my collar, my sabre and my spurs do not impose on you. Lilly, however, looks with respect on a man of action. I know she adores soldiers, while you ——."

"Still, I have twice married a soldier," replied I laughing.

. . . .

During meals, at the upper end of the table where my father and his old friends gave the tone, and where Frederick and I also sat (the young folks at the other end had their own talk to themselves), politics was the chief subject; that was the favourite material for conversation with the old gentlemen. The negotiations for peace which were in progress gave sufficient ground for this display of wisdom, for it is a firm conviction of most people that political events form the most sterling matter for conversation and that most suited for serious men. From gallantry and out of friendly regard for my female weakness of intellect, one of the generals said by the way: "These things can hardly interest our young friend Baroness Martha; we should only speak about them when we are alone. Eh! fair lady?"

I defended myself from this and begged them seriously to continue the subject. I took a real and an anxious interest in the proceedings of the military and diplomatic world. Not from the same point of view as these gentlemen, but it was of great moment to me to follow to its ultimate conclusion "the Danish question," whose origin and course I had studied so carefully during the war. Now, after these battles and victories the fate of the disputed duchies must surely be settled, and yet the questions and the doubts were always going on. The Augustenburg—that famous Augustenburg on account of whose immemorial rights all the contest had been lighted up—was he then installed now? Nothing of the kind. Nay, a new pretender arrived on the scene. Glücksburg and Gottorp, and all the lines and branch lines, whatever their names were, which I had been painfully committing to memory, were not enough. Now Russia stepped in and opposed to the Augustenburg an *Olden*burg! However, the result of the war up to this point was that the duchies were to belong neither to a Glücks- nor to an Augusten- nor to an Olden- nor to any other -burg, but to the allied victors. The following I found out were the articles of the conditions of peace then in progress :—

1. "Denmark surrenders the duchies to Austria and Prussia."

I was pleased with that. The allies would now, of course, hasten to give up the countries, which they had conquered not for themselves but for another, to that other.

2. "The frontiers will be accurately defined."

That again is quite right, if only these definitions could have a little more stability; but it is pitiable even to see what ever-lasting shiftings these blue and green lines on the maps have to suffer unceasingly.

3. "The public debts will be allocated in proportion to the populations."

That I did not understand. In my studies I had not got up to questions of political economy and finance. I took interest in politics only so far as they bore on peace and war, for this was the vital question to me as a human being and a wife.

4. "The duchies bear the cost of the war."

That again was to some extent intelligible to me. The country had been devastated, its harvests trampled down, its sons massacred; some reparation was due to it : so let it pay the expenses of the war.

"And what news is there about Schleswig-Holstein?" I myself asked, as the conversation had not yet been brought into the field of politics.

"The latest news is," said my father, "on August 13 that Herr v. Beust has put the question before the assembly of the Bund, with what right can the allies accept the *cession* of the duchies from a king whom the Bund has never recognised as their lawful possessor?"

"That is truly a very reasonable objection," I remarked, "for it surely means that the Protocol-Prince is not the legitimate lord of German soil, and now you accept it solemnly from Christian IX."

"You don't understand, dear," interrupted my father. "It is only an impudence, a trick of this Herr v. Beust, nothing else. The duchies, besides, belong to us already, for we have conquered them."

"But surely not conquered them for yourselves? for the Augustenburg."

"That again you do not understand. The reasons, which before the outbreak of a war are put forward by the cabinets as the motive for it, retreat into the background as soon as the battles are once engaged. *Then* the victories and defeats bring out quite new combinations; then kingdoms diminish or increase, or shape themselves in relations before unforeseen."

"These reasons then are really no reasons, but only pretexts?" I asked.

"Pretexts? no," said one of the generals, coming to my father's aid; "motives rather, starting-points for the events which then shape themselves according to the scale of the results."

"If *I* had had to speak," said my father, "I would really not have given in to any peace negotiations after Duppel and Alsen; all Denmark might have been conquered."

"What to do with it?"

"Incorporate it in the German Bund."

"Why, your speciality is only that of an Austrian patriot, dear father. What business is it of yours to enlarge Germany?"

"Have you forgotten that the Hapsburgs were German emperors, and may become so again?"

"That would rejoice you?"

"What Austrian would it not fill with joy and pride?"

"But," remarked Frederick, "suppose the other great power of Germany cherishes similar dreams?"

My father laughed outright.

"What! the crown of the Holy Romano-German Empire on the head of a Protestant kingling? Are you in your senses?"

"Whether now or at another time," said Dr. Bresser, "a quarrel will occur between the two powers over the object for which they have fought in alliance. To conquer the Elbe provinces, that was a trifle; but what to do with them? That may yet give occasion to all kinds of complications. Every war, however it may turn out, inevitably contains within itself the germ of a succeeding war. Very naturally; for an act of violence always violates some right. Sooner or later this right raises its claims, and the new conflict breaks out, is then again brought to a conclusion by force pregnant with injustice, and so on, *ad infinitum*."

A few days later a fresh event occurred. King William of Prussia paid a visit to the emperor at Schönbrunn. Extraordinarily warm reception, embraces, the Prussian Eagle hoisted, Prussian popular hymns played by all the military bands, triumphant huzzahs. To me this news was satisfactory, for by it the evil prophecies of Dr. Bresser were put to shame, that the two powers would get into a quarrel with each other over the countries they had joined in liberating. The newspapers also gave expression on all hands to this consolatory assurance.

My father was equally pleased with the friendly news from Schönbrunn. Not, however, from the point of view of peace, but of war. "I am glad," he said, "that we have now a new ally. In alliance with Prussia we can, just as easily as we have conquered the Elbe provinces, get Lombardy back again."

"Napoleon III. will not consent to that; and Prussia will certainly not be willing to embroil herself with him," one of the generals said. "Besides, it is a bad sign that Benedetti, the bitterest enemy of Austria, is now ambassador at Berlin."

"But tell me, gentlemen," I cried out, folding my hands

together, "why do not all the civilised states in Europe form an alliance? That surely would be the simplest way."

The gentlemen shrugged their shoulders, smiled in a superior fashion, and gave me no answer. I had plainly given utterance again to one of those silly things which "the ladies" are in the habit of saying, when they venture into the, to them, inaccessible region of the higher politics.

.   .   .   .

The autumn had come, peace was signed at Vienna on October 30, and with it had come the time when my darling wish, Frederick's retirement, could be carried out. But man proposes, and circumstances master him. An event occurred— a heavy blow for me—which brought to nothing the plans we had cherished so joyfully. It was simply this: the house of Schmidt & Sons failed, and my whole private fortune was gone.

This bankruptcy was also a sequel of the war. The shot and shells shatter not only the walls against which they are aimed, but, through this destruction, banking houses and financial companies over a wide area fall to pieces also.

I was not brought thereby, as so many others were, to beggary; for my father would not let me want for anything. But the plan of retirement had to be quite given up. We were no longer independent persons. Frederick's pay was now our sole substantial resource. Even if my father could assure me a sufficient allowance, it was out of the question under such circumstances that Frederick should quit the service. I myself could not suggest it to him. What sort of a part would he be playing, in the eye of my father?

There was nothing to do, we had to submit. "Destiny" in Aunt Mary's phrase. I have not much to tell of the affliction which this great pecuniary loss caused me; it was a question of several hundred thousand florins; for there are no long entries in my diary about it, and even my memory—which has experienced since then so many impressions of far deeper pain —bears no longer any very lively traces of these incidents. I

12

only know that I was chiefly sorry for the beautiful castle in
the air which we had been building—retirement, purchase of
an estate, a life independent and apart from the so-called
"world"—in other things the loss did not hurt me so much.
For, as I have said, my father would during his life not allow
me to want for anything, and would afterwards leave me a
sufficiency, and my son Rudolf was sure of wealth in the future.
One thing comforted me: there was not the slightest prospect
of any war; one might hope for ten or twenty years of peace.
Till then ——

Schleswig-Holstein and Lauenburg were finally given
over by the treaty of October 30 to the free disposition of
Prussia and Austria. These two, now the best of friends, were
to share in a brotherly way the advantages so accruing, and find
no cause for quarrelling over them. Nowhere on the whole
political horizon was there any "black spot" visible to one's
consideration. The shame of the defeat we had sustained in
Italy was sufficiently atoned by the military glory we had gained
in Schleswig-Holstein, and so there was no longer any occasion
for military ambition to conjure up new campaigns. And I was
also pacified with the following consideration. That war had
come so short a time since, I took as a pledge that it would not
be very soon repeated. Sunshine follows after rain and in the
sunshine one forgets the rain. Even after earthquakes and
eruptions of volcanoes men build up new dwellings again and
do not think of the danger of a repetition of the past catastrophe.
A chief element in our life's energy appears to reside in forgetfulness.

We took up our winter quarters in Vienna. Frederick had
now got employment in the Ministry of War, a business which
he at any rate preferred to barrack life. This year my sisters
and Aunt Mary had gone to spend the carnival at Prague.
That Conrad's regiment was then quartered in the Bohemian
capital was perhaps only a coincidence. Or could this circumstance have had any influence on their choice of a winter resort?
When I gave a hint of this to my sister Lilly she blushed deeply

and answered with a shrug of her shoulders: "Why, you must know that I do not want him".

My father repaired to his old dwelling in the Herrengasse. He proposed to us that we should settle down with him as he had room enough: but we preferred to live by ourselves, and hired an *entresol* on the Franz Joseph's Quay. My husband's pay and the monthly allowance made me by my father amply sufficed for our modest housekeeping. We had indeed to renounce subscriptions to opera-boxes, court balls—in fact, all going into "society". But how easily did we renounce it! It was indeed a pleasure to us that my pecuniary losses made this quiet way of life necessary, for we loved a quiet way of life.

To a small circle of relatives and friends our house was always open. In particular, Lori Griesbach, the friend of my youth, often visited us—almost more often than I liked. Her talk, which had before appeared to me sorely superficial, I now found so insipid as to be quite wearisome; and her intellectual horizon, whose narrowness I had always perceived, seemed now still more restricted. But she was pretty and lively and coquettish. I understood that in society she turned many men's heads, and it was said that she had no objection to be made love to. What was very unpleasant to me was to perceive that Frederick was very much to her taste, and that she shot many darts out of her eyes at him, which were evidently intended to fix themselves in his heart. Lori's husband, the ornament of the Jockey Club, the race-course, and the *coulisses*, was well known to be so little true to her that a slight imitation on her side would not have deserved too strong condemnation. But that Frederick should serve as the medium of her revenge— I had a good deal to say against that. I jealous! I turned red as I caught myself in this agitation. I was, in truth, so sure of his heart. No other woman, none in the world, could he love as he did me. Ah, yes, *love*, but a little blaze of flirtation? *that* might perhaps have flashed up by the side of the soft glow which was consecrated to me.

Lori did not in any way conceal from me how much Frederick attracted her.

"I say, Martha! you are really to be envied to have such a charming husband," or "You should keep a good look-out on this Frederick of yours, for all the women I know are running after him".

"I am quite certain of his fidelity," I replied to this.

"Don't flatter yourself; to think of 'fidelity' and 'husband' being coupled together! That is impossible. For example, you know how my husband ——"

"Good heavens! you may perhaps have been wrongly informed. Besides, surely all men are not alike!"

"Yes, they are—all—believe me. I know none of our gentlemen who do not. . . . Among those who pay me attention are several married men. And what is their object? Certainly not to give me or themselves exercises in fidelity to marriage."

"I suppose they know you will not listen to them. And do you think Frederick belongs to this crew?" I asked with a smile.

"That is more than I can tell you, you little goose. But for all that it is very good of me to let you know how much I am struck with him. Now, all you have to do is to keep your eyes open."

"My eyes are wide open already, Lori, and they have before now observed with displeasure several attempts at coquetry on your part."

"Oh, that's it! Then I must disguise it better in future."

We both laughed, but I still felt that in the same way as behind the jealousy which I pretended for fun a real movement of this passion lay hid, so behind the chat with which she affected to tease me there lay a germ of truth.

The arrangement to marry my son Rudolf one day to Lori's little Beatrix was still kept intact. It was of course more in play than in reality—the main question whether the children's hearts would beat for each other could only be decided by the

future. That in a worldly point of view my Rudolf would be
a most eligible match was certain, and so much the more
fastidious might he be in choosing. Beatrix indeed promised
to be a great beauty, but if she took after her mother in
coquetry and shallowness of mind she would not be one I
should desire for a daughter-in-law. But all that was in the
far distance.

Lori's husband had not shared in the Schleswig-Holstein
campaign, and that annoyed him much. Lori too was grieved
at this "ill-luck".

"Such a nice victorious war," she complained. "Griesbach
would have been sure to have got a step by this time. However, the comfort is that in the next campaign ——"

"What are you thinking of?" I broke in. "There is not the
least prospect of that. Do you know any cause for it? What
should a war be waged about now?"

"What for? Really I have nothing to do with that. Wars
come—and there they are. Every five or six years something
breaks out. That is the regular course of history."

"But surely some reasons must exist for it."

"Perhaps, but who knows what they are? Certainly I don't,
nor my husband either. I asked him in the course of the late
war 'What is the exact thing they are fighting about down
there?' 'I don't know,' he replied, shrugging his shoulders,
'it is all the same to me. But it is a bore that I am not
there,' he added. Oh, Griesbach is a true soldier. The 'why'
and 'what for' of the wars are not the business of the soldiers.
The diplomatists settle that amongst themselves. I never
bothered my brains about all these political squabbles. It is
not the business of us women at all—we should besides understand nothing of it. When once the storm has broken we have
only to pray ——"

"That it may strike our neighbours and not ourselves—that
is certainly the most simple plan."

.   .   .   .

"Dear Madam,—A friend—or perhaps an enemy, no matter

—a person who knows but wishes to remain unknown—takes this means of informing you that you are being betrayed. Your husband, so seeming virtuous, and your friend who wants to pass for an innocent, are laughing at you for your good-humoured confidence—you poor blinded wife. I have my own reasons for wishing to tear the mask off both their faces. It is not from goodwill to you that I so act, for I can easily imagine that this detection of two persons dear to you may bring you more pain than profit—but I have no goodwill to you in my heart. Perhaps I am a rejected adorer, who is taking his revenge this way. What matters the motive? The fact is there, and if you wish for proofs I can furnish them to you. Besides, without proofs you would give no credit to an anonymous letter. The accompanying 'billet' was lost by Countess Gr——"

This astounding letter lay on our breakfast-table one fine spring morning. Frederick was sitting opposite to me, busied with *his* letters, while I read and re-read the above ten times over. The note which accompanied the traitorous epistle was enclosed in an envelope of its own, and I put off tearing it open.

I looked at Frederick. He was deep in a morning paper; still he must have felt the look which I fixed on him, for he let the newspaper fall, and with his usual kindly, smiling expression, turned his face to me.

"Hollo, what is the matter, Martha? Why are you staring at me in that way?"

"I wanted to know whether you are still fond of me."

"Oh, no, not for a long time," he said jestingly. "Really I have never been able to bear you."

"That I do not believe."

"But now I begin to see —— But you are quite pale. Have you had any bad news?"

I hesitated. Should I show him the letter? Should I first look at the piece of evidence which I held in my hand still unbroken? The thoughts whirled through my head—my

Frederick, my all, my friend and husband, him whom I trusted and loved—could he be lost to me? Unfaithful, he! Oh, it must have been only a momentary intoxication of the senses—nothing more. Was there not enough indulgence in my heart to forgive it, to forget it, to regard it as having never happened? But to be false! How would it be, if his heart, too, had turned from me; how, if he preferred the seductive Lori to me?

"Well, do speak. You seem quite to have lost your voice. Show me the letter which has so shocked you," and he stretched his hand out for it.

"There it is for you." I gave him the letter I had just read —the enclosure I kept back. He glanced over the informer's writing. With an angry curse, he crumpled up the paper, and sprang from his seat.

"Infamous!" he cried, "and where is the proof he speaks of?"

"Here, not opened. Frederick, say one word only, and I throw the thing into the fire. I do not want to see any proofs that you have betrayed me."

"Oh, my own one!" He was now by my side, and embraced me closely. "My treasure! Look into my eyes. Do you doubt me? Proof or no proof—is my word enough for you?"

"Yes," I said, and threw the paper into the fire.

But it did not fall into the flames, but remained close to the bars. Frederick jumped up to get it, and picked it out.

"No, no! we must not destroy that. I am too curious. We will look at it together. I do not recollect ever writing anything to your friend which could lead to the inference of a relation which does not exist."

"But you have smitten her, Frederick. You have only to throw your handkerchief to her."

"Do you think so? Come, let us look at this document. Right, my own hand. Oh, look here! It is surely the two lines which you dictated to me some weeks back, when you had hurt your right hand."

" My Lori ! come. I am anxiously expecting you to-day at five P.M. MARTHA (still a cripple)."

" The finder of this note did not understand the meaning of the parenthesis. This is really a funny confusion. Thank God that this grand proof was not burned ; now my innocence is plain. Or have you still any suspicion ? "

' " No ; after you had looked in my face I had no more. Do you know, Frederick, I should have been very unhappy, but I should have forgiven you ? Lori is coquettish, very pretty. Tell me, has not she made advances to you ? You shake your head. Well, truly, in this matter you have not only the right but almost the duty of deceiving even me ; a man cannot betray a lady's favour whether he accepts or rejects it."

" And so you would have forgiven me a false step ? Are you not jealous ? "

" Yes ; in a way that tears my heart. If I think of you at another's feet ; sipping joy from another's lips ; grown cold to me ; all desire dead—it is horrible to me. Yet, it was not the death of your love that I feared. Your *heart* would under no circumstances turn cold to me, that I am sure of ; our souls are surely so interwoven with each other. But ———"

" I understand. But you need by no means think of me that my feeling for you is like that of a husband after the silver wedding. We have been married too short a time for that ; so long as the fire of youth glows in me (for indeed I am forty years old already), it burns for you. You are the only woman on earth to me. And should some other tempta-tion in reality again assail me, my will is quite strong enough to keep it away from me. The happiness which is contained in the consciousness of having kept one's plighted troth, the proud repose of conscience with which a man can 'say of himself that he has kept the firmly-tied bond of his life in every respect sacred—all this is to me too noble to allow it to be destroyed by a passing intoxication of the senses. You have besides made so perfectly happy a man of me, my Martha, that I am raised as far above everything—above all intoxication, all amusement, all pleasure—as the possessor of ingots of gold above the gain of copper pieces."

With what delight did such words as these sink into my heart! I was expressly thankful to the anonymous letter-writer, for helping me to this delightful scene. And I transferred every word into my red book. I can still reproduce the entry here, under date 1/4/1865. Ah, how far, how far back is all that!

Frederick, on the contrary, was highly incensed against the slanderer. He swore that he would find out who had been guilty of the composition, so as to punish the actor as he deserved. I found out the same day what the origin and aim of the writing was. Its *result*, which was that Frederick and I were thenceforth drawn a little closer together, its originator could hardly have foreseen.

In the afternoon I went to my friend Lori to show her the letter. I wanted to let her know that she had an enemy by whom she was falsely exposed to suspicion, and I wanted to laugh with her over the chance that my dictated note had been so misconstrued.

She laughed more than I expected.

"So you were shocked at the letter?"

"Yes, mortally; and yet I had nearly burned the enclosed note."

"Oh! then the whole joke would have missed fire."

"What joke?"

"You would have believed to the end that I had really betrayed you. Let me take this opportunity to make you a confession, that I did in an hour of delirium—it was after the dinner at your father's at which I sat next to Tilling, and it was because I had drunk too much champagne—that I did then, so to say, offer him my heart on a salver."

"And he?"

"And he answered me very much to the purpose, that he

loved you above all other things and was firmly resolved to remain true to you to death. The whole joke was contrived to teach you to prize this phenomenon better."

"What is this joke that you keep talking of?"

"Why, you must know, inasmuch as the letter and the envelope come from me."

"From you? I know nothing about it."

"Have you then not turned the enclosure round? See here—on the back of it is written my name and the date—April 1."

CHAPTER IX.

" BROUGHT nearer—ever nearer ! I have found out that this capacity of approximation of loving hearts belongs to the class of things of which divisibility is an example—things which have no limits. One might have believed that a particle might have become so small already that nothing smaller could be conceived, and yet it is susceptible of division into two halves ; and so one might think that two hearts might be already so fused together that a more intimate union could not be possible, and yet some external influence acts, and the atoms— the two hearts—embrace and inter-penetrate each other still more firmly, and closer—ever closer."

This was the effect of Lori's sufficiently tasteless April fooling; and such was the effect of another external event which happened soon after ; *viz.*, a violent nervous fever which attacked me and laid me on a sick bed for six weeks. It was indeed a sad event, and yet how fruitful it was in happy recollections for me, and how powerful in its influence on the process sketched above—I mean the "bringing nearer and nearer" of two so closely attached hearts ; whether it was the fear of losing me which made me still dearer to my husband, or whether it was that his love had merely become more noticeable to me by his behaviour as sick nurse—in short, during this nervous fever and after it I still more and still more surely felt that I was beloved, than before.

I was also truly afraid of dying—first, because it would have given me horrible pain to lose a life which seemed to me so rich in beauty and happiness, and to leave my dear ones: Frederick with whom I wished so much to grow to old age, Rudolf whom I wished so much to train up to manhood ; and secondly, too, not in respect to myself but with regard to Frederick, the thought of death was horrible to me because I knew as well as one can know anything that the pain of laying me in the grave would be to the bereaved one well-nigh intolerable. No! No! People who are happy, and people who are beloved by those they hold dear, cannot feel any contempt for Death. The chief ingredient in the latter is contempt for life. On my sick bed, where sickness buzzed around me with its deadly power, as the warrior on the battlefield hears the buzz of the bullets around him, I was able to enter perfectly into the feelings of those soldiers who love their lives and who know that their death will plunge hearts they love into despair.

"There is but one thing," said Frederick in reply to me when I communicated this thought to him, "in which the soldier has the advantage of the fever-patient—the conscious- ness of duty fulfilled. Still I agree with you in this : to die with indifference, to die with joy, as we are on all hands told to do, is what no happy man can do—only those could who were exposed in former times to all the ills of life, or those who have nothing left to lose in a peaceful existence, or such as can only free their brethren from shame and an intolerable yoke by their own death !"

When the danger was over how I enjoyed my recovery—my

new birth! That was a feast for both of us, like the happiness of our re-union after the Schleswig-Holstein war, but still different. Then the joy came with a single stroke, and here little by little, and, besides, since that time we were closer to each other—ever closer.

My father had visited me daily during my illness, and shown much concern; but for all that I knew that he would not have taken my death to heart overwhelmingly. He was much more attached to his two younger daughters than to me, and the dearest of all to him was Otto. I had become to some extent estranged from him by my two marriages, and particularly by the second, and perhaps also by my totally different way of thinking. When I was completely recovered, which was in the middle of June, he removed to Grumitz, and gave me a warm invitation to come to him there with my little Rudolf. But I preferred, since Frederick was prevented from leaving the city by his duties, to take my country holiday quite close to Vienna, where my husband could visit me daily, and so I hired a summer lodging at Hietzing.

My sisters, still under Aunt Mary's protection, travelled to Marienbad. In her last letter from Prague, Lilly wrote to me as follows, amongst other matters: " I must confess to you that Cousin Conrad begins to be by no means displeasing to me. During several cotillons I was in the humour to have said ' Yes' if he had put the important question. But he omitted to take the decisive step at the *right* moment. When it was settled that we were to leave the city he did, it is true, make me an offer again, but then I had again an impulse to refuse. I have become so used to do this to poor Conrad that when he used the accustomed form to me: ' Will you not now become my wife, Lilly?' my tongue replied quite automatically: 'I have no idea of doing so'. But this time I added: ' Ask me again in six months '. That means that I am going to examine my heart during the summer. If I long after him in his absence, if the thought of him (which now follows me almost uninterruptedly day and night) does not quit me when I am at

Marienbad ; if neither there nor in the ensuing shooting season any other man succeeds in making an impression on me, why, then, the perseverance of my obstinate cousin will have prevailed."

Aunt Mary wrote to me about the same time. (This happens to be the only letter of hers which I have kept.)

" My dear child,—This has been a fatiguing winter campaign ! I shall be not a little glad when Rosa and Lilly have found partners. *Found* they have, plenty of them ; for, as you know, each has refused in the course of the carnival half-a-dozen offers, not counting the perennial Conrad. Now the same drudgery is to begin again at Marienbad. I should like to have gone to Grumitz to spend some time, above all things, or to you ; and instead of this I am obliged to play over again the tiresome and thankless part of chaperon to these pleasure-seeking girls.

" I am very glad to hear that you are quite well again. Now that the danger is over, I may say that we were in great trouble —your husband used for some time to write us such despairing letters—every moment he was in fear of seeing you die. But let us thank God that it was not destined so to be. The novena which I kept at the Ursulines for your recovery also, perhaps, helped to preserve you. The Almighty designed to spare you for your little Rudi. Kiss the dear little boy and tell him to keep hard at his learning. I send him with this a couple of little books, *The Pious Child and his Guardian Angel*, a charming story, and *Our Country's Heroes*, a collection of war-sketches for boys. A taste for such things cannot be instilled too early into the young. Your brother Otto, for instance, was not five years old when I used to tell him about Alexander the Great, and Cæsar, and other famous conquerors ; and it is a real pleasure to see what a spirit he has now for everything heroic.

" I have heard that you prefer to remain for the summer in the neighbourhood of Vienna, instead of going to Grumitz. You are quite wrong there. The air of Grumitz would suit you much better than that dusty Hietzing ; and poor papa will be quite bored all alone. Probably it is on your husband's

account that you will not go away; but it seems to me that the
duty of a daughter also should not be quite neglected. Tilling,
too, could surely come to Grumitz for a day sometimes. To be
so very much together is not altogether good for married folks—
trust to my experience of life. I have noticed that the best
marriages are those in which the couple are not always sitting
prosing together, but allow each other a little latitude. Now,
good-bye; spare yourself—so as not to get a relapse—and think
again about Hietzing. May heaven preserve you and your
Rudi. This is the constant prayer of your affectionate

"AUNT MARY.

"P.S.—Your husband has, I know, relatives in Prussia (happily he is not so arrogant as his countrymen), so ask him what
they are saying there about the political situation. It is surely
very grave."

This letter of my aunt made me reflect again that there was
a "political situation". During all this time I had not troubled
myself about anything of the sort. I had, it is true, read a good
deal both before and after my illness, as usual, daily and weekly
papers, reviews and books, but the leading articles in the
journals remained unnoticed, since I no longer debated with
myself the anxious question: "War or no war?"; the chatter
about home and foreign politics possessed no interest for me.
The postscript of the letter quoted above looked serious, and it
occurred to me to look up what I had neglected and inform
myself about our present position:

"What does Aunt Mary mean by her expression 'threatening'?
you least arrogant among the Prussians," I asked my husband,
as I gave him the letter to read. "Is there then a political
situation at the present time?"

"There is one, as there is weather, always—more's the pity
—and one is also as changeable and treacherous as the other"

"Well, tell me then. Are they talking still about these complicated duchies? Have they not done with them yet?"

"They are talking about them more than ever. They have
not done with them in the least. The Schleswig-Holsteiners

have now a great fancy to get free of the Prussians—the 'arrogant' Prussians we are called in the latest form of speech.
'Sooner Danish than Prussian,' say they, repeating a signal
given them by the central states. Do you know that the
hackneyed 'Meerumschlungen' song is now sung with this
variation :—

"'Schleswig-Holstein stammverwandt Schmeisst die Preussen
aus dem Land'?"[1]

"And what has happened to the Augustenburg ? Have they
got him then ? O do not tell me, Frederick, do not tell me
that they have *not* got him ! It was on account of this, the
only rightful heir, for whom the poor countries oppressed by
the Danes were longing so, that the whole war had to be waged
which might have cost me *you !* Leave me then at least the
consolation that this indispensable Augustenburg has been
reinstated in his rights, and is reigning over the undivided
duchies. I take my stand on this word 'undivided'. It is an
old historical right, which has been assured to them for several
centuries, and the foundation of which I had trouble enough
in investigating."

"It is going badly with your historical rights, my poor
Martha," said Frederick laughing. "No one says anything
at all about Augustenburg now, except himself in his protests
and manifestoes."   .

From this time I began again to look into the political complications, and found out as follows : Absolutely nothing had
really been settled or recognised, in spite of the Protocol signed
at the time of the Peace of Vienna. Since that, the Schleswig-
Holstein question had been brought into all sorts of stages,
but now was "debated" more than ever. The Augustenburg
and the Oldenburg had made haste, since the abdication which
had taken place on the part of the Glücksburg, to make
reclamation before the assembly of the Bund. And Lauenburg
was eagerly desirous to be incorporated in the kingdom of

---

[1] Schleswig-Holstein, brother-land, kick the Prussians out of the
country.

LAY DOWN YOUR ARMS.

Prussia. No one knows exactly what the allies were going to
try to do with the conquered provinces. Each of these two
powers attributed to the other a design of overreaching the
other.

"What is this Prussia up to now?"   Such was the question,
indicating mischief, which Austria, the central states, and the
duchies kept always asking. Napoleon III. advised Prussia
to annex the duchies up to North Schleswig, where they speak
Danish, but Prussia was not thinking of that for the moment.
At last, on February 22, 1865, her claims were formulated to
this effect: Prussian troops to remain in the countries; the
latter to put their defensive forces under Prussian leadership,
with the exception of a contingent of troops of the Bund.
The harbour of Kiel to be occupied. Posts and telegraphs to
be Prussian; and the duchies to be compelled to join the
Zollverein.

Of these demands our Minister, Mensdorf-Pouilly, complained.
I do not know why. And still further (again, I have no idea why—
presumably out of envy, that distinctive feature in the conduct of
"external relations"), the central states complained also. They
vehemently demanded that the Augustenburg should with all
speed be at once inducted into the government of the duchies.
Austria, however, had something to say also, and what she said
was this. She treated the Augustenburg as non-existent, was
willing to consent to the possession by Prussia of the Kiel
harbour, but stood out against the right of recruiting and pressing sailors.

And so the quarrel went on without cessation. Prussia
declared that her demands were made only in the interests of
Germany; that she did not wish for annexation; Augustenburg
might enter on his inheritance if he accepted the demands laid
down; but if these necessary and moderate claims were not
granted, then (with voice raised to the pitch of threatening) perhaps she would be compelled to demand more.
Against this menacing voice other voices were raised in scorn,
in mockery, in provocation. In the central states and in

13

Austria public opinion became daily more and more embittered against Prussia and especially against Bismarck. On June 27 the central states accepted a motion to request information from the Great Powers; but, as giving information is not the habit of diplomacy but keeping everything snug and secret, the Great Powers negotiated in private. King William travelled to Gastein, the Emperor Francis Joseph to Ischl, Count Blome flitted hither and thither between them, and an agreement was arrived at on certain points: the occupation was to be half Austrian and half Prussian. Lauenburg, according to her own wish, was to be united to Prussia. For this Austria was to receive as compensation two and a half millions of thalers. This last result was not calculated to inspire me with patriotic joy. What good could this insignificant sum do to the thirty-six millions of Austrians? even if it was to be divided among them, which was not the case. Would it replace the hundreds of thousands which, for example, I had lost with Schmidt & Sons? Or still more the losses of those who were mourning for their dear ones? What pleased me was a treaty which was signed at Gastein on August 14. "Treaty," the word sounds so promising of peace. It was not till afterwards that I learned that international treaties very often only serve, by means of opportune violations of them, to introduce what is called a *casus belli*. Then it is only necessary for one party to charge the other with "a breach of treaty," and immediately the swords spring out of their sheaths with all the appearance of a defence of violated rights.

Still the Gastein treaty brought me repose. The quarrel seemed to be laid aside. General Gablenz—handsome Gablenz —for whom all we ladies had a slight penchant, was Stadtholder in Holstein, Manteuffel in Schleswig. I had at last to give up my favourite security, enacted in the year 1460, that the countries should remain together for ever "undivided". As far as concerned my Augustenburg, for whose rights I had with so much trouble got up some warmth, it happened that this prince went on one occasion into his country and received the homage of his adherents, on which Manteuffel signified to him that if he ever ventured to come into those parts again without permission, he would unquestionably have him arrested. Whoever cannot see in that a good joke of Muse Clio's can have no comprehension of the comicalities of history.

In spite of the Gastein treaty, the situation would not calm down, and as I now, being alarmed by Aunt Mary's letter and the explanations of it which I received, resumed the regular perusal of the political leading articles and collected intelligence from all sides about the opinions which gained currency, I was in a position to follow once more with accuracy the phases of the varying strife. That the latter would lead to a war, I did not apprehend. Such legal questions would have to be brought to an issue in the legal way, *i.e.*, by weighing the claim of right on the two sides, and by a sentence consequent on this. All these consultative meetings of ministers and assemblies, these negotiating statesmen and monarchs in friendly intercourse, would surely settle the debated points which were in themselves so trivial. It was with more curiosity than anxiety that I followed the course of this incident, the different stages of which I find noted in my red volumes.

October 1, 1865. In the assembly of delegates at Frankfort the following conclusions were accepted: (1) The right of the people of Schleswig-Holstein to decide on their own destiny remains in force. The Gastein treaty is rejected by the nation as a breach of right. (2) All representatives of the people are to refuse all taxes and expenses to such Governments as assert the policy of violence hitherto followed.

October 15. The Prussian crown-syndic gave his judgment on the hereditary rights of Prince Augustenburg. The father of the latter had renounced for himself and his posterity his succession to the throne for a sum of one and a half million of specie thalers. The duchies were surrendered in the treaty of Vienna—the Augustenburg had no claims at all upon them.

An impudence—an assumption—such were the terms applied to this speech delivered at Berlin, and "the arrogance of Prussia" became a catchword. "We must protect ourselves against it," was accepted as a dogma on all hands. "King

William seems disposed to play the part of a German Victor Emmanuel." "Austria's secret motive is to reconquer Silesia," "Prussia is paying court to France," "Austria is paying court to France," *et patati, et patata,* as the French say. *Tritsch tratsch* is the German name for it, and it does not go on more busily in the coffee-house coteries of country towns than between the Cabinets of Great Powers.

The winter brought my whole family back to Vienna. Rosa and Lilly had amused themselves very much in the Bohemian watering-places, but neither was engaged. Conrad's affairs were in an excellent way. In the shooting season he was to come to Grumitz, and, although at this crisis the decisive word had not yet been spoken, still both were inwardly convinced that they would end in being united.

Neither at this autumn shooting season did I make my appearance, in spite of my father's pressing persuasions. Frederick could not get any leave, and to separate from him was to exist in such sorrow as I would not expose myself to without necessity. A second reason for not passing any length of time at my father's was that I did not wish to expose my little Rudolf to his grandfather's influence, whose effort always was to inspire the child with military tastes. The inclination for this calling, to which I was thoroughly averse as a profession for my son, had been awakened in him without this. Probably it was in his blood. The scion of a long race of soldiers must, by nature, bring warlike instincts into the world with him. In the works on natural science, whose study we were now pursuing more eagerly than ever, I had learned about the power of heredity, of the existence of so-called "congenital instincts," which are nothing but the impulse to put in action the customs handed down from our ancestors.

On the boy's birthday his grandfather was careful to bring him again a sabre.

"But you know, father," I remonstrated, "that my son will certainly not become a soldier, and I must really beg you seriously ——"

"What, do you want to tie him to his mother's apron-strings? I hope you will not succeed there. Good soldiers' blood is no liar. Let the fellow only grow up, and he will soon choose his profession for himself, . . . and there is no finer one than that which you want to forbid him."

"Martha is frightened," said Aunt Mary, who was present at this conversation, "of exposing her only son to danger, but she forgets that if one is destined to die, that fate will overtake one in one's bed as surely as in battle ——"

"Then, suppose 100,000 men to have fallen in a war, they would all have been killed in peace, too?"

Aunt Mary was not at a loss for an answer. "It was the destiny of these 100,000 to die in war."

"But if men had the sense not to begin any war," I suggested.

"Oh! but that is an impossibility," cried my father, and then the conversation turned again into a controversy such as my father and I used often to wage, and always on the same lines. On the one side, the same assertions and principles; on the other, the same counter assertions and opposite principles. There is nothing to which the fable of the hydra is so applicable as to some standing difference of opinion. No sooner have you cut one head off the argument, and settled yourself to send the second the same way, when, lo! the first has grown again. Thus my father had one or two favourite positions in favour of war which nothing could uproot:—

1. Wars are ordained by God Himself—the Lord of Hosts—see the Holy Scriptures.

2. There have always been wars, and consequently there always will be wars.

3. Mankind, without this occasional decimation, would increase at too great a rate.

4. Continual peace relaxes, effeminates, produces—like stagnant water—corruption; especially the degeneration of morals.

5. Wars are the best means for putting in practice self-sacrifice, heroism—in short, the firmer elements of the character.

6. Men will always contend. Perfect agreement in all their views is impossible; divergent interests must be always impinging on each other, consequently everlasting peace is a contradiction in terms.

None of these positions—in particular none of the "consequentlies" contained in them — could be kept standing if stoutly attacked. But each of them served the defender as a bulwark, if compelled to let another of them fall, and while the new bulwark was being reduced to ruins he had been setting the old one up again. For example, if the champion of war, driven into a corner, has to confess that peace is more worthy of humanity, more rich in blessing, more favourable to culture, than war, he says: "Oh, yes; war is an evil, but it is inevitable"; and then follow Nos. 1 and 2. Then if one shows that it could be avoided and how—by alliances of states, arbitration courts and so forth—then comes the reply: "Oh, yes; war could be avoided, but it ought not"; and then come in Nos. 4 and 5. Then if the advocate of peace upsets these objections, and goes on to prove that on the contrary "war hardens men and dehumanises them". "Oh, yes; I allow that, but —" No. 3. This argument, too, is overthrown, for it is admitted that Nature herself will see that "the trees do not grow up to the sky," and wants no assistance from man to that end. This, again, turns out not to be the result which the possessor of force has in view in making war. Granted, but No. 1. And so there is no end to the debate. The advocate of war is always in the right; his reasoning moves in a circle, where you may always follow, but can never catch him. "War is a horrible evil, but it must exist. I grant it is not a necessity, but it is a great good." This want of consecutiveness, of logical honesty, all those people incur who defend a cause on principles which are not *axiomatic*, or else with no principles, merely from instinct, and to that end will make use of all such phrases or commonplaces as may have come to their ears, and which have obtained currency, in the maintenance of that cause. That these arguments do not proceed from the same points of view, that accordingly they not only do not support each other, but even do directly neutralise each other, makes no matter to them. It is not because this or that reasoning has originated from their own reflections, or is in harmony with their own convictions, that it comes into their train of argument; they merely use to bolster the latter up, without any selection, the conclusions which others have thought out.

All this might not have been so clear to me at that time, when I was disputing with my father on the topic of peace and war; it was not till later on that I had accustomed myself to follow with attention the movements of the intellect in my own and other people's heads. I only recollect that I always came away from these discussions in the highest degree fatigued and excited, and I now see that this fatigue proceeded from this "pursuing in a circle" which my father's way of argument necessitated. The conclusion was, however, every time a compassionate shrug of the shoulders on his part, with the words: "You do not understand that"; words which, as he was treating of military matters, sounded certainly very well deserved in the mouth of an old general as addressed to a young lady.

. . . .

New-Year's Day, 1866. We were all sitting, with our punch and New-Year's cakes, assembled round my father's table when the first hour of this eventful year struck. It was a cheerful feast. We celebrated an engagement with the end of the old year—Conrad and Lilly's. As the hand pointed to twelve, and a *feu de joie* was fired in the street, my enterprising cousin threw his arm round the young lady, who was sitting beside him, pressed, to the surprise of us all, a kiss on her lips, and then asked:—

"Will you take me in '66?" .

"Yes, I will," she replied, "and I love you, Conrad."

Then followed on all hands a clinking of glasses, embracing, handshaking, felicitations, and blessings without end.

"The health of the lovers," "Long live Conrad and Lilly,"

" God bless your union, my children," " Heart-felt congratulations, cousin," " Happiness to you, sister," and so on, and so
on. A joyful and peaceful frame of mind took possession of us
all. Perhaps not quite free of envy in all, for as Death represents the most mournful and most lamentable of events, so
love—the love which is sanctioned by the life-giving union—is
the most joyful and the most enviable. I indeed could detect
no trace of envy in myself, for the happiness which had only
just become a promise to the new bride [1] had long since been
my actual and firm possession ; it was rather a feeling of doubt
that crept over me. " Such perfect bliss as was prepared for
me by Frederick can hardly fall to poor Lilly's lot. Conrad is,
it is true, a very amiable man, but there is but *one* Frederick."

My father brought to an end the tumult of congratulations
by tapping on his glass with the signet ring on his little finger
and rising to speak. He spoke somewhat to this effect : " My
dear children and friends, the year '66 begins well. To me it
is bringing in its very first hour the fulfilment of a cherished
wish, for I have long looked forward to having Conrad for my
son-in-law. Let us hope that this prosperous year may also
bring our Rosa under the yoke, and to you, Martha and Tilling,
a visit from the stork. To you, Doctor Bresser, may it bring
many patients, though this as far as I see hardly goes with the
many wishes for good health that we have all been exchanging ;
and to you, dear Mary, may it present (that is, provided that it
has been destined for you, for I know and honour your fatalism)
a pitched battle or a plenary indulgence, or whatever it is that
you are wishing for. You, my Otto, may it endow with eminent
' distinction ' in your final examination, and with all possible
soldierly virtues and acquirements, so that you may one day
become the ornament of the army and the pride of your old
father. And to the latter also I must try and get something
good to come ; and since he is one who knows no higher wish
than for the good and the glory of Austria, I hope the coming
year may bring some great conquest to the country—Lombardy,

---

[1] *Braut*, an engaged girl.

or—who knows ?—the province of Silesia. One cannot tell to what all this is preliminary, but it is by no means impossible that we may take back again from the insolent Prussians that country which was stolen from the great Maria Theresa."

I recollect that the close of my father's toast "threw a chill" on us. Lombardy and Silesia !—truly none of us felt any pressing need for them. And the underlying wish for "war," *i.e.*, fresh lamentation, more death pangs, that surely did not accord with the tender joyfulness which this hour, made sacred by a new bond of love, had awakened in our hearts. I even permitted myself to reply :—

"No, dear father; to-day is the New Year for the Italians and Prussians also, so we will not wish any destruction for them. May all men in the year '66 and in the years that are to follow grow more united and more happy !"

My father shrugged his shoulders. "You enthusiast !" said he pityingly.

"Not at all," said Frederick in my defence. "The wish expressed by Martha has no taint of enthusiasm, for its fulfilment is assured to us by science. Better and more united and more happy are men constantly becoming, from the beginning of all things to the present day, but so imperceptibly, so slowly that a little span of time, like a year, may not show any visible progress."

"If you believe so firmly in everlasting progress," remarked my father, "why are you so often complaining about reaction—about relapse into barbarism ?"

"Because"—Frederick took out a pencil and drew a spiral on a sheet of paper—"because the march of civilisation is something like *this*. Does not this line, in spite of its occasional twist backwards, always move steadily onwards ? The year which is commencing may, it is true, represent a twist, especially if, as seems likely, another war is going to be waged. Anything of that sort pushes culture a long way back in every aspect, material as well as moral."

"You are not talking much like a soldier, my dear Tilling,"

"I am talking, my dear father-in-law, of a general proposition. My view about this may be true or false; whether it is soldierly or not is another question. At any rate truth can only be in any matter one way. If a thing is red, should one man call it blue on principle, because he wears a blue uniform; and black, if he wears a black cowl?"

"A what?" My father was in the habit, if any discussion did not go quite as he liked, to affect a little difficulty of hearing. To reply to such a "what" by repeating the whole sentence was what few people had the patience to do, and the best way was to give up the argument.

Afterwards, the same night, when we had got home, I put my husband under examination.

"What was that you said to my father? That there was every appearance that there would be another fight this year? I will not have you go into another war; I will not have it."

"What is the use, dear Martha, of this passionate 'I will not'? You would certainly be the first to withdraw it in face of the facts. By how much more visibly war stands at the gate, by so much the more impossible would it be for me to apply for my discharge. Immediately after Schleswig-Holstein it might have been feasible."

"Ah, that unlucky Schmidt & Sons!"

"But now when new clouds are gathering ——"

"Then you really believe that ——"

"I believe that these clouds will disperse again. The two great powers will not tear each other to pieces for those northern countries. But now that it seems threatening again, retirement would have a cowardly look. You must see that too?"

I was obliged to be guided by this reasoning. But I clung to the hopeful phrase: "These clouds will disperse again".

I now followed with anxiety the development of political events, and the opinions and prophecies about them that were current in the newspapers and public speeches. "Be prepared!" "Be prepared!" was the cry now. "Prussia is silently preparing." "Austria is silently preparing." "The Prussians assert that we are preparing, and it is not true, it is they who are preparing." "You lie." "No, it is not true that we are preparing." "If they prepare, we must prepare also. If we leave off our preparations, who knows if they will?" And so the note of preparation sounded in my ear in all possible variations.

"But then what is all this clang of arms for, if one is not to take them in hand?" I asked, to which my father answered in the old phrase :—

"*Si vis pacem, para bellum;* we, that is, are only preparing out of precaution".

"And the other side?"

"With a view of attacking us."

"But they also are saying that their action is only a precaution against our attack."

"That is malice."

"And they say that we are malicious."

"Oh, they say that only as a pretext, to be better able to make their preparations."

So again an endless circle, a serpent with his tail in his mouth, whose upper and lower end is a double dishonesty. It is only by producing an impression on an enemy, who desires war, that the method of fighting him by preparations can be effective on the side of peace, but two equal powers, both desirous of peace, cannot possibly act on that system, unless each is firmly persuaded that the other is deceiving him with hollow phrases. And this persuasion becomes the more firm, the more one knows that one is oneself hiding the same views as one charges on one's adversary under similar phrases. It is not only the augurs, the diplomatists also know well enough about each other, what each has in his mind behind the public ceremonies and modes of speech. The preparation for war lasted on both sides during the early months of the year. On March 12 my father burst into my room radiant with joy.

"Hurrah!" he shouted.   "Good news."

"Disarmament?" I asked delighted.

"What for?   On the contrary, this is the good news: Yesterday, a great Council of War was held. It is really splendid what an armed power we are masters of! The arrogant Prussians had best take care. We are prepared any hour to take the field with 800,000 men! And Benedek, our best strategist, is to be commander-in-chief with unlimited power. I say this to you, my child, in confidence. Silesia is ours, whenever we choose."

"Oh God! Oh God!" I groaned, "must this scourge come on us once more? Who—who can be so devoid of conscience as from ambition, from greed of territory——"

"Calm yourself, we are not so ambitious, nor are we greedy of territory. What we desire (that is to say not I exactly, for to me it would be quite the right thing to get our own Silesia back again), but what the Government desire is to keep peace: *that* they have asserted often enough, and the enormous strength of our active army, as it comes out in the communication yesterday made to the Council of War by the emperor, will inspire all other powers with due respect. Prussia, to begin with, will certainly sing small, and leave off trying to speak in a commanding tone. Thank God, we shall have our say in Schleswig-Holstein too, and I am sure we shall never endure that the other great power should by too great an extension of its dominion conquer for itself a preponderance in Germany. That is a matter which touches our honour, our 'prestige' as the French call it, perhaps our existence, but you cannot understand it. The whole affair is a contest for hegemony, the miserable Schleswig is the last thing in it, but this splendid Council of War has shown plainly *which* takes the first place and *which* is to dictate conditions to the other, the successors of the little Electors of Brandenburg or those of the long line of Romano-German Emperors! I consider peace as certain. But if the others are going on still to behave them. selves in an impudent and arrogant way, and so to make war inevitable, then our victory is assured, and with it conquests which are absolutely incalculable. It were to be wished that it would break out ——"

"Oh yes! and you do wish it too, father, and the whole Council of War seems to be with you! Then, I should like it better if you said it out plainly! Only do not let us have this falsehood—this assurance to the people and the friends of peace that all this purchasing of weapons and demands for war-credits are only for the purpose of your beloved peace. If you are already showing your teeth and closing your fists, do not whisper soft words all the while. If you are trembling with impatience to draw the sword, do not make believe that it is only from precaution that you are laying your hand on the hilt."

So I went on talking for a while with trembling voice and rising passion, while my father was too much taken aback to answer a word, and at last I ended by bursting into tears.

Now followed a time of fluctuating hopes and fears. To-day it was " Peace is secure," to-morrow " War inevitable". Most persons were of the latter view. Not so much because the situation pointed to a bloody arbitrament, but on this account, that if once the word " war " has been pronounced there may be a good deal of debating one way and the other, but experience shows that the end always is war. The little invisible egg which contains the *casus belli* is brooded over so long that at last the monster creeps out of it.

Daily did I note in the red volumes the phases of the varying strife, and thus I knew at that time, and still know to-day, how the eventful " war of '66 " was prepared and how it broke out. Without these entries I might easily find myself in the same ignorance about this precise piece of history as most men are who live where history is being played out. The great majority of the people usually know nothing about why or how a war exists. They only see it coming for a certain time, and then it is there. And when it is there people make no more inquiries about the petty interests and differences of opinion which brought it about, but are then only busied with the mighty events to which its progress gives birth. And when it is over at last, what one remembers chiefly are the terrors and losses we have personally experienced, the conquests and triumphs that have marked its course, but on the political grounds for its origin no one wastes a thought. In the many works of history which appear after every campaign under the title of "The war of the year so and so historically and strategically described," or something to that effect, all the old motives for the strife and all the tactical movements of the campaign in question are recounted, and any one who takes an interest in such things can pick out the explanation from the literature in which it is wrapped up, but in the remembrance of the people such histories certainly do not live. Even of the feelings of hatred and enthusiasm, of embitterment and hope of victory, with which the whole population greets the commencement of the war—feelings expressed in the common saying: "This is a very popular war"—even of these feelings all is wiped out after a year or two.

On March 24 Prussia issued a circular note in which she complained of the threatening preparations of Austria. Then why do we not disarm, if we do not wish to threaten? Why, how can we? For on March 28 you see it is enacted on the side of Prussia that the fortresses in Silesia and two *corps d'armée* are to be put on a war footing.

March 31. Thank God! Austria declares that all the rumours in circulation about her secret preparations are false. It has never even entered into her head to attack Prussia. And on this she founds the demand that Prussia shall suspend her measures of warlike preparation. Prussia replies that she has not the remotest idea of attacking Austria, but that it has become compulsory, in consequence of the late preparations, to be prepared for attack.

And so the responsive song of the two voices goes on without pause :—

My preparations are defensive.
  Your preparations are offensive.
I must prepare because you are preparing.
  I am preparing because you prepare.
    Then let us prepare,
    Yes, let us go on preparing.

The newspapers give the orchestral accompaniments to this duet. The leading articles revel in what is called conjectural politics. It was all poking up, baiting, bragging, slandering. Historical works on the Seven Years' War were published with the avowed intention of renewing the old enmity.

Meanwhile the exchange of notes went on. In that of April 7 Austria again officially denied her preparations, but laid stress on an oral expression said to have been used by Bismarck to Count Carolyi that "it would be easy to disregard the Gastein treaty". Must, then, the destiny of nations depend on anything that two noble diplomatists may have said to one another, in a more or less good humour, about treaties? And what kind of treaties can those be after all, whose contents remain dependent on the good-will of the contracting parties, and are not assured by any higher Court of Arbitration?

Prussia answered this note on April 15, that the charge was untrue; but she was obliged to persist in asserting that Austria had really made preparations on the frontier; and on this she founded the justification of her own preparations. If Austria were in earnest about not attacking she would first disarm.

To this the Vienna Cabinet replied: "We will disarm on the 25th of this month, if Prussia promises to do the same on the following day".

Prussia declared herself ready.

What a breathing again! So then, in spite of all threatening signs, peace will be preserved! I noted this change joyfully in the red book.

But prematurely. New complications arose. Austria declared that she could only disarm in the north, but not in the south at the same time, since she was threatened in that quarter by Italy.

To which Prussia replied : " If Austria does not disarm *altogether*, we shall also remain in a state of preparation ".

Now Italy expressed herself to the effect that it had never, in the faintest way, entered into her mind to attack Austria, but that after this last declaration she was under the necessity of at least making counter preparations.

And so this charming song of defence was now sung by three voices.

I allowed myself to be again in a measure lulled to sleep by this melody.   After such loud and repeated protestations, neither surely *can* attack, and unless one of them attack, there can be no war.   The principle that it is only defensive wars that can be justified has now taken such firm possession of the public conscience that surely no Government can any more undertake an invasion of a neighbouring country ; and if none but mere defensive troops are ranged opposite each other, however threatening their armies are, however determined they may be to defend themselves to the knife, still they cannot actually break the peace.

What a delusion ! Beside "the offensive" there are, I find, many other ways of commencing hostilities.   There are demands and interventions regarding some small third country, and which have to be resisted as unfair ; there are old treaties which are declared to be violated, and for the upholding of which recourse must be had to arms; and, finally, there is "the European equilibrium," which would be endangered by the acquisition of power by one state or the other.   And so energetic steps are demanded to prevent such acquisition. It is not avowed ; but one of the most violent impulses to fight is the hate which has long been stirred up, and which at last presses on to the death-dealing combat, as ardently and with the same natural force as long-cherished love to the life-giving embrace.

Events now began to tread on each other's heels.   Austria

declared for the Augustenburg so decisively that Prussia characterised it as a breach of the Gastein treaty, and discovered in that a plainly hostile intention; the consequence of which was that the preparations on both sides were carried to their highest point. And now Saxony also began to do the same. The excitement was universal, and became more violent every day. "War in sight, war in sight," was the announcement of every newspaper and every speech. I felt as if I were at sea and a storm approaching.

The most hated and most reviled man in Europe then was called Bismarck. On May 7 an attempt was made to assassinate him. Did Blind, the perpetrator of the deed, wish to avert this storm? And *would* he have averted it?

I received letters from Prussia from Aunt Cornelia, from which it seemed that in that country the war was anything but desired. While with us there prevailed universal enthusiasm for the idea of a war with Prussia, and we looked with pride on our "million of picked soldiers," inward contention reigned there. Bismarck was no less reviled and slandered in his own country than in ours; the report went that the Landwehr would refuse to go out to the "fraternal war," and it was said that Queen Augusta threw herself at her husband's feet to pray for peace. Oh! how glad should I have been to kneel at her side, and how gladly would I have hurried off all my sister-women—yes, all—to do the same. It is this, and this alone, that should be the effort of all women: "Peace, peace. Lay down your arms."

If our beautiful empress had also thrown herself at her husband's feet, and with tears and lifted hands had begged for disarmament—who knows? Perhaps she did—perhaps the emperor himself also wished to preserve peace, but the pressure proceeding from the councils, and the speakers, and the shouting and the writing was such as no one man—even on the throne—could stand against.

On June 1 Prussia declared to the assembly of the Bund that she would at once disarm if Austria and Saxony set the example. Against that came a direct accusation from Vienna that Prussia had for a long time been planning, in concert with Italy, an attack on Austria, and on that account the latter now desired to call the whole Bund to arms, in order to request it to undertake the decision of the case of the duchies. She desired at the same time to call the Estates of Holstein to co-operate.

Against this declaration Prussia lodged a protest—inasmuch as it overturned the Gastein treaty. That being so the position reverted to the Vienna treaty, *i.e.*, to the common condominium. The consequence was that Prussia had also the right to occupy Holstein—as on her side Austria was permitted to occupy Schleswig. And the Prussians at once moved into Holstein. Gablenz withdrew without sword drawn, but under protest.

Bismarck had previously said in a circular letter: "We have found no disposition at all to meet us at Vienna. On the contrary, expressions have fallen from Austrian statesmen and councillors of the emperor which have reached the ear of the king from authentic sources (*tritsch tratsch*), and which prove that the ministers wish for war at any price (to wish for public slaughter, what a fearful accusation !), partly because they hope for success in the field, partly to get free of internal difficulties, and to eke out their own shattered finances by contributions from Prussia (statecraft)."

The Press was now completely warlike, and of course (as the patriotic custom is) sure of victory. The possibility of defeat must be entirely left out of view by every loyal subject whom his prince summons to the battle. Numerous leading articles pictured Benedek's entry into Berlin, and also the sack of that city by the Croats. Some even recommended to raze the capital of Prussia to the ground. "Sack," "raze to the ground," "ride over spurs in blood"—these are expressions which do not indeed any longer express the popular conception in modern times of what is right; but they have, since the days of our school-studies of the ancient histories of war, been always clinging to people; and they have been so often recited in the histories of battles learned by heart, so often written down in our essays in German, that if a man has to write an article on the subject of war in a newspaper, such expressions drop from his pen spontaneously. Contempt for the enemy cannot be too strongly expressed—for the Prussian troops the Vienna newspapers had no other term than "the tailors". Adjutant-General Count Grünne expressed himself thus : "We shall chase off these Prussians with a flea in their ear". That is the kind of way to make a war quite "popular". That sort of thing strengthens the national confidence.

June 11. Austria proposes that the Bund shall take action against Prussia's helping herself in Holstein, and mobilise the whole army of the Bund. On June 14 this proposition is put to the vote, and by nine votes to six—accepted ! Oh ! those three votes ! How much grief and how many shrieks of pain have made groaning echo to those three voices !

It is done—the ambassadors have received their dismissal. On the 16th the Bund requested Austria and Bavaria to go to the assistance of the Hanoverians and Saxons, who were already attacked by Prussia.

On the 18th the Prussian war manifesto appeared, and at the same time the manifesto of the Emperor of Austria to his people, and the proclamation of Benedek to his troops. On the 22nd Prince Frederick Charles published his orders to his army, and thus commenced the war. I copied the four original documents at the time. Here they are :—

King William says :—

Austria will not forget that her princes were once the rulers of Germany, and will not regard modern Prussia as a co-partner, but only as a hostile rival. Prussia, it is held, must be opposed in all her efforts, because whatever profits Prussia injures Austria. The old unblessed jealousy has again burst out into a fierce flame. Prussia is to be weakened, destroyed, disinherited. With her no treaties are to be any longer in force. Wherever we look in Germany we are surrounded by foes, and their war-cry is " Humiliation for Prussia". Up to the last moment I have sought for and kept open the way to a friendly solution. Austria refused.

On the other hand, the Emperor Francis Joseph expresses himself thus :—

The latest events prove incontestably that Prussia is now setting open force in the place of right. Thus has the most impious of wars— a war of Germans against Germans—become inevitable. To answer for all the misery it will bring on individuals, families, neighbours and districts, I summon those who have brought it about before the judgment-seat of history, and of the Eternal and Almighty God.

" The opposite party " is always the one that wishes for war. The " opposite party " are always charged with setting up force in the place of right. Why, then, is it anyhow possible, consistently with public law, that this can happen? An "impious" war, because it is one of "Germans against Germans". Quite true. The point of view is a higher one, which, beyond " Prussia " and " Austria," raises the wider conception of Germany. But take one step more and we shall reach that still higher unity in the light of which every war—men against men, especially civilised men against civilised—will necessarily appear an impious fratricide. And to " summon before the judgment-seat of history "—what is the use of that? History, as it has been managed hitherto, has never pronounced any other judgment than a worship of success. When any one comes out of a war as conqueror the guild of historical scribblers fall in the dust before him, and praise him as the fulfiller of his "mission of educative culture". And "before the judgment-seat of Almighty God ". Yes ; but is not this He who is represented as the producer of the fights, is not the same almighty, irresistible will equally concerned with the outbreak as with the course of the war? Oh, contradiction on contradiction ! And this is what must certainly take place always, whenever the truth is hidden under hypocritical phrases—when an attempt is made to hold equally holy two principles which are mutually destructive, such as war and justice, or national hatred and humanity, or the God of Love and the God of Battles.

And Benedek says:—

We are standing opposed to a war power which is composed of two halves—Line and Landwehr. The first is formed exclusively of young fellows who are not accustomed either to fatigue or privation, who have never taken part in any considerable campaign. The second consists of untrustworthy, discontented elements, who would like better to overthrow their own Government, which they dislike, than to have to fight us. The enemy has also, in consequence of the long period of peace, not a solitary general who has had the opportunity of educating himself on the field of battle. Veterans of Mincio and Palestro, you will, I think, count it as a special point of honour, acting under your old and tried leaders, not to yield to such antagonists even the smallest advantage. The enemy has for a long time been pluming himself upon his quick-firing needle gun; but I think, my men, that will not do him much good. We shall most likely leave him no time for that, but charge him home at once with the bayonet and the butt. As soon as, with God's help, the enemy has been beaten and compelled to retreat, we shall follow on his traces, and you will rest from your toils in the foeman's country, and demand in the amplest measure those refreshments which a victorious army will have fully merited.

Finally Prince Frederick Charles says:—

Soldiers! the faithless and covenant-breaking Austria has now for some time, without any declaration of war, disregarded the frontiers of Prussia in Upper Silesia. So I might have equally considered myself entitled to cross the Bohemian frontier without any declaration of war. But I have not done so. To-day I have forwarded a regular declaration of war, and to-day we tread the territory of our enemies, in order to protect our own country. May our commencement have God's sanction. [Is this the same God with whose help Benedek promised to strike down the enemy?] Let us rest our cause in His hands, who guides the hearts of men, who decides the fate of nations and the result of battles, as it is written in the Scriptures. Let your hearts beat for God and your hands strike the foe. In this war, as you know, Prussia's dearest interests, nay, the continued existence of our beloved Prussia, are in question. The enemy avows, in the most open manner, the wish to dismember and humiliate her. Shall then the rivers of blood which your fathers and mine poured out under Frederick the Great, and that which we lately poured out at Düppel and Alsen, have been poured out in vain?

Never! we will maintain Prussia as she is, and make her stronger and more powerful by victory. We will show ourselves worthy of our fathers. We rely on the God of our fathers that He will be gracious to us, and bless the arms of Prussia! So, now, forward with our old battle-cry: " With God for king and fatherland. Long live the king."

CHAPTER X.

The Austro-Prussian war.—My husband with the army.—
Parting letters.—Dr. Bresser.—The course of the war.—
Victory of Custozza.—Austrian reverses in Bohemia.—
War correspondence in the newspapers.—Discussions with
my father.—A long letter to my husband.

So it had come again—this greatest of all misfortunes—and
was greeted by the populace with the accustomed rejoicing.
The regiments marched out (in what state were they to return?)
and wishes for victory, and blessings, and the shouting of the
street boys were their accompaniment.

Frederick had been ordered to Bohemia some time previously,
even before war had been declared; and just when matters
were in such a position as to enable me to entertain a confident
hope that the quarrel about the duchies, so unblessed and so
contemptible, would be settled amicably. And, therefore, this
time I was spared the heart-rending leave-taking which precedes
the setting off of one's beloved directly "to the war". When
my father brought me the news in triumph: "Now it is off," I
had been already alone for a fortnight. And for some time I
had quite made my mind up to this news, as a criminal in his
cell has made up his mind to the reading of the death-sentence.

I bowed my head and said nothing.

"Keep up a good heart, my child. The war will not last
long; in a day or two we shall be in Berlin. And as your husband came back from Schleswig-Holstein, so he will come back
from this campaign, but covered with much greener laurels. It
may, indeed, be unpleasant for him, being himself of Prussian

(215)

extraction, to fight against Prussia, but after he entered into the Austrian service he became one of us body and soul. Those Prussians! the arrogant windbags! they want to turn us out of the Bund! they will soon repent it; if Silesia becomes ours again, and if the Hapsburgs ———"

I stretched out my hand: "Father—one request—leave me to myself".

He might have imagined that I felt the need of giving my tears full vent; and as he was an enemy to all scenes of emotion, he willingly granted my wish and took his departure.

I, however, did not weep. I felt as if a numbing stroke had fallen on my head. Breathing heavily, staring blindly, I sat motionless for some time. Then I went to my writing-table, opened the red volume, and made this entry :—

"The sentence of death is pronounced. A hundred thousand men are to be executed. Will Frederick be among them? And I also, as a consequence. Who am I that I should not perish like the rest of the hundred thousand? I wish I were dead already."

From Frederick I received the same day a few hasty lines.

"My wife, be of good cheer; keep your heart up! We have been happy—no one can take that from us—even if to-day for us, as for so many others, the decree has gone forth—'It is finished'. (The same thought here as I expressed in my red book about the many others who were sentenced.) To-day we go to meet 'the enemy'. Perhaps I shall recognise there a few comrades in battle at Düppel and Alsen—possibly my little cousin Godfrey. . . . We are to march on Liebenau with the advanced guard of Count Clam-Gallas. From this time there will be no more leisure for writing. Do not look for any *letters* for you. At the most, if opportunity offers, a line, as a token that I am alive. But before that I should like to find one single word which could comprehend in itself the whole of my love that I might write it here for you in case it might be my last. I can find only this word—'Martha'. You know what that means for me."

Conrad Althaus had also to march. He was full of fire and delight in battle, and animated by sufficient hatred of the Prussians to make him start off with pleasure; still his parting was hard for him. The marriage licence had arrived only two days before the order to march.

"Oh, Lilly, Lilly," he cried with pain, as he said adieu to his affianced bride, "why did you delay so long to accept me? Who knows now whether I shall come back again?"

My poor sister was herself full of repentance. Now for the first time there sprang up passionate love for him she had slighted so long. When he was gone she sank into my arms in tears.

"Oh, why did I not say 'yes' long ago! I should now have been his wife."

"Then, my poor Lilly, the parting would have been all the more painful for you."

She shook her head. I well understood what was going on in her mind, perhaps more clearly than she understood herself; to be obliged to part with love-longings still unfulfilled, and, perhaps, destined to remain for ever unfulfilled; to see the cup torn from their lips, and possibly shattered, before they had had a single draught—that might well be doubly torturing.

My father, sisters, and Aunt Mary now removed to Grumitz. I was easily persuaded to go there too with my little son. As long as Frederick was away, my own hearth seemed extinguished —I could not stay there. It is strange. I felt myself just as much a widow, to have done with life just as thoroughly, as if the news of the outbreak of war had been at the same time the news of Frederick's death. Occasionally in the midst of my dull grief, a brighter thought would break in : "He is alive and surely may come back"; but along with it an idea of horror would rise again : "He is writhing and agonising in intolerable pains ; he is fainting in a trench ; heavy waggons are driving over his shattered limbs ; flies and worms are crawling over his open wounds ; the people who are clearing the field of battle take the stiffened object lying on the ground for dead, and are shovelling him still alive along with the dead into the damp trench : there he comes to himself and ——"

With a loud scream I woke up from such images as these.

"What is the matter with you now, Martha," said my father in a scolding tone. "You will drive yourself out of your senses if you brood in this way and cry out so ; why will you summon up such foolish pictures out of your fancy ? It is sinful."

I had indeed often given expression aloud to these ideas of mine, and this irritated my father extremely.

"Sinful," he went on, "and improper and nonsensical. Such cases as your excited fancy pictures, do no doubt occur once in a thousand times among the common men, but a staff-officer, as your husband is, is not left to lie on the field. Besides, as a general rule, folks should not think about such horrid things. Such conduct involves a kind of sacrilege, a profanation of war, in keeping these pitiful details before one's eyes instead of the sublimity of the whole. One should not think about them."

"Yes, yes, not think about it," I replied, "that is always the custom of mankind in the presence of any human misery— 'don't think about it,' that is the support of all kinds of barbarity."

Our family doctor, Dr. Bresser, was not at this moment at Grumitz, he had voluntarily placed himself at the disposal of the army medical department, and had started for the theatre of war, and the idea occurred to me also whether I should not go too, as a sick-nurse. Yes, if I could have known that I should be in Frederick's neighbourhood, be at hand in case he was wounded, I would not have hesitated. But for others ? No, there my strength broke down, my spirit of sacrifice failed. To see them die, hear the death-rattle, want to give help to hundreds begging for help, and have no help to give, to bring on myself all this pain, this disgust, this grief, without thereby getting to Frederick, on the contrary diminishing thereby the chance of meeting again, for the nurses themselves ran into various kinds of danger to their lives. No; that I would not do. Besides my father informed me that a private person like myself was altogether inadmissible for nursing in a field hospital, that this office could only be exercised by soldiers of the army medical service, or at the most by sisters of charity.

"To pluck charpie," he said, "and prepare bandages for the Patriotic Aid Society, that is the only thing that you ladies can do to help the wounded, and that my daughters ought to do diligently, on that I bestow my blessing."

And it was now to this occupation that my sisters and I devoted many hours of every day. Rosa and Lilly worked with gently compassionate, almost happy-looking faces. As we heaped up the fine threads under our fingers into soft masses, or folded up the strips of linen in beautiful order together, the occupation affected the two girls like an office of charitable nursing: they fancied themselves soothing the burning pains and staunching the bleeding wounds, hearing the sighs of relief and seeing the grateful glances of those on whom they attended. The picture they so formed of the condition of a wounded man was then almost a pleasant one. Enviable soldiers! who, delivered from the dangers of the raging fight, were now stretched on clean soft beds, and there would be nursed and pampered up to the time of their recovery, lulled for the most part in a half-unconscious slumber of luxurious fatigue, waking up again occasionally to the pleasant consciousness that their lives were saved, and that they would be able to return to their friends at home and relate to them how they had received their honourable wounds at the battle of ——.

Our father also encouraged them in this innocent way of looking at it. "Bravo, bravo, girls! working again to-day! You have now again prepared delights for a number of our brave defenders. What a relief it is to get a pad of charpie like that on a bleeding wound! I can tell you a tale about that. Long ago, when I got that bullet in my leg at Palestro ——" and so on, and so on.

I however sighed and said nothing. I had heard other

histories of wounds than those which my father loved to relate, histories which bore about the same relation to the usual veterans' anecdotes, as the realities of the life of a poor shepherd do to the pastoral pictures of Watteau.

The Red Cross.   I knew through what an impulse of popular sympathy, shocked to the most painful degree, that institution had been called into life.   In its time I had followed the debate which took place at Geneva on the subject, and had read the tract by Dunant, which gave the impetus to the whole thing.   A heart-rending cry of woe was that tract! The noble patrician of Geneva had hurried to the field of Solferino, in order to give what aid he could ; and what he found there he related to the world.   Innumerable wounded men, who had been lying there for five or six days without any assistance. He would have liked to save them all ; but what could he, a single person, do, what could the other few individuals, in the face of this mass of misery ?   He saw men whose lives might have been saved by a drop of water, by a mouthful of bread. He saw men who, still breathing, had to be buried in fearful haste. . . .   Then he spoke out ; said what had often been admitted, but now found an echo for the first time, *vis.*, that the means for nursing and rescue at the disposal of the army administration had not grown in proportion to the requirements of a battle.   And so the "Red Cross" was founded.

Austria had at that time not yet adhered to the Geneva Convention.   Why ?   Why is there resistance opposed to everything that is new, however rich in blessing, and however simple it may be ?   Because of the law of laziness, the power of holy custom.   "The idea is very fine, but impracticable," is the saying. I often heard my father repeat these arguments of hesitation used by several of the delegates at the Conference of 1863. " Impracticable, and, even if practicable, yet in many points of view unbecoming.   The military authorities could not allow that private action on the field of battle was admissible.   In war tactical aims must have the priority over the friendly offices of humanity; and how could this private action be surrounded with proper guarantees against the existence of espionage? And the expenses! Is not war costly enough already? The voluntary nurses would, through their own material wants, fall as a burden on the provision department; or, if they are to supply themselves in the country occupied, will there not arise a regrettable difficulty for the army administration through the purchase of the articles necessary for the service, and the immediate raising of their price?"

Oh, this official wisdom! so dry, so well-instructed, so real, so redolent of prudence, and so unfathomably stupid!

. . . .

The first engagement between our troops in Bohemia and the enemy took place on June 25 at Liebenau. My father brought us this news with his usual triumphant mien.

"That is a grand beginning," he said; "you can see heaven is on our side. It is significant that the first with whom these windbags had to do were the troops of our celebrated 'Iron Brigade'. You know, of course, the Poschach Brigade which defended Königsberg in Silesia so valiantly—they will give them all they want!" (However, the next news from the seat of war showed that after five hours' fighting this brigade, forming part of the advanced guard of Clam-Gallas, retreated to Podol. Also that Frederick was there—which I did not know —and that in the same night Podol, which had been barricaded, was attacked by General Horn, and the fight renewed by the bright moonlight; which also I heard later.) "But," continued my father, "even more splendid than in the north is the beginning of matters in the south. At Custozza we have gained a victory, children, more glorious than any but one. I have always said it: Lombardy must become ours! Are you not delighted? I regard the war as already decided; for if we get done with the Italians, who do at any rate set a regular trained army in the field against us, we shall not find it hard to deal with these 'tailors' apprentices'. This Landwehr—it is really an impudence—but it is just of a piece with the whole Prussian conceit to take the field against regular armies with such stuff. There are these fellows, torn away from the workbench and the writing-desk ; they are not inured to any hardship, and so it is impossible that they can stand in the field against soldiers proof against blood and steel. Just look there—at what the *Wiener Zeitung* of June 24 writes in its 'original correspondence'— surely that is good news : 'In Prussian Silesia cattle plague has broken out, and, as is understood, in a highly threatening form'."

"'Cattle plague,' 'threatening form,' 'joyful news,'" I said with a slight shake of the head ; "nice things people must take pleasure in in times of war. However, one good thing is that black and yellow posts are erected on the frontiers, so that the plague cannot cross."

But my father did not hear, and went on reading his pleasant intelligence :—

Fever is raging among the Prussian troops at Neisse. The un-healthy marsh-land, the bad treatment and the miserable shelter of the troops accumulated in the villages around, must necessarily produce such results. In Austria we have no idea of the treatment of the Prussian soldiery. The nobles believe themselves entitled to give any orders they please to the "common folk". Six ounces of pork per man is all—and that for men who are not experienced soldiers.

"The newspapers are all full of capital news ; above all, the account of the glorious day of Custozza. You should keep these papers, Martha."

And I have kept them. It is what people should always do ; and when a new national quarrel is impending, then read, not the most recent newspapers, but those dating from the former war, and then you will see what weight to attach to all their prophesying and boasting, and even to their accounts and intelligence. *That* is instructive.

From the seat of war in the north—from headquarters of the Army of the North—they write to us as follows, on the subject of the Prussian plan of campaign (I) : "According to the latest advices, the Prussian army has shifted its headquarters to Eastern Silesia. (Then follows in the usual tactical style a long narrative of the projected movements and positions contemplated by the enemy, according to which the gentleman who furnished the news most have had a much clearer picture before him than Moltke and Roon.) According to this, it seems to be the object of the Prussians to anticipate in this way our march on Berlin by their own in which, however, they will hardly succeed, having regard to the precautions taken (with which again ' our special correspondent ' is much more familiar than Benedek). Favourable accounts may be looked for from the northern army with the utmost confidence, even if they do not arrive so quickly as the popular longing desires them to do. They will, however, thereby become more decisive and more important."

The new *Frankfurter Zeitung* relates a pleasant interlude, the march of Austrian troops of Italian nationality through Munich, as follows :—

Among the troops passing through Munich were some battalions of the line. They, like the rest of the troops passing through the Bavarian capital, were entertained in the garden of an inn situated near the station. Any one might convince himself with what delight these Venetians testified to their joy in fighting the foes of Austria (perhaps too "any one" might have imagined that drunken soldiers would willingly show enthusiasm for anything they were told to be enthusiastic about). In Würzburg the station was filled by the rank and file of an Austrian regiment of infantry of the line. As far as could be ascertained the whole consisted of Venetians. They were received with equal friendliness (*i.e.*, were made equally drunk) ; and the men could not find words to express with sufficient warmth their joy and their determination to fight against the truce-breakers (of two parties at war with each other the other is always "the truce-breakers"). The hurrahs were endless. (Could not this " Mr. Any One," who was thus lounging about the railway station, and so edified by the cries of the soldiery, find out that there is nothing so contagious as hurrahing—that a thousand voices shouting together are not the expression of a thousand unanimous sentiments, but simply exemplify the working of the natural instinct of imitation ?)

At Böhmisch-Trübau Field-Marshal Benedek communicated to the Army of the North the three bulletins relative to the victory of the Army of the South, and added the following order of the day :—

In the name of the Army of the North, I have despatched the following telegram to the commander of the Army of the South: Field-Marshal Benedek and the whole northern army to the glorious and most

illustrious commander-in-chief of the brave southern army with joyful
admiration, sends most hearty congratulations on the news of the famous
day of Custozza. The campaign in the south is opened with a new and
glorious victory for our arms. Glorious Custozza shines on the escut-
cheon of the imperial army.

Soldiers of the Army of the North! You will receive the news with
shouts of joy. You will move to battle with increased enthusiasm, so
that we also may very soon inscribe names of fame on that same shield, and
announce to the emperor a victory from the north also towards which
our warlike ardour burns, and which your valour and devotion will conquer, to the cry "Long live the emperor".

                                                    BENEDEK.

To the foregoing telegram the following answer from Verona
reached Böhmisch-Trübau:—

The Army of the South and its commander return their thanks to
their beloved ex-commander and his brave army. Convinced that we
also shall soon have to send our congratulations for a similar victory.

"Convinced! Convinced!" . . .

"Does not your heart leap up, my children, when you read
such things?" shouted my father in delight. "Can you not
rise up to a sufficient height of patriotic feeling to throw into
the background your private circumstances at the sight of such
triumphs, you, Martha, to forget that your Frederick, and you,
Lilly, that your Conrad is exposed to some danger? Danger
which probably they will come out of safe and sound: and even
to succumb to which—a fate which they share with the best
sons of our country—would redound to their fame and honour.
There is not a soldier who would not willingly die to the call,
'For our country!'"

"If, after a lost battle, a man is left lying with shattered
limbs on the field," I replied, "and lies there undiscovered for
four or five days and nights in indescribable agonies from thirst
and hunger, rotting while still alive, and so perishes, knowing
all the while that his death has not helped his country you talk
of one bit, but has brought his loved ones to despair, I should
like to know whether all this time he is gladly dying to the
call you speak of."

"You are outrageous, and besides you speak in such shrill tones, quite unbecoming for a lady."

"Oh yes, the true word, the naked reality, is outrageous, is shameless. Only the phrase which by thousandfold repetition has become sanctioned is 'proper,' but I assure you, father, that this unnatural 'joy in dying' which is thus exacted from all men, however heroic it may seem to him who uses the phrase, sounds to me like a *spoken death-knell*."

. . . .

Among Frederick's papers, many years later, I found a letter which in those days I sent to the seat of war. This letter shows as clearly as possible with what feelings I was filled at that time.

" Grumitz, *June* 28, 1866.

" Dear one,—I am not alive. Fancy that in the next room people are debating whether I am to be executed in the next few days or no, while I have to wait outside for their decision. During this period of waiting I do indeed breathe, but can I call it *living !* The next room, in which the question is to be decided, is called Bohemia. But no, my love, the picture is hardly yet correct. For if it were only a matter of *my* life or death, the anxiety would not be so great. For my anxiety concerns a far dearer life than my own ; and my fear is concerned even with something still worse than your death—with your possible agony in dying. Oh that all this were over, over ! Oh that our victories would come in speedy succession ; not for the sake of the victory, but of the end !

" Will these lines ever reach you ? and where, and how ? Whether after a hot day's fight or in camp, or perhaps in hospital ? In any case it will do you good to get news of your dear ones. If I can write nothing but what is mournful—and what else but what is mournful can be felt during this time, when the sun is darkened by the great black pall hoisted up in the name of 'our country,' to fall down on the country's sons? —still my lines will bring you refreshment, for I am dear to you, Frederick—I know how dear, and my written word rejoices and

15

moves you, as would a soft touch from my hand. I am near you, Frederick—be assured of that—with every thought, with every breath, by day and night. Here, in my own circle, I move and act and speak mechanically. My innermost self, *that* belongs to you, *that* never leaves you for a moment ; only my boy reminds me that the world still contains for me a thing which is not you. The good little fellow—if you knew how he asks and cares for you ! We two talk together of nothing but 'papa'. He knows well, like a boy of sharp perceptions, what object fills my heart ; and however little he may be (you know that !) he is already in a sense a *friend* of his mother. I even begin to speak with him as with a reasonable being, and for this he is thankful. I, on my part, am thankful to him for the love he shows to you. It is so seldom that children get on well with their step-parents. It is true there is nothing of the stepfather about you—you could not be more tender and kind to a child of your own, my own tender and kind one ! Yes, kindness, great, soft, and mild, is the foundation of your being ; and what does the poet say ?   'As heaven is vaulted by one single great sapphire, so the greatness of character of a noble man is formed of one single virtue, kindness.' In other words, I love you, Frederick ! That is still always the refrain of all my thoughts about you and your qualities. I love you so confidingly, with such assurance. I *rest* in you, Frederick, warm and soft—that is when I have you, of course. Now when you are again torn from me, my repose is naturally gone. Oh, if the storm were only over, over ; if you all were only in Berlin to dictate terms of peace to King William ! For my father is firmly convinced that this will be the end of the campaign ; and from all that is heard and read here, I also must believe him.   'As soon as, with God's help, the enemy is struck down '—so runs Benedek's proclamation—' we will follow on his track, and you shall repose in the country of the foe, and enjoy those refreshments —— ' and so on. What, then, are these refreshments ? At this day no general dare say openly, and without circumlocution : 'You shall plunder, burn, murder, and ravish,' as they used to say in the middle ages to excite their hordes.   Now, at the most, all that could be kept before their eyes as a reward would be the free distribution of beer and sausages; but that would be a little tame, and so it was put figuratively—'those refreshments,' and so on. Every one may make out of that what he pleases.   The principle that in 'the country of the foe' is to be found the reward of war is still maintained in military language. . . . And how will you feel in 'the foeman's land,' which is really your own ancestral country, where your friends and your cousins are living?   Will you 'refresh' yourself by laying Aunt Cornelia's pretty villa even with the ground?   ' Enemy's country ;' that is really a fossilised conception of those times when war was openly what its *raison d'etre* proclaims it, a piracy ; and when the enemy's country attracted the combatant as a land of prey which promised him a recompense.

"I am talking now with you, as I used in those happy hours when you were at my side, and when, after the reading of some book of the progressive school, we used to philosophise with each other about the contradictions of our times, so intimately, so entirely understanding and supplementing each other.   In my circle there is no one—no one—with whom I could talk about matters of that kind.   Doctor Bresser would have been the only one with whom ideas condemnatory of war could be exchanged ; and he also is now gone—himself drawn into this horrible war—but with the purpose of healing wounds, not inflicting them ; another contradiction really, this 'humanity' in war: an essential contradiction.   It is about the same as 'enlightenment' in faith.   One thing or the other ; but humanity and war, reason and dogma, *that* will not do.   The downright, burning hatred of the enemy, coupled with an entire contempt for human life, that is the vital nerve of war, exactly as the un-questioning suppression of reason is the fundamental condition of faith.   But we live in a time of compromise.   The old institutions and the new ideas are working with equal power. And so people, who do not wish to break entirely with the old and who cannot entirely comprehend the new, make an attempt to fuse the two together; and it is this which generates this mendacious, inconsistent, contradictory, half-and-half system under which spirits who thirst for truth, accuracy, and completeness so groan and suffer.

"Ah, why do I compose all this treatise! You will at the present time be scarcely disposed for such generalisations, as you used to be in our happy hours of chat. You hear raging round you a horrible reality, with which you have to reckon. How much better would it be if you could accept it with the simple assurance of ancient times, when the warlike life was to the soldier a proud pleasure and a delight. Better also would it be if I could write to you, as other wives do, letters full of wishes for prosperity, confident promises of victory, and incitements to your courage. Girls of the present day are educated in patriotism, so that at the proper time they might cry to their husbands: 'Go on, die for your country—that is the most glorious of deaths'; or, 'Come back with victory, and then we will reward you with our loves. In the meantime we will pray for you. The God of battles, who protects our army, He will hear our prayers. Day and night our intercession is rising up to heaven, and we are sure to take His favour by storm. You will come back crowned with fame. We never tremble for an instant, for we are worthy comrades of your valour. No! no! the mothers of your sons must be no cowards if they would raise up a new race of heroes; and even if we have to give up what is dearest to us—for king and country no sacrifice is too great!'

"That would be the right letter for a soldier's wife, would it not? But not such a letter as you would wish to read from your wife—from the partner of your thoughts, from her who shares your disgust at the old blind delusion of mankind. Oh, such disgust—so bitter, so painful that I cannot describe it to you. When I picture to myself these two armies, composed of individuals with the gift of reason, and for the most part kind and gentle men, how they are rushing on each other, to annihilate each other, desolating at the same time the unfortunate land,

in which they cast aside the villages they have 'taken' like
cards in their game of murder.   When I picture all this, I feel
inclined to shriek out: 'Do bethink you!' 'Do stop!'   And
out of the 100,000, 90,000 individuals would certainly be glad
to stop; but the mass is compelled to go on in its fury.

But enough; you will prefer to hear the accounts and the news
from home.   Well, then, we are all well.   My father is constantly
in the highest state of excitement over present events.   The
victory of Custozza fills him with radiant pride.   He behaves as
if he had won it himself.   In any case he regards the splendour
of that day as so bright that the reflection which falls on
him as an Austrian and a general makes him completely
happy.   Lori, too, whose husband, as you know, is with
the Army of the South, writes me a letter of triumph about
this same Custozza.   Do you recollect, Frederick, how jealous
I was for a quarter of an hour about this same good Lori?
And how I came out after that attack with stronger love
and stronger trust in you?   Oh, if only you had betrayed me
then ; if only you had sometimes a little ill-treated me ; then
I should perhaps bear your absence now more easily.   But to
know that *such* a husband is in the storm of bullets !   Let me
go on with my news.   Lori has offered to spend the remainder
of her grass-widowhood in Grumitz, along with her little
Beatrix.   I could not say 'no'; yet frankly any society is at
the present time disagreeable to me.   I want to be alone, alone
with my longing for you, the extent of which no one but you
can measure.   Next week Otto begins his vacation.   He laments
in every letter that the war should have begun before, instead
of after, his admission to officer's rank.   He hopes to God that
the peace will not ' break out ' before he leaves the academy.
That word ' break out ' is not perhaps the one he used, but in
any case it expresses his meaning, for peace appears to him a
threatening calamity.   It is indeed the way they are brought
up.   As long as there are wars men must be brought up to be
war-loving soldiers ; and so long as there are war-loving soldiers
there must be wars.   Is that our eternal, inevitable circle ?

No, God be thanked! For *that* love, in spite of all school training, is constantly diminishing. We found the proof of this diminution in Henry Thomas Buckle. Do not you recollect? But I don't want any printed proof; a glance into your heart, your noble human heart, my Frederick, is enough to demonstrate this to me. Let me get on with my news. From all our landed connections and acquaintances in Bohemia we get on all sides epistles of lamentation. The march of the troops through the country, even if they are marching to victory, devastates it and sucks everything out of it. And how if once the enemy should advance into it, if the fight should be played out in their neighbourhood, there where their possessions, their châteaux and fields are situated? All is ready for flight, all their effects packed up and their treasures buried. Adieu to our happy tours among the Bohemian Spas; adieu to the pleasant visits to the country houses; adieu to the brilliant autumn hunting parties; and, in any case, adieu to the usual revenues from farms and businesses. The harvests are trampled down, the factories, if they are not battered down and burned, are robbed of their labourers. ' It is indeed a real misfortune,' they write, 'that we live exactly on the border-land; and it is a second misfortune that Benedek did not assume the offensive with more vigour, so as to fight out the war in Prussia.' Perhaps it might also be called a misfortune that the whole political quarrel could not have been adjusted before a court of arbitration, but that the murderous devastation must be carried out on Bohemian or Silesian soil (for in Silesia also, if we believe the accounts of trustworthy travellers, there are really men and fields and crops). But that idea does not occur to anybody!

"My little Rudolf is sitting at my feet while I am writing. He sends you a kiss, and his love to our dear Puxl. We both miss him much, the good, merry little dog; but, on the other hand, he would have missed his master sadly, and he will be a diversion and a companion to you. Give Puxl both our loves. I shake his paw, and Rudi kisses his dear black snout.

"And now, good-bye for to-day, my all on earth!"

CHAPTER XI.

The Austrian reverses increase.—Sketches from the seat of war, showing its realities, as viewed by a soldier who abhors war.—Death of poor Puzl.—My husband avows his determination never to serve in another campaign.

" NEVER was such a thing heard of—defeat after defeat. First the village of Podol, barricaded by Clam-Gallas, carried by storm, taken in the night by moonlight, and by the light of the conflagration. Then Gitchin conquered. The needle-gun, the cursed needle-gun, mows our troops down by whole ranks at a time. The two great army corps of the enemy, that commanded by the Crown Prince and that under Prince Fr. Karl, have joined, and are pressing forward against Münchengrätz." Thus sounded the terrible news, and my father communicated it with as great a degree of lamentation as he had shown joy in telling us the victorious news from Custozza. But his confidence was not yet shaken.

" Let them come, all of them, all, into our Bohemia, and be annihilated there, to the last man. There is no escape there, no retreat for them ; we hem them in, we encircle them, and the enraged country folks themselves will give them the finishing stroke. It is not altogether so advantageous as you might suppose to operate in an enemy's country ; for in that case you have not only the army but the whole population against you. The people poured boiling water and oil on the Prussians from the windows of the houses at ——."

I uttered a low sound of disgust.

"What would you have?" said my father, shrugging his shoulders. "It is horrible, I grant, but it is war."

"Then at least never assert that war ennobles men. Confess that it unmans them, makes them tigers, devils. Boiling oil! Uh!"

"Self-defence, which is enjoined on us, and righteous retribution, my dear Martha. Do you think that our people like the bullets of their needle-guns? Our brave fellows have to be exposed, like defenceless cattle in a slaughter-house, to this murderous weapon. But we are too numerous, too disciplined, too warlike, not to conquer these 'tailors' for all that. At the beginning one or two failures have taken place; that I admit. Benedek ought to have crossed the Prussian frontier at once. I have my doubts whether this choice of a general was quite a happy one. If it had been determined to send the Archduke Albert there and give Benedek the Army of the South— but I will not despond too soon. Up to the present there have really been only some preliminary engagements which have been magnified by the Prussians into great victories. The decisive battles are still to come. We are now concentrating on Königgrätz; there we shall await the enemy, a hundred thousand strong. There our northern Custozza will be fought."

Frederick was to fight there too. His last letter, arrived that morning, brought the news: "We are bound for Königgrätz".

Up to this time I had had tidings regularly. Though in his first letter he had prepared me for his being able only to write little, yet Frederick had made use of every opportunity to send me a word or two. In pencil, on horseback, in his tent, in a hasty scrawl only legible by me, he would write on pages torn out of his note-book letters destined for me. Some he found opportunities for sending, and some did not come into my hands till the campaign was over.

I have kept these memorials up to the present hour. They are not careful, polished descriptions of the war, such as the war correspondents of the papers offer in their despatches, or the historians of the war in their publications; no sketches of

battles worked up with all the technicalities of strategical
details; no battle-pictures heightened with rhetorical flights,
in which the narrator is always occupied in letting his own
imperturbability, heroism, and patriotic enthusiasm shine out.
Frederick's sketches are nothing of this sort, I know. But what
they are, I need not decide. Here are some of them :—

" In bivouac. Outside the tent, it is indeed a mild, splendid
summer night; the heavens, so great and so indifferent, full of
shining stars. The men are lying on the earth, exhausted by
their long, fatiguing marches. Only for us, staff officers, have
one or two tents been pitched. In mine there are three field-
beds. My two comrades are asleep. I am sitting at the table,
on which are the empty grog glasses and a lighted candle. It
is by the feeble, flickering light of this (a draught of wind comes
in through the open flap) that I am writing to you, my beloved
wife. I have left my bed to Puxl, he was so tired, the poor
fellow ! I am almost sorry I brought him with me; he too is,
as our men say the Prussian Landwehr are, ' not used to the
hardships and privations of a campaign '. Now he is snoring
sweetly and happily—is dreaming, I fancy, very likely, of his
friend and patron, Rudolf, Count Dotzky. And I am dreaming of you, Martha; I am silly, I know, but I see your dear
form as like you as the image of a dream sitting in yonder
corner of the tent on a camp-stool. What longing seizes me
to go thither and lay my head on your bosom. But I do not
do so, because I know that then the image would disappear.

" I have just been out for an instant. The stars are shining
as indifferently as ever. On the ground a few shadows are
gliding—those of stragglers. Many, many men are left behind
on the road; these have now slipped in here drawn on by the
light of our watch-fires. But not all; some are still lying in
some far-off ditch or cornfield. What a heat it was during this
forced march ! The sun flamed as if it would boil your brains,
add to that the heavy knapsack and the heavy musket on their
galled shoulders ; and yet no one murmured. But a few fell
out and could not get up again. Two or three succumbed to

sunstroke and fell dead at once. Their bodies were put on an ambulance waggon.

"This June night, however illuminated by moon and stars, and however warm it may be, is still disenchanted. There are no nightingales or chirping crickets to be heard, no scents of rose and jasmine to be breathed. All the sweet sounds are drowned by the noise of snorting or neighing horses, by the men's voices and the tramp of the sentries' tread; all sweet scents overpowered by the smell of the harness and other barrack odours. Still all that is nothing; for now you do not hear the ravens croaking over their feast, you do not smell gunpowder, blood, and corruption. All that is coming—*ad majorem patriæ gloriam*. It is worth noting how blind men are. In looking at the funeral piles which have been lighted 'for the greater glory of God' in old times, they break out into curses over such blind, cruel, senseless fanaticism, but are full of admiration for the corpse-strewn battlefields of the present day. The torture chambers of the dark middle ages excite their horror, but they feel pride over their own arsenals. The light is burning down—the form in that corner has disappeared. I will also lie down to rest, beside our good Puxl."

.	.	.	.	.	.	.	.	.	.

"Up on a hill, amidst a group of generals and high officers, with a field-glass at his eye—that is the situation in a war which produces the greatest æsthetic effect. The gentlemen who paint battle pieces and make illustrations for the journals know this too. Generals on a hill reconnoitring with their glasses are represented again and again; and just as often a leader pressing forward at the head of his troops on a horse, as white and light-stepping as possible, stretching his arm out towards a point in the background all in smoke, and turning the head towards those rushing on after him, plainly shouting ' Follow me, lads!'

" From my station on this hill one sees really a piece of battle poetry. The picture is magnificent, and sufficiently distant to have the effect of a real picture, without the details, the horrors, and disgusts of the reality; no gushing blood, no death-rattles, nothing but elevated and magnificent effects of line and colour. Those far-extended ranks of the army corps winding on, that unbounded procession of infantry regiments, divisions of cavalry, and batteries of artillery, then the ammunition train, the requisitioned country waggons, the pack horses, and, bringing up the rear, the baggage. The picture comes out still more imposing if, in the wide country stretched out beneath the hill, you can see, not merely the movements of *one*, but the meeting of two armies. Then how the flashing sword-blades, the waving flags, the horses rearing up like foaming waves, mingle with each other, while amongst them clouds of smoke arise, forming themselves in places into thick veils which hide all the picture, and when they lift show groups of fighters. Then, as accompaniment, the noise of shots rolling through the mountains, every stroke of which thunders the word Death! Death! Death! through the air. Yes, that sort of thing may well inspire battle lays. And for the composition, too, of those contributions to the history of the period which are to be published after the conclusion of the campaign, the station on the hill-top offers favourable opportunities. There, at any rate, the narrative can be made out with some exactness. The X Division met the enemy at N, drove him back, reached the main bulk of the army; strong forces of the enemy showed themselves on the left flank—and so on, and so on. But one who is not on the hill, peering through his field-glass, one who is himself taking part in the action, he can never, *never* relate the progress of a battle in a way worthy of belief. He sees, feels, and thinks of only what is close to him. All the rest of his narrative is from intuition, for which he avails himself of the old formulas. 'Look, Tilling,' one of the generals said to me, as I was standing near him on the hill. 'Is not that striking? A grand army, is it not? Why, what are you thinking about?' What was I thinking about, my Martha? About you. But to my superior officer I could not say so. So I answered, with all due deference, some untruth. 'All due deference'

and 'truth' have besides little to do with each other. The
latter is a very proud fellow, and turns with contempt from
all servility."

   .   .   .   .

  " The village is ours—no, it is the enemy's—now ours
again—and yet once more the enemy's ; but it is no longer a
village, but a smoking mass of the ruins of houses.

  " The inhabitants (was it not really *their* village ?) had left it
previously and were away—luckily for them, for the fighting in
an inhabited place is something really fearful ; for then the
bullets from friend and foe fall into the midst of the rooms and
kill women and children.   One family, however, had remained
behind in the place which yesterday we took, lost, re-took, and
lost again—namely, an old married couple and their daughter,
the latter in childbed.   The husband is serving in our regiment.
He told me the story as we were nearing the village. ' There,
colonel, in that house with the red roof, is living my wife with
her old parents.   They have not been able to get away, poor
creatures ; my wife may be confined any moment, and the old
folks are half-crippled ; for God's sake, colonel, order me there !'
Poor devil ! he got there just in time to see the mother and
child die ; a shell had exploded under their bed.   What has
happened to the old folks I do not know.   They are probably
buried under the ruins ; the house was one of the first set on
fire by the cannonade.   Fighting in the open country is terrible
enough, but fighting amongst human dwellings is ten times
more cruel.   Crashing timber, bursting flames, stifling smoke ;
cattle run mad with fear ; every wall a fortress or a barricade,
every window a shot-hole.   I saw a breastwork there which was
formed of corpses.   The defenders had heaped up all the slain
that were lying near, in order, from that rampart, to fire over on
to their assailants.   I shall surely never forget that wall in all
my life.   A man, who formed one of its bricks, penned in
among the other corpse-bricks, was still alive, and was moving
his arm.

  " ' Still alive '—that is a condition, occurring in war with a

thousand differences, which conceals sufferings incalculable.
If there were any angel of mercy hovering over the battlefields
he would have enough to do in giving the poor creatures—men
and beasts—who are 'still alive' their *coup de grâce*."

. . . .

"'To-day we had a little cavalry skirmish in the open field.
A Prussian cavalry regiment came forward at a trot, deployed
into line, and then, with their horses well in hand and their
sabres above their heads, rode down on us at a hand gallop.
We did not wait for their attack, but galloped out against the
enemy. No shots were exchanged. When a few paces from
each other both ranks burst out into a thundering 'hurrah'
(shouting intoxicates; the Indians and Zulus know that even
better than we do); and so we rushed on each other, horse to
horse, knee to knee; the sabres whistled in the air and came
down on the men's heads. Soon all were huddled together too
close to use their weapons; then they struggled breast to breast,
and the horses, getting wild and frightened, snorted and plunged,
reared up, and struck about them. I too was on the ground
once, and saw—no very pleasant sight—a horse's hoof striking
out within a hair's breadth of my temples."

. . . .

"Another day of marching, with one or two skirmishes. I
have experienced a great sorrow. Such a mournful picture
accompanies me. Among the many pictures of woe which
are all around me this ought not so to strike me, ought not to
give me such pain. But I cannot help it; it touches me
nearly, and I cannot shake it off. Puxl—our poor, happy,
good, little dog—oh, if I had only left him at home with his
little master, Rudolf! He was running after us, as usual.
Suddenly he gave a shriek of pain; the splinter of a shell had
torn off his fore-leg. He could not come after us, so is left
behind, and is 'still alive'. Between twenty-four and forty-
eight hours have passed, and he is 'still alive'. 'Oh master!
my good master!' his cries seemed to say. 'Do not leave
poor Puxl here! His heart will break!' And what especially

pains me is the thought that the faithful dying creature must misunderstand me. For he saw that I turned round, that I must have understood his cry for help and yet was so cold and so cruel as to leave him there. Poor Puxl could not understand that a regiment advancing to the attack, out of whose ranks comrades are falling and are left on the ground, cannot be ordered to halt for the sake of a dog who has been hit. He has no conception of the higher duty which I had to obey: and so the poor true heart of the dog is complaining of my unmercifulness. Only think of troubling oneself about such trumpery in the midst of the 'great events' and gigantic misfortunes which fill the present time. That is what many would say, with a shrug of the shoulders; but not you, Martha, not you. I know that a tear will come into your eyes for our poor Puxl."

. . . .

"What is happening there? The execution party is drawn out. Has a spy been caught? One? Seventeen this time. There they come, in four ranks, each one of four men, surrounded by a square of soldiers. The condemned men step out, with their heads down. Behind comes a cart with a corpse in it; and bound to the corpse the dead man's son—a boy of twelve, also condemned.

"I could not look on at the execution, and withdrew; but I heard the firing. A cloud of smoke rose from behind the walls. All were dead, the boy included."

. . . .

"At last a comfortable night's lodging in a little town! The poor little nest! Provisions, which were to have served the people for months, we have taken on requisition. 'Requisition!' Well, it is one good thing to have a pretty recognised name for a thing. However, I was at least glad to have got a good night's lodging and a good night's food; and—let me tell you a story:—

"I was just going to lie down in bed, when my orderly announced that a man of my regiment was there, and earnestly

begged for admission, as he had something for me. 'Well,
let him come in ;' and the man entered. And before he went
out I had rewarded him handsomely, shaken him by both hands,
and promised to look after his wife and children. For what he
brought me, the fine fellow, had given me the greatest pleasure,
and had freed me from a pain under which I had been suffering for the last thirty-six hours. It was my Puxl. Injured, it
is true—honourably wounded—but still alive, and so happy to
be with his master, by whose behaviour he must certainly have
seen that he had been wrong in charging him with want of
fondness for him. Ah, that was indeed a scene of re-union.
First of all, a drink of water ! How good it was ! He interrupted his greedy drinking ten times to bark out his joy to me.
Then I bound up the stump of his leg for him, set before him
a tasty supper of meat and cheese, and put him to sleep on
my bed. We both slept well. In the morning when I woke
he licked my hand again and again in token of thanks. Then
he stretched out his poor little leg, breathed deep, and—was
no more. Poor Puxl ! It is better so."

. . . .

" What is all I have seen to-day ? If I shut my eyes, what
has passed before them comes with terrible distinctness into my
memory. 'Nothing but pain and pictures of horror,' you will
say. Why then do other men bring such fresh, such joyful
images away with them from war ? Ah, yes ! These others
close their eyes to the pain and the horror. They *say nothing
about them.* If they write, or if they narrate, they give themselves no trouble to paint their experiences after nature ; but
they occupy themselves in imitating descriptions which they
have read, and which they take as models, and in bringing out
those impressions which are considered heroic. If they occasionally tell also of scenes of destruction, which contain in
themselves the bitterest pain and the bitterest terror, nothing
of either is to be discovered in their tone. On the contrary,
the more terrible the more indifferent are they, the more
horrible the more easy. Disapprobation, anger, excitement ?

Nothing of all this. Well, perhaps instead of this, a slight
breath of sentimental pity, a few sighs of compassion. But
their heads are soon in the air again. 'The heart to God, and
the hand against the foe.' Hurrah, Tra-ra-ra !

" Now look at two of the pictures which impressed themselves
on me.

"Steep, rocky heights. Jägers nimble as cats climbing up
them. The object was to 'take' the heights, from the top of
which the enemy was firing. What I see are the forms
of the assailants who are climbing up, and some of them
who are hit by the enemy's shot, suddenly stretch both
arms out, let their muskets fall, and with their heads falling
backwards, drop off the height, step by step, from one rocky
point to another, smashing their limbs to pieces.

" I see a horseman at some distance obliquely behind me,
at whose side a shell burst. His horse swerved aside, and came
against the tail of mine, then shot past me. The man sat still
in the saddle, but a fragment of the shell had ripped his belly
open, and torn all the intestines out. The upper part of his
body was held on to the lower only by the spine. From the
ribs to the thighs nothing but one great bleeding cavity. A
short distance further he fell to the ground, with one foot still
clinging in the stirrup, and the galloping horse dragging him on
over the stony soil."

. . . .

" An artillery division is sticking fast in a part of the road
which is steep and soaked with rain. The guns are sinking
deeper than their wheels in the morass. It is only with the
most extreme exertion, dripping with sweat, and animated by
the most unmerciful flogging, that the horses can get forward.
One, however, dead beat before, now can do no more.
Thumping him does no good; he is quite willing, but he
cannot. He literally *can* not. Cannot that man see this, whose
blows are raining down on the poor beast's head ? If the cruel
brute had been the driver of a waggon in the service of some
builder, any peace officer, even I myself, would have had him

arrested. But this gunner, who has to get his death-laden carriage forward anyhow, is only doing his duty. The horse, however, cannot know this. The tortured, well-meaning, noble creature, who has exerted himself to the utmost limit of his vital power, what must he think in his inmost heart of such hard-heartedness and such want of sense? Think, as animals do think, not in words and conceptions, but in feelings, and feelings which are all the more lively for wanting expression. There is but *one* expression for it, the shriek of pain ; and he did shriek, that poor horse, till at last he sank down, a shriek so long drawn and so resounding, that it still rings in my ear, that it haunted me in my dream the next night—a horrible dream in other respects. I thought that I was—how can I ever tell you the story? dreams are so senseless that language conformable to sense is hardly adapted to their reproduction— that I was the sense of pain in such an artillery horse—no, not one, but in 100,000, for in my dream I had quickly summed up the number of the horses slaughtered in one campaign, and thus this pain multiplied its effect at once a hundred-thousandfold. The men *know* at least why their lives are exposed to danger. They know whither they are going, and what for ; but we poor unfortunates know nothing—all around us is night and horror. The men seem to go with pleasure to meet their foes, but we are surrounded by foes—our own masters, whom we would love so truly, to serve whom we spend our last energies, they rain blows on us, they leave us lying helpless ; and all that we have to suffer besides, the fear that makes the sweat of agony run from our whole body, the thirst—for we too suffer from fever—oh, that thirst ! the thirst of us poor bleeding, maltreated 100,000 horses ! . . . Here I woke, and clutched the water bottle. I was myself suffering from burning, feverish thirst."

.   .   .   .

" Another street fight in the little town of Saar. To the noise of the battle-cries and the shots is joined the crashing of timber and the falling of walls. A shell burst in one of the

16

houses, and the pressure of the air, caused by its explosion, was so powerful that several soldiers were wounded by the ruins of the house which were borne along by the air. A window flew over my head with the window-sash still in it. The chimney-stack tumbled down, the plaster crumbled into dust and filled the air with a stifling cloud that stung one's eyes. From one lane to another (how the hoofs rang on the jagged pavements) the fight wound on, and reached the market-place. In the middle of the square stands a high pillar of the Virgin. The Mother of God holds her child in one arm and stretches the other out in blessing. Here the fight was prolonged—man to man. They were hacking at me, I was laying about me on all sides. Whether I hit one or more of them I know not: in such moments one does not retain much perception. Still two cases are photographed on my soul, and I fear that the market-place at Saar will remain always burned into my memory. A Prussian dragoon, strong as Goliath, tore one of our officers (a pretty, dandified lieutenant—how many girls are perhaps mad after him) out of his saddle, and split his skull at the feet of the Virgin's pillar. The gentle saint looked on unmoved. Another of the enemy's dragoons—a Goliath too—seized, just before me almost, my right-hand man, and bent him backwards in his saddle so powerfully that he broke his back—I myself heard it crack. To this also the Madonna gave her stony blessing."

.   .   .   .

"From a height to-day the field-glass of the staff officer commanded once more a scene rich in changes. There was, for instance, the collapse of a bridge as a train of waggons was moving across it. Did the latter contain wounded? I do not know. I could not ascertain. I only saw that the whole train —waggons, horses, and men—sank into the deep and rushing stream and there disappeared. The event was a 'fortunate' one, since the train of waggons belonged to the 'blacks'. In the game now being played I designate 'us' as the white side. The bridge did not collapse by accident; the whites, knowing that their adversaries had to cross it, had sawn through the pillars—a dexterous stroke that.

"A second prospect, on the other hand, which one might view from the same height represented one of the follies of the "whites". Our Khevenhüller Regiment was directed into a morass, from which it could not extricate itself, and they were all, except a few, shot down. The wounded fell into the morass, and there had to sink and be smothered, their mouth, nose, and eyes filled with mud, so that they could not even utter a cry. Oh yes ! it must be admitted to have been an error of the man who commanded the troops to go there ; but ' to err is human,' and the loss is not a great one—might represent a pawn taken—a speedy, lucky move of castle or queen, and all is right again. The mud, it is true, remains in the mouth and eyes of the fallen, but that is a very secondary consideration. What is reprehensible is the tactical error ; that has to be wiped out by some later fortunate combination, and then the leader implicated in it may still be decorated with grand orders and promotions. That lately our 18th battalion of Jägers in a night battle was firing for several hours on our King of Prussia Regiment, and the error was not found out till break of day ; that a part of the Gyulai Regiment was led into a pond—these are little oversights, such as may happen even to the best players in the heat of a game."

. . . .

"It is decided—if I come back from this campaign, I quit the service. Setting everything else aside, if one has learned to regard anything with such horror as war produces in me, it would be a continual lie to keep in the service of that thing. Even before this, I went, as you know, to battle unwillingly, and with a judgment condemnatory of it ; but now this unwillingness has so increased, this condemnation has become so strengthened, that all the reasons which before determined me to persevere with my profession have ceased to operate. The sentiments derived from my youthful training, and perhaps also, to some extent, inherited, which still pleaded with me in favour of the military life, have now quite departed from me in the course of the horrors I have just experienced. I do not know whether it is the studies, which I undertook in common with you, and from which I discovered that my contempt for war is not an isolated feeling, but is shared by the best spirits of the age, or whether it is the conversations I have had with you, in which I have strengthened myself in my views by their free expression and your concurrence in them ; in one word, my former vague, half-smothered feeling has changed into a clear conviction, a conviction which makes it from this time impossible to do service to the war god. It is the same kind of change as comes to many people in matters of belief. First they are somewhat sceptical and indifferent, still they can assist at the business of the temple with a certain sense of reverence. But when once all mysticism is put aside, when they rise to the perception that the ceremony which they are attending rests on folly, and sometimes on cruel folly, as in the case of the religious death-sacrifices, then they will no longer kneel beside the other befooled folks, no longer deceive them-selves and the world by entering the now desecrated temple. This is the process which has gone on with me in relation to the cruel worship of Mars. The mysterious, supernatural, awe-inspiring feeling which the appearance of this deity generally awakes in men, and which in former times obscured my senses also, has now entirely passed away for me. The liturgy of the bulletins and the ritual of heroic phraseology no longer appear to me as a divine revelation ; the mighty organ-voice of the cannon, the incense-smoke of the powder have no charm more for me. I assist at the terrible worship perfectly devoid of belief or reverence, and can now see nothing in it except the tortures of the victims, hear nothing but their wailing death-cries. And thence comes it that these pages, which I am filling with my impressions of war, contain nothing except pain seen with pain."

CHAPTER XII.

Ruin of the Austrian cause at Königgrätz.—Dr. Bresser at the seat of war.—I resolve to join him and seek for my husband. —Aspect of the railway station and line in a time of defeat. —The journey.—The regimental surgeon's experiences of the horrors of war.—I arrive at the seat of war and meet Dr. Bresser and Frau Simon.—Night journey to Horonewos.— The horrors I saw there.—I sink exhausted under them, and am carried back by Dr. Bresser to Vienna.—My father takes me home, and there I am joined by my husband, who had been wounded.

THE battle of Königgrätz had been fought. Another defeat! And this time as it seemed a decisive one. My father communicated the news to us in such a tone as he would have used in announcing the end of the world.

And no letter, no telegram from Frederick. Was he wounded? dead? Conrad gave his *fiancée* news of himself—he was untouched. The lists of the slain had not yet arrived, it was only known that there were 40,000 killed and wounded at Königgrätz; and the latest news I had had ran: "We are moving to-day to Königgrätz".

On the third day still not a line. I wept and wept for hours: I could weep just because my grief was not quite hopeless; if I had known that all was over, there would have been no tears for my load of woe. My father too was deeply depressed. And my brother Otto was mad with thirst for revenge. It was announced that corps of volunteers were to be formed in Vienna. He wanted to join them. It was further announced that

(245)

Benedek was to be removed from his command and the victorious Archduke Albert summoned to the north to take his place, and then perhaps there might yet be a rally; the overweening enemy, who wanted altogether to annihilate us, might be beaten back, as he would be caught on his march on Vienna. Fear, rage, pain filled all minds; all pronounced the name of "the Prussians" as if they were all that is detestable.   My only thought was Frederick—and no news—none !

A few days afterwards arrived a letter from Dr. Bresser. He was busy in the neighbourhood of the battlefield in giving what assistance he could.   The need, he wrote, was without limit, mocking all power of imagination.   He had joined a Saxon physician, Dr. Brauer, who had been despatched by his government to give them information from actual inspection on the state of affairs.   In two days a Saxon lady was to arrive—Frau Simon, a new Miss Nightingale—who since the outbreak of the war had been busy in the hospitals of Dresden, and who had offered to undertake the journey to the fields of battle in Bohemia in order to render assistance in the hospitals adjacent. Dr. Brauer, and Dr. Bresser with him, were going, on a day named, at seven in the evening, to Königinhof, the nearest station to Königgrätz to which the railway was still open, to await the courageous lady there.   Bresser begged us to send if possible a quantity of bandages and such things to that station, so that he might receive them there himself.

I had hardly read this letter before my resolution was taken. I would take the box of bandages myself.   In one of those hospitals which Frau Simon was to visit possibly lay Frederick. I would join her and find the dear sufferer—nurse him—save him.   The idea seized me with compelling force—so compelling that I held it to be a magnetic influence from afar, derived from the longing wish with which the dear one was calling for me.

Without telling any one in my family of my purpose—for I should only have encountered resistance on all hands—I embarked on the journey a few hours after the receipt of Bresser's letter. I had given out that I wanted to look out the things which the doctor required, in Vienna, and send them off myself, and so I managed to get away from Grumitz without difficulty. From Vienna I meant to write to my father " I am off to the seat of war ". It is true that doubts arose in me—my incapacity and want of experience, my horror of wounds, blood, and death —but I chased these doubts away. What I was doing I was compelled to do. The gaze of my husband was fixed on me, in prayer and supplication. From his bed of pain he was stretching his arms out after me, and " I am coming, I am coming," was all I was able to think of.

I found the city of Vienna in unspeakable excitement and confusion. Disturbed faces all round me. My carriage came across a number of carriages full of wounded men. I was always looking to see whether Frederick might be among them. But no ! His longing cry, which vibrated in my vitals, rang from far away, from Bohemia. If he had been sent off home the news would have come to us simultaneously.

I drove to an hotel. From thence I went to look after my purchases, sent the letter which I had prepared for Grumitz, got myself equipped in a travelling costume most adapted for rough work, and drove to the Northern Station. I wanted to take the first train that was starting, so as to reach my destination in good time. I had a single fixed idea under whose domination I carried out all my movements.

At the station all was in a bustle of life, or should I say a bustle of death ? The halls, the waiting-room, the platform, all full of wounded, some of them at their last gasp. And a corresponding crowd of people, sick nurses, soldiers of the sanitary depart- ment, sisters of mercy, physicians, men and women of all ranks and occupations, who had come there to see whether the last train had brought one of their relations ; or again, to distribute presents, wine and cigars, among the wounded. The officials and servants, busy everywhere in pushing back the folks who were pushing forward. They wanted to send me off too.

" What do you want there ? Make way ! you are forbidden

to give out things to eat and drink. Go to the committee; your presents will be taken in there."

"No, no," I said; " I want to set off. When does the next train start ?"

It was long before I could get information in reply to this. Most of the departure trains, I found at last, were suspended, in order to keep the line open for the arrival trains which were coming in, one after another, laden with the wounded. For the day there were absolutely no more passenger trains. There was only one with the reserve troops that were being sent forward, and another exclusively reserved for the service of the Patriotic Aid Society, which had to take away a number of physicians and sisters of mercy, and a cargo of necessary material to the neighbourhood of Königgrätz.   .

"And could not I go by that train ?"

"Impossible."

I heard, ever plainer and more beseeching, Frederick's cry for help, and could not get to him. It was enough to drive one to despair. Then I espied at the entrance of the hall Baron S——, vice-president of the Patriotic Aid Society, whose acquaintance I had first made in the year of the war of '59. I hastened to him.

"For God's sake, Baron S——, help me. Surely you recognise me ?"

" Baroness Tilling, the daughter of General Count Althaus. Of course, I have that honour. What can I do to serve you ?"

"You are sending off a train to Bohemia. Let me travel by it ! My dying husband is pining for me. If you have a heart—and your action surely proves how fair and noble your heart is—do not reject my prayer !"

There were still all kinds of doubts and difficulties, but in the end my wish was granted. Baron S—— called one of the physicians despatched by the Aid Society, and recommended me to his protection as a fellow-traveller.

There was still an hour before our departure. I wanted to

go into the waiting-room, but every available space had been
turned into an hospital. Wherever you looked, you saw cowering, prostrate, bandaged, pale forms. I could not look at
them. The little energy which I possessed I had to save up
for my journey, and for its object. I could not venture to
expend here anything of the stock of strength, of compassion,
or of power of assistance which was at my command—all
belonged to him—to him who was calling for me.

Meantime, there was no corner to be found in which a
painful scene could be spared me. I had taken refuge on the
platform, and there I was brought face to face with the most
grievous of all sights, the arrival of a long train, all whose
carriages were full of wounded, and the disembarkation of the
latter. The less seriously wounded got out by themselves, and
managed to get themselves forward; but most had to be
supported, or even carried altogether. The available stretchers
were at once occupied, and the remaining patients had to
wait till the bearers returned, lying on the floor. Before my
feet, at the spot where I was sitting on a box, they laid a man
who made, without cessation, a continuous gurgling sound. I
bent down to speak a word of sympathy to him, but I started
back in horror, and covered my face with both hands. The
impression on me had been too fearful. It was no longer a
human countenance—the lower jaw shot away, one eye welling
out, and, added to that, a stifling reek of blood and corruption.
I should have liked to jump up and run away, but I was deadly
sick, and my head fell back against the wall behind me. "Oh
what a cowardly, feeble creature I am," I said, reproaching
myself; "what have I to do in these abodes of misery, where I
can do nothing, nothing, to help, and am exposed to such
disgust?" Only the thought of Frederick rallied me again.
Yes, for him, even if he were in the condition of the poor
wretch at my feet, I could bear anything. I would still embrace
and kiss him, and all disgust, all horror would be drowned in
that all-conquering feeling—love. "Frederick, my Frederick,
I am coming." I repeated half-aloud this fixed thought of mine

which had seized me at the time I read Bresser's letter, and had never quitted me.

A fearful notion passed through my brain—what if this man should be Frederick ?   I collected all my forces, and looked at him again.   No, it was not he.

.   .   .   .

The anxious hour of waiting did, however, come to an end. They had carried off the poor gurgling fellow.   "Lay him on the bench there," I heard the regimental doctor order ; " he is not to be brought back into hospital.   He is already three parts dead."   And yet he must surely have still understood the words, this three-parts-dead man ; for with a despairing gesture he raised both his hands to heaven.

Now I was sitting in a carriage with the two physicians and four sisters of mercy.   It was stiflingly hot, and the carriage was filled with the smell of the hospital and sacristy—carbolic acid and incense.   I was unspeakably ill.   I leaned back in my corner, and shut my eyes.

The train began to move.   That is just the time when every traveller brings before his mind's eye the object towards which he is being taken.   I had often before travelled over the same ground ; and then there lay before me a visit to a château full of guests, or a pleasant bathing-place—my wedding-tour, a blessed memory, was made on this same route, to meet with a brilliant and loving reception in the metropolis of " Prussia ". What a different sound that last word has assumed since then ! And to-day ?   What is our object to-day ?   A battlefield and the hospitals round it—the abodes of death and suffering.   I shuddered ——

" My dear lady," said one of the physicians, "I think you are ill yourself.   You look so pale and so suffering."

I looked up ; the speaker had a friendly, youthful appearance. I guessed that this was his first service on being recently promoted to the rank of surgeon.   It was good of him to devote his first service to this dangerous and laborious duty !   I felt grateful to these men who were sitting in the carriage with me for the relief which they were in the act of bringing to the sufferers. And to the self-sacrificing sisters—really of mercy— I paid heartfelt admiration and thanks. Yet what was it that each of these good men had to bestow? An ounce of help for 1000 hundredweights of need. These courageous nuns must, I thought, bear in their hearts for *all* men that overmastering love which filled mine for my own husband; as I had felt just now that if the fearfully disfigured and repulsive soldier who was gurgling at my feet had been my husband, all my repulsion would have vanished, so these women must have felt towards every brother-man, and surely through the power of a higher love—that for their chosen bridegroom, Christ. But alas! here also these noble women brought an ounce only—one ounce of love to a place where 1000 hundredweights of hatred were raging!

"No, doctor," I replied to the sympathetic question of the young physician. "I am not ill, only a little exhausted."

The staff-surgeon now joined in the conversation.

"Your husband, madam, as Baron S—— told me, was wounded at Königgrätz, and you are travelling thither to nurse him. Do you know in which of the villages around he is lying?"

No, I did not know.

"My destination is Königinhof," I replied. "There a physician awaits me who is a friend of mine—Dr. Bresser."

"I know him. He was with me when we made a three days' examination of the field of battle."

"Examined the field of battle!" I repeated with a shudder. "Let us hear."

"Yes, yes, doctor, let us hear," begged one of the nuns. "Our service may bring us into the position of helping at an examination of the kind."

So the regimental surgeon began his narration. Of course I cannot give the exact words of his description; and, again, he did not speak in a single flow of words, but with frequent interruptions, and almost with reluctance, being only compelled to speak by the persistent questions with which the curious nuns and I assailed him. The narration, however, though sketchy, formed a series of perfect pictures before my mind's eye, which impressed themselves so on my memory that I can even now make them pass before me. In other circumstances I should not have so clearly comprehended and retained the doctor's sketches—one always forgets so easily what one has heard or read—but at that time the narratives made almost the impression of an experience. I was in a state of high nervous tension and excitement. My fixed thought of Frederick, which had gained the mastery over me, made me represent Frederick to myself as a person concerned in each scene described; and on that account they remained fixed in my mind as painful things I had myself experienced. Later on I noted down the events related by the regimental surgeon in the red book, just as if they had taken place before my own eyes.

. . . .

The ambulance was placed behind a hillock which protected it. The battle was raging on the other side. The ground quavered, and the heated air quavered. Clouds of smoke were rising, the artillery was roaring. Now the duty was to send out patrols to repair to the scene of battle, pick out the badly wounded, and bring them in. Is there anything more heroic than such going into the midst of the hissing rain of bullets, in the face of all the horrors of the fight, exposed to all the perils of the fight, without allowing oneself to be penetrated by its wild excitement? According to military conceptions this office is not distinguished. On "the Sanitary Corps" no smart, active, handy, young fellow will serve. No man in it turns the girls' heads. And a field doctor, even if one is no longer called by that name, but "regimental surgeon," can he nevertheless hold a comparison with any cavalry lieutenant?

The corporal of the Sanitary Corps ordered his people towards some low ground against which a battery had opened its fire. They marched through the dark veil of the powder smoke and the dust and the scattered earth to a point where a cannon ball, which struck the ground at their feet, bounded in front of them. They had only gone a few paces when they began to meet with wounded men, men slightly wounded, who were crawling to the ambulance, either alone or in pairs, giving each other mutual support. One sank down; but it was not his wounds which had sapped his strength, it was exhaustion. "We have eaten nothing for two days, made a forced march of twelve hours, got into the bivouac, and then, two hours afterwards, came the alarm and the fight."

The patrol went forward. These men would find their way for themselves, and manage to take their exhausted comrade with them. Aid must be reserved for others still more in need of aid.

On a heap of rocks, forming part of a precipitous declivity, lies a bleeding mass. There are a dozen soldiers lying there. The sanitary corporal stops and bandages one or two of them. But these wounded men are not carried off; those must first be fetched in who have fallen in the centre of the field. Then, perhaps, on their return march, these men can be picked up here.

And again the patrol goes on, nearer to the battle. In ever thicker swarms wounded men are tottering on, painfully creeping forward, singly or together. These are such as can still walk. The contents of the field flasks is distributed amongst these, a bandage is applied to such wounds as are bleeding, and the way to the ambulance pointed out to them. Then forward again. Over the dead—over hillocks of corpses. Many of these dead show traces of horrible agonies. Eyes staring unnaturally, hands grasping the ground, the hair of the beard staring out, teeth pressed together, lips closed spasmodically, legs stiffly outstretched. So they lie.

Now through a hollow way. Here they are lying in heaps, dead and wounded together. The latter greet the sanitary patrol as angels of rescue, and beg and shriek for help. With broken voices, weeping and lamenting, they shout for rescue, for a gulp of water. But alas! the provisions are almost exhausted, and what can these few men do? Each ought to

have a hundred arms to be able to rescue them all. Yet each
does what he can. Then sounds the prolonged tone of the
sanitary call. The men stop and break off from their work of
aid. "Do not desert us! Do not desert us!" the poor injured
men cry; but the signal horn calls again and again, and this,
plainly distinguishable from all other noises, is evidently going
further afield. Then also an adjutant comes in hot haste.
"Men of the Sanitary Corps?" "At your command," replies
the corporal. "Follow me."

Evidently a general wounded. It is necessary to obey and
leave the rest. "Patience, comrades, and keep a good heart;
we will return." Those who hear and those who say it know
that it is not true.

And again they go further: following the adjutant, at the
double quick, who spurs on in front and points the way.
There is no halting on the way, although on the right hand and
on the left resound shrieks of woe and cries for help; and
although also many bullets fall among those who are thus
hurrying on, and stretch one and another on the ground—only
onwards and over everything. Over men writhing with the pain
of their wounds, men trodden down by horses tearing over
them, or crushed by guns passing over their limbs, and who,
seeing the rescue corps, mutilated as they are, rear themselves
up for the last time. Over them, over them!

.   .   .   .

This sort of thing goes on for pages of the red book. The
relation that the regimental surgeon gave of the march of a
sanitary patrol over the battlefield contains many similar, and
even more painful things, such as the description of moments
when bullets and shells fall in the midst of the dressers and
tear up new wounds; or when the course of the battle brings
the fight on to the dressing station itself, right up on to the
ambulance, and sucks in the whole *personnel* of the sanitary
corps, with the physicians and with the patients into the
whirl of the fighting or fleeing or pursuing troops; or when
frightened riderless horses all abroad come across the way, and

overturn the stretcher on which a severely wounded man is lying, who is now dashed to the earth all shattered. Or this, the most gruesome picture of all—a farmyard, into which a hundred wounded men had been carried, bandaged, and made comfortable—the poor wretches, glad and thankful that their rescue had been effected. Then a shell came and set the whole on fire. A minute afterwards the hospital was in flames. The shrieks, or rather the howls, which resounded from this abode of despair, and which in its wild agony drowned all the other noises, will remain for ever in the memory of any one who heard it. Ah me! it remains for ever in my memory too, though I did not hear it; for, as the regimental surgeon was telling it, I fancied again that Frederick was there—that I heard his shriek out of the burning place of torture.

"You are getting ill, dear madam," said the narrator, breaking off. "I must have tried your nerves too much."

But I had not yet heard enough. I assured him that my momentary weakness was the consequence merely of the heat and of a bad night, and I was not too tired to ask for the rest. I kept feeling still that I had not yet heard enough; that of the infernal circles that were being described, the description had not yet been given of the lowest and most hellish; and when once the thirst for the horrible has been awakened it is impossible to stop till it has been slaked by the most horrible of all. And I was right, for there is something more hideous than a battlefield during the fight, *viz.*, one afterwards.

No more thunder of artillery, no more blare of trumpets, no more beat of drum; only the low moans of pain and the rattle of death. In the trampled ground some redly-glimmering pools, lakes of blood; all the crops destroyed, only here and there a piece of land left untouched, and still covered with stubble; the smiling villages of yesterday turned into ruins and rubbish. The trees burned and hacked in the forests, the hedges torn with grape-shot. And on this battle-ground thousands and thousands of men dead and dying—dying without aid. No blossoms of flowers are to be seen on wayside or meadow;

but sabres, bayonets, knapsacks, cloaks, overturned ammunition waggons, powder waggons blown into the air, cannon with broken carriages. Near the cannon, whose muzzles are black with smoke, the ground is bloodiest. There the greatest number and the most mangled of dead and half-dead men are lying, literally torn to pieces with shot; and the dead horses, and the half-dead which raise themselves on their feet—such as they have left them—to sink again; then raise themselves up once more and fall down again, till they only raise their head to shriek out their pain-laden death-cry. There is a hollow way quite filled with corpses trodden into the mire. The poor creatures had taken refuge there no doubt to get cover, but a battery has driven over them, and they have been crushed by the horses' hoofs and the wheels. Many of them are still alive—a pulpy, bleeding mass, but "still alive".

And yet there is still something more hellish even than all this, and that is the appearance of the most vile scum of humanity, as it shows itself in war—*i.e.*, the appearance and the activity of "the hyenas of the battlefield". "Then slink on the monsters who grope after the spoils of the dead, and bend over the corpses and over the living, mercilessly tearing off their clothes from their bodies. The boots are dragged off the bleeding limbs, the rings off the wounded hands, or to get the ring the finger is simply chopped off, and if a man tries to defend himself from such a sacrifice, he is murdered by these hyenas; or, in order to make him unrecognisable, they dig his eyes out."

I shrieked out loud at the doctor's last words. I again saw the whole scene before me, and the eyes into which the hyena was plunging his knife were Frederick's soft, blue, beloved eyes.

"Pray, forgive me, dear lady, but it was by your own wish ——"

"Oh yes; I desire to hear it all. What you are now describing was the night which follows the battle; and these scenes are enacted by the starlight?"

" And by torchlight. The patrols which the conquerors send out to survey the field of battle carry torches and lanterns, and red lanterns are hoisted on signal poles to point out the places where flying hospitals are to be established."

" And next morning, how does the field look ? "

"Almost more fearful still. The contrast between the bright, smiling daylight and the dreadful work of man on which it shines has a doubly-painful effect. At night the entire picture of horror is something ghostly and fantastic. By daylight it is simply hopeless. Now you see for the first time the mass of corpses lying around on the lanes, between the fields, in the ditches, behind the ruins of walls. Everywhere dead bodies—everywhere. Plundered, some of them naked ; and just the same with the wounded. These who, in spite of the nightly labour of the Sanitary Corps, are still always lying around in numbers, look pale and collapsed, green or yellow, with fixed and stupefied gaze, or writhing in agonies of pain, they beg any one who comes near to put them to death. Swarms of carrion crows settle on the tops of the trees, and with loud croaks announce the bill of fare of the tempting banquet. Hungry dogs, from the villages around, come running by and lick the blood from their wounds. There are a few hyenas to be seen who are still carrying on their work hastily further afield. And now comes the great interment."

" Who does that—the Sanitary Corps ? "

" How could they suffice for such a mass of work ? They have fully enough to do with the wounded."

" Then troops detailed for the work ? "

"No. A crowd of men impressed, or even offering themselves voluntarily—loiterers, baggage people, who are supporting themselves by the market stalls, baggage waggons and so forth, and who now have been hunted away by the force of the military operations, together with the inhabitants of the cottages and huts—to dig trenches—good large ones, of course—wide trenches, for they are not made deep—there is no time for that. Into these the dead bodies are thrown, heads up or heads

17

down just as they come to hand. Or it is done in this way:
A heap is made of the corpses, and a foot or two of earth is
heaped up over them, and then it has the appearance of a
tumulus. In a few days rain comes on and washes the
covering off the festering dead bodies ! but what does that
matter? The nimble, jolly gravediggers do not look so far
forward. For jolly, merry workmen they are, that one must
allow. Songs are piped out there, and all kinds of dubious
jokes made—nay, sometimes a dance of hyenas is danced
round the open trench. Whether in several of the bodies that
are shovelled into it or are covered with the earth life is still
stirring, they give themselves no trouble to think. The thing
is inevitable, for the stiff cramp often comes on after wounds.
Many who have been saved by accident have told of the danger
of being buried alive which they have escaped. But how many
are there of those who are not able to tell anything ! If a man
has once got a foot or two of earth over his mouth he may
well hold his tongue."

"Oh my Frederick, my Frederick !" I groaned in my
heart.

"That is the picture of the next morning," said the surgeon,
in conclusion. "Shall I go on further and tell you what
happens next evening ? "

" I will tell you that, doctor," I broke in. " One of the two
capitals of the powers engaged has received the telegraphic
news of the glorious victory. And there in the morning, while
the hyena dance is going on round the trench, they are singing
in the churches: ' Now thank we all the Lord,' and in the
evening there the mother or the wife of one of the men buried
alive is putting a lighted candle or two in the window-sill
because the city is illuminated."

" Yes, madam, that is the comedy which is being played at
home. Meanwhile, on the field of battle, the tragedy is still
far from played out by the second sunset. Besides those who
are carried to the hospital or the trench, there still remain the
' missing '. Hidden behind some thick brushwood, in the

fields of standing corn, or amongst the ruins of buildings, they have escaped the sight of the bearers or the buriers, and for them begins now the martyrdom of an agony which lasts many days and nights—in the burning heat of midday—in the dark shadows of midnight, crouched on stones and thistles, in the stench of the corpses around and of their own putrefying wounds—a prey, while still quivering, for the feasting vultures."

. . . .

What a journey that was! The regimental surgeon had long ceased to speak, but the scenes he had described went on continually presenting themselves before my mind's eye. To escape from this train of thoughts which persecuted me, I began to look out of the carriage window and try to find distraction in the prospect of the country. But here also pictures of the horrors of war presented themselves to my vision. It is true that no violent devastation had taken place in this neighbourhood, there were no ruined villages smoking there, "the enemy" had effected no lodgment there, but what was raging there was perhaps still worse, *viz.*, the *fear* of the enemy. "The Prussians are coming! the Prussians are coming!" was the signal of alarm through the whole region, and though in travelling past one did not hear the words, yet even from the carriage window their effect was plainly to be seen. Everywhere on all the roads and lanes were people flying, leaving their homes with bag and baggage. Whole trains of waggons were moving inland, filled with bedding, household furniture and provisions, all evidently packed up in the greatest haste. On the same car would be some little pigs, the youngest child, and one or two sacks of potatoes, beside it on foot man and wife and the elder children; that is how I saw a family making their escape as they moved down a road near me. Where were the poor creatures going? They themselves very likely did not know, it was only away, away from "the Prussians". So men flee from the roaring fire, or the rising flood.

Frequently a train passed us on the other line—wounded,

always and again wounded—always once more the ashy faces, the bandaged heads, the arms in slings. At the stations especially one might feed on this sight in all its variations to satiety. All the large or small platforms, on which one usually sees the travelling population waiting or cheerfully standing or walking about, were now filled with prostrate or cowering figures. They were the invalid soldiers who had been brought from the field- or private-hospitals in the neighbourhood, and were waiting for the next train which might serve for the transport of the wounded. There they might have to lie for hours; and who knows how many removals they have already passed through! From the battlefield to the first-aid station, from thence to the ambulance, from thence to a movable hospital, then to the village, and now to the railway, whence they have still the journey to Vienna before them; then from the station to the hospital, and from thence, after all these long tortures, perhaps back to their regiment—perhaps to the churchyard. I was so sorry—so sorry—so terribly sorry for these poor fellows! I should have liked to kneel down before each of them and whisper a few words of compassion to him. But the doctor would not allow me. When we got out at a station he gave me his arm and took me into the stationmaster's office. There he brought me some wine, or some other refreshment.

The nurses carried on their work of mercy here also. They gave the wounded men drink and food, such as they could hunt up, but often there was nothing to be had. The provisions in the refreshment rooms were generally exhausted. This movement at the stations, especially at the large ones, had a bewildering effect on me. It seemed to me like an evil dream. All this running hither and thither, this confused pell-mell —troops marching out, people flying away, sick-bearers, heaps of bleeding and complaining soldiers, sobbing women wringing their hands, shouts, harsh words of command— crowds on all hands, no free passage anywhere—baggage being sent in, war material, cannons—on another side horses and bellowing cattle, and amongst them the continuous sound of the telegraph—trains rushing through filled, or crowded rather, with the reserves coming up from Vienna. These soldiers were brought along in third and fourth class carriages—nay, also in baggage and cattle trucks—just in the same way as cattle to be slaughtered, and regarding it as a matter of fact, I could not repress the thought: " What else were they in reality ? Were they not like the cattle marked out for slaughter—were they not, like them, sent to the great political market, where business is done in food for powder—what the French call *chair-à-canon* ?" A mad roar—was it a war song?—pealed out and drowned the rattling sound of the wheels—one minute, and the train was gone. With the speed of the wind it bore a portion of its freight to certain death. Yes, certain death. Even if no individual can say of himself that he is sure to fall, yet a certain percentage of the whole must and will fall. An army marching to the field, as they sweep along the high road on foot or on horseback, may have a touch of antique poetry about it ; but for the railroad of our modern day, the symbol of culture binding nations together, to serve as the means for promoting barbarism let loose - that is a thing altogether too inconsistent and horrible. And what a false ring also has the telegraph signal used in this service—that splendid sign of the triumph of the human intellect, which has enabled us to propagate thought with lightning speed from one land to another. All these inventions of the new era which are designed to promote the intercourse of nations, to lighten, beautify, and enrich life, are now misapplied by that old-world principle which aims at dividing the peoples and annihilating life. Our boast before savages is : " Look at our railroads, look at our telegraphs ; we are civilised nations "; and then we use these things to increase a hundredfold our own savagery.

My being forced to torture myself with such thoughts as these, and these only, as I waited at the station or pursued my way in the train, made my grief still more deep and bitter. I almost envied those who merely wrung their hands and wept in simple pain, who did not rise up in wrath against the whole hideous comedy, who accused no one—not even that " Lord of armies " of whom yet they believed that He was so, and that it was He who was keeping suspended over their heads the misery that had come to them.

. . . .

It was late at night when I got to Königinhof. My travelling companions had been obliged to get out at an earlier station. I was alone, in fear and anxiety. How if Dr. Bresser were prevented from coming ? What step could I then take in this place ? Besides I was, so to speak, broken on the wheel by the journey, quite unnerved by all the experiences of grief and terror that I had passed through. If it had not been for my longing for Frederick I should have wished now for nothing but death. To be able to lie down, go to sleep, and never wake again in a world where things go on so horribly and so madly ! But preserve me from one thing at least, to live on and know that Frederick is among the "missing " !

The train stopped. Tired and trembling, I alighted and took out my hand-baggage. I had taken with me a hand-basket, with some linen for myself and charpie and bandages for the wounded, and also my travelling dressing-case. This I had taken quite mechanically, in the belief in which I was brought up that one could not exist without the silver cases and baskets, the soaps and essences, the brushes and combs. Cleanliness, that virtue of the body, corresponding to honour in the soul, that second nature of educated humanity, what a lesson had I now to learn, that there can be no thought of it at such times as these ! That, however, is only consistent—war is the negation of education, and therefore all the triumphs of education must be annihilated by it ; it is a step backwards into barbarism and must therefore have everything that is barbarous in its train, and amongst others that thing which to the cultured man is so utterly abominable—dirt.

The chest with materials for the hospitals, which I had looked out for Dr. Bresser in Vienna, had been given over with

the other chests to the care of the Aid Committee, and who
could tell when and where they would be delivered? I had
nothing with me except my two pieces of hand-baggage, and a
bag of money round my neck containing a few hundred florin
notes. With a tottering step I crossed the rails to the platform.
There, in spite of the lateness of the hour, the same confusion
prevailed as at the other stations, and the same picture was
always repeated. Wounded men—wounded men. No, not
the same picture, one still worse. Königinhof was a place
which was over-full of these unfortunates, there was not an
unoccupied room in the whole village, and now they had
brought the sick in crowds to the railway station, where, hastily
bandaged up, they were lying about everywhere — on the
ground—on the stones.

It was a dark, moonless night, the scene was illuminated
only by three or four lamps on the pillars. Exhausted and
thirsting for sleep, almost for the sleep of death, I sank on the
unoccupied corner of a bench and put my luggage on the
ground in front of me.

At first I had not the courage to look about me and see
whether amongst the number of men who were busy passing
to and fro here one might be Dr. Bresser. I was almost
persuaded that I should not meet him. It was at least ten
chances to one that he would be prevented from coming, or
that he would get here at another hour than the one fixed, for
there was no longer any regularity in the service, my train had
certainly arrived much later than was fixed by the railway
regulations. Regulations—another civilised conception, and so
it was now set aside along with the rest.

My undertaking seemed to me now a perfect lunacy. This
fancied call from Frederick—could I then believe in mystical
things of that sort? It certainly had no foundation whatever.
Who knows? Frederick was perhaps on his way home, perhaps
he was dead; why was I seeking for him here? Another voice
began now to call upon me, other arms were stretched out to
meet me. Rudolf, my son, how he would have been asking

for "mamma" and not been able to get to sleep without his
mother's kiss when he bade "good-night". Whither should I
turn here if I did not find Bresser? And the hope of finding
him had of a sudden become as small as the hope of the lucky
number among 100,000 lots. Luckily I had my bag of money
—the possession of bank notes affords always a means of
getting out of difficulties. Mechanically I felt the place where
the bag should have been hanging. Good God! the strap by
which it had been fastened had been torn off, and the bag was
gone—was lost! What a blow! And yet I had not recourse
to any complaint against my destiny. I could not lament:
"How hard fortune is hitting me!" for, at a time when misfortune was falling in floods on all sides, to complain about a
little misfortune of one's own would have made one blush for
one's own selfishness. And besides, for me there was only one
possibility which could alarm me—Frederick's death; all the
rest was nothing.

I began to look at all the people present. No Dr. Bresser.
What to do now? To whom to address myself? I stopped one
of the men passing ——

"Where can I find the stationmaster?"

"You mean the director of the Sick Depôt—Staff-surgeon
S——. He is standing there."

He was not the person I meant, but perhaps he would
be able to give me information about Dr. Bresser. I
approached the place he pointed out. The staff-surgeon was
speaking to a gentleman standing near him.

"It is a pity," I heard him say. "Here and at Turnau
depôts have been founded for all the hospitals of the theatre of
war. Gifts are flowing in in masses—linen, food, bandages as
much as you can wish, but what is to be done with them?
How are they to be unpacked? how sorted? how sent out?
We have no hands. We could occupy a hundred active
officers."

I was just going to speak to the staff-surgeon when I saw a
man hurrying towards him in whom—O joy!—I recognised

Dr. Bresser. In my excitement I fell on the neck of my old family friend.

"You! you! Baroness Tilling! Whatever are you doing here?"

"I am come to help—to nurse. Is not Frederick in one of your hospitals?"

"I have seen nothing of him."

Was this a disappointment or a relief? I do not know. He was not there, and therefore either dead or unhurt . . . besides, Bresser could not possibly know all the wounded in the neighbourhood. I must search through all the hospitals myself.

"And Frau Simon?" I asked next.

"She has been here now some hours. A splendid woman! quick in decision, prudent. Just now she is busied in getting the wounded who are lying here carried into empty railway trucks. She has discovered that in a village near, at Horone-wos, the need is the greatest. She is going there, and I am to accompany her."

"And I also, Dr. Bresser, let me go with you."

"Baroness Martha, where are you thinking of going? You, so delicate and unaccustomed to such hard, bitterly hard work as this?"

"What else have I got to do here?" I said, interrupting him. "If you are my friend, doctor, help me to carry out my purpose. I will really do anything, perform any service. Introduce me to Frau Simon as a volunteer nurse; but take me with you—for mercy's sake take me with you."

"Very well; your will shall be done. The brave lady is there. Come."

.   .   .   .

When Dr. Bresser brought me to Frau Simon and introduced me to her as a sick nurse she nodded, but turned away at once to give some order. I was not able to see her features in the dubious light.

Five minutes later we were on our journey to Horonewos.

A country waggon which had just brought some wounded from that place served as our conveyance. We sat upon the straw which was perhaps still bloody from its former freight. The soldier who sat by the driver held a lantern which threw a flickering light on our road. " An evil dream—an evil dream." Such was more and more the impression of what I was going through. The only thing which brought to my mind the reality of my situation, and which at the same time gave me repose, was Dr. Bresser's company. I had placed my hand in his, and his other arm supported me.

" Lean on me, Baroness Martha, my poor child," he said softly.

I did lean on him as well as I could, but what a position of torture it was! When one has been accustomed during the whole of one's life to repose upon cushioned seats, carriages on well-hung springs, and soft beds, how heavy it falls on one all at once, after an exhausting day's travel, to be sitting on a jolting country cart, the hard planks of which are cushioned only by a layer of bloody straw. And yet I was uninjured. What then must those have felt who were hurried over stock and stone in such a conveyance as that with shattered limbs and their bones sticking out of their skin ?

My eyelids closed with a leaden weight. A painful feeling of sleepiness tortured me. Sleep was indeed impossible from the discomfort of my position—every limb was aching—and from the excitement of my nerves, but the somnolence which I could not shake off had the more terrible effect on me. Thoughts and images, as confused as the visions of fever, whirled through my brain. All the scenes of horror which the regimental surgeon had described repeated themselves before my spirit, partly in the very words of the narrator, partly as delusions of sight and hearing, called up by those words. I kept seeing the gravediggers shovelling in the dead, saw the hyenas sneaking up, heard the shrieks of those who were being sacrificed in the burning lazaretto, and between whiles words came in as if they were pronounced aloud in the accents of the regimental surgeon, such as carrion crows, market folks, sanitary patrols. That, however, did not prevent me from hearing the conversation that was being carried on half aloud by my companions in the cart.

"A part of the routed army fled to Königgrätz," Dr. Bresser said ; "but the fortress was closed and the fugitives were fired on from the walls—especially the Saxons, who in the twilight were mistaken for Prussians. Hundreds plunged into the ditches of the fort and were drowned. The flight was checked by the Elbe, and the disorder reached its height. The bridges were so overcrowded by horses and cannon that the infantry could find no room. Thousands flung themselves into the Elbe—even the wounded."

"It must be a horrible state of things at Horonewos," said Frau Simon. "All abandoned by its inhabitants—village and castle. The whole of the inner rooms destroyed and yet filled with helpless wounded men. What joy will the refreshments we are bringing give the wretched men ! But it will not be enough—not enough l"

"And our medical aid is also not enough," added Dr. Bresser. "There should be a hundred of us, in order to do what is required; we are in want of instruments and medicines; and would even these help us ? The overcrowding of these places is such as to threaten the outbreak of dangerous epidemics. The first care is always this, to send away as many wounded as possible, but their condition is usually such that no conscientious man would take the responsibility of their transport—to send them off means to kill them, to leave them there means to introduce hospital gangrene—a sad alternative l The horrors and miseries I have seen in these days since the battle of Königgrätz exceed all conception. You must prepare yourself for the worst, Frau Simon."

"I have the experience of many years and courage. The greater the misery, the higher rises my determination."

"I know, your fame has preceded you. I, on the contrary, when I see so much misery feel all my courage sink, and it strikes me to the heart. To hear hundreds — nay, thousands—of men in want of help, praying for help, and not to be able to help —it is hideous! In all these ambulances which have been set up in the most hasty way around the field of battle we have been in want of restoratives—above all things, there is no water. Most of the wells around have been made unserviceable by the inhabitants, far and wide there is not a piece of bread to be obtained. All rooms that have a roof over them, churches, country houses, châteaux, huts, all are filled with sick. Everything in the shape of a carriage has been sent off with its load of wounded. The roads in all directions are covered with such carts of hell, for in truth the sufferings carried by those wheels are hellish. There they lie—officers, petty officers, soldiers, disfigured by dirt and dust and blood till they are unrecognisable—with wounds for which there is no human help available, uttering cries of pain, shrieks which are hardly human; and yet those who can still cry are not the most pitiable."

"Then many die on the way."

"Certainly, or after they are unloaded they finish quietly and unobserved on the first bundle of straw on which they have been left to die. Some quietly, but others raving and raging in a desperate fight with Death, uttering such curses as might make your hair stand on end. It must have been curses like these that that Mr. Twining of London heard who made the following proposal at the Geneva Conference: 'Would it not be well, if the condition of a wounded man leaves not the slightest hope of recovery, in such a case to give him first the consolations of religion, then, as far as the circumstances allow, leave him a moment for reflection and then put an end to his agony in the least painful way possible? This would prevent his dying a few moments later, with fever in his brain, and perhaps blasphemies against God on his tongue.'"

"How unchristian!" cried Frau Simon.

"What, to give him the *coup de grâce!*"

"No, but the idea that a blasphemous expression wrung

from the soul of a man in the midst of unbearable tortures could imperil his soul. The Christian's God is not so unjust as that, and assuredly will take every fallen warrior into His grace."

"Mahomet's paradise was assured to every Mussulman who had killed a Christian," replied Bresser. "Believe me, my dear Frau Simon, all those deities who have been represented as leaders of wars, and whose assistance and blessing the priests and commanders promise as the wages of murder, all of them are as deaf to blasphemies as to prayers. Look up there ; that star of the first magnitude, with reddish light, it is only seen twinkling or rather shining, for it does not twinkle, over our heads every second year, that is the planet Mars, the star dedicated to the God of War, that god who was so feared and reverenced in old times that he had by far more temples than the Goddess of Love. Of old on the field of Marathon, in the narrow pass of Thermopylæ, that star shed a bloody light on the battles of men, and to him rose up the curses of the fallen who accused him of their misfortune, while he indifferent and peaceful, then as now, was circling round the sun. Hostile stars ? there are no such things. Man has no enemy except man, but he is savage enough. And no other friend either," added Bresser after a short pause; "of that you yourself are giving an example, magnanimous lady. You are ——"

"O doctor," interrupted Frau Simon ; "look there, that flame on the horizon, it is surely a village in flames ——"

I opened my eyes and saw the red glare.

"No," said Dr. Bresser, "it is the moon rising."

I tried to get into a more comfortable position, and sat up for a time. I kept constantly preventing myself from closing my eyes, for that state of half-slumber, with the consciousness of not being asleep, in which the most horrible fancy-pictures carried on their wild procession, was far too painful. Better to take part in the conversation of the other two, and tear myself away from my own thoughts. But the gentleman and lady were dumb. They were looking towards the place where now

the luminary of night was really rising.   And again in spite of
me my eyes closed for a space.   This time it *was* sleep.   In
the one second during which I felt that I was going to sleep,
that the world around me was ceasing to exist, I felt such a
delight in annihilation that the brother of my benefactor, Death,
would have been quite welcome to me.

I do not know how long a space I passed in this negatively
happy state of removal from existence, but I was torn out of it
suddenly and forcibly.   It was no noise, no shock that woke
me, but a vapour of intolerably poisoned air.

"What is that?"

The others called out the same question at the same time
as I did.

Our waggon turned round a corner, and at the side of the
way we found the answer.   Brightly lighted by the moon there
stood up a white wall, probably of a church.   Anyhow, it had
served as a cover from gunshot.   At its foot, heaped up, lay
numerous corpses.   It was the smell of putrefaction, which
rose up from their dead bodies, that had broken my sleep.   As
we drove by, a thick crowd of ravens and crows rose screaming
from the heap of dead, fluttered for a time, as a black cloud
against the clear background of the sky, and then settled down
again to their feast.

"Frederick! my Frederick!"

"Calm yourself, Baroness Martha," said Bresser consolingly.
"Your husband could not have been present there."

The soldier who was driving had pressed his team on in order
to get away the quicker from the neighbourhood of the mephitic
vapour—the conveyance clattered and jolted as if we were in
wild flight.   I thought the horses had run away . . . trembling
fear took hold on me.   With both hands I clasped Bresser's
arm, but I could not help turning my head back to look *there*
at that wall, and—was it the deceptive light of the moon, or
was it the movements hither and thither of the birds as they
came back to their booty?   I thought that the whole troop of
the dead rose up, and that the corpses all stretched their

arms towards us, and made ready to pursue us. I would have shrieked, but my throat was closed by fear and would not obey my impulse.

.   .   .   .

Again the waggon turned round the corner of a street.

"Here we are—this is Horonewos," I heard the doctor say, and he ordered the driver to stop.

"What are we to do with the lady?" said Frau Simon complainingly. "She will be rather a hindrance than any help."

I collected myself. "No, no," I said, "I am better now; I will do all I can to help you."

We found ourselves in the middle of the village at the gate of a château.

"We will first do here what there is to do," said the doctor. "The château, which is deserted by its owners, must be filled from cellar to roof with wounded."

We got out. I could hardly keep on my feet, but stiffened myself with all my force, so as not to give in.

"Forward," said Frau Simon. "Have we all our luggage? What I am bringing with me will give the people some refreshment."

"There are restoratives and bandages in my box too," said I.

"And my hand-bag contains instruments and medicines," added Bresser. Then we gave the needful orders to the soldiers who accompanied us; two were to wait with the horses and the others come with us.

We passed under the gate of the château. Stifled sounds of woe proceeded from various sides. All was dark.

"Light! the first thing is to strike a light!" called out Frau Simon.

Alas! we had brought all possible things with us—chocolate, meat essence, cigars, strips of linen, but no one had thought of a candle. There was no means of illuminating the darkness which surrounded us and the poor fellows. Only a box of lucifers, which the doctor had in his pocket, enabled us for a few seconds to see the terrible pictures which filled this abode of the wretched. The foot slipped on the floor, slippery with blood, if one tried to go on. What was to be done? To the hundred despairing men who were groaning and sighing here a few more people had come to despair and sigh. " What is to be done? What is to be done?"

" I will find out the clergyman's house," said Frau Simon, " or get some assistance somewhere else in the village. Come, doctor, you conduct me with your lucifer-matches to the egress, and you, Frau Martha, remain here meanwhile."

Here, alone, in the dark, amongst all these wailing people, in this stifling odour? What a situation! I shuddered to the marrow of my bones. But I said nothing against it.

" Yes," I replied, " I will remain on this spot, and wait till you come back with the light."

" No," cried Bresser, putting his arm through mine. " Come with us. You must not be left behind in this purgatory, amongst men who may be in the delirium of fever."

I was thankful to my friend for this speech, and clung tight to his arm. To stop behind in these rooms might perhaps have driven me mad with fear. Ah, I was still a cowardly, helpless creature, not brought up to the misery and the horror into which I had now plunged. Why had I not kept at home? Still, supposing I should find Frederick again? Who could tell whether he might not be lying in these same dark rooms, which we were just quitting? As we went out I called out his name more than once, but the answer which I hoped for and feared: " Here I am, Martha," was not returned.

We got again into the open air. The waggon was standing in the same place. Dr. Bresser decided that I should get in again.

" Frau Simon and I are going meanwhile into the village to seek for aid, and you shall remain here."

I willingly submitted, for my feet could hardly carry me. The doctor helped me to get up and arranged a convenient seat for me with the straw that was lying about. Two soldiers remained behind with the waggon. The rest Frau Simon and the doctor took along with them.

After about half-an-hour the whole expedition came back. No success. The parsonage was destroyed, like everything else, and empty. All the houses in ruins ; no light to be obtained anywhere. So there was nothing else to be done except to wait till day dawned. How many of the poor wretches in whom our coming had already roused hope, and whom our aid might still have saved, might perhaps die during this night?

What a long, long night that was ! Though in reality only between three and four hours passed before sunrise, how endless these hours necessarily seemed to us, their course being marked, not by the ticking of a clock, but by the helpless cries of fellow-men for aid.

At last the morning dawned. Now we could act. Frau Simon and Dr. Bresser took the road again to see whether they could rouse up some of the concealed inhabitants of the village. They succeeded. Out of the ruins here and there one or two peasants crawled forth, at first morose and distrustful. When, however, Dr. Bresser spoke to them in their own language, and Frau Simon urged them with her soft voice, they agreed to give their services. It was necessary before all things to recruit all the other hidden villagers, so that they might help in the work —bury the dead that were lying about, get the wells into working order so as to procure water for the living, collect the field kettles that lay scattered about the roads so as to have vessels, empty the knapsacks of the slain and the dead, and use the linen they contained for the wounded. Now arrived also a Prussian staff-surgeon with men and aid materials, and then the work of bringing help to these poor creatures could be undertaken with some success. Now the moment was come for me too, when I might perhaps discover him at whose fancied call I had undertaken this luckless journey, and whose recollection whipped up to some extent my failing powers.

Frau Simon betook herself, under the conduct of the

18

Prussian surgeon, first to the château, where most of the wounded were lying. Dr. Bresser chose to search through the other places in the village. I preferred to keep with my friend, and went along with him. That Frederick was not lying in the château the doctor had discovered by a previous look round it.

We had hardly gone a hundred paces when loud cries of pain smote on our ears. They came from the open door of the little village church. We went in. There more than a hundred men were lying on the hard stone pavement, severely wounded, crippled. With feverish, wandering eyes they shrieked and cried for water. I had nearly sunk down even on the threshold; still I walked through the whole row. I was seeking for Frederick. He was not there.

Bresser with his people set themselves to attend to the poor fellows. I leaned against a side altar, and contemplated the scene of woe with infinite horror.

And *this* was the temple of the God of Love! These were the wonder-working saints who were there folding their hands so piously in the niches and on the walls, and lifting up their heads with the golden glories round them! "Oh Mother of God—holy Mother of God, one drop of water; have mercy on me!" I heard a poor soldier pray. That prayer he had probably been addressing all the long day to the gaudily-painted dumb image. Ah poor men! Till you yourselves have listened to the command of love which God has put into your own hearts you will always call in vain upon God's love. So long as cruelty is not overcome in your own selves you have nothing to hope from the compassion of heaven.

.   .   .   .

Ah, how much I had to see and to go through in the whole of this same day! It would in truth be the simplest way and the most pleasant to pursue the narrative no further. One shuts one's eyes and turns away one's head when something altogether too horrid presents itself—even the recollection has the power to make one shut one's eyes. And if there is no

more power to help (and what can be altered in this stony
past ?) why torture oneself and others by writing up these
horrors ?

Why ? I will answer the question afterwards. Now I can
only say I *must* do it.

More still. I will not merely tax my own memory that I
may be able to relate what I have in view, for my powers of
perception were far too weak to bear the burden of the events,
but I will also add what Frau Simon, Dr. Bresser, and the Saxon
inspector of field hospitals, Dr. Naundorff, told me. As in
Horonewos, so also in many of the villages in this neighbourhood, Hell had set up branch establishments. It was so in
Sweti, in Hradeck, in Problus. So in Pardubitz, where, when the
Prussians first took possession of it, "over *one thousand* severely
wounded men, operations and amputations, were lying about,
some dying, some already dead, corpses mixed with those in
the act of death, and those who envied them their end,
many with nothing on but bloody shirts, so that no one could
tell even what countrymen they were. All those who had still
a spark of life in them were shrieking for water and bread,
writhing with the pain of their wounds, and begging for death
as a blessing."

"Rossnitz," writes Dr. Bauer in his letters—"Rossnitz, a
place whose picture will live in my memory till the hour of my
death—Rossnitz, whither I was sent by the St. John's Society
six days after the murderous fight, and where the greatest
misery which the human fancy can picture was still reigning
down to that day. I found there 'R.' of ours with 650
wounded, who were lying in wretched barns and stables
without any nursing in the midst of death and half-dead men,
some of them lying for days in their own offal. It was here
that after the erection of the funeral mound of the fallen
Lt.-Col. von F—— I was so overcome with pain that *for an
hour I poured out the hottest tears* and could hardly regain self-
control in spite of the expenditure of all my moral force.
Though as a medical man I am accustomed to look at human

suffering in all its forms, and in the exercise of my profession have learnt to bear the shrieks of tortured human nature, yet here in very truth tears which I could not repress welled from my eyes. It was here in Rossnitz that when, on the second day, I found that our powers were not equal to cope with such misery, I lost courage and left off dressing the wounds."

"In what condition were these 600 men?" It is Dr. Naundorff who is speaking this time. "It is impossible to depict it accurately. Flies were feeding on their open wounds, which were covered with them; their gaze, flaming with fever, wandered about asking and seeking for some help—for refreshment, for water and bread! Coat, shirt, flesh and blood formed in the case of most of them one repulsive mass. *Worms were beginning to generate in this mass and to feed on them.* A horrible odour filled every place. All these soldiers were lying on the bare ground; only a few had got a little straw on which they could repose their miserable bodies. Some who had nothing under them but clayey, swampy ground had half sunk into the mud it formed; they had not the strength to get out of it. Others lay in a puddle of horrible filth which no pen could consent to describe."

"In Masloved," so says Frau Simon, "a place of about fifty houses, there were lying, eight days after the battle, about 700 wounded. It was not so much their shrieks of agony as their abandonment without any consolation which appealed to heaven. In one single barn alone sixty of these poor wretches were crowded. Every one of their wounds had originally been severe, but they had become hopeless in consequence of their unassisted condition, and their want of nursing and feeding; almost all were gangrenous. Limbs crushed by shot formed now mere heaps of putrefying flesh, faces a mere mass of coagulated blood, covered with filth, in which the mouth was represented by a shapeless black opening, from which frightful groans kept welling out. The progress of putrefaction separated whole mortified pieces from these pitiable bodies.

The living were lying close to dead bodies which had begun to fall into putrefaction, and for which the worms were getting ready.

"These sixty men, as well as the greater number of the others, lay for a week in the same situation. Their wounds were either not dressed at all, or only in a most imperfect way—since the day of the battle they lay there, incapable of moving from the spot—only scantily fed, and without sufficient water. The bedding under them corrupting with blood and excrement—that is how they passed eight days! living corpses —through whose quivering limbs a stream of poisoned blood hardly circulated. They had not been able to die, and yet how could they expect ever again to return to life? Which is the more astonishing in this matter," says Frau Simon, in concluding her tale, "the eternal living force of human nature, which could endure all this and yet go on breathing, or the want of efficient assistance?"

What is most astonishing, according to my way of looking at it, is, that men should bring each other into such a state— that men who have seen such a sight should not sink on their knees and swear a passionate oath to make war on war—that if they are princes they do not fling the sword away—or if they are not in any position of power, they do not from that moment devote their whole action in speech or writing, in thought, teaching or business to this one end—Lay down your arms.

. . . .

Frau Simon—she was called the Mother of the Lazarettos —was a heroine. For weeks she stayed in that neighbourhood and bore all privations and dangers. Hundreds were saved by her agency. Day and night she worked, provided, directed. Sometimes she was doing the lowest offices beside the sick-beds, sometimes ordering the transport of wounded, sometimes requisitioning necessaries. When she had provided assistance in one place, she hastened without any rest to another; she got a copious supply from Dresden, and conveyed it in spite of all opposing difficulties to the points where

help was needed. She undertook to represent the Patriotic
Aid Society on the soil of Bohemia, and made a position for
herself there equal to that which Florence Nightingale took in
the Crimea. And as to me? Exhausted, comfortless, overpowered by pain and disgust, I had no power to render any
help. Even in the church—our first station—I had fallen
fainting with fatigue on the steps of that altar of the Virgin,
and Dr. Bresser had a good deal of trouble to bring me round
again. Thence I tottered a little further by his side, and we
got into just such a barn as Frau Simon has depicted. In the
church there was at least a large space, in which the poor
fellows lay side by side; here they were crowded upon each
other, or in each other's arms, in heaps or rolls. Into the
church there had come nurses—probably some sanitary corps
on its march through—and these had given some help, though
insufficient. But here they were mere castaways quite undiscovered—a crawling whining mass of half-putrefied remains of
men. Choking disgust laid hold of my throat, the bitterest
grief of my breast. I felt as if my heart was breaking in two,
and I gave utterance to a resounding shriek. This shriek is
the last thing remaining in my memory of that scene.

.   .   .   .

When I came to my senses again, I found myself in a
railway carriage in motion. Opposite me sat Dr. Bresser.
When he perceived that I had opened my eyes, and was
looking about me astonished and questioning, he took my
hand.

"Yes, yes, Lady Martha," he said, "this is a second-class
carriage. You are not dreaming. You are here in company
with a slightly wounded officer and your friend Bresser, and we
are on our way to Vienna."

So it was. The doctor had brought a detachment of
wounded from Horonewos to Königinhof, and from thence
another detachment had been given into his charge to transport
to Vienna. Me, in my fainting state, fainting in both senses
of the word, he had taken with him and was bringing home.

I had shown myself to be entirely useless and incapable in those abodes of misery, only a hindrance and a burden. Frau Simon was very glad when Dr. Bresser got me out of the way. And I was obliged to allow that it was better so. But Frederick? I had not found him. Thank God that I had not found him, for then all hope was not dead, and if I had been obliged to recognise my beloved husband among those shapes of woe, I should have gone mad. Perhaps I should find at home a letter for me from my Frederick! This hope, no, it would be too much to say "hope," but the thought of this bare possibility poured balm into my wounded soul. Yes, wounded. I felt my inmost soul wounded. The gigantic woe which I had seen had cut so deep into my own heart that I felt as if it would never be healed again completely. Even if I were to find my Frederick again, even if a long future of brilliancy and love were granted me, could I ever forget that so many others of my poor human brothers and sisters had had to bear such unspeakable misery? And must go on bearing it till they come to see that this misery is no fatality but a crime.

I slept almost the whole way. Dr. Bresser had given me a slight narcotic, so that a longer and sounder sleep might to some extent calm my nerves, which had been so shattered by the occurrences at Horonewos.

When we arrived at the Vienna station, my father was already there to take me away. Dr. Bresser, who thought of everything, had telegraphed to Grumitz. It was not possible for him himself to see me there, for he had his wounded to see into the hospital, and wished then to return to Bohemia without delay.

My father embraced me in silence, and I also did not find a word to say. Then he turned to Dr. Bresser.

" How can I thank you? If you had not taken this little crazy thing under your protection ——"

But the doctor pressed our hands hastily.

" I must go," he said. " I have duty to do. May you get home safely. The young lady wants forbearance, your excellency.

She has had a terrible shaking. No reproaches, no questioning.
Get her quick to bed. Orange-flower water—rest. Good-bye.'
And he was gone.

My father put my arm in his and led me through the crowd
to the exit. There again a long row of ambulance waggons
was standing. We had to go some distance on foot till we
could get to the place where our carriage was waiting.

The question : " Has any news of Frederick come during this
while?'' rose several times to my lips, but I could not find
courage to give voice to it. At last, when we had driven some
distance, while my father kept silence all the way, I brought it
out.

" Not up to yesterday," was the reply. " It is possible that
we may find news to-day. It was, of course, yesterday,
immediately after the receipt of the telegram, that I left for the
city. Oh, what a fright you have given us, you silly creature !
To go to the battlefields, where you might meet the most
cruel enemies, for these folks are just like savages. They are
perfectly intoxicated with the victories of their needle-rifle,
and all ; they are no disciplined soldiers, these landwehr fellows ;
from such men you may be sure of the worst outrages, and you—
a lady—to run into the midst of them—you —— However,
the doctor just now ordered me not to scold you."

" How is my son Rudolf?''

" He is crying and moaning about you, seeking you all over
the house, will not believe that you could have gone away
without giving him a parting kiss. And do not you ask after
the rest? Lilly, Rosa, Otto, Aunt Mary? You seem to me
altogether so indifferent."

" How are they all? Has Conrad written?''

" They are all well. A letter arrived yesterday from Conrad.
Nothing has happened to him. Lilly is happy. You will see
that good news will very soon arrive about Tilling too.
Unfortunately there is nothing good to be hoped in a
political point of view. You have surely heard of the
great calamity?''

"Which? In the present state of things I have seen nothing but great calamities."

"I mean Venice. Our beautiful Venice given away—made a present of to that intriguer Louis Napoleon, and that after such a brilliant victory as we won at Custozza! Instead of getting back our Lombardy to give up our Venice as well! It is true that by this means we get free from our enemies in the South, have Louis Napoleon too on our side, and can now with our whole force take our revenge for Sadowa, chase the Prussians out of our country, follow them up and gain Silesia for ourselves. Benedek has committed great mistakes, but now the chief command will be put into the hand of the glorious commander of the Army of the South. But you make no reply? Well, then, I will follow Bresser's prescription and give you repose."

After a drive of two hours we arrived at Grumitz.

As our carriage drove into the court of the château my sisters ran out to meet me.

"Martha! Martha!" both of them shouted from a distance. "He is there."

And again at the carriage door: "He is there".

"Who?"

"Frederick, your husband."

.   .   .   .

Yes, so it was. It was the day before, late in the evening, that Frederick had been brought with a consignment of wounded from Bohemia to Vienna and from thence here. He had received a bullet in his leg, a wound which rendered him for the moment unfit for service and in need of nursing, but was entirely free from danger.

But joy is also hard to bear. The news then shouted to me by my sisters, so entirely without preparation, that "Frederick was there," had just the same effect as the terror of the past days—it deprived me of consciousness.

They were obliged to carry me from the carriage into the château, and put me to bed. Here, whether from the after-

effect of the narcotic, or the violence of the shock of joy, I
spent several hours in unconsciousness, sometimes slumbering,
sometimes delirious.   When I came to myself and found
myself in my own bed I believed myself to have awoke from
a dreadful dream, and thought I had never left Grumitz.
Bresser's letter, my resolution to start for Bohemia, my
experiences there, the homeward journey, the news of Frederick's return home—all was a dream.

I looked up.   My *femme de chambre* was standing at the
foot of the bed.   " Is my bath ready ? " I asked.   " I want to
get up."

Now Aunt Mary rushed forward out of a corner of the room.

" Oh Martha ! poor dear, are you at last awake and restored
to your senses ?   God be praised.   Yes, yes ; get up and take
your bath.   That will do you good, when one is covered, as
you are, with the dust of the roads and railways."

" Dust from railways ; what do you mean ? "

" Quick ; get up.   Netty, get everything ready.   Frederick
is almost dying with impatience to see you."

" Frederick—my Frederick ? "

How often had I during these last days called out this name,
and with what pain !   But now it was a cry of joy—for now I
had comprehended.   It was no dream.   I had been away and
come back again, and was to see my husband.

A quarter of an hour afterwards I went into his room, alone.
I had requested that no one should go with me.   No third
person should be present at our meeting.

" Frederick ! "   " Martha ! "   I rushed to the couch on
which he lay and sobbed on his bosom.

CHAPTER XIII.

*My delight in the restoration of my husband.— The war practically
at an end : but the Prussians continue their advance on
Vienna. —Life at Grumits.—Military education.—My
brother Otto.—Description of the flight of a routed corps.—
Peace imminent.—Victory of Lyssa.—Plans for the future.
—Conrad's return.—The soldier's delight in war.*

THIS was the second time in my life that my beloved husband
had been restored to me from the dangers of war.

Oh ! the blessedness of having him once more with me.
How was it that I, just I, had succeeded in emerging out of the
flood of woe in which so many had sunk, on to a safe and happy
shore ?   Happy for those who in such circumstances can raise
their eyes with joy to heaven and send up warm thanks to their
Guide above.   By this thanksgiving, which, because it is spoken
in humility, they take to be humble, and of which they have
no conception how arrogant and self-important it is in reality,
they feel themselves relieved, inasmuch as they have, according
to their own opinion, given a sufficient discharge for the benefit
which has accrued to them, and which they call grace and
favour.   I could not put myself in that position.   When I
thought of the wretches whom I had seen in those abodes of
misery, and when I thought of the lamentable mothers and
wives whose dear ones had been hurried into torture and death
by the same destiny as had so favoured me—when I thought
of this I found it impossible to be so immodest as to take this
favour as having been sent by God, and one for which I was
entitled to give thanks.   It appeared to me that just as, a little

while before, Frau Walter, our housekeeper, had swept her broom over a cupboard on which a swarm of ants who scented sugar were collected, so fate had swept over the Bohemian battlefields. The poor busy black things were mostly crushed, killed, scattered ; but a few remained uninjured. Now, would it have been reasonable and proper in them if they had sent up their heartfelt thanks for this to Frau Walter? No. I could not entirely banish the woe out of my heart by means of the joy of meeting again, however great that were. I neither could nor did I wish to do so. I was not able to help—to dress wounds, nurse, wait on the sick—like those sisters of mercy and the courageous Frau Simon had done ; my strength was not sufficient for that. But the mercy which consists in compassion, that I had offered up to my poor brother-men, and that I could not withdraw from them again in my selfish contentment. I could not forget.

But if I might not triumph and give thanks yet I well might *love*—might clasp the beloved one to my heart with a hundred-fold the former tenderness. "Oh Frederick, Frederick!" I repeated amidst our tears and caresses, "have I got you again?"

"And you wanted to seek me out and nurse me ? How heroic and how foolish, Martha !"

"Foolish ! Yes, there I agree with you. The appealing voice which drew me on was imagination—superstition—for you were not calling for me. But heroic? No. If you knew how cowardly I showed myself when face to face with misery ! It was only you, if you had been lying there, that I could have nursed. I have seen horrors, Frederick, that I can never forget. Oh ! this beautiful world of ours, how can people so spoil it, Frederick? A world in which two beings can so love each other as you and I do, in which there can glow such a fire of bliss as is our union, how can it be so foolish as to rake up the flames of hate which brings death and woe in its train ? "

"I also have seen something horrible, Martha—something that I can never forget. Just think of Godfrey v. Tessow rushing wildly upon me with uplifted sword—it was in the cavalry action at Sadowa."

" Aunt Rosalie's son ? "

" The same ; he recognised me in time, and let the blade sink which he had already raised."

" He acted in that directly contrary to his duty. How? To spare an enemy of his king and country, under the worthless pretext that he was his own dear friend and cousin."

" Poor fellow! He had scarcely let his arm fall when a sabre whistled over his head. It was my next man, a young officer, who wanted to defend his lieutenant-colonel, and ——"

Frederick stopped and covered his face with both hands.

" Killed ? " I asked shuddering. He nodded.

" Mamma, mamma," resounded from the next room, and the door was burst open. It was my sister Lilly, leading little Rudolf by the hand.

" Forgive me if I interrupt your *tête-à-tête* on meeting again, but this boy was too ardently eager to see his mamma to be denied."

I hastened to the child and pressed him passionately to my heart. Ah ! poor, poor Aunt Rosalie !

On the very same day the surgeon who had been summoned by telegraph from Vienna arrived at the château and undertook the treatment of Frederick's wound. Six weeks of the most perfect rest, and his cure would be complete.

That my husband should quit the service was a point perfectly settled between us two. Of course, this could not be carried out till the war was at an end. The war might, however, be practically looked on as over. After the renunciation of Venice the conflict with Italy was ended, Napoleon's friendship secured, and we should be in a position to conclude peace on moderate terms with the northern conqueror. Our emperor himself was most ardently desirous to put an end to the unlucky campaign, and would not expose his capital to a siege also. The Prussian victories in the rest of Germany, joined to the entry of the Prussians into Frankfort-on-the-Main which took place on July 16, invested our adversaries with a halo, which, like all success, extorted admiration even from our countrymen, and awoke a sort of belief that it was an historical mission which was thus being carried out by Prussia through the battles she had won. The words "suspension of hostilities," "peace," having been once let drop, one could count on their taking effect as certainly as in the times when a threatening of war has once found vent one may reckon on its breaking out sooner or later. Even my father himself admitted that under the stress of circumstances a suspension of hostilities was desirable ; the army was debilitated, the superiority of the needle-gun must be recognised, and an advance of the enemy's troops on the capital, the blockade of Vienna, and along with that the destruction of Grumitz, these were possibilities which were not particularly alluring to even my warlike papa. His trust in the invincibility of the Austrian troops had then received a severe shock by present facts, and it is, speaking generally, a predisposition of the human mind to infer from the events passing before us that they will recur in a series, that on one success another success will follow, on one misfortune a fresh misfortune. So it is better to stop in the run of bad luck—the time of satisfaction and of vengeance will come one day.

Vengeance ! and always repeated vengeance ! Every war must leave one side defeated, and if this side can only find satisfaction in the next war, a war which must naturally produce another defeated side craving satisfaction, when is it to stop ? How can justice be attained, when can old injustice be atoned, if fresh injustice is always to be employed as the means of atonement ? It would never suggest itself to any reasonable man to wash out ink spots with ink and oil stains with oil, it is only blood which has always to be washed out with new blood ! The frame of mind prevailing at Grumitz was on the whole a gloomy one. In the village panic reigned. "The Prussians are coming. The Prussians are coming" was always the cry of terror which they kept uttering still, in spite of the hopes of peace which were cherished in many

quarters ; and people were packing up their treasures at home
or burying them out of sight. Even in the château Aunt Mary
and Frau Walter had taken care that the family plate had been
put in a secret place of concealment. Lilly was in constant
anxiety about Conrad, of whom there had been no news for
several days ; my father found himself wounded in his patriotic
honour, and we two, Frederick and I, in spite of the bliss
which lay deep in our hearts on account of our re-union, had
been most painfully shaken by the miseries of the time which
we had experienced, and with which we so warmly sympathised.
And from all sides flowed in constantly fresh food for this pain.
In all the correspondence in the papers, in all our letters from
relatives and acquaintance, there was nothing but complaints
and lamentations. First there was a letter from Aunt Rosalie,
who had not yet learned her unhappiness, but who spoke in
such moving terms of the fear in which she was of having to
lose her only child—a letter over which we two shed bitter
tears. And in the evening, when we sat all together, there was
no more of cheerful chatter, seasoned with jokes, music, card-
playing and interesting reading, but always, whether spoken or
read, only histories of woe and death. We read nothing but
newspapers, and these were filled with " war," and nothing
but " war," and our talk related chiefly to the experiences
which Frederick and I had brought back from the Bohemian
battlefields. My departure thither had been, it is true, taken
very ill by them all, but for all that they listened eagerly as I
related the events there, partly from my own observation,
partly from what I had been told. Rosa was an enthusiast
for Frau Simon, and swore that, if the war was going to continue, she would join the Saxon Samaritans. Papa, of course,
protested against this.

" With the exception of the sisters of charity and the sutlers
no woman has any business in a war. You must surely see
how useless our Martha showed herself to be. That was an
unpardonable prank of yours, you silly child. Your husband
ought to chastise you properly for it."

Frederick stroked my hand.

"Yes, it was a folly, but a noble one."

If I spoke of the horrors which I had seen with my own eyes, or which my travelling companions had related to me, in quite naked terms, I was often interrupted reproachfully by my father or Aunt Mary, with: "How can people repeat such dreadful things?" or, "Are you not ashamed, as a woman, as a gently bred lady, to take such ugly words into your mouth?" This exhausted my patience.

"Oh, away with your prudery! away with your affected decorum! Any cruelties may be committed, but it is not permitted to name them. Gently bred ladies are not to know anything about blood and filth, but they may embroider the flags which are to wave over this bath of blood ; maidens may not know anything of the cause which is to render their lovers incapable of reaping the reward of their love, but they are allowed to promise them that reward, in order to inspire their martial ardour. *Death* and killing do not offer anything improper for you—well-bred ladies as you are—but at the bare mention of the things which are the sources of the implanted *life*, you must blush and look aside. That is cruel ethics I would have you know—cruel and cowardly. This looking aside—with the bodily and the spiritual eye—it is to this that is due the persistence of so much misery and injustice. If one had but the courage to look steadily whenever one's fellow-creatures are pining in pain and misery, and the courage to reflect on what one saw ——"

" Don't get excited," interrupted Aunt Mary ; "however much we might look, and however much we might reflect, we should never be able to chase evil from the earth. It is now, once for all, a vale of misery, and will ever remain so."

" It will not," I replied ; and so at least I had the last word.

.   .   .   .

" The danger that peace will be concluded is coming steadily nearer," said my brother Otto complainingly one day.

We were sitting at the time at the family table again,

Frederick on the sofa near us, and some one had just read
out of the newspapers the tidings that Benedetti had arrived in
Bohemia, obviously entrusted with the mission of suggesting
proposals for peace.

My little brother—he was indeed big enough by this time,
but I had got into the habit of calling him so—my little brother
was in fear of nothing so much as that the war would come to
a speedy end, and it would not be his lot to chase the enemy
out of the country. For the news had just come from the
Neustadt that in case hostilities had to be resumed, then at the
next period of calling out the reserves—*i.e.*, next August 18—
not only the recruits of the last year, but also a large proportion
of the last but one would have to go at once into active service.
This prospect delighted the young hero. Straight from the
academy into the field ! What rapture ! Just so a school-girl
looks out into the world—to her first ball. She has learned to
dance ; the Neustadt scholar has learned to shoot and fence.
She longs to display her powers under a blazing chandelier in
evening dress, to the accompaniment of the orchestra ; and he
longs no less for the smart uniform and the great artillery
dance.

My father was of course pleased in the highest degree at his
darling's martial ardour.

" By easy, my brave boy," he said in reply to Otto's sigh over
the threat of peace, patting him the while on the shoulder.
" You have a long life before you. Even if the campaign were
to come to an end now, it must break out again in a year or
two."

I said nothing. Since my outbreak against Aunt Mary I had,
on Frederick's advice, formed and carried out the resolution
to avoid these painful disputes on the subject of war as far as
possible. It would lead to nothing but bitter feelings ; and
after having seen the traces of the grim scourge with my own
eyes I had so increased my hatred and my contempt for war that
all defence of it cut into my soul like a personal insult. About
Frederick we were indeed at one—he was to quit the service ;

and I was also clear on this point, that my son Rudolf should not be put into any military institution where the whole of the education is directed—and *must*, to be consistent, be directed —to awaken in the young a longing for deeds of war. I once asked my brother what might be the views which were put before the students on the subject of war. His replies came to something like what follows: War was represented as a necessary evil (thus, at any rate, *evil*—a concession to the spirit of the age) but at the same time as the chief excitant of the noblest of human virtues—such as courage, the power of self-renunciation and the spirit of sacrifice, as the bestower of the greatest glory, and lastly, as the mightiest factor in the development of civilisation. The mighty conquerors and founders of the so-called universal empires—Alexander, Cæsar, Napoleon —were quoted as the most exalted specimens of human greatness, and recommended for admiration. The successes and advantages of war were set forth in the liveliest colours, while they passed over in complete silence the drawbacks which inevitably come in its train, its barbarising influence, its ruinous effects, the moral and physical degeneration it causes. Yes, assuredly, for the same system was pursued in my case—in the education of girls—and it was thus that was kindled in my childish spirit the admiration of warlike laurels which at first inspired me. If I had even myself been full of regret that the possibility of plucking these laurels did not beckon me on, as it did the boys, could I now take it ill in a boy if such a possibility filled him with joy and with impatience?

And so I answered nothing to Otto's complaint, but quietly went on with my reading. I was, as usual, reading a newspaper, and that was filled, as usual, with news from the theatre of war.

" Here is an interesting correspondence of a physician who accompanied the retreat of our troops. Shall I read it aloud?" I asked.

" The retreat?" cried Otto. " I had rather not hear about

that. Now, if it were the history of the retreat of the foe, hotly pursued ——"

"As a general principle it surprises me," remarked Frederick, "that any one should tell the tale of a flight which· he has accompanied. That is an episode of war which the people concerned in it generally pass over in silence."

"An orderly retreat is however not a flight," interposed my father. "We had one in '49. It was under Radetzky ——"

I knew the story and prevented its continuation by inter-posing.

"This account was sent to a medical weekly paper, and, therefore, was not intended for military circles. Listen."

And without further request for permission I read out the passage.

"It was about four o'clock when our troops began the retreat. We doctors were fully occupied dressing the wounded —to the number of some hundreds—who could bear removal. Suddenly cavalry broke in on us, and spread themselves beside and behind us, over hills and fields, accompanied by artillery and baggage-waggons, towards Königgrätz. Many riders fell and *were stamped to pieces* by the horses that came behind. Waggons overturned and crushed the foot-men, who were pressed in among them. We were scattered away from the dressing station, which disappeared all at once. They shouted to us: "Save yourselves!" While this cry went on we heard the thunder of the cannon, and splinters of shell began to fall amongst our crowd. And so we were carried for-ward by the press without knowing whither. I despaired of my life. My poor old mother, my dear espoused bride, farewell! On a sudden we had water before us, on the right a railway embankment, on the left a hollow way stopped up with clumsy baggage- and sick-waggons, and behind us an innumerable crowd of horsemen. We began to wade through the water. Now came the order to cut the traces of the horses, to save the horses, and leave the waggons behind. The waggons of the wounded also? Yes, those too. We on foot were almost in despair : we were wading again over our knees in water, every moment in fear of being shot down or drowned. At last we got into a railway station, which again was closely barred. ' Many broke through the barrier, the rest leaped over it. I with thousands of the infantry soldiers ran on. Now we came to a river, waded through it, then clambered over some palisades, passed again through a second river up to our necks, clambered up some rising ground, leaped over fallen trees, and arrived about one A.M. at a little wood, where we sank down from exhaustion and fever. About three o'clock we marched —that is, some of us, another part had to remain and die there—we marched on still dripping with wet and shuddering with cold. The villages were all empty—no men, no provisions, not even a drop of drinking water ; the air was poisoned, corpses covering the corn-fields ; bodies black as coal, with the eyes fallen from their sockets ——"

"Enough ! enough !" cried the girls.

"The censorship should not allow the publication of things of that sort," said my father. "It might destroy a man's love for the profession of a soldier."

"And especially the love for war, which would be a pity," I murmured half aloud.

"As a general rule," he went on, "about these episodes of flight, the people who have been present at them should observe a decorous silence, for it is surely no honour to have borne a part at a general 'Sauve qui peut'. The fellow who, by shouting 'Save yourselves,' gives the signal for scampering should be shot down on the spot. One coward raises the shout, and a thousand brave men are demoralised thereby and obliged to run with him."

"Exactly so," replied Frederick, "just as when one brave man shouts 'Forward' a thousand cowards are obliged to rush on, and thus are really animated by a merely momentary courage. Men cannot in general be divided so sharply into courageous and cowards, but every one has his moments of more or less courage and those of more or less cowardice.

And especially when one is dealing with masses of men each individual is dependent on the condition of his comrades. We are gregarious animals, and are under the domination of gregarious feelings. Where one sheep leaps over the others leap after him, where one man rushes on shouting ' Hurrah' the others shout and rush after him, and where one dashes down his musket into the corn in order to run away the others run after him. In the one case ' our brave troops' get praised, in the other their proceedings are passed over in silence, yet they are all the same persons. Yes, they are the very same men who, obeying in each case a common impulse, behave and feel at one time courageously, at another cowardly. Bravery and fear are to be regarded, not as fixed qualities, but rather as states of the spirits, just like joy and grief. I, during my first campaign, was once involved in the whirl of one of these panic flights. In the official account of the Etat-major, it is true, the affair was passed over in a few words as an ' orderly retreat ' ; but in fact it was a thorough rout. They rushed on, madly raging in indescribable confusion ; arms, knapsacks, shakos, and cloaks were cast away; no word of command could be heard ; panting, shrieking, hounded on by despair, the disbanded battalion streamed on, with the enemy pursuing and firing after them. That is one of the many gruesome phases of war—the most gruesome, when the two adversaries figure no longer as warriors but as hunter and prey. Thence arises in the hunter the most cruel lust of blood ; in the prey the most bitter fear of death. The pursued, hunted and spurred by fear, get into a kind of delirium, all the feelings and sentiments in which they have been educated, and which animate a man as he is rushing into battle, such as love of country, ambition, thirst for noble deeds —all these are lost to the fugitive. He is filled with one impulse only, in its greatest force, liberated from all restraint, and that the most vehement which can assume the mastery of a living being—the impulse of self-preservation : and this, as danger comes nearer, rises to the highest paroxysm of terror."

. . . .

Frederick's recovery progressed surely. The feverish outer world, too, seemed to come nearer to recovery. The word " Peace" was always being spoken more frequently and always louder. The advance of the Prussians, who found no longer any opposition on the way, and who were quietly drawing on towards Vienna, by way of Brünn, the keys of which were delivered by the burgomaster to King William, this advance was more in the nature of a military promenade than an operation of war, and on July 26 a regular suspension of arms at Nikolsburg was ended by the preliminaries of peace.

My father had a great delight in the reception of the news of Admiral Tegethoff's victory at Lyssa. Italian ships blown into the air, the *Affundatore* destroyed, what a satisfaction ! I could not with perfect honesty take my share in his joy. Speaking generally, I could not understand why, since Venice had already been surrendered, these naval actions should be fought at all. So much, however, is certain, that there broke out over this event the most lively shout of joy, not from my father only, but from all the Viennese papers. The fame of a victory in war is a thing which has been swollen up to such a size through the traditions of a thousand years, that even from the mere news of one some share of pride is spread over the whole population. If anywhere a general of your country has beaten a general of a foreign country, every single subject of the state in question is congratulated, and since each man hears that all the rest are rejoicing, a thing which in itself is exhilarating, why, each man ends by rejoicing, in fact. This is what Frederick called "feeling in droves".

Another political event of those days was that Austria at length joined the Geneva convention.

" Well, are you contented now ? " asked my father as he read the news. " Do you agree that war, which you are always calling a barbarity, is always becoming more humane as civilisation progresses ? I too am indeed in favour of carrying on war humanely : the wounded should have the most careful nursing and all possible relief. . . . Even on strategic principles, which in the long run are surely the most important in warlike matters, by a proper treatment of the sick very many may become fit for service again, and be replaced in the ranks in a shorter space of time."

"You are right, papa. Material to be used again, that is the chief thing. But after the things which I have seen, no Red Cross will be enough, even if they had ten times as much of men and means, to conjure away the misery which one battle brings with it ——"

"No, indeed, not to conjure it away, but to mitigate it. What cannot be prevented, one must always seek to mitigate."

"Experience teaches that no sufficient mitigation is possible. I should therefore wish the maxim to be inverted, 'What cannot be mitigated ought to be prevented'."

It began to be a fixed idea with me, that war must cease. And every individual *must* contribute, all that he is able, to bring mankind nearer to this end, were it but by the thousandth part of a line. I could not get away from the scenes which I had witnessed in Bohemia. Especially at night, when I woke out of a sound sleep, I would feel that sore pain at my heart, and felt at the same time in my conscience the admonition, just as if some one was giving me the command, " Stop it, prevent it, do not suffer it". It was not till I was wide awake and thought on what I was that the perception of my impotence came over me. What then was I to stop or to prevent? A man might as well order me, in face of the sea swelling with winds and waves, "Not to suffer it, dry it up". And my next thought was, especially as I listened to his breathing, one of deep happiness, " I have Frederick again," and I would plunge into this idea as vividly as I could, and then I would put my arm round him as he lay beside me, even at the risk of wakening him, and kiss his lips.

My son Rudolf had really reason to be jealous of his stepfather, and this feeling was actually aroused in the boy's heart, especially since recent days. That I had gone away from Grumitz without bidding him good-bye, that after my return

my first wish was not to embrace *him*, that as a general rule
I did not move from my husband's side for almost the whole
day—all this put together caused the poor little fellow one fine
morning to throw himself weeping on my neck, and sob out:
"Mamma, mamma, you do not love me a bit".

"What nonsense are you talking, child?"

"Yes—only—only papa. I—I will not grow up at all—if
you no longer like me."

"No longer like you—you my treasure!" I kissed and
caressed the weeping child. "You, my only son, my pride,
the joy of my future. I love you so—so above—no, not above
everything—but infinitely."

After this little scene, my love for my boy came more vividly
into my feelings. In the days just past, I had in fact been
so much engrossed by my fears for Frederick, that poor Rudolf
had got thrust a little into the background.

The plans which Frederick and I had made up between
ourselves for the future were as follows: After the war was
over, to quit the military service, and retire to some small,
cheap place, where Frederick's pension as colonel, and what
I could contribute, would suffice to keep up our little household. We rejoiced over this solitary independent life together,
as if we had been a pair of young lovers. By means of the
events of our recent experience, we had been taught thoroughly
that we each formed the whole world to the other. Little
Rudolf, moreover, was not excluded from this fellowship. His
education was a main business in filling up the existence we
were planning. We were not to pass our days therein in
idleness and without any aim; amongst other things we had
marked out a whole list of studies, which we were to pursue
in common. In especial, there was among the sciences a
branch of the science of law, *international*, to which Frederick
intended to devote himself particularly. His aim was, quite
apart from all utopian and sentimental theory, to investigate
the practical side of national peace. By means of the perusal
of Buckle—to which I had given him the impulse—by means

of an acquaintance with the newest acquisitions in natural philosophy, which had been revealed to him in the works of Darwin, Büchner, and others, the conviction had come before him that the world was arriving at a new phase of knowledge, and to make this knowledge his own, as far as possible, appeared to him sufficient to fill up life, along with domestic pleasures.

My father, who meanwhile knew nothing of our views, was making quite other plans for the future on our behalf. "You will now, Tilling, be colonel at an early age, and in ten years you will certainly be general. A fresh war will no doubt break out again about that time, and you may get the command of an entire *corps d'armée*, or who knows but that you may reach the rank of commander-in-chief, and perhaps the great happiness may come to you of restoring the arms of Austria to their full glory, which is now for the moment obscured. When we have once adopted the needle-gun, or perhaps some still more effectual system, we shall soon have the best in a war with these gentlemen of Prussia."

"Who knows," I suggested, "perhaps our enmity with Prussia will cease. Perhaps we shall some day conclude an alliance with them."

My father shrugged his shoulders. "If women would only abstain from talking politics!" he said disdainfully. "After what has taken place, we have to chastise these insolent fellows, we have to get the annexed (as they call them—I call them 'plundered') states back to their severed allegiance; that is what our honour demands, and the interest of our position amongst the Powers of Europe. Friendship—alliance with these transgressors? Never! unless they came and begged humbly for it."

"In that case," remarked Frederick, "we should perhaps set our feet on their necks. Alliances are sought and concluded only with those whom one respects, or who can offer one protection against a common foe. In state-craft the ruling principle is egotism."

"Oh yes," my father replied, "if the *ego* means one's

country, everything else is certainly to be subordinated to it, and everything is certainly allowable and commanded which seems serviceable to its interests."

"It is, however, to be wished," answered Frederick, "that in the behaviour of communities the same elevated civilisation should be reached, as has banished from the behaviour of individuals the rough self-worship, resting on fist-law, and that the view should prevail more and more that one's own interests are really most effectually furthered by avoiding damage to those of foreigners, or rather in union with the latter."

"Eh?" asked my father, with his hand to his ear.

But Frederick could not, of course, repeat this long sentence and illustrate it, and so the discussion ended.

. . . .

"I shall be at Grumitz to-morrow at one o'clock.—Conrad."

Everybody can imagine the delight which this telegram caused Lilly. No other arrival is hailed with such joy and rapture as that of one returning from the wars. It is true that in this case there was not also what is the favourite subject of the common ballads and engravings, *vis.*, "The conqueror's return"; but the human feelings of the loving sweetheart would not be interfered with by patriotic considerations, and if Conrad had "taken" the city of Berlin, I believe this would not have availed to heighten the warmth of Lilly's reception of him.

To him, of course, it would have been better if he had come home along with troops who had been victorious, if he had contributed to conquer the province of Silesia for his emperor. Meantime, the very fact of having fought is in itself an honour for a soldier, even if he is one of the beaten, nay, one of the fallen: the latter is even more especially glorious. Thus Otto told us that in the academy at Wiener-Neustadt the names of all the students were inscribed on a table of honour, to whom the advantage had befallen of having been left dead on the battlefield, *Tué à l'ennemi*, they say in France; and in that country, as everywhere else, it is a much-prized ancestral distinction. The more progenitors one can point out in one's family who have lost their lives in battles, whether won or lost, the prouder is the descendant of it, the more value may he set on his name, the less value on his life. In order to show oneself worthy of one's slain ancestors, one must have a lively joy of one's own in slaying, active and passive. Well, so much the better is it, that, as long as war exists, there should also be found people who see therein elevation and inspiration, nay, even pleasure. The number, however, of these people is daily becoming less, while the number of the soldiers becomes daily greater. Whither must this finally lead? To its becoming *intolerable*. And whither will this lead?

Conrad did not think so deeply. His way of looking at it was excellently expressed by the well-known song of the lieutenant in the "Dame Blanche": "Oh, what delight is a soldier's life, what delight!" To hear him speak, one might have actually envied him the expedition of which he had just formed part. My brother Otto was really filled with this envy. This warrior returned from his baptism of blood and fire, who even before looked so knightly in his hussar uniform, and who was now also adorned with an honourable scar over his chin, received in the shower of bullets, who had perhaps given their quietus to so many of the foe, he seemed to him now surrounded by a nimbus of glory.

"It was not a successful campaign, that I must admit," said Conrad, "but I have brought back from it one or two grand reminiscences."

"Tell us, tell us," Lilly and Otto besought him.

"Well, I cannot give you many details; the whole thing lies behind me like a dream, the powder gets into one's head in such a strange way. The intoxication, in fact, or the fever, the martial fire, in a word, begins from the moment of marching. The parting from one's love indeed comes hard on one; it was the one hour in which my breast was full of tender pain, but when one is once off with one's comrades; when the thought is, now I am going on the highest duty which life can lay on a man, *vis.*, to defend my beloved country; when, then, the

musicians struck up *Radetsky's March*, and the silken folds of
the flags rustled in the wind, I must confess, Lilly, that at that
moment I would not have turned back—no, not into the arms
of my love.   Then I felt that I should never be worthy of that
love except by doing my duty out there by the side of my
brethren.   That we were marching to victory we did not
doubt.   What did we know about the horrible needle bullets ?
It was they alone that were the cause of our defeat.   I tell you
they fell on our ranks like hail.   And we had also bad leaders.
Benedek, you will see, will yet be brought before a court-
martial.   We should have attacked.   If I should ever become
a general my tactics would be to advance, always advance,
play a forward game, invade the enemy's country.   That
surely is only another kind, and the most weighty one too, of
defence :—

> If it must be so, go forward—forward go.
> The way is found by never looking back,

as the poet says.   However, that is nothing to the point ; the
emperor has not put me in command, and so I am not responsible for the tactical blunders : the generals must see how they
are to settle with their military superiors and with their own
consciences ; we, officers and soldiers, did our duty—we
had to fight, and fight we did.   And that is a grand sensation
in itself.   The very expectation, the very excitement one feels
when one rushes on to the foe and when the word goes round
'Now it is afoot,' this consciousness that in that moment a
portion of the world's history is being enacted, and then the
pride, the joy in one's own courage, Death right and left, great
and mysterious, and yet one bids him a manly defiance ——"

"Just like poor Godfrey Tessow," murmured Frederick to
himself.   "Well, of course, it is the same school."

Conrad went on eagerly.

"One's heart beats higher, one's pulse flutters, there awakes
--and that is the peculiar rapture of it—there wakes the joy of

battle. The rage, the hate of the foe blazes up, and at the same time the most burning love for one's menaced country, while the onward rush, the hewing down at them becomes a delight. One feels transported into another world from that in which one grew up, a world in which all the ordinary feelings and ways of looking at things are changed into their opposites. Life is changed into plunder ; killing becomes a duty. Only, however, heroism, the most magnificent self-sacrifice, are left surviving—all other conceptions have perished in the tumult. Then add the powder-smoke, the battle-cries. I tell you it is a state of things to which no parallel is to be found elsewhere. At the most, perhaps, the same fire may glow through one in the lion or tiger hunt, when one stands in the face of the maddened wild beast, and ——"

" Yes," broke in Frederick, "the fight against an enemy who threatens you with death, the longing, proud desire of conquering him fills you with peculiar enjoyment—pray forgive me the word, Aunt Mary—as indeed everything which sustains or expands life is guaranteed to us by Nature through the reward of joy. As long as man was in peril from savage assailants, on two legs or four, and could only protect his life by killing the latter, battle became one of his delights. If in the midst of a fight the same pleasure creeps through our veins still though we are civilised men, it is only a reminiscence of heredity. And at the present time, when there are in Europe no more savages or beasts of prey, in order that this delight may not vanish from us entirely, we have invented artificial assailants for ourselves. This is what goes on. Attention ! You wear blue coats, and those men there red coats. As soon as we clap hands three times the red coats will be turned for you into tigers, and the blue coats will become wild beasts to them. So now—one, two, three ; blow the charge, beat the attack ; and now you can set off, and devour each other; and after 10,000—or always in proportion to the rise in the magnitude of armies—100,000 artificial tigers have devoured each other with mutual delight in battle at Xdorf, then you have the battle of

Xdorf, which is to become historical; and then the men who clap hands assemble round a green congress table in Xstadt, rule lines for altered frontiers on the map, haggle over the proportion of contributions, sign a paper which figures in the historical annals as the Peace of Xstadt, clap their hands three times once more, and say to the redcoats and the bluecoats surviving ' Embrace each other, men and brethren ' ! "

.   .   .   .

CHAPTER XIV.

The Prussians advance on Vienna.—Prussian officers quartered at Grumitz.—My brother Otto's warlike ardour.—He gets into trouble.—A grand dinner to the self-invited guests. Sudden engagement of my sister Rosa to Prince Henry von Reuss.—General felicity and enjoyment.—Departure of the Prussians.—Outbreak of cholera at Grumitz.—The château is infected.—First some of the servants, then my sisters, then Otto die of cholera, and lastly my father dies from heart disease, cursing war with his last breath.—Conrad's suicide.

THERE were Prussians quartered everywhere in the neighbourhood, and now Grumitz had to come into the circle.

Though the suspension of hostilities was already in force, and peace was almost certain, yet general fear and mistrust reigned throughout the people. The idea that these spike-helmeted tigers would tear them to pieces if they could was not easily eradicated out of the people. The three claps of the hand at Nicolsburg had not yet availed to undo the effect of the three claps of the declaration of war, and to make the country-folk look on the Prussians again in the light of brothers. The very name of the opposing nation gathers round it in war time a whole host of hateful implied meanings. It is not merely the distinctive name of a nation hostile for the moment, but it becomes the synonym for "enemy," and comprises in itself all the repugnance which that word expresses.

And so it happened that the folks in the neighbourhood trembled, as before wolves broken loose, if a Prussian quarter-

(303)

master came there to procure lodging for his troops. With some besides fear hatred also was expressed, and these thought they were discharging a patriotic duty if they did anything to injure a Prussian, if they sent a rifle bullet out of some place of concealment after "the foe". This had often taken place, and if the guilty party was caught he was executed without much circumstance. These examples had the effect of making the people suppress their hatred and receive without opposition the soldiers quartered on them. Then they found to their no small amazement that "the enemy" really consisted of nothing but good-humoured, friendly fellows, who paid their way honestly.

One morning, it was early in August, I was sitting in the bow-window of the library and looking out through the open window. From this point was a long view over the surrounding country. I thought I saw from a distance a troop of cavalry moving along the high road in our direction.

"Prussians coming for quarters," was my first thought. I adjusted a telescope which stood in the bow, and looked towards the point in question. Right; it was a troop of about ten riders with waving black and white little flags on the points of their lances. And among them a man on foot, in hunting costume. Why was he walking in this way between the horses? A prisoner? The glass was not powerful enough. I could not make out whether the man I took for a prisoner might not be one of our own foresters.

Still it was right to warn the inhabitants of the château of the fate impending over them. I hastily left the library to look for papa and Aunt Mary. I found both in the drawing-room. "The Prussians are coming, the Prussians are coming," I announced to them breathlessly. One is always glad to be able to be the first to communicate important tidings.

"Devil take them," was my father's rather inhospitable exclamation, while Aunt Mary hit on the right thing to do, as she said: "I will immediately give Frau Walter her orders for the necessary preparations".

"And where is Otto?" I asked. "Some one must acquaint him, and warn him not to let his hatred of the Prussians peep out anyhow, and not to be uncivil to the guests."

"Otto is not at home," replied my father. "He went out early to-day after the partridges. You should have seen him, how well his hunting-dress sat on him. He grows a fine fellow. My delight is in him."

Meanwhile the house filled with noise. Hasty steps were heard, and excited voices.

"They are come already—those windbags," muttered my father. .

The door was dashed open, and Franz, the *valet de chambre*, rushed in.

"The Prussians—the Prussians," he shouted, in the same tone as one calls "Fire, fire!"

"Well, they won't eat us," growled my father.

"But they are bringing a man with them--a man from Grumitz," the man went on in a trembling voice. "I do not know who it is. He has fired on them; and who would not like to fire on such a scum? But it is all over with him."

Now one heard the tramp of horses and tumult of voices together. We went down to the ground floor and looked through the windows which opened out into the courtyard. At that moment the Uhlans came riding in, and in their midst, with pale, defiant face, Otto, my brother.

My father uttered a shriek and hurried down the steps. My heart stood still. The scene before us was horrible. If Otto had really fired at the Prussian soldiers, which seemed very like him —— I dared not think of the conclusion.

I had not the courage to go after my father. Consolation and assistance in all sorrows I always sought from Frederick only. So I collected myself in order to betake myself to Frederick's room. But before I got there, my father came back again and Otto after him. By their bearing I saw that the danger was over. The hearing of the matter had given the following result: The shot had been discharged accident-

20

ally. When the Uhlans came riding on, Otto wanted to see them close, ran across the field, stumbled, fell down into a ditch, and in doing so discharged his gun. At the first moment the statement of the young sportsman was doubted by the men. They took him in their midst and brought him to the château as their prisoner. But when it came out that the young gentleman was the son of General Althaus, and was himself a military student, they accepted his explanation.

" The son of a soldier, and himself a future soldier, might well fire on hostile soldiers in honourable fight, but not in time of truce, and not like an assassin." On this speech of my father's the Prussian subaltern had set the young man free.

" And are you really innocent ? " I asked Otto. " For from your hatred of the Prussians it would not surprise me if ——"

He shook his head.

" I shall, I trust, have plenty of opportunities in the course of my life to fire at a few of them ; but not from behind, not without exposing my heart, too, to their bullets."

" Bravo, my boy ! " cried my father, delighted by these words.

I could not share his delight. All these phrases, in which *life*, whether one's own or another's, is tossed about so contemptuously and so boastfully, have a repellent tone for me. But I was glad at heart that the matter had passed over thus. How horrible would it have been for my poor father if these men had shot down the presumed malefactor without more ado! In that case the unhappy war by which our house had hitherto been spared would have yet plunged it into misery.

The detachment in question had come in the regular way to take up quarters. Schloss Grumitz had been selected as the habitation of two colonels and six officers of the Prussian army. The men were to be lodged in the village. Two men were to be set as sentinels in the courtyard of the château.

An hour or two after the settlement of the quarters the involuntary and self-invited guests made their entry into our house. We had been prepared for the event for several days, and Frau Walter had seen that all the guest chambers and beds were in readiness. The cook also had laid in plenty of provisions, and the cellar held a sufficient number of full barrels and old bottles. The Prussian gentlemen should not find any scarcity in our house.

. . . .

When the company in the château mustered in the drawing-room that day at the sound of the dinner-bell the room presented a brilliant and lively picture. The gentlemen, all excepting Minister " To-be-sure," who was our guest for the moment, all in uniform, the ladies in full dress. For the first time for a long while we were all in our glory—Lori especially—the lively Lori—who had arrived that same day from Vienna, had, on the news that foreign officers were to be present, unpacked her fine dresses, and adorned herself with fresh roses. The object, no doubt, was to turn the head of one or other of the members of the enemy's army. Well, as far as I was concerned she might have conquered the whole Prussian battalion, so she left Frederick undazzled. Lilly, the happy *fiancée*, wore a light blue robe. Rosa, who also seemed very happy to have the chance once more of showing herself off to young cavaliers, was dressed in pink muslin ; and I, feeling that war time, even if one has no person to mourn, is always a time of mourning, put on a black dress.

I recollect still the singular impression which it made on me when I entered the drawing-room, in which the rest were already assembled. Glitter, cheerfulness, distinguished elegance, the well-dressed ladies, the smart uniforms—what a contrast to the scenes of woe, filth, and terror that I had seen so short a time since. And it is these same glittering, cheerful, elegant personages who of their own accord set this woe in motion, who refuse to do anything to abolish it, who on the contrary glorify it, and by means of their gold lace and stars testify the pride which they find in being the agents and props of this system of woe !

My entrance broke up the conversation which was being

carried on in the different groups, since all our Prussian guests
had to be introduced to me, most of them distinguished-
sounding names ending in "ow" and in "witz," many "vons,"
and even a prince—one Henry—I don't know of what number
—of the house of Reuss.

Such then were our enemies! perfect gentlemen with the
most exquisite manners in society.   Well, certainly one knows
as much as this: that if war is to be carried on at the present
day with a neighbouring nation one has not to do with Huns
and Vandals ; but for all that it would be much more natural
to think of the enemy as a horde of savages, and it requires
some effort to look upon them as honourable and civilised
citizens.   "God, who drivest back by Thy mighty protection
the adversaries of those who trust in Thee, hear us graciously
as we pray for Thy mercy, so that the rage of the enemy having
been suppressed we may praise Thee to all eternity."   This
was the prayer daily offered by the priest at Grumitz.   What
conception must there have been formed by the common people
of this "raging enemy"?   Certainly not anything like these
courteous noblemen who were now giving their arms to the
ladies present to take them to dinner. . . . Besides this, God
this time had listened to the prayer of the other side and had
suppressed *our* rage—the foaming, murderous foe who through
the might of the Divine protection (which, to be sure, we called
the needle-gun) had been driven back were *ourselves*.   Oh!
what a pious concatenation of nonsense!   I was thinking something to this effect as we were sitting down in a brilliant row at the
table, adorned with flowers and dishes of fruit.   The silver,
too, had been brought out of its hiding-place at the order of
the master of the house.   I was seated between a stately
colonel, ending in "ow," and a tall lieutenant in "itz"; Lilly,
of course, by her lover's side.   Rosa had been taken in to
dinner by Prince Henry, and the naughty Lori had once again
succeeded in getting my Frederick as her next-door neighbour.
But what of that?   I was not going to be jealous.   He was
assuredly *my* Frederick, my very own.

The conversation was very abundant and very lively. "The Prussians" evidently felt highly pleased, after the toils and privations they had gone through, to be sitting down again at a well-furnished table and in good company; and the consciousness that the campaign which was ended had been a victorious one must certainly have contributed to raise their spirits. But even we, the vanquished, did not allow anything of grudge or humiliation to appear, and did all we could to play the part of the most amiable of hosts. To my father it must have cost some self-control, as I could judge from knowing his sentiments, but he played his part throughout with exemplary courtesy. The one who was most dejected was Otto. It was visibly against the grain for him, with the hatred which he had been cherishing against the Prussians in these late days, with his eagerness to chase them out of the country, to have now to reach the pepper and salt for this same foe in the most polite manner, instead of being allowed to pierce him with a bayonet. The topic of the war was carefully avoided in the conversation; the foreigners were treated by us as if they had been pleasure-travellers who happened to be passing through our neighbourhood, and they themselves with still greater caution avoided even hinting at the real state of things—*vis.*, that they were stationed here as our conquerors. My young lieutenant even tried, quite in earnest, to pay his court to me. He swore, by his honour and credit, that there was no such pleasant place in the world as Austria, and that there (shooting sidewards a needle-gun glance) the most charming women in the world were to be found. I do not deny that I too coquetted a little with the smart son of Mars, but that was to show Lori Griesbach and her neighbour that in a certain given case I was capable of having my revenge; the folks opposite, however, remained quite as undisturbed as I myself was really at the bottom of my heart. It would have been more reasonable and more to the purpose, however, if my dashing lieutenant had directed his killing glances to the fair Lori. Conrad and Lilly in their character of engaged persons (and such folks should really be always put behind a grating) exchanged loving glances quite openly, and whispered and clanked their glasses together by themselves, and played all sorts of other drawing-room turtle-dove tricks. And as it seemed to me a third flirtation began on the spot to develop itself. For the German prince—Henry the So and So —kept conversing in the most pressing way with my sister Rosa, and as it went on his countenance became a picture of the most unconcealed admiration.

When we rose from table, we went back into the drawing-room, in which the chandelier, which had now been lighted, diffused a festive glow.

The door on to the terrace was open. Outside was the warm summer night, flooded by the gentle light of the moon. The evening star shed its rays over the grassy expanse of the park, fragrant with hay, and mirrored itself in glittering silver on the lake which spread out in the background. . . . Could that really be the same moon which a short time ago had shown me the heap of corpses against the church wall surrounded by the shrieking birds of prey? And were these people inside—just then a Prussian lieutenant opened the piano to play one of Mendelssohn's "Lieder ohne Worte"—could they be the same as were laying about them with their sabres a short time since to cleave men's skulls?

After a time Prince Henry and Rosa came out too. They did not see me in my dark corner, and passed by me. They were now standing, leaning on the balustrade, near, very near each other. I even believe that the young Prussian—the foe— was holding my sister's hand in his. They were speaking low, but still some of the prince's words reached me. "Charming girl . . . sudden, conquering passion . . . longing for domestic happiness . . . the die is cast . . . for mercy's sake do not say 'No'. Do I then inspire you with disgust?" Rosa shook her head. Then he raised her hand to his lips and tried to put his arm round her waist. She, like a well-brought-up girl, disengaged herself at once.

Ah! I would almost have preferred that the soft moonlight

had then and there shone on the kiss of love. . . . After all the pictures of hate and bitter woe which I had been obliged to witness a short time ago, a picture of love and sweet pleasure would have seemed to me like some compensation.

"Oh! is it you, Martha?"

Rosa had now become aware of me, and was at first very much shocked that any one should have been listening at this scene, but then pacified that it was only me.

The prince, however, was in the highest degree discomposed and perplexed. He stepped towards me.

"I have just made an offer of my hand to your sister, gracious madam. Kindly say a word in my favour. My action may perhaps seem to both of you somewhat sudden and presumptuous. At another time I should myself perhaps have proceeded more cautiously and more modestly; but in these last few weeks I have been accustoming myself to advance quickly and boldly—no hesitation or trembling was allowed then—and the practice which I formed in war I have now involuntarily again exercised in love. Pray forgive me, and be favourable to me. You are silent, countess? Do you refuse me your hand?"

"My sister," said I, coming to Rosa's assistance, who was standing there in deep emotion with her head turned aside, "cannot surely be expected to decide her fate so quickly. Who knows whether our father will give his consent to a marriage with 'an enemy'; who knows again whether Rosa will return an inclination so suddenly kindled?"

"I know," she replied, and stretched out both her hands to the young man; and he pressed her warmly to his heart.

"Oh, you silly children," I said, and drew back a few paces to the drawing-room door, to watch that—at least at *that* moment—no one should come out.

. . . .

On the following day the betrothal was celebrated. My father offered no opposition. I should have thought that his hatred of the Prussians would have made it impossible for him to receive into his family a hostile warrior and a victor ; but whether it was that he separated altogether the individual question from the national (a common method of action—for one often hears people protest: "I hate them as a nation, not as individuals," though there is no sense in it, no more sense than if one were to say: "I hate wine as a drink, but I swallow each drop with pleasure" ; still a phrase need not be rational in order to be popular, quite the contrary), or whether it was that ambition got the upper hand and an alliance with a princely house flattered him, or, finally, that the sudden love of the young folks so romantically expressed touched him—in short, he said yes, and with seeming heartiness. Aunt Mary was less disposed to agree. "Impossible !" was her first exclamation. "The prince is surely of the Lutheran sect." But in the end she comforted herself with the consideration that Rosa would probably convert her husband. The deepest resentment it awoke was in Otto's heart. "How would you like it," he said, "supposing the war was to break out again, that I should chase my brother-in-law out of the country?" But to him also the famous theory of the difference between nation and individual was explained, and to my astonishment—for I could never understand it—he understood it.

How quickly and easily does one in happy circumstances forget the misery one has gone through. Two pairs of lovers, or, if I may venture to say so, *three*—for Frederick and I, the married ones, were not much less in love with each other than the betrothed —well, so many pairs of lovers in the little company gave an air of felicity to everything. For the next day or two Schloss Grumitz was an abode of cheerfulness and worldly enjoyment. I, too, gradually felt the pictures of terror of the past weeks fading out of my remembrance. It was not without reproaches of conscience that I became aware how my compassion, which had been so burning a short time since, was at some moments quite gone. It is true that sounds of mourning still came pealing from the world without, the complaints of people who in the war had lost goods or money or lives of those dear to them, accounts of threatened financial catastrophes, of the outbreak of pestilence. It was said that the cholera had shown itself among the Prussian troops; a case had even been reported in our village, but only a doubtful one, it is true: "It might be diarrhœa, which occurs every summer," was the consolatory remark. Let us only chase away troubled thoughts and anxious fears with: "It is nothing," or "It has passed over," or "It will not come"; all this is so easy to say. All that is wanted is a vigorous shake of the head and the unpleasant facts are gone.

"I say, Martha," said the happy *fiancée* to me one day, "this war was indeed a horrible thing, and yet I must bless it; without it should I ever have been so immeasurably happy as I am now? Should I ever have had the opportunity of making Henry's acquaintance? And as to him, would he ever have found a bride to love him so?"

"Very well, dear Rosa. I shall be happy to share this view of it with you. Let your two hearts made happy be weighed against the many thousands of hearts that have been broken."

"But it is not only individual destinies that are concerned, Martha. In the gross and on the whole war also brings great gain to those who conquer, and therefore to a whole nation. You must hear Henry talk on that subject. He says Prussia shines out grandly. In the army universal exultation reigns, and enthusiastic thankfulness and love for the generals who have led it to victory. And in this way there arises for German civilisation, for commerce—or perhaps he said for the prosperity of Germany, I have forgot the exact term—its historical mission—in short, you should hear him talk himself."

"Why, does not your *fiancé* prefer to speak of your love rather than of political and military matters?"

"Oh, we speak about everything, and everything he says sounds like music in my ears. I feel that it is so good for him that he is proud and happy to have joined in fighting out this war for his king and country ——"

"And carried away for himself so dear a sweetheart as his booty," I added, to finish her sentence.

His future son-in-law suited my father very well, and who would not have been pleased with such a grand young man? Still he gave him his sympathy and his blessing with all kinds of protestations and restrictions.

"You are dear to me in every respect, dear Reuss—as a man and as a soldier and as a prince"—this is what he said to him repeatedly, and in various modes of speech—"but as a Prussian officer of course I reserve to myself the right, despite any family connection, of wishing for nothing so much as a future war, in which Austria may pay back handsomely the present victory snatched from her. The political question must be separated altogether from the personal. My son will one day —God grant that I may live to see it—take the field against the Prussian state. I myself, if I were not too old, and if my emperor were to summon me to it, would at once accept a command to fight William I., and especially his overbearing Bismarck. This does not prevent me from recognising the military virtues of the Prussian army, and the strategic science of its leaders; and from thinking it quite a matter of course that in the next campaign you, at the head of your battalion, should try to storm our capital, and set fire to the house in which your father-in-law lives—in short ——"

"In short," said I, one day breaking in on a rhapsody of this kind, "confusions in terms and inconsistencies of fact twine round each other like the *infusoria* in a putrefying drop of water. It is always so, when you pen up together conceptions repugnant to each other. To hate the whole and love its parts, to want to have one way of thinking as members of a nation and another as a man. That will not do; it must be one thing or another. So I approve of the Indian chief's way of looking at it. He entertains for the adherent of a different tribe—as to which he does not even know that it consists of individuals— no other wish than to scalp him."

"But my dear girl, Martha, such savage feelings do not suit

he stage of our civilisation, which has grown more cultured
nd more humane."

" Rather say that our present stage of civilisation does not
uit the savagery which has come down to us from old times.
s long as this savagery, that is, so long as the spirit of war is
ot cast out, our much-valued 'humanity' cannot be looked
n as *reasonable*. For surely now as to the speech you made
ist now, in which you assured Prince Henry that you would
ive him as a son-in-law and hate him as a Prussian, value him
early as a man, and abominate him as an officer, that you give
im your paternal blessing with pleasure, and at the same time
low him the right, in given circumstances, of firing on you,
rgive me, my dear father, but will you really uphold this as
asonable ? "

" What are you saying ? I do not catch a word."

The favourite deafness had again come on at the right
oment.

. . . .

After a few days all became quiet again at Grumitz. The
ldiers quartered on us had to march off, and Conrad had
en ordered to join his regiment. Lori Griesbach and the
inister had already departed before.

The marriage of my two sisters had been postponed till
:tober. Both were to be married on the same day at
:umitz. Prince Henry was to quit the service ; now that he
d finished this glorious campaign in which he had earned
stinction, he could easily do this, and so repose on his
irels, and on his estates.

The partings of the two pairs of lovers were painful and
rful at the same time. They promised to write to each other
ery day, and the certain prospect of bliss so near made the
guish of parting seem not so severe.

Certain prospect of bliss ? There is in reality no such
ng, and assuredly least of all in seasons of war. Then
sfortunes hover around "as thick as the swarms of gnats in
: air," and the chances that you may be standing on a spot

that will be spared by the descending scourge are at best but small.

True, the war was over. That is, it had been proclaimed that peace was concluded. A word is sufficient to unchain the horrors, and thence one is apt to think that a word will also suffice to remove them again, but no spell has in reality that power. Hostilities may be suspended, and yet hostility may persist. The seed of future war is sown, and the fruit of the war just ended spreads still further, in wretchedness, savagery, and plagues. Yes, no falsehood and no "not thinking of it" was any good now, the cholera was raging through the country.

It was on the morning of 8th August. We were all seated at the breakfast-table and reading our correspondence which had just come by the post. The two *fiancées* had fastened on the love letters that had come for them, I was turning over the newspapers. From Vienna the news was :—

The cholera death-rate is rising considerably. Not only in the military but also in the civil hospitals many cases have been already reported, which must be looked on as genuine Asiatic cholera, and energetic measures are being taken on all sides to check the progress of the epidemic.

I was about to read the passage aloud when Aunt Mary, who had in her hand a letter from one of her friends in a neighbouring château, gave a cry of horror.

"Horrible! Betty writes me that in her house two persons have died of cholera, and now her husband is ill also."

"Your excellence, the schoolmaster wishes to speak to you."

The gentleman announced followed the footman into the room. He looked pale and bewildered.

"Count, I tell you, with all deference, that I must close the school. Two children were taken ill yesterday, and to-day they are dead."

"The cholera?" we cried out.

"I think it is. I think we must give it that name. The so-called diarrhœa which broke out among the soldiers quartered here, and of which twenty of them died, was the

olera. Great terror prevails in the village, because the
ctor who came here from town has affirmed without any
ncealment that the horrible disease has now beyond doubt
ken hold of the population of this place."

"What sound is that," I asked, listening, "that one hears?"

"That is the passing-bell, baroness," announced the school-
aster. "Some one must be lying at his last gasp. The
ctor tells us that in town the passing-bell absolutely never
ps ringing."

We all looked round at each other, pale and speechless.
here it was again—Death—and each one of us saw his bony
nd stretched out in the direction of some dear one's head.

"Let us flee!" suggested Aunt Mary.

"Flee? whither?" answered the schoolmaster. "The pest
s by this time spread everywhere round."

"Oh, far, far away, over the frontier ——"

"But a cordon will be drawn there, over which no one will
allowed to pass."

"Oh, that would be horrible! Surely no one would hinder
ople from quitting a land stricken with pestilence?"

"Assuredly, the healthy neighbourhoods will protect them-
lves against infection."

"What is to be done? what is to be done?" And Aunt
ary wrung her hands.

"To await God's will," answered my father. "You are
sides such a believer in destiny, Mary, I cannot understand
ur desire for flight. Every one's fate finds him, wherever he

But, at the same time, I should like it better if you, children,
uld depart; and you, Otto, see that you touch no more fruit."

"I will telegraph at once to Bresser," said Frederick, "to
nd on disinfectants."

What happened immediately after this I am no longer able
set down in detail, because the scene at the breakfast-table
s the last which at that time I entered in the red book. I
n only tell the events of the next few days from memory.
ar and anxiety filled us all—yes, all. Who, in a time of

epidemic, could help trembling when living amongst those
dear to him? For the sword of Damocles was always suspended
over the dear one's head, and even to die oneself, so terribly
and so uselessly, who is there that such a thought would not
fill with horror? The chief proof of courage consists in this,
not to think about it.

To flee? The idea had occurred to myself also, so as to get
my little Rudolf into a safe place.

My father, in spite of all his fatalism, insisted on flight for
the others. The whole family were to be off next day. He
alone determined on remaining, in order not to abandon his
household and the inhabitants of the village in their danger.
Frederick declared in the most decisive manner his determination to remain, and this involved at once my decision. I
would never voluntarily leave my husband.

Aunt Mary with the two girls and with Otto and Rudolf
were to depart as quickly as possible—whither? That was not
yet settled. In the first place, to Hungary—as far away as
possible. The fiancées did not make any opposition whatever,
but were busy in helping to pack. To die, when the new
future promised the fulfilment of the warm desires of love, is,
a tenfold delight in living, would be to die tenfold.

The boxes had been brought into the dining-room, so that
with the united assistance of all the work might go on quicker.
I was bringing a package of Rudolf's clothes under my arm.

" Why does not your maid do that? " asked my father.

" I do not know where Netty has got to. I have rung for
her several times, and she does not come, so I prefer to wait
on myself."

" You spoil your people," said my father angrily, and he gave
orders to a footman to look for the girl everywhere and bring
her there immediately.

After a time the man who had been sent returned, looking
confused.

" Netty is lying down in her room. She is—she has—she
is ——"

"Well, can't you speak?" thundered my father. "What is the matter with her?"

"She is already—quite black."

A cry burst out of all our mouths. So the horrible spectre was already present in our own very house.

Now, what should we do? Could one leave the poor girl to die unaided? But whoever went near her brought death on himself almost certainly, and not only on himself, he spread it again more widely among the rest. Ah! a house like that, into which the pest has penetrated, is like one encircled by robbers, or as if it were in flames; everywhere and in every corner and place, at every step and move, Death is grinning at you.

"Fetch the doctor immediately," was my father's order "And you, children, hurry your departure."

"The doctor went back to town an hour ago," was the servant's reply to my father's direction.

"Oh, dear! I feel so ill," now cried Lilly, and she turned pale to her very lips, and clutched at the arm of her chair.

We ran to her: "What is the matter with you?"—"Don't be foolish"—"It is only fear".

But it was not fear, there was no doubt what it was. We had to carry the poor thing to her room, where she was seized at once with violent vomiting and the other symptoms. This was the second case of cholera in the château in this same day.

It was horrible to see my poor sister's sufferings. And no doctor at hand! Frederick was the only one who could perform the duty of one, as well as he might. He ordered what was wanted—warm fomentations, mustard poultices to the stomach and the legs, ice in fragments, champagne. Nothing did any good. These means, which are sufficient for slight attacks of cholera, could not save in this case. But at least they gave the patient and the bystanders the comfort of knowing that *something* was being done. When the attacks had subsided, the cramps followed, quiverings and tearings of the whole frame till the very bones cracked. The poor thing tried to lament, but could not, for her voice failed, the skin turned blue and cold, the breath stopped.

My father was running up and down, wringing his hands. Once I put myself in his way.

"This is war, father," I said. "Will not you curse it?"

He shook me off and gave no reply.

In ten hours Lilly was dead. Netty, my poor lady's maid had died before—alone, in her room. We were all of us busy about Lilly, and of the servants, none had ventured to go near one who had "already turned quite black".

.   .   .   .

Meanwhile Dr. Bresser had arrived. He himself brought the medicines which we had telegraphed for. I could have kissed his hands as he walked into the midst of us to devote his self-sacrificing services to his old friends. He at once took on himself the command of the establishment. He had the two corpses carried into a remote chamber, barred up the rooms in which the poor things had died, and made us all submit to a powerful disinfecting process. An intense carbolic odour now penetrated all the rooms, and to this day, whenever this smell meets me, those dreadful days of cholera rise before my imagination.

The intended flight had to be postponed a second time. On the very day of Lilly's death, the carriage was standing ready which was to convey away Aunt Mary, Rosa, Otto, and my little boy, when the coachman, seized by the invisible destroyer, was forced to get off the coach-box again.

"Then I will drive you," said my father, when the news was brought to him. "Quick, is everything ready?"

Rosa came out. "Drive on," she said, "but I must stop behind. I am going Lilly's way."

And she spoke truth. The break of day dawned on this second young bride too in the chamber of death.

Of course, in the horror of this new calamity, the departure of the others was not carried out.

In the midst of my anguish, of my raging fear, the deepest scorn again seized me for that gigantic folly which had voluntarily called forth so great a calamity. My father, when Rosa's corpse had been carried out, had sunk on his knees, with his head against the wall.

I went to him, and took him by the arm. "Father," I said, "this is war." No answer. "Father, do you hear? Now or never, will you now curse war?"

He, however, collected himself.

"You remind me of it—this misfortune shall be borne with a soldier's courage. It is not I alone, the whole country has to offer its sacrifice of blood and tears."

"What comfort then has come to the country from the sufferings of you and your brethren? What comfort from the lost battles? What from these two girls' lives cut short? Father! Oh do me this kindness for the love of me!—curse war! See here "—I drew him to a window, and just then a black coffin was being brought on a car into the courtyard—"See here; that is for our Lilly, and to-morrow another such for our Rosa, and the day after perhaps a third; and why, why?"

"Because God has willed it so, my child."

"God—always God. All that, however, is folly. All savagery, all the arbitrary action of men, hiding itself under the shield of God's will."

"Do not blaspheme, Martha! Do not blaspheme now when God's chastening hand is so visibly ——"

A footman came into the room.

"Your excellency, the carpenter will not carry the coffin into the chamber where the countesses are lying, and no one will venture into it."

"Not you, either, coward?"

"I could not alone."

"Then I will help you. I will myself see to my daughters;" and he strode to the door.

"Back," he cried to me, as I was following him; "you must

not go with me.   You must not die as well as me—think of your child."

What could I do?   I hesitated.   That is the most torturing thing in such circumstances—not to know at all *where* one's duty lies.   If one pays to the sick and the dead the loving service which one's heart yearns to do, then one spreads the germs of the evil wider again, and brings danger on the others who have as yet been spared.   One would be willing to sacrifice oneself; but one knows that in risking this one risks sacrificing others also.

In such a dilemma there is only one helpful way—to give up life, not one's own merely, but also that of all one's dear ones—to assume that all is done with, and for each one to stand by the other in his hours of suffering, as long as they last. Looking backward, looking forward—all that must cease. Together!   On the deck of a sinking ship, no means of escape —" let us hold each other in our arms—close, close as possible, to the last moment ; and adieu, fair world ".

This resignation had come over us all.   The plan of flight had been given up; every one went to the bed of every patient, and of every one who had died.   Even Bresser no longer tried to keep us from this, the only humane way of acting.   His neighbourhood, his energetic, unresting rule gave us a certain feeling of security.   Our sinking ship was at least not without a captain.

Oh that cholera week in Grumitz!   Over twenty years have passed since then, but I still feel a shudder through my bones and marrow when I think of it.   Tears, wailing, heart-rending death-scenes, the smell of carbolic acid, the cracking of the bones of those seized with cramp, the disgusting symptoms, the incessant tolling of the death-bell, the interment—no, the huddling away—of the dead, for in such cases there is no funeral pomp.   All the order of life given up ; no meal times— the cook was dead.   No going to sleep at nights.   Here and there a morsel snatched standing, and a doze as one sat in one's chair in the morning hours.   Outside, as though from the irony of indifferent Nature, the most splendid summer weather; the joyous song of the blackbird, the luxuriant colours of the flower-beds. In the village, death without cessation. All the Prussians who were left behind were dead.

"I met the man who buries the dead to-day," said Francis, our *valet de chambre*, "as he was coming back from the church-yard with his empty carriage. 'One or two more taken there?' I asked. 'Oh yes; six or seven—about half-a-dozen every day, sometimes even more ; and it does happen sometimes that one or other gives a grunt or so inside the hearse there; but that makes no matter, in he goes into the trench, the d——d Prussian."

Next day the monster died himself, and another man had to take up his office—at that time the most laborious in the place. The post brought nothing but sorrow—news from all quarters of the ravages of the pest ; and love letters—letters to remain for ever unanswered—from Prince Henry, who knew nothing of what was going on. To Conrad I had sent a single line to prepare him for the awful event—"Lilly very ill". He could not come immediately, the service detained him. It was not till the fourth day that the poor fellow rushed into the house.

"Lilly!" he cried. "Is it true?" He had heard of the misfortune as he was on the way.

We said yes.

He remained unnaturally still and tearless.

"I have loved her many years," was all he said, low to himself. Then aloud: "Where is she lying? In the churchyard? Good-bye. She is waiting for me."

"Shall I come with you?" some one offered.

"No, I prefer going alone."

He went, and we saw him no more. On the grave of his sweetheart he put a bullet through his brains.

So ended Conrad Count Althaus, captain-lieutenant in the Fourth Regiment of Hussars, in his twenty-seventh year.

At another time the tragic nature of this event would have produced a very shocking effect; but now, how many young officers had not the war carried off immediately, this one only indirectly! And at the moment when we heard of his deed a new misfortune had occurred in our midst which called for all the anguish of our hearts. Otto, my poor father's adored and only son, was seized by the destroying angel. His sufferings lasted the whole night and the next day, with alternations of hope and despair; about 7 P.M. all was over. My father threw himself on the corpse with such a thrilling shriek that it pealed through the whole house. We could hardly tear him from the dead body. And oh! the cries of agony that now ensued; for hours and hours long the old man poured out howling, roaring, rattling shrieks of desperation. His son—his pride—his Otto —his all!

To this outburst succeeded on a sudden a stiff, dumb apathy. He had not had the strength to attend the burial of his darling. He lay on a sofa, motionless, and, it almost seemed, unconscious. Bresser ordered him to be undressed and put to bed.

After an hour he seemed to awake. Aunt Mary, Frederick and I were at his side. For a time he looked about him with a questioning look, and then sat up and tried to speak. He could not, however, pronounce a word and was struggling for breath, with a puzzled face of anguish. Then he began to shake and to throw himself about, as if he were attacked by those terrible cramps which are the last symptoms of the cholera, though he had not shown any of the other symptoms of it. At last he got out one word—"Martha!"

I fell on my knees at his bedside.

"Father, my poor, dear father!"

He held his hands over my head.

"Your wish," said he with difficulty, "may be fulfilled. I curse—I cur——"

He could get no further and sank back on his pillow.

In the meantime, Bresser had come in, and, in answer to our

anxious questions, gave us his opinion that a spasm of the heart had caused my father's death.

"The most terrible thing," said Aunt Mary after we had buried him, "is that he departed with a curse on his lips."

"Don't trouble about that, aunt," I said, to console her. "If that curse fell from the lips of everybody—yes, of everybody—it would be a great blessing to humanity."

.   .   .   .

Such was the cholera week at Grumitz. In the space of seven days nine inhabitants of the château had been snatched away: my father, Lilly, Rosa, Otto, my maid Netty, the cook, the coachman, and two grooms. In the village, during the same time, over eighty persons died.

Stated in this dry way all this sounds like a noteworthy statistical fact, or if it stands recorded in a tale book, like an extravagant play of the author's fancy. But it is neither so dry as the one nor so romantically terrible as the other. It is a cold, intelligible fact, full of sadness.

It was not Grumitz alone in our neighbourhood that was so hardly hit. Whoever chooses to search the annals of the neighbouring villages and châteaux may find there plenty of similar cases of enormous calamity. For example, there is Schloss Stockern, in the vicinity of the little town of Horn. Of the family which inhabited it, during the time from the 9th to the 13th of August, 1866, and also after the departure of the Prussian troops quartered there, four members of the family—Rudolf aged twenty, his sisters Emily and Bertha, and his uncle Candide; and, besides them, five of the servants succumbed to the plague. The youngest daughter, Pauline von Engelshofen, was spared. She afterwards married a Baron Suttner, and she, even now, still tells with a shudder the tale of the cholera week at Stockern.

At that time such a resignation to woe and death had come over me that I was in daily expectation that Death, whose characters had been stamped on the land for the last two months, would carry off myself and my loved ones. My

Frederick, my Rudolf; I actually wept for them in anticipation. And yet, along with all this, and in the midst of my trouble, I still had sweet moments. Such were when leaning on my husband's breast, and encircled by his loving arms, I could pour my tears out on his faithful heart. How gently then would he speak words to me, not of consolation, but of fellow-feeling and love ; so that my own heart warmed and expanded to them. No, the world is not so bad, I was compelled against my will to think. The world is not all lamentation and cruelty. Compassion and love are alive in it—at present, it is true, only in individual souls, not as an all-pervading law and a prevailing normal condition. Still they are *present ;* and just as these feelings glow in us twain, sweetening, by means of their gentle contact, even this time of suffering, just as they dwell in many other, nay, in *most* other souls, so they will one day come to an outbreak, and will dominate the general relations of the human family. The future belongs to goodness.

CHAPTER XV.

WE passed the remainder of the summer in the neighbourhood of Geneva. Dr. Bresser's powers of persuasion had at last succeeded in moving us to fly from the infected country. I at first strove against leaving so quickly the graves of my family, and, as I have said, I was filled with such a resignation to death that I had become wholly apathetic, and held every attempt at flight to be useless; but in spite of all this Bresser was certain to conquer when he represented to me that it was my maternal duty to carry little Rudolf out of the way of danger as well as I could.

That we chose Switzerland as our place of refuge resulted from Frederick's wish. He wanted to become acquainted with the men who had called the "Red Cross" into life, and to gain information on the spot about the proceedings of the conferences which had been held, as well as about the further aims of the convention.

Frederick had given in his resignation of the military service,

(327)

and as a preliminary had received half-a-year's leave till his request should be granted. I had now become rich, very rich. The death of my father, and of my brother and two sisters, had put me in possession of Grumitz and of the whole family property.

"Look here," I said to Frederick, when the title deeds were delivered to me from the notary's, "what would you say if I were now to praise the war which has just passed because of the advantages which have fallen to my share from its consequences?"

"Why, that you would not then be my Martha. Still I understand what you mean. The heartless egotism, which is capable of rejoicing over material gains that proceed out of the ruin of others—this impulse which every individual, even if he is base enough to feel it, still takes all possible care to hide—is proudly and openly confessed by nations and dynasties. 'Thousands have perished in untold sufferings; but we have thereby increased in territory and in power: so let there be praises and thanks to Heaven for the successful war!'"

We lived very quietly, and retired, in a small villa situated on the shore of the lake. I was so oppressed by the scenes through which I had gone, that I would have absolutely no intercourse with any strangers. Frederick respected my mourning, and made no attempt whatever to recommend me the vulgar resource of "diversion" as a cure for it; I owed it to the graves at Grumitz—and my tender husband saw this well—to grieve over them for some time in perfect quiet. Those who had been hurried so speedily and so cruelly out of this fair world should not be equally quickly and coldly stolen also out of the place of memory which they held in my mourning heart.

Frederick himself went often into the city, in order to follow up the object of his stay here—the study of the Red Cross question. Of the results of this study I do not retain any clear recollection. I did not at that time keep any diary; and thus what Frederick communicated to me of the experiences he met with has for the most part passed out of my recollection. I only recollect clearly one impression which the whole of my surroundings made on me—the quiet, the ease, the cheerful activity of the people whom I happened to see, as if they were living in a most peaceful, most good-humoured time. There was hardly anywhere even an echo of the war that had just ended, or at the most in a conversational tone, as if it had contributed one more interesting event—nothing more— which might furnish pleasant matter for talk along with the rest of European gossip: as if the awful thunder of the cannonades on the Bohemian battlefields had had nothing more tragic in them than a new opera by Wagner. The thing belonged now to history, and had for its result some alterations in the atlas; but its horror had passed out of recollection, or perhaps had never been present to these neutrals; it was forgotten; the pain was over; it had vanished. The same with the news- papers. I read French newspapers chiefly; all the interest was concentrated about the Universal Exhibition in Paris which was in preparation for 1867; about the court festivities at Compiègne; about literary celebrities (two new geniuses had come to light who caused much discussion, Flaubert and Zola); about the events of the drama—a new opera by Gounod—a new leading part designed by Offenbach for Hortense Schneider; and so forth. The little exciting duel which the Prussians and Austrians had fought out *là bas en Bohème* was an event that had already become to some extent a thing of the past. Ah! what lies three months back or at thirty miles' distance, what is not being played out in the domain of the Now and the Here, is a thing which the short feelers of the human heart and the human memory cannot reach! We quitted Switzerland towards the middle of October. We betook ourselves back to Vienna, where the course of the business of my inheritance required my presence. When this business was despatched, our intention was to stay for a considerable time at Paris. Frederick had it in his mind to smooth the way with all his power for the idea of a league of peace; and his view was that the projected Universal Exhibition offered the best opportunity

for setting on foot a congress of friends of peace, and he also
thought Paris the most appropriate place for giving actual
vitality to what was a matter of international concern.

"I have," he said, "renounced the trade of war, and that I
have done from convictions gained in actual war. I will now
work for these convictions. I enter the service of the peace
army. A very small army indeed, it is true, and one whose
combatants have no other shield or sword than the sentiment
of justice and the love of humanity. Still, everything which has
ultimately become great has started from small or invisible
beginnings."

"Ah!" I sighed; "it is a hopeless beginning. What can you
—a single man—achieve against that mighty fortress, thousands
of years old, and garrisoned by millions of men?"

"Achieve? I? I am not really so foolish as to hope that
I personally shall bring about a conversion. I was only saying
just then that I wished to enter the *ranks* of the peace-army.
When I had my place in the army of war, did I, do you suppose,
hope that *I* should save my country, that *I* should conquer a
province? No; the individual can only *serve*. And still
further, he *must* serve. A man who is penetrated by any cause
cannot do better than work for it—than devote his life to it,
even if he knows how little this life, in and by itself, can contribute towards its victory. He serves because he must; not only
the state, but our own conviction, if it is enthusiastic, lays on
us the duty of defending it."

"You are right, and if at length there are enough millions
animated by the enthusiasm of this duty, then that thousand-
year-old fortress will be abandoned by its garrison and must
fall."

From Vienna, I made a pilgrimage to Grumitz, whose
mistress I had now become. But I did not even enter the
château. I only laid down four wreaths in the churchyard,
and drove back again. After my most important matters of
business were put in order, Frederick proposed a little journey
to Berlin, in order to pay a visit to Aunt Cornelia, who was so

much to be pitied. I assented. During our absence I put my little son Rudolf in the charge of Aunt Mary. The latter had been cast down more than I can describe by the events of the cholera week at Grumitz. Her whole love, her whole interest in life, she now concentrated on my little Rudolf. I even hoped that she might be somewhat diverted and raised in her spirits by having the child with her for a time.

We left Vienna on November 1. We broke our journey in Prague, intending to spend the night there. Next day, instead of pursuing our journey to Berlin, we made a new pilgrimage.

"All Souls' Day," said I. "How many poor dead bodies are lying on the battlefield in this neighbourhood, for whom even this day of honour to the graves does nothing, because they have no graves. Who will pay them a visit?"

I looked at him for a while in silence. Then, half aloud, I said:—

"Will you?"

He nodded. We understood one another, and in an hour we were on our way to Chlum and Königgrätz.

．　．　．　．　．　．　．　．　．　．

What a prospect. An elegy of Tiedge came into my mind.

Oh, sight of horror! mighty prince, come, see,
　And o'er this awful heap of mouldering clay
Swear to thy folk a gentler lord to be,
　And give to earth the light of peaceful day.

Great leader, when thou thirstest for renown,
　Come, count these skulls, before the solemn hour
When thine own head must lay aside its crown,
　And in Death's silence ends thy dream of power.

Let the dread vision hover o'er thee ever
　Of these sad corpses here around thee strown,
And then say, does it charm thee, the endeavour
　Upon men's ruins to erect thy throne?

Yes, unfortunately it will charm men, so long as the histories of the world, i.e., those who write them, build the statues of their heroes out of the ruins of war, so long as they offer their crowns to the Titans of public murder. To refuse the laurel crown, to give up fame, would be nobler. Is that what the poet means? The first thing to do should be to despoil the thing, which it should appear so beneficent to renounce, of its glory, and then there would be no ambitious man any longer to grasp after it.

It was twilight already when we got to Chlum, and from thence walked on, arm in arm, to the battlefield, near at hand, in silent horror. A mist was falling, mingled with very fine snowflakes, and the dull branches of the trees were bent by the shrill-sounding pipe of a cold November wind. Crowds of graves, and the graves of crowds, were all around us. But a churchyard?—no. No pilgrim weary of life had there been invited to rest and peace; there, in the midst of their youthful fire of life, exulting in the fullest strength of their manhood, the waiters on the future had been cast down by force, and had been shovelled down into their grave mould. Choked up, stifled, made dumb for ever, all those breaking hearts, those bloody mangled limbs, those bitterly-weeping eyes, those wild shrieks of despair, those vain prayers.

On this field of war it was not lonely. There were many —very many—whom All Souls' Day had brought hither, from friends' and enemies' country, who were come here to kneel down on the ground where what they loved most had fallen. The train itself which brought us was full of other mourners, and thus I had heard now for several hours weeping and wailing going on around me. "Three sons—three sons, each one more beautiful and better and dearer than the others, have I lost at Sadowa," said to us an old man who looked quite broken down. Many others, besides, of our companions in the carriage mingled their complaints with his—for brother, husband, father. But none of these made so much impression on me as the tearless, mournful "Three sons—three sons" of the poor old man.

On the field one saw on all sides, and on all the roads, black figures walking, or kneeling, or painfully staggering along and breaking out from time to time into loud sobs. There were only a few there who were buried by themselves—few crosses or stones with an inscription. We bent down and deciphered, as well as the twilight permitted, some of the names.

"Major v. Reuss of the Second Regiment of the Prussian Guards."

"Perhaps a relation of the one engaged to our poor Rosa," I remarked.

"Count Grünne. Wounded, July 3. Died, July 5."

What might he not have suffered in those two days! Was he, I wondered, a son of the Count Grünne who uttered, before the war, the well-known sentence: "We are going to chase the Prussians away—wet foot"? Ah, how frantic and blasphemous! how shrilly out of tune sounds of a surety every word of provocation spoken before a war when one stands on a place like this! Words, and nothing more, boasting words, scornful words, spoken, written and printed; it is *these* alone that have sown the seed of fields like these.

We walk on. Everywhere earth heaps, more or less high, more or less broad, and even there where the earth is not elevated, even under our feet, soldiers' corpses are perhaps mouldering!

The mist grows thicker constantly. "Frederick, pray put your hat on, you will take cold."

But Frederick remained uncovered, and I did not repeat my warning a second time.

Among the mourners who were wandering about here were also many officers and soldiers, probably such as had themselves shared in the nobly contested day of Königgrätz, and now were making a pilgrimage to the place where their fallen comrades were sleeping.

We had now come to the spot where the largest number of warriors, friend and foe together, lay entombed. The place was walled off like a churchyard. Hither came the greatest number of mourners, because in this spot there was most chance that their dear ones might be entombed. Round this enclosure the bereaved ones were kneeling and sobbing, and here they hung up their crosses and their grave-lights.

A tall, slender man, of distinguished, youthful figure, in a general's cloak, came up to the mound. The others gave place reverently to him, and I heard some voices whisper: "The emperor".

Yes, it was Francis Joseph. It was the lord of the country, the supreme lord of war, who had come on All Souls' Day to offer up a silent prayer for the dead children of his country, for his fallen warriors. He also stood with uncovered and bowed head there, in agonised devotion, before the majesty of Death.

Long, long he stood without moving. I could not turn my eyes away from him. What thoughts must be passing through his soul, what feelings through his heart, which after all was, as I knew, a good and a soft heart? It came into my mind that I could feel with him, that I could think the thoughts at the same time as he, which were passing through that bowed head of his.

You, my poor, brave fellows, dead, and what for? No, we have not conquered. My Venice—lost. So much lost—ah, so much! and your young lives too. And you gave them so devotedly—for me. Oh, if I could give them back to you! I, for my part, never desired the sacrifice; it was for you, for your country, that you, the children of my country, were led forth to this war! And not by my means; no, not though it was at my order, for was I not *compelled* to give the order? The subjects do not exist for my sake. No, I was called to the throne for their sakes, and any hour have I been ready to die for the weal of my people. Oh, had I followed the impulse of my heart, and never said "Yes," when all around me were shouting "War!" "War!" Still, could I have resisted them? God is my witness that I could not. What impelled me, what forced me, at this moment, I do not know exactly, only so much I know, that it was an irresistible pressure from without, from yourselves, ye dead soldiers! Oh, how mournful,

mournful, mournful ! How I have suffered for it all ! and now
you are lying here, and on other battlefields, snatched away by
grape-shot and sabre-cuts, by cholera and typhus ! Oh, if I had
said " No ! " You begged me to do so, Elizabeth. Oh, if I
had said it ! The thought is intolerable that —— Oh, it is
a miserable, imperfect world—too much, too much of woe !

During the whole time that I was thinking thus for him, I
fastened my eyes on his features, and now—yes, just as I came
to " too much—too much of woe "—now he covered his face
with both hands, and broke out into a hot flood of tears.

So passed All Souls' Day on the battlefield of Sadowa.

.   .   .   .

We found the city of Berlin in the height of jubilation.
Every counter-jumper and every street-loafer bore on his countenance a certain consciousness of victory. " We have given
the fellows there a good licking." That appears anyhow to
be a very elevating feeling, and one which may be spread over
the whole population. Still, in the families which we visited,
we found many people deeply cast down, those, that is to say,
who had one never to be forgotten lying dead on the German
or Bohemian battlefields. For my own part, I feared most the
meeting with Aunt Cornelia again. I knew that her handsome
son Godfrey was her idol, her all, and I could judge of the pang
which the poor bereaved mother must now be experiencing. I
had only to fancy to myself that my Rudolf, if I had brought
him up to manhood—no, that thought I absolutely refused to
think out.

Our visit was announced. With a beating heart I entered
Fr. v. Tessow's house. Even in the ante-chamber, the mourning
which reigned in the house was perceptible. The footman who
opened the door for us wore a black livery ; in the great reception-room, the chairs of which were covered over with chair
covers, there was no fire lighted ; and the mirrors and pictures
on the walls were all covered with crape. From hence, the
door into Aunt Cornelia's bedroom was opened for us, and she

received us there. It was a very large room, divided into two
by a curtain, behind which the bed stood; and it served Aunt
Cornelia now as her regular reception-room. She no longer
quitted the house at all, except every Sunday to go to the
cathedral, and very seldom her room, except for one hour
every day, which she spent in what had been Godfrey's study.
In this everything was left standing or lying as he had left it
on the day of his departure. She took us into it, in the course
of our visit, and made us read a letter, which he had laid on
his portfolio.

"My own dear Mother,—I know well that you will come here
after my departure, and then you will find this letter. My personal departure is over. So much the more will it please and
surprise you to find one *more* line, to hear one more last word
from me, and indeed a joyful, hopeful one. Be of good cheer.
I shall come back again. Two hearts, that hang together so
entirely as ours do, fate will not tear asunder. I have settled
that I am now going to serve through a fortunate campaign,
gain stars and crosses, and then make you a grandmother six
times over. I kiss your hand, I kiss your dear soft forehead.
O you most adored of all little mothers."

"YOUR GODFREY."

When we went into Aunt Cornelia's room, she was not alone.
A gentleman in a long black coat, recognisable at the first
glance as a clergyman, was sitting opposite to her.

She got up and came to meet us. The clergyman rose at
the same time from his seat, but remained standing in the
background.

What I expected occurred. When I embraced the old lady
both of us, she and I, broke out into loud sobs. Frederick
also did not remain dry-eyed as he pressed the mourner to his
heart. In this first minute no word at all was spoken. All
that one can say at such a moment, at one's first meeting after
a severe misfortune, is sufficiently expressed by tears.

She led us back to the place where they were sitting, and pointed us to chairs that stood there. Then, after drying her eyes, she made the introduction.

"My nephew, Colonel Baron Tilling—Herr Mölser, head military chaplain and consistorial councillor."

Silent bows were exchanged.

"My friend and spiritual adviser," she proceeded, "who has allowed me to lay on him the burden of instructing me in my trouble."

"But who unfortunately has not succeeded in instilling into you the proper resignation, the proper joy in bearing the cross, my valued friend," said he. "Why is it that I have always to witness a fresh outburst of these very foolish tears?"

"Oh, forgive me! When I last saw my nephew with his sweet young wife, my Godfrey was there."

She could speak no further.

"Your son was there, in this sinful world, still exposed to all temptations and dangers, while now he has gone into the bosom of the Father, after meeting with the most glorious and most blessed of deaths for king and country.

"You, colonel," turning now to my husband, "who have just been introduced to me as a soldier, can assist me to give to this afflicted mother the consolation that her son's fate is an enviable one. You must know what delight in death animates the brave warrior; the resolve to offer his life as a sacrifice on the altar of his country glorifies for him all the pain of departing this life; and, though he sinks in the storm of the battle amidst the thunder of the artillery, yet he expects to be transferred to the great army on high, and to be present when the Lord of Sabaoth holds muster above. You, colonel, have come back in the number of those to whom Divine Providence has granted a righteous victory."

"Forgive me, reverend consistorial councillor, I was in the Austrian service."

"Oh, I thought —— Oh, really," replied the other, quite confused. "A grand, brave army too is the Austrian." He

22

rose. "But I will not intrude longer. You will be wishing, doubtless, to talk of family matters. Farewell, dear lady ; in a few days I will come again. Till then, raise your thoughts to the All-merciful, without whose will not a hair falls from our heads, and who causes all things to serve for the good of those that love Him—even sorrow and suffering, even privation and death. I salute you with all devotion."

My aunt shook his hand.

"I hope I shall see you soon. Very soon, pray."

He bowed to us all, and was stepping towards the door when Frederick detained him.

"Reverend consistorial councillor, may I ask you a favour?"

"Pray tell me what it is, colonel."

"I conclude from your conversation that you are penetrated equally by the religious and the military spirit. In that case you might do me a great pleasure."

I listened with interest. What could Frederick mean?

"The fact is," he continued, "that my little wife here is full of scruples and doubts of all sorts. Her opinion is that, from a Christian point of view, war is not quite permissible. I, of course, know to the contrary, for there is no alliance closer than that between the professions of priest and soldier, but I have not the eloquence to make this clear to my wife. Would you then, reverend consistorial councillor, so far favour us as to give us, to-morrow or next day, an hour of your conversation, with the view ——"

"Oh, with great pleasure," the clergyman said, interrupting him. "Will you give me your address?"

Frederick gave him his card, and the day and hour of the visit he asked for were fixed at once. Then we remained alone with our aunt.

"Does your intercourse with this friend really afford you consolation?" asked Frederick.

"Consolation? There is no consolation for me any more here below. But he speaks so much and so beautifully about the things which I like most to hear of—about death and mourning, about the cross and sacrifice and resignation—he paints the world which my poor Godfrey had to leave, and from which I long to be released, as such a vale of misery, of corruption, of sin, and of advancing ruin. . . . And so it seems to me a little less mournful that my child has been called away. He is assuredly in heaven, and here on this earth ——"

"The powers of hell often prevail. That is true. I have again seen proof of that close to me," replied Frederick thoughtfully.

The poor lady next questioned him about the two campaigns that he had passed through—the one with, the other against, Godfrey. He had to relate hundreds of details, and in doing so he was able to give the bereaved mother the same comfort that he once brought me back from the war in Italy, namely, that the lamented one had died a rapid and painless death. It was a long and a mournful visit. I also again recounted there all the details of the horrible cholera week, and my experiences on the Bohemian battlefields. Before we left, Aunt Cornelia took us into Godfrey's room, where I wept bitter tears anew at the perusal of the letter which I have quoted above, and of which at a later period I begged a copy.

.   .   .   .

"Now explain to me," I said to Frederick, as we got into our carriage, which was in waiting in front of Aunt Cornelia's villa, "why you asked the consistorial councillor ——"

"To a conference with you? Do not you understand? That is to serve me as material for study. I want to hear once more—and this time to take note of—the arguments by which priests defend public murder. I put you forward as the leader in the fray. It better becomes a young lady to nourish a doubt from the Christian point of view as to the lawfulness of war than a 'gallant colonel'!"

"But you know that my doubt is not from a religious, but a humanitarian point of view."

"We must not lay this at all before the reverend consistorial councillor, or else the discussion would be transferred to a different field. The efforts after peace of free thinkers suffer from no internal inconsistency, but it is this very inconsistency existing between the maxims of Christianity and the orders of military authorities which I should like to hear explained by a military chaplain, *i.e.*, a representative of militant Christianity."

The clergyman was punctual in his arrival. The prospect was evidently an inviting one for him of having to preach a sermon of instruction and conversion. I on the contrary looked forward to the conversation with somewhat painful feelings, for the part assigned to me in it was a dishonest one. But, for the good of the cause to which Frederick had devoted his services henceforth, I was easily able to put some constraint on myself, and comfort myself with the proverb: "The end justifies the means".

After the first greetings—we were all three seated on low, easy-chairs before the fire—the consistorial councillor began thus :—

"Allow me, dear lady, to enter on the object of my visit. The matter is to remove from your soul some scruples, which are not destitute of some apparent grounds, but which can easily be refuted as sophistical. You think, for example, that Christ's command to love your enemies, and also the text, 'He who takes the sword shall perish by the sword,' are inconsistent with the duties of a soldier, who no doubt is empowered to injure the enemy in body and life."

"Certainly, reverend councillor, this inconsistency seems to me irreconcilable. Then there occurs also the express command of the Decalogue, 'Thou shalt not kill'."

"Oh, yes, to a superficial judgment there is some difficulty in that, but on penetrating deeper all doubt vanishes. As regards the fifth commandment, it would be more correctly given (as it is actually in the English version of the Bible): 'Thou shalt not murder'. Killing for necessary defence is not murder. And war is in reality only necessary defence on a large scale. We can and we ought, following the gentle precept of our Saviour, to love our enemies, but that does not mean that we are not to venture to defend ourselves from open wrong and violence."

"Then does it not follow of course from this that only defensive wars are justifiable, and that no sword-stroke ought to be given till the enemy has invaded the country? But if the opposing nation proceeds on the same principle, how then can the battle ever begin? In the late war it was your army, reverend councillor, which first crossed the frontier, and ——"

"If one wishes to keep the foe off, dear lady, as we have the most sacred right to do, it is utterly unnecessary to put off the favourable opportunity, and to wait until he has first invaded one's country. On the contrary, the sovereign must, under all circumstances, have freedom to anticipate the violent and unjust. In doing so he is following the written word: 'He who takes the sword shall perish by the sword'. He presents himself as God's servant and avenger on the enemy, because he strives to make him, as he has taken the sword against him, perish by the sword."

"There must be some fallacy in that," I said, shaking my head. "It is impossible that these principles should justify both parties equally."

"And as to the further scruple," pursued the clergyman, without noticing my remark, "that war is of and by itself displeasing to God, this must depart from every Christian who believes in the Bible, for the Holy Scriptures sufficiently prove that the Lord Himself gave commands to the people of Israel to wage wars, in order to conquer the promised land, and He granted them victory and His blessing on their wars. In Numbers xxi. 14, a special 'book of the wars of the Lord' is spoken of. And how often in the Psalms is the assistance celebrated which God has granted to His people in war! Do you not know what Solomon says (Proverbs xxi. 31): 'The horse is prepared against the day of battle, but safety is of the Lord'? In Psalm cxliv. David thanks and praises the

Lord, his strength, 'who teacheth his hand to war, and his fingers to fight'."

"Then a contradiction prevails between the Old and the New Testament—the God of the ancient Hebrews was a warlike Deity, but the gentle Jesus proclaimed the message of peace, and taught love to neighbour and to enemy."

"In the New Testament also, Jesus speaks in a figure (Luke xiv. 31) without the least blame of a king who is going to make war against another king. And how often, too, does not the Apostle Paul use figures from the military life? He says (Rom. xiii. 4) that the magistrate does not bear the sword in vain, but is God's servant—a revenger on him that doeth evil."

"Well, then, in that case the contradiction I mean exists in the Holy Scripture itself. By your showing me that it is present in the Bible you do not remove it."

"There one sees the superficial and at the same time arrogant method of judgment which seeks to exalt one's own weak reason above the Word of God. Contradiction is something imperfect, ungodlike; and if I show that a thing is in the Bible the proof is complete that in itself—however incomprehensible it may be to the human understanding—it can contain no contradiction."

"Unless the presence of contradiction does not much rather prove that the passages in question cannot possibly be of Divine origin." This answer trembled on my lips, but I suppressed it, in order not to change entirely the object of the discussion.

"Look here, reverend councillor," said Frederick, now mingling in the conversation, "a chief captain of artillery in the seventeenth century has laid down much more forcibly than you have done the justifiability of the horrors of war by an appeal to the Bible. I extracted the passage and have read it to my wife, but she did not sympathise with the spirit expressed in it. I confess the thing seems to me—well, a little strong—and I should like to hear your view about it. If you will allow me I will fetch the paper." So he took a sheet of paper out of a drawer, unfolded it, and read :—

War was invented by God Himself and taught to men. God posted the first soldier with a two-edged sword in front of Paradise, to keep out of it Adam, the first rebel. You may read in Deuteronomy how God, by means of Moses, gives people encouragement to victory and even gives them His priests for advanced guard.

The first stratagem was practised at the city of Ai. In this war of the Jews the sun had to stand and show light in the firmament for two whole days together in order that the war and the victory might be followed up, and many thousands put to the sword and their kings hung up. All the horrors of war are permitted by God, for the whole of Holy Writ is full of them, and proves satisfactorily that regular war is an invention of God Himself, and that therefore every man can with a clear conscience serve in it, and can live and die in it. He is permitted to burn his enemy, or brand him, flay him, shoot him down, or hack him to pieces. All this is just, let others judge as they please about it. God in these passages has forbidden nothing, but has permitted the most horrible ways of destroying men.

The prophetess Deborah nailed the head of Sisera, the leader in that war, to the earth. Gideon, chosen by God as the leader of the people, revenged himself on the princes of Succoth, who had refused him some provisions, like a soldier; sword and fire were too poor, they were thrashed and torn in pieces with thorns; and, as before, this was righteous in the sight of God. The royal prophet David, a man after God's own heart, invented the most cruel tortures for the vanquished children of Ammon at Rabboth—he had them hewed with sabres, caused chariots to drive over them, cut them with knives, and dragged them through the places where they made the bricks, and so did he in all the towns of the children of Ammon. Besides this ——

"That is horrible, abominable!" broke in the chief chaplain. "It could only be a rough soldier of the savage times of the Thirty Years' War to whom it would appear natural to produce examples like these out of the Bible, in order to found thereon a justification for their cruelties against the enemy. We preach quite other doctrine now—nothing more is to be striven for in war than to make your adversary incapable of harm—even up to his death—but without any evil design against the life of any individual. If any such design enters in, or even any murderous desire or any cruelty against those who are defenceless, in such a case killing in war is exactly as immoral and as impermissible as in peace. No doubt in past centuries, when the adventurous

delight in feud and quarrel prevailed, when leaders of Lands-
knechts and vagrant persons carried on war as a trade, in such
times an artillery captain might write in that style; but in
the present day armies are not put into the field for gold
and booty, not without knowing for whom or for what, but
for the highest ideal objects of mankind—for freedom,
independence, nationality; for justice, faith, honour, purity and
morality ——"

" You, reverend consistorial councillor," I interposed, "are at
least milder and more humane than the artillery captain.   And
thus you have no proofs out of the Bible to allege for the lawfulness of cruelty, in which our forefathers of the middle ages,
and presumably also the ancient Hebrews, took a pleasure; and
yet it is the same book, and the same Jehovah, and He cannot
have become milder—and everybody still gets from Him as much
support as suits his views."

On this I received a slight sermon of rebuke for my want of
reverence for the Word of God, and for my want of judgment
in reading it.

Still I succeeded in leading the conversation back again to
our especial subject; and now the consistorial councillor
launched out into a long dissertation, and one which this time
was allowed to be uninterrupted, about the connection between
the military and Christian spirits; he spoke of the religious
devotion " which is indwelling in the oath to the standard, when
the colours are carried solemnly, with the accompaniment of
music, into the church, with the guard of honour of two officers
with drawn swords; and there the recruit marches out for the
first time in public with helmet and side-arms, and for the first
time follows the colours of his company, unfolded now before
the altar of the Lord torn as they are and stained with the
honourable marks of the battles in which they have been
carried".   He spoke of the prayer offered every Sunday in
church: "Preserve the royal commander of the army, and all
true servants of their king and country.   Teach them as Chris-
tians to think of their end, and grant that their service may be

blessed, to the honour and the good of the country." "God with us," he went on, "is, as you know, the motto on the belt-buckle with which the foot-soldier buckles on his side-arms, and this watchword should give him confidence. If God be with us, who can be against us? Then there are also the universal days of public prayer and humiliation which are ordered at the commencement of a war that the people may beg for God's help in prayer, both in the comfortable hope of His support and in the confidence through that support of gaining a victorious termination. What devotion does there not lie in this for the departing warrior! How mightily does this exalt his delight in battle and in death! He can with comfort enter into the ranks of the warriors when his king calls for him, and can reckon on victory and blessing for the cause of right. God the Lord will no more deprive our people of this than His people Israel of old, if only it is with prayers to Him that we carry on the work of battle. The intimate alliance between prayer and victory, between piety and valour, easily follows—for what can more assure one of joy in the prospect of death than the confidence that if our last hour should strike in the confusion of the battle we shall find favour at the hands of the Judge in heaven? Fidelity and faith, in union with manliness and warlike virtue, belong to the oldest traditions of our people."

He went on in this tone for a long time more—now with oily mildness, with sunken head, in the softest tones speaking of love, humility, "little children," salvation, and "precious things"—now with military voice of command, with a proud, erect attitude, talking of strict morals and stern discipline—sharp and cutting—of sword and shield. The word "joy" was never used otherwise than in composition with death, battle, and dying. From the point of view of the army chaplain, to kill and to be killed seemed to be the most exquisite delights in life. Everything else is exhausting, sinful pleasure. Verses, too, were recited. First this of Körner:—

Father, do Thou guide me!
Guide me to victory—guide me to death!
Lord, I confess Thy command.
Lord, as Thou willest, so guide me!
God, I confess Thee.

Then the old popular song of the Thirty Years' War :—

No happier death on earth can be
  Than one good stroke from mortal foe,
On fresh green turf, in breezes free—
  No woman's tears, no cries of woe:
No grim deathbed, whence, lone and slow,
From life's gay scene your soul must go.
Like swathes of grass, in lusty row,
'Mid shouting friends, Death lays you low.

And then the song by Lenau of the war-loving armourer :—

Peace steals on, and, mining slowly,
  Saps our vigour, dims our story.
While she boasts her "influence holy,"
  Cobwebs gather o'er our glory.
Hark! then sounds War's joyous rattle.
Wounds may yawn, blood flow, in battle!
We need yawn in sloth no longer,
War's pruning makes mankind the stronger.

And, to conclude, the saying of Luther :—

"When I look at war as a thing that protects wife, child, house, land, goods, and honour—and in doing so gains peace and secures it—in that view war is a right precious thing".

"Oh, yes; if I look at the panther as a dove, in that case the panther is a very gentle beast," I remarked unheard.

The military chaplain did not allow himself to be disturbed in his flow of eloquence; and, when he ended and took leave. I found myself with two convictions: that war from the Christian point of view is a justifiable, and in and by itself is a precious, thing. It was visibly a very agreeable thing to him to have, by means of this rhetorical victory, both fulfilled the duty of his profession, and in doing so rendered a considerable service to the foreign colonel; for, as he rose to go, and we expressed to him our thanks for the trouble he had been so good as to undertake, he deprecatingly rejoined :—

"It is for me to thank you for having given me an opportunity of chasing away your doubts through my feeble word (whose entire efficacy is to be ascribed to the Word of God, which I have so often quoted), doubts which are of such a nature as to bring nothing but pain to a person who is not only a Christian but a soldier's wife. Peace be with you."

"Oh," I groaned, when he was gone, "that was a torture !"

"Yes," said Frederick; "it was. Our want of straightforwardness especially was uncomfortable to me, and particularly the false premises under which we got him to display his eloquence. At one moment I was on the point of saying to him : 'Stop, reverend sir, I myself entertain the same views against war as my wife, and what you are saying only serves, as far as I am concerned, to enable me to see more clearly the weakness of your arguments'. But I held my tongue. Why interfere with an honest man's conviction—a conviction which is besides the foundation of his profession in life ? "

"Conviction ? Are you certain of that ? Does he really believe that he is speaking the truth, or does he purposely deceive his common soldiers, when he promises them an assured victory through the assistance of a God of whom he nevertheless must know this—that He is invoked in exactly the same way by the enemy ? These appeals to 'our people' and to 'our cause' as the only righteous one, and one which is God's cause too, were surely only possible at a time when one people shut out all other peoples, and considered itself as the only one entitled to exist—the only one beloved of God. And then all these promises of heaven, with the view of more easily procuring the sacrifice of earthly life, all these ceremonies, consecrations, oaths, hymns which are intended to awaken in the breast of the man ordered into war that 'joy in death' (repulsive words to me !) which they so admire ; is it not——"

"Everything has two sides, Martha," said Frederick interrupting me. "It is because we deprecate war that everything which supports and excuses it, everything which veils its horrors, appears hateful to us."

"Yes, of course; because the hateful thing is upheld thereby."

"But not thereby only. All institutions stand on roots of a thousand fibres, and as long as they exist it must be a good thing that those feelings and methods of thought should persist by which they are excused, by which they are rendered not only tolerable, but even beloved. How many a poor fellow is helped through his death-agony by that same 'joy in death' into which he has been educated! how many a pious soul relies in all confidence on the help of God of which he has been assured by the preacher! how much innocent vanity and proud feeling of honour are awakened and satisfied by those ceremonies! how many hearts beat higher at the sound of those hymns! From the total of the pain which war has brought on men, we must at least deduct that pain which war poets and war preachers have contrived to sing away and lie away."

. . . .

We were summoned away from Berlin very hurriedly. A telegram announced to me that Aunt Mary was very ill and wished to see me.

I found the old lady given up by her physicians.

"It is my turn now," she said. "For my own part I am right willing to go. Since my poor brother and the three children were snatched away, this world has had no more joy for me. Apart from anything else, I shall never more have the strength to bear up after such a blow. I shall find the others there above. Conrad and Lilly are also united there; it was not ordained that they should be united here on earth."

"If they had finished their arrangements in proper time . . ." I was disposed to say in opposition, but I stopped myself. I could not surely raise any discussion with this dying person, and still less try to unsettle her about her favourite theory of "pre-ordination".

"I have one comfort," she went on, "that you at least, dear Martha, remain behind happy; the cholera has spared you, and that proves clearly that it is ordained for you to grow old in company. Only try to make of your little Rudolf a good Christian and a good soldier, so that his grandfather up in heaven may still find his joy in him."

Even on this point I preferred to keep silence, for I was firmly resolved to make no soldier of my son.

"I will pray for you incessantly, so that you may live long and happily."

Of course I did not dwell on the inconsistency that an "inevitable destiny" could be influenced in one's favour by incessant prayer; but I interrupted the poor creature by begging her not to exhaust herself with talking, and, in order to distract her attention, told her about our doings in Switzerland and Berlin. I also related how we met Prince Henry, and that he had caused to be erected in the park of his castle a marble monument in memory of the bride whom he had lost as soon as won.

Three days afterwards poor Aunt Mary fell asleep, resigned and calm, fortified with the sacrament for the dying, which she had herself begged for and which she received with devotion; and thus were all my relations gone from the earth, all those in whose midst I had been brought up.

In her will the entire inheritance of her little fortune was left to my son Rudolf, and as his trustee Minister "To-be-sure" was nominated.

This circumstance brought me now into frequent contact with this old friend of my father. He was also pretty nearly the only visitor at our house. The deep mourning into which the unhappy week at Grumitz had plunged me caused me as a matter of course to live in perfect retirement. Our plan of settling in Paris could not be carried out till all my affairs were put in order, and in any case several months more would be necessary for that.

Our friend the Minister, who, as I have said, formed almost the whole of our society, had in these latter days either received

or obtained his discharge—I never quite fathomed the matter—
but in short he had withdrawn into private life, but he was still
as fond as ever of busying himself about politics.   He continually contrived to turn the conversation on to this his favourite
theme, and we also willingly took our share in it.   As Frederick
was now occupying himself so busily with the study of international law, any discussion was welcome to him which touched
on this province.   After dinner (Mr. "To-be-sure"—for we always
between ourselves made use of this nickname for him—was
always asked to dine at our house twice a week) the two gentlemen would plunge into a long political conversation ; but in
doing this my husband took care not to let this conversation
turn into the political gossip which he so hated, but was careful
to lead it to views of more general interest.   In this, to be sure,
Mr. "To-be-sure" could not always follow him, for in his character
as an inveterate diplomatist and official he had accustomed himself to follow what is called "practical politics"—a thing which
is directed merely to the private interests which lie nearest to
hand and knows nothing about the theoretical questions of social
science.

I sat by, busy over some needlework, and took no share in
the conversation—a thing which seemed quite natural to the
Minister ; for politics is, as is well known, far "too high a thing"
for ladies ; he was sure that I was thinking all the time of other
things, whilst I, on the contrary, was listening very attentively,
since it was my business to impress the tenor of this dialogue
on my memory, in order to transfer it afterwards into the red
book.   Frederick made no secret of his opinions, though he
knew what a thankless part it is to set oneself to oppose what
is generally received, and to defend ideas whilst they are in the
stage when—even if they are not condemned as subversive—
still they are derided as fantastic.

"I am in a position to-day to communicate to you an
interesting piece of news, dear Tilling," said the Minister one
afternoon with an air of importance.   "People in government
circles—that is to say, in the ministry of war—are ventilating

the idea of introducing a universal liability to service amongst us also."

"What? the same system which before the war was so universally condemned and derided among us? 'Tailors in arms,' and so on?"

"To be sure we had a prejudice against it a short time since. Still, it has rendered good service to the Prussians you must allow. And, in fact, from the moral point of view, and even from the democratic and liberal point of view, for which you occasionally appear so enthusiastic, it is surely a just and elevating thing that every son of his fatherland, without any regard to his position or stage of education, should have to fulfil the same duties. And from a strategic point of view, could little Prussia have been always victorious if she had not had the Landwehr; and if the latter had been introduced amongst us before, should we have been always beaten?"

"Well, the meaning of that is, that if we had had more material, the material which our enemy had would not have served him. Ergo—if the Landwehr were introduced everywhere it would not benefit anybody. The war game would be played with more pieces, but the game nevertheless depends still on the luck and the ability of the players. I will suppose that all the European powers have introduced the obligation of universal defence; the proportion of forces in that case remains exactly the same, the only difference would be that, in order to come to a decision, instead of hundreds of thousands, millions would have to be slaughtered."

"But do you think it just and fair that a part only of the population should sacrifice themselves in order to protect the dearest possessions of the others, and that these others, chiefly because they are rich, should be entitled to stop quietly at home? No, no; that will cease with this new law. Then there will be no more buying-off—every one will have to take his part. And it is especially the educated—the students—those who have some learning, who will contribute the elements of intelligence and therefore of victory."

"The other side has the same elements ready to hand, and so the advantages to be gained from educated petty officers neutralise each other. On the other hand, what remains (and equally to both sides) is the loss of material of priceless mental worth, of which the country is deprived by the fact that the most educated, those who might have promoted its civilisation by means of inventions, works of art, or scientific inquiry, are set up in rank and file to be marks for the enemy's shot ——"

"Oh, well! for making inventions, and producing works of art, and investigating skull-bones, and all sorts of things of that kind, which do not advance the position of the state's power one drachm ——"

"Hm!"—"What?" "Oh, nothing; go on."

"For all that there remains plenty of time for people. And besides they need not serve for the whole of their life; but a few years of strict discipline are assuredly good for everybody, and make them only so much the more competent to fulfil their other duties as citizens. We must in the present state of things pay the blood tax some time—so it ought to be divided between all equally."

"There would be something to say for that, if it fell less heavily on individuals on that account. But that would not be the case; the blood tax would not be *divided* by that measure, but increased. I hope the project may not be carried out. There is no seeing whither it may lead. One state would then try to outvie the other in strength of army, till at last there would no longer be any armies, but only armed nations. More people would be constantly drawn into the service; the length of service would be constantly increased; the incidence of war taxes and the costs of armaments constantly greater;—so that without fighting each other the nations would all come to ruin in making preparations for war!"

"But, dear Tilling, you look too far."

"One can never look too far. Everything a man undertakes he ought to think out to its remotest consequence —at least as far as his mind reaches. We were likening war just now to a game at chess. Politics also is of the same nature, your excellency, and those are only very feeble players who look no further forward than a single move, and are quite pleased with themselves if they have got into a position in which they can threaten a pawn. I want to develop the thought of defensive forces constantly increasing and the universal extension of liability to military service still more widely, till we reach the extremest verge, *i.e.*, where the mass becomes excessive. What then, if after the greatest numbers and the furthest limits of age are reached, one nation should take it into its head to recruit regiments of women too? The others must imitate it. Or battalions of boys? The others must imitate it. And in the armaments—in the means of destruction—where can the limit be? Oh this savage, blind leap into the pit!"

"Calm yourself, dear Tilling. You are a genuine faddist. If you could only point me out a means to do away with war it would be a perfect benefit, to be sure. But as that is not possible, every nation must surely endeavour to prepare itself for it as well as possible, in order to assure itself of the greatest chance of winning in the inevitable 'struggle for existence'— that is the cant word of the fashionable Darwinism, is it not?"

"If I should choose to suggest to you the means of doing away with wars, you would again call me a silly faddist, a sentimental dreamer rendered morbid by the 'humanitarian craze' —that, I think, is the cant word in favour with the war party, is it not?"

"To be sure, I cannot conceal from you that no practical foundation exists for the realisation of such an ideal. One must calculate with the actual factors. In these are classed the passions of men; their rivalries; the divergences of interests; the impossibility of coming to an agreement on all questions."

"But that is not necessary. When disagreements begin an arbitration tribunal—not force—is to decide."

23

"The sovereign states would never betake themselves to such a tribunal—nor would the peoples."

"The peoples? The potentates and diplomatists would not —but the people? Just inquire, and you will find that the wish for peace is warm and true in the people, while the peaceful assurances which proceed from the governments are frequently lies, hypocritical lies—or at least are regarded as such on principle by other governments. That is precisely what is called 'diplomacy'. And the peoples will go on ever more and more calling for peace. If the general obligation of defence should extend, the dislike of war will increase in the same proportion. A class of soldiers animated with love for their calling is, of course, imaginable; their exceptional position, which they take for a position of honour, is offered to them as a recompense for the sacrifices which it entails, but when the exception ceases the distinction ceases also. The admiring thankfulness disappears which those who stay at home offer to those who go out in their defence,—because then there will be no one to stay at home. The war-loving feelings which are always being suggested to the soldier—and in so doing are often awakened in him—will be more seldom kindled; for who are those that are of the most heroic spirit, who are most warm in their enthusiasm for the exploits and dangers of war? Those who are safe against them—the professors, the politicians, the beer-shop chatterers—the chorus of old men, as it is called in 'Faust'. When the safety is lost, that chorus will be silenced. Besides, if not only those devote themselves to the military life who love and praise it, but all those also are forcibly dragged into it who look on it with horror, that horror must work. Poets, thinkers, friends of humanity, timid persons, all these will, from their own points of view, curse the trade they are forced into."

"But they will beyond doubt have to keep silent about this way of thinking, in order not to pass for cowards—in order not to expose themselves to the displeasure of the higher powers."

"Keep silence? Not for ever. As I talk—though I have

myself kept silence long—so will the others also break out into speech. If the thought ripens, the word will come. I am an individual who have come to the age of forty before my conviction acquired sufficient strength to expand itself in words. , And as I have required two or three decades, so the masses will perhaps require two or three generations—but speak they will at last."

CHAPTER XVI.

THE New Year, '67 ! We kept the Sylvester Night quite alone, my Frederick and I. When it struck twelve,—

"Do you recollect," I asked with a sigh, "the speech my poor father made in proposing a toast last year at this same hour? I do not dare to wish you good fortune now. The future sometimes hides something so unexpectedly terrible in its bosom ; and no wish has ever availed to turn it aside."

"Then let us use the turn of the year, Martha, as an occasion not for thinking of what is coming, but for looking back into the year which has just flown by. What sufferings you have had to endure, my poor, brave wife! So many of your dear ones buried—and those days of horror on the battlefields in Bohemia."

"I do not grieve that I have seen the cruel things that took

(356)

place there.   Now I can at least participate with all the might
of my soul in your efforts."

"We must bring up your—or rather *our*—Rudolf with a view
of his pushing these efforts further.   In his time a visible mark
will perhaps arise above the horizon—hardly in ours.   What a
noise the people are making in the streets! they are greeting
with shouts the new year in spite of the sufferings which the
old one (that was greeted in the same way) brought on them.
Oh, how forgetful men are!"

"Do not chide them too much for their forgetfulness,
Frederick.   We too are beginning to brush away from our
memory the sufferings of the past, and what I feel is the bliss
of the present—the bliss of having you, my own one.   We
were not to speak of the future I know; still I think that the
future we have before us is good.   United, loving, sufficient in
ourselves, rich—how many exquisite enjoyments can not life
still offer us!   We will travel, will make acquaintance with the
world, the world that is so fair!   Fair so long as peace prevails ;
and peace may now last for many, many years!   But if war is
to break out again, you are no longer involved in it; and
Rudolf too is not threatened, since he is not going to be a
soldier."

"But if, according to Minister To-be-sure's information,
every man should be obliged to share in the defence——"

"Oh, nonsense.   So what I mean is, we will travel; we will
bring up our Rudolf to be a pattern man ; we will follow our
noble aim—the propaganda of peace ; and we—we will love
each other!"

The carnival this same year brought with it once more balls
and pleasures of all sorts ; but my mourning kept me away from
all such things.   But what astonished me was that the whole of
society did not abstain from such mad goings on.   Surely
there must have been a loss in almost every family ; but, as it
seemed, folks set all that at nought.   A few houses, it is true,
remained closed, especially among the aristocracy ; but there
was no want of opportunities for the young people to dance,

and the most favoured partners were, of course, those who had
come back from the battlefields of Italy and Bohemia ; and the
naval officers were those most *fêted*, especially those who had
fought at Lissa. Half the lady world had fallen in love with
Tegethoff, the youthful admiral, as they had done with the
handsome General Gablenz after the campaign of Schleswig-
Holstein. "Custozza" and "Lissa" were the two trump-cards
which were everywhere played in any conversation about the
war which was over. Along with this, the needle-gun and
Landwehr came in—two institutions which must be introduced
as speedily as possible—and then future victories were assured
to us. Victories? when and over whom? On this point
people did not speak out ; but the idea of revenge, which is
wont to accompany the loss of a game, even if it be only a game
at cards, was hovering over all the utterances of the politicians.
If even we did not ourselves take the field once more against
the Prussians, perhaps there might be others who would take
it on themselves to avenge us. All appearances seemed to
show that France would get into a quarrel with our conquerors,
and then they might get paid off for a good deal. The thing
had even got a name in diplomatic circles—"La Revanche de
Sadowa". Such was the triumphant announcement to us of
Minister To-be-sure.

It was at the beginning of spring that once more a certain
"black spot" appeared on the horizon—a "question" as they
call it. The news also of French preparations provided the
conjectural politicians with what they love so—"the prospect
of war". The question this time was called that of Luxembourg.

Luxembourg? What was there then of such great importance
to the world in that? On this subject I had again to embark
in studies similar to those about Schleswig-Holstein. The
name was indeed familiar to me only from Suppé's "Jolly
Companions," in which, as is well known, a Count of Luxembourg "spends all he has in dress—dress—dress". The result
of my studies was as follows :—

Luxembourg belonged according to the treaties of 1814 and

1816 (Ah! there we have it! treaties—they contain ready-made the root of a national quarrel—a fine institution these treaties) to the King of the Netherlands, and at the same time to the German Bund. Prussia had the right to garrison the capital. Now, however, as Prussia had renounced her share in the old Bund, how could she keep the right of garrison? That was the point—the "question". The peace of Prague had in fact introduced a new system into Germany, and thereby the connection with Luxembourg had been dissolved; why then did the Prussians maintain their right of garrison? "To be sure" that was an intricate affair, and the most advantageous and righteous way of settling it would be to slaughter fresh hundreds of thousands—that every "enlightened" politician must allow. The Dutch had never attached any importance to the possession of the Grand Duchy; the king also—William III.—attached no importance to it, and would have been happy to cede it to France for a sum to be paid into his privy purse; so *private* negotiations now commenced between the king and the French Cabinet. Exactly; secrecy is always the essence of all diplomacy. The peoples are not to know anything of the matters in dispute; as soon as the latter are ripe for decision they have the right to bleed for them. Why and wherefore they are fighting each other is a question of no importance.

It was not till the end of March that the king made the official announcement, and on the same day as that on which his assent was telegraphed to France, the Prussian ambassador at the Hague was informed of it. On that began negotiations with Prussia. The latter appealed to the guarantees of the treaties of 1859, the foundations on which the kingdom of Holland stood. Public opinion in Prussia (What is meant by public opinion? Possibly the writers of leading articles) was indignant that the old German Reichsland should be torn away; and in the Reichstag of North Germany, on April 1, there were heated questions on the subject. Bismarck, it is true, remained cool about Luxembourg; but nevertheless he set on foot preparations against France on this occasion, and they of course were followed by counter preparations on the French side. Ah, how well I know that tune! At that time I trembled sorely for fear of a new fire being lighted in Europe. No want of people to poke it—in Paris, Cassagnac and Emile de Girardin, in Berlin, Menzel and Heinrich Leo. Have then such provokers of war even the remotest notion of the gigantic enormity of their transgression? I hardly think so. It was at this time—as I first heard the tale many years after—that Professor Simson used the following expression in the presence of the Crown Prince Frederick of Prussia about the question in dispute :—

"If France and Holland have already come to an agreement, that signifies war ".

To which the crown prince in hot excitement and alarm replied :—

"You have never seen war; if you had seen it, you would not pronounce the word so quietly. I have seen it; and I say to you that it is the highest duty, if it be anyhow possible, to avoid it."

And this time it was avoided. A conference met at London, which, on May 11, led to the wished-for peaceable solution. Luxembourg was declared neutral and Prussia drew her troops out. The friends of peace breathed again, but there were plenty of people who were discontented at this turn of affairs. Not the Emperor of the French—he wished for peace—but the French "war party". In Germany too there were voices raised to condemn the behaviour of Prussia. "Sacrifice of a fortress," "submission looking like fear," and other things of the kind. But every private person also, who on the sentence of a court gives up his claim to any possessions, shows the same submission. Would it be better for him not to bow to any tribunal, but to settle the matter with his fists? The result achieved by the conference of London may in such doubtful questions be *always* achieved, and the leaders of states can always find that avoidance possible, which Frederick the Noble, afterwards Frederick III., called the *highest duty*.

.   .   .   .

In May we betook ourselves to Paris to visit the exhibition. I had not yet seen the World's Capital, and was quite dazzled by its splendour and its life. At that time especially, the empire was standing at its highest pitch of splendour, and all the crowned heads of Europe had collected there; and at that time above all others, Paris presented a picture of splendour the most joyful and the most secure of peace. The city appeared to me at that time not like the capital of a single country, but like the capital of Internationality; that city which three years afterwards was to be bombarded by its eastern neighbour. All the nations of the earth had assembled in the great palace in the Champ de Mars for the peaceful—nay profitable, because productive not destructive—strife of business competition. Riches, works of art, marvels of manufactory were brought together here, so that it must have excited pride in every beholder to have lived in a time so progressive and so full of promise of further progress; and along with this pride must naturally have arisen the purpose never more to hamper the march of that development of civilisation which was spreading enjoyment all round, by the brutal rage of destruction. All these kings, princes, and diplomatists who were assembled here as guests of the emperor and empress could not surely be thinking amidst all the civilities that were interchanged, the courtesies and the good wishes, of exchanging next time shots with their hosts or one another? No. I breathed again. This really splendid exhibition *fête* seemed to me the pledge that now an era of long, long years of peace had begun. At most against an incursion of Tartar hordes, or something of that sort, these civilised people might draw the sword; but against each other!—we were never more to see that it was hoped. What strengthened me in this opinion was a communication that reached me from a well-informed trustworthy source

about a favourite plan of the emperor for a *general disarmament.*
Yes. Napoleon III. was strong on that point. I have it from
the mouth of his nearest relations and most trusted friends,
and on the next convenient opportunity he was going to
communicate to all the European governments a proposal for
reducing their military establishments to a minimum. That
was good to hear; it was at any rate a more reasonable idea
than that of a general increase of forces. In this way the well-
known demand of Kant would be granted, which is thus
formulated in par. 3 of the "Preliminary Article to an Everlasting Peace":—

Standing armies (*miles perpetuus*) are in time to cease absolutely.
They are a constant menace of war to other states, in consequence of the
readiness to appear always prepared for war; they provoke them to over-
pass each other in the mass of preparations which know no limit (oh,
prophetic glance of wisdom!); and inasmuch as the costs of maintaining
peace become at last more burdensome than a short war, they are themselves causes of offensive war, in order to get rid of this burden.

What government could decline a proposition such as that
which France was meditating without unmasking its lust of
conquest? What nation would not revolt against such a
refusal? The plan must succeed.

Frederick did not share my confidence.

"In the first place," he said, "I doubt whether Napoleon
will make the proposal. The pressure of the war party will
hinder him. As a general rule the occupants of thrones are
prevented by those who surround them from the exercise of
those great efforts of individual will, which fall quite outside of
the usual pattern. In the second place, one cannot give to a
living being the command to cease to exist in this sort of way.
It straightway sets itself on its defence ——"

"Of what living being are you speaking?"

"Of the army. That is an organism, and as such has powers
of life development and of self-maintenance. At the present
time this organism is just in its prime, and, as you see—
for the system of universal defence will surely be introduced

into other countries—is just on the point of being powerfully extended."

"And yet you want to fight against it?"

"Yes; but not by stepping up to it and saying 'Die, thou monster!' for the organism in question would hardly do me the kindness to stretch itself dead at my feet on that summons. But I am fighting against it in appearing on behalf of another living form, which is still only in its fragile bud, but which, as it gains in power and extent, will crush the other out. It is your fault to begin with, Martha, that I talk in these scientific metaphors. It was you who first led me to study the works of the modern students of nature. From this there has arisen in me the view that the phenomena of social life also can not be understood in their origin, or foreseen in their future course till one conceives of them as existing under the influence of eternal laws. Of this most politicians and people in positions of high dignity have no notion—not the faintest; the worthy soldier certainly not. A few years ago it had not entered my head either."

We were living in the Grand Hotel on the Boulevard des Capucines. It was occupied chiefly by English people and Americans. We met few of our own people—the Austrians are not fond of travel. Besides, we sought for no acquaintance. I had not put off my mourning, and we cherished no wish for company. Of course I had my son Rudolf with me. He was now eight years old, and a wonderfully clever little fellow. We had hired a young Englishman, who performed the duties partly of tutor, partly of nursery governess to the boy. In our long visits to the exhibition-palace, as well as our numerous excursions into the neighbourhood, we could not, of course, always take Rudi with us; and besides, the time was also now come for him to begin to learn.

New—new—new—to me, was the whole of this world here open to us. All the men who had come together from the four corners of the earth—the richest and most distinguished from every quarter—these *fêtes*, this expenditure, this turmoil. I was literally deafened by it. But, interesting and full of enjoyment as it was to me to receive into my mind these surprising and overpowering impressions, yet, when alone, I wished myself out of all this hubbub again, and in some remote peaceful spot, where I could live in quiet retirement along with Frederick and my child—nay, my *children*, for I was looking forward confidently to the joy of motherhood again. It is wonderful, indeed—and I find it often noted in the red volumes—how in retirement the longing rises for events and exploits, for experiences and enjoyments; and again, in the midst of the latter, for solitude and tranquillity.

We kept ourselves apart from the great world. We had merely paid a visit to the house of our ambassador, Metternich, and had let it be known there that on account of our domestic afflictions we did not desire any *entrée* into Court circles or society. On the other hand, we sought to make the acquaintance of a few prominent political and literary personages, partly from self-interest and for our mental improvement, partly with a view to "the service" into which Frederick had entered. In spite of the slight hopes he had of any perceptible result from his efforts, he never allowed it to escape him, and he put himself into communication with numerous influential persons, from whom he might gain assistance in his career, or at least information as to its position. We had at that time commenced a little book of our own—we called it *The Protocol of Peace*—into which all news, notices, articles, and so forth, bearing on the subject, were to be sedulously entered. The history also of the idea of Peace, as far as we could gain a knowledge of it, was incorporated in the *Protocol;* and along with this the expressions of various philosophers, poets, priests, and authors on the subject of "Peace and War". It had soon grown into an imposing little volume; and in course of time —for I have carried on this composition down to the present day—it has grown into several little volumes. If one were to compare it with the libraries which are filled with works on strategical subjects, with the untold thousands of volumes containing histories of wars, studies on war, and glorification of

war, with the text-books of military science and military
tactics, and guides for the instruction of recruits and artillery,
with the chronicles of battles and annals of *états-majors*,
soldiers' ballads and war songs : well, then, I allow that the
comparison with these one or two poor little volumes of peace-
literature might humiliate one, on the assumption that one
might measure the power and value—especially the future
value—of a thing by its size. But if one reflects that a single
grain of seed hides in itself the virtual power of causing the
growth of an entire forest, which will displace whole masses
of weeds, though spread over acres of country, and further
reflects that an idea is in the mental kingdom what a seed
is in the vegetable, then one need not be anxious about the
future of an idea, merely because the history of its development
may be as yet contained in one little manuscript.

I will here produce a few extracts taken from our *Protocol
of Peace* for the year 1867. On the first page was placed a
compressed historical survey.

Four hundred years before Christ, Aristophanes wrote a comedy—
"Peace"—into which a humanitarian tendency enters.

The Greek philosophy—afterwards transplanted to Rome—admitted
a striving after "the unity of humanity" from Socrates, who called himself a "citizen of the world," down to Terence, to whom "nothing human
was foreign," and Cicero, who represents the "love of the human race" as
the highest grade of perfection.

In the first century of our era appears Virgil with his famous fourth
eclogue which prophesies universal peace to the world under the mytho-
logical image of the return of the golden age.

In the middle ages, the Popes often strove, though in vain, to
interpose as arbitrators between states.

In the fifteenth century the idea occurred to a king of forming a
"league of peace". This was Geo. Podiebrad of Bohemia, who wished
to put an end to the wars of the emperor and the Pope ; for this purpose
he betook himself to King Louis XI. of France, who however did not fall
in with the proposal.

At the close of the sixteenth century, King Henry IV. of France
conceived the plan of a European confederation of states. After he had
delivered his country from the horrors of the religious war, he wished to

see toleration and peace assured for all future time. He wished to see the sixteen states of which Europe then consisted (for Russia and Turkey were reckoned parts of Asia) combined into a Bund. Each of these sixteen states was to have the right of sending two members to a "European Council," and to this council, consisting thus of thirty-two members, the task was to be entrusted of maintaining the religious peace, and avoiding all international conflicts. And then if every state would bind itself to submit to the decisions of the council, every element of European wars would be thereby removed. The king communicated this plan to his Minister, Sully, who heartily accepted it and straightway commenced negotiations with the other states. Elizabeth of England, the Pope, Holland, and several others were actually won over; only the House of Austria would have offered resistance, because territorial concessions might have been demanded from her, which she would not have granted. A campaign would have been necessary to overcome this resistance. France would have contributed the main army, and she would have renounced beforehand any extension of territory; the sole aim of the campaign and the sole condition of peace imposed on the House of Austria would have been their entrance into the league of states. All the preparations were already completed, and Henry IV. meant to take the command of the army in person, when on May 13, 1610, he fell under the dagger of an insane monk.

None of his successors nor any other sovereign took up again this glorious plan for procuring happiness for the nations. Rulers and politicians remained true to the old war-spirit; but the thinkers of all countries did not allow the idea of peace to fall to the ground again.

In the year 1647 the sect of the Quakers was founded, and the condemnation of war was its fundamental principle. In the same year William Penn published his work on the future peace of Europe, which he founded on the plan of Henry IV.

In the early part of the eighteenth century appeared the famous book of the Abbé de S. Pierre, entitled *La Paix Perpétuelle*. At the same time a Landgrave of Hesse sketched out the same plan, and Leibnitz wrote a favourable comment on it.

Voltaire gave out the maxim "Every European war is a civil war". Mirabeau, in the memorable session of August 25, 1790, spoke the following words:—

"The moment is perhaps not far off now when Freedom, as the unfettered monarch of both worlds, will fulfil the wish of philosophers, to free mankind from the sin of war, and proclaim universal peace. Then will the happiness of the people be the only aim of the legislator, the only glory of the nations."

In the year 1795 one of the greatest thinkers of all time, Emmanuel

Kant, wrote his treatise "On Eternal Peace". The English publicist, Bentham, joins with enthusiasm the ever-increasing number of the defenders of peace—Fourrier, Saint Simon, etc. Beranger sang "The Holy Alliance of Peace," Lamartine "La Marseillaise de la Paix". In Geneva Count Cellon founded a "Peace Club," in whose name he entered into a propagandist correspondence with all the rulers of Europe. From Massachusetts In America comes "the learned blacksmith," Elihu Burritt, and scatters his *Olive Leaves* and *Sparks from an Anvil* about the world in millions of copies, and takes the chair in 1849 at an assembly of the English Friends of Peace. In the Congress of Paris, which wound up the Crimean War, the idea of peace gained a footing in diplomacy, inasmuch as a clause was added to the treaty which provided that the Powers pledged themselves in future conflicts to submit themselves previously to mediation. This clause contains in itself a recognition of the principle of a court of arbitration, but it has not been acted upon.

In the year 1863 the French Government proposed to the Powers to call a congress, before which was to be brought the consideration of proposals for a general disarmament, and for the avoidance of future wars.

But this proposal found no support whatever from the other Governments.

. . . .

And now, my hour of trial was again drawing nigh.

But it was so different this time from that other in which Frederick had to leave me—to fight for the Augustenburger. This time he was at my side—the husband's proper post—diminishing through his presence and through his sympathy the sufferings of his wife. The feeling that I had him there was to me so calming and so happy that in it I almost forgot my physical discomfort.

A girl! It was the fulfilment of my silent hope. The joys connected with a son had already been given to us by my little Rudolf: we could now, in addition to these, taste those joys which such a fine little daughter promised to her parents. That this little Sylvia of ours would grow into a paragon of beauty, grace, and comeliness we did not doubt for a single moment. How childish we both of us became over the cradle of this child ; what sweet fooleries we spoke and acted there, I will not even try to tell. Others than fond parents would not understand it, and all of them have no doubt been just as silly themselves.

But how selfish happiness makes us I   There came now a time for us, in which we really were far too forgetful of every-thing which lay outside of our domestic heaven.   The terrors of the cholera week kept taking always more and more in my memory the shape of a vanished evil dream ; and even Frederick's energy in the pursuit of his aim gradually abated. And it was no doubt discouraging, wherever one knocked at any doors with these ideas, to meet with shrugs of shoulders, compassionate smiles, if not a regular setting to rights.   The world, as it seems, is fond not only of being cheated, but also of being made miserable.   Wherever one tries to put forward any proposals for removing misery and woe, they are called " Utopian—a childish dream "—and the world will not listen to them.

Still Frederick did not let his aim fall quite out of sight.   He plunged ever deeper into the study of international law, and got into correspondence by letter with Bluntschli and other men learned in this branch.   At the same time, and here with my companionship, he diligently followed other studies, chiefly natural science.   He formed a plan for writing a great work on " War and Peace ".   But, before setting to work on it, he wanted to prepare himself for it and instruct himself by long and comprehensive researches.   " I am, it is true," he said, " an old royal and imperial colonel, and it would shame most of my equals in age and rank to dip into schooling.   When one is an elderly man of office and rank one thinks oneself usually clever enough to act independently.   I myself a few years since had that respect for my own individuality.   But when I had suddenly attained to a new point of view, in which I got an insight into the modern spirit, then the consciousness of my want of knowledge came over me.   Ah yes I   Of all the gains that have now been made in the matter of new discoveries in all provinces of knowledge, there was nothing at all taught in my youth—or rather the reverse was taught—so I must now, in spite of the streaks of grey on my temples, begin again at the beginning."

The winter after Sylvia's birth we spent at Vienna in perfect quiet. Next spring we travelled to Italy. To travel and make acquaintance with the world was indeed a part of our new programme of life. We were independent and rich, and nothing hindered us from carrying it out. Small children are a little troublesome in travelling; but if one can take about a sufficient train of *bonnes* and nurses, the thing can be done. I had taken into my establishment an old servant who had once been nurse to me and my sisters, and then had married an hotel steward, and now was left a widow. This "Mistress Anna" was worthy of my fullest confidence, and in her hands I could leave my little Sylvia at home with perfect security, at any time when we—*i.e.*, Frederick and I—left our headquarters for several days on some excursion. Rudolf would have been just as well seen after by Mr. Foster, his tutor; but it often happened that we took the little eight-years-old boy with us.

Happy, happy times! Pity that I then neglected the red books so much! It was exactly at this time that I might have entered so much that was beautiful, interesting and gay; but I neglected it, and so the details of that year have mostly faded out of my recollection, and it is only in rough outline that I can now recall a picture of it.

In the *Protocol of Peace* I did find an opportunity to make a gratifying entry. This was a leading article signed B. Desmoulins, in which the proposal was made to the French Government that it should put itself at the head of the European states by giving them the example of disarmament:—

In this way France will make herself sure of the alliance and of the honest friendship of all states, which will then have ceased to be afraid of France, while they would desire her sympathy. In this way the general disarmament would commence spontaneously—the principle of conquest would be given up for ever, and the confederation of states would quite naturally form a Court of International Law, which would be in a position to settle in the way of arbitration all disputes which could never be decided by war.   In so acting, France would have gained over to her side the only real and only lasting power—namely, right—and would have opened for humanity, in the most glorious manner, a new era.   (*Opinion Nationale*, July 25, 1868.)

This article, of course, got no attention.

In the winter of 1868-69 we went back to Paris, and this time, for we wished to make acquaintance with life, we plunged into the "Great World".

It was a rather tiring process ; but yet for a time it was very pleasant.   In order to have some home, we had hired a small residence in the quarter of the Champs Elysées, whither we also could sometimes invite in turn our numerous acquain-tance, by whom we were invited every day to a party of some kind or other.   Having been introduced by our ambassador at the Court of the Tuilleries, we were invited for the whole winter to the Mondays of the empress, and, besides this, the houses of all the ambassadors were open to us, as well as the *salons* of Princess Mathilde, the Duchess of Mouchy, Queen Isabella of Spain, and so on.   We made the acquaintance also of many literary magnates, not of the greatest, however, I mean Victor Hugo, as he was living in exile, but we met Renan, Dumas *père et fils*, Octave Feuillet, George Sand, Arsène Houssaye, and some others.   At the house of the last named we also were present at a masked ball.   When the author of the *Grandes Dames* gave one of his Venetian *fêtes* in his splendid little hotel, on the Avenue Friedland, it was the custom that the real *grandes dames* should go there under the protection of their masks along with the "little ladies," well-known actresses and so forth, who were making their diamonds and their wit sparkle here.

We were also very industrious visitors to the theatres.   At least three times a week we spent our evenings either at the Italian opera, where Adelina Patti, just married to the Marquis de Caux, was enchanting the audience, or at the *Théâtre Français*, or even at one of the little boulevard theatres to see Hortense Schneider as the Grand Duchess of Gerolstein, or some of the other celebrities of operetta or vaudeville.

It is wonderful, however, how, when one is once plunged into this whirl of splendour and entertainments, this little "great world" appears to one all of a sudden so terribly important; and the laws which prevail therein of elegance and *chic* (it was even then called *chic*) as laying on one a kind of solemnly undertaken duty. To take at the theatre a less distinguished place than a stage-box; to appear in the Bois with a carriage whose equipage should not be faultless; to go to a court ball without putting on a toilette of 2000 francs, "signed" by Worth; to sit down to table (Madame la Baronne est servie), even if one had no guests, without having the finest dishes and the choicest wines served by the solemn *maître d'hôtel* in person and several lackeys, all these would have been serious offences. How easy, how very easy it becomes to one, when one is caught up in the machinery of such an existence as this, to spend all one's thoughts and feelings on this business, which is really devoid of all thought and feeling, and in doing this to forget to take any part in the progress of the real world outside, I mean the universe, or in the condition of one's own world within, I mean domestic bliss. This is what might perhaps have happened to me, but Frederick preserved me from it. He was not the man to allow himself to be torn away and smothered by the whirlpool of Parisian "high-life". He did not forget, in the world in which we were moving, either the universe or our own hearth. An hour or two in the morning we still kept devoted to reading and domestic life; and so we accomplished the great feat of enjoying happiness even in the midst of pleasure.

For us Austrians there was much sympathy cherished at Paris. In political conversations there was often a talk about a *Revanche de Sadowa*, certainly in the sense that the injustice done to us two years before was to be made good again —as if *anything of that sort* could make it *good* again. If blows are

only to be wiped out by fresh blows, then surely the thing
can never cease.   It was just to my husband and me, because
he had been in the army and had served the campaign in
Bohemia, it was just to us that people thought they could say
nothing more polite or more agreeable than a hopeful allusion
to the *Revanche de Sadowa* which was in prospect, and which
was already treated of as an historical event which would assure
the European equilibrium, and was itself ensured by diplomatic
arrangements.   A slap to be administered to the Prussians on the
next opportunity was a necessity in the school-discipline of
the nations.   Nothing tragical would come of the matter, only
enough to check the arrogance of certain folks.   Perhaps even
the whip hanging up on the wall would' be enough for this
purpose; but if that arrogant fellow should try any of his saucy
tricks he had received fair warning that it would come down
upon him in the shape of the *Revanche de Sadowa.*

We, of course, decisively put aside all such consolations.   A
former misfortune was not to be conjured away by a fresh
misfortune, nor an old injustice to be atoned for by a new
injustice.   We assured our friends that we wished for nothing,
except that we might never see the present peace broken again.
This was also essentially the wish of Napoleon III.   We had
so much intercourse with persons whose position was quite
close to the emperor, that we had plenty of opportunities of
becoming acquainted with his political views, as he gave utterance to them in his confidential conversation.   It was not only
that he wished for peace at the moment—he cherished the
plan of proposing to the powers a general disarmament.   But,
for the moment, he did not feel his own domestic position in
the country secure enough to carry this plan out.   There was
great discontent boiling and seething among the populace;
and in the circle immediately surrounding the throne there
was a party which laboured to represent to him that his throne
could only be rendered secure by a successful foreign war—just
a little triumphal promenade to the Rhine, and the splendour
and stability of the Napoleonic dynasty were secured.   *Il faut
faire grand,* was the advice of his counsellors.   That the war.

which was in prospect the year before on the Luxembourg question, had come to nothing, and was displeasing to them; the preparations on both sides had gone on so grandly, and then the matter had been adjourned. But in the long run a fight between France and Prussia was certainly inevitable. They were incessantly urging on further in this direction. But only a feeble echo of these matters came to us. One is accustomed to hear that sort of thing resounding in the journals, as regularly as the breakers on the shore. There is no occasion to fear a storm on that account. You listen quite tranquilly to the band which is playing its lively airs on the beach—the breakers form only a soft unheeded bass accompaniment to them.

This brilliant way of life, only too overburdened with pleasure, reached its highest pitch in the spring months. At that time there were added long drives in the Bois in open carriages, numerous picture exhibitions, garden parties, horse-races, picnics, and with all this no fewer theatres, or visits, or dinner or evening parties, than in the depth of winter. We then began to long much for repose. In fact, this sort of life has never its true attraction, except when some flirtation or love affair is combined with it. Girls who are in search of a husband, women who want a lover, or men who are in search of adventures, for these every new *fête*, where it is possible they may meet the object of their dream, possesses a new interest, but for Frederick and me? That I was inflexibly true to my lord, that I never by a single glance gave any one the occasion to approach me with any audacious hopes, I may say, without any pride of virtue—it was a mere matter of course. Whether, under different relations, I should also have resisted all the temptations to which, in such a whirl of pleasure, pretty young ladies are exposed, is more than I can say; but when one carries in one's heart a love so deep and so full of bliss as I felt for my Frederick, one is surely armed against all danger. And as far as he was concerned, was he true to me? I can only say, that I never felt any doubt about it.

When the summer had returned to the land, when the Grand Prix was over, and the different members of society began to quit Paris, some to Trouville or Dieppe, Biarritz or Vichy, others to Baden Baden, and a third set to their châteaux, Princess Mathilde to St. Gratien, and the court to Compiègne, then we were besieged with requests to select the same destinations for travel, and with invitations to country-houses ; but we were decidedly indisposed to prolong the campaign of luxury and pleasure which we had carried out in the winter, into a summer one also. I did not wish to return at once to Grumitz. I feared too much the reawakening of painful memories ; besides, we should not have found there the solitude we desired, on account of our numerous relations and neighbours. So we chose once more for our resting-place a quiet corner of Switzerland. We promised our friends in Paris that we would come back next winter, and went on our summer tour with the joy of schoolboys going for their holidays.

Now succeeded a time of real refreshment. Long walks, long hours of study, long hours of play with the children, and no entries in the red volumes—which last was a sign of freedom from care, and spiritual peace.

Europe also seemed at that time tolerably free from care, and peaceful. At least no "black spots" were anywhere visible. One did not even hear any more talk about the famous *Revanche de Sadowa*. The greatest trouble which I experienced at that time was caused by the universal obligation for defence which had been introduced a year before amongst us Austrians. That my Rudolf some time or other *must* become a soldier—that was a thing I could not bear. And yet folks dream of freedom !

Frederick tried to comfort me. " A year of ' volunteering ' is not much." I shook my head.

" Even if it were but a day ! No man ought to be compelled to take upon himself a certain office, which perhaps he hates, even for a single day ; for during that day he must make a show of the opposite of what he feels—must pretend that he is doing joyfully what he really hates—in short, he is obliged to lie, and I wanted to bring up my son to be true, before all things."

"Then he ought to have been born one or two centuries later, my dearest," replied Frederick. "It is only the perfectly free man who can be perfectly true; and we are still poorly off for both things—freedom and truth—in our days; that becomes clearer and clearer to me the deeper I plunge into my studies."

Now, in this retirement Frederick had twice the leisure for his work, and he set about it with true ardour. However happy and content we were with our life in this solitude, still we remained firm in our determination to spend next winter in Paris again. This time, however, it was not with the view of amusing ourselves, but in order to do something practical towards the fulfilment of the task of our lives. In this, it is true, we did not cherish any *confidence* that we should attain anything; but when a man sees even the possibility of the shadow of a chance offered him to contribute anything towards a cause which he recognises as the holiest cause on earth, he feels it to be a duty which he cannot refuse, to try this chance. Now, in recapitulating, during our familiar talks, the recollections of Paris, we had thought also of that plan of the Emperor Napoleon which had come to our ears by the communications of his confidants—I mean the plan for proposing disarmament to the great powers. It was on this that we based our hopes and our projects. Frederick's researches had brought into his hand Sully's *Memoirs*, in which the plan of Henry IV. for peace is described in all its details. We meant to convey an abstract of this to the Emperor of the French; and at the same time to try, through our connections in Austria and Prussia, to prepare both these Governments for the propositions of the French Government. I could set this on foot by the means of Minister To-be-sure, and Frederick had at Berlin a relative who was in an influential political position, and stood very well at court.

In December, which was the time we meant to move to

Paris, we were prevented. Our treasure, our little Sylvia, fell ill. What anxious hours those were! Napoleon III. and Henry IV. of course were then put in the background—our child dying !

But she did not die. In two weeks all danger was over. Only the physician forbade us to travel during the worst of the winter's cold. So we put off our departure till March.

This sickness and recovery, the danger and the preservation —what a shock they had given our hearts ! and how much— though I thought that no longer possible—they had brought them more near to each other still ! To tremble in unison before a horrid disaster—one which each fears the more from seeing the other's despair, and to weep tears of joy in common when this disaster has been averted—are things which have a most mighty influence in welding souls together.

.   .   .   ,   .   .   .   ,   .   .

Forebodings? No, there were none. If there had been Paris would not have made on me the cheerful impression of promised pleasure which it did on one sunny afternoon of March, 1870, on our arrival. One knows now what horrors were brooding over that city after a very short interval ; but not the faintest anticipation of trouble arose in my mind.

We had already hired beforehand, through the agent, John Arthur, the same little palace in which we had lived last year, and at its door was waiting for us our *maître d'hôtel* of the previous year. As we drove across the Champs Elysées to reach our dwelling, it was just the hour for the Bois, and several of our old acquaintances met us and exchanged joyful recognitions. The numerous little barrows of violets which were dragged about the streets of Paris that year filled the air with the promise of spring; the sunbeams were sparkling and playing in rainbows on the fountains of the *Rond-point*, making little reflections on the carriage lamps and the harness of the many carriages. Amongst others, the beautiful empress was driving in a carriage harnessed *à la Daumont*. She passed us, and, recognising me, made a gesture of salutation.

There are some special pictures or scenes which photograph or phonograph themselves on our memory, along with the feelings that accompany them, and some of the words that are spoken at them. "This Paris is truly lovely," cried Frederick at this point, and my feeling was a childish self-congratulation at the coming treat. Had I known what was coming to me, and to this whole city, now bathed in splendour and rejoicing!

This time we abstained from throwing ourselves, as we had done the year before, into the whirlpool of worldly amusements. We announced that we would not accept any dancing invitations, and kept ourselves apart from the great receptions. Even the theatre we did not visit so often—only when some piece made a great impression—and so it came about that we spent most evenings at home alone, or in the society of a few friends.

As to our plans with regard to the idea of the emperor about disarmament, we got on but badly with them. Napoleon III. had not, indeed, given up his idea altogether, but the present time, it was said, was not at all suited for carrying it out. In the circle around the throne a conviction had grown up that that throne stood on no very firm footing—a great discontent was boiling and seething among the people, in order to repress which all the police and censorship regulations were made more stringent, and the only consequence of this was greater discontent. The only thing, said certain people, which could give renewed splendour and security to the dynasty would be a successful campaign. It is true there was no near prospect of this, but all mention of disarmament would be a total and complete mistake, for thereby the whole Bonaparte-nimbus would be destroyed, which was undoubtedly founded on the heritage of glory of the first Napoleon. We had also received no very cheering answers to our inquiries on these subjects from Prussia and Austria. There people had entered on an epoch of expansion of the "defensive forces" (the word "army" began to be unfashionable), and the word "disarmament" fell on this like a gross discord. On the contrary, in order to obtain the blessings of peace, the "defensive power" must be increased—the French were not to be trusted—the Russians neither—and the Italians, most certainly not—they would fall on Triest and Trent at once, if they had the opportunity—in short, the only thing to do was to nurse the Landwehr system with all the care possible.

"The time is not ripe," said Frederick, on our receiving communications such as these, "and I must, I suppose, in reason give up the hope that I personally may be able to help in hastening the ripening of that time, or even see the fruits I long for blossoming. What I can contribute is mean enough. But from the hour that I saw that this thing, however mean, is my duty, it has in spite of all become the greatest thing of all to me, so I keep on."

But if for the present the project of disarmament had been dropped, I had yet one comfort—there was no war in sight. The war party which existed in the court and among the people, and whose opinion was that the dynasty must be "rebaptised in blood," and that another little taste of glory must be provided for the people, were obliged to renounce their plan of attack and their bewitching "little campaign on the Rhine frontier". For France possessed no allies; great drought prevailed in the country; a dearth of forage was to be anticipated; the army horses had to be sold; there was no "question" in agitation; the contingent of recruits had been diminished by the legislative body; in short, so Ollivier declared from the tribune—" the peace of Europe is assured ".

Assured! I rejoiced over the word. It was repeated in all the papers, and many thousands rejoiced with me. For what can there be better for the majority of men than assured peace?

How much, however, that security which was announced by a statesman on June 3, 1870, was worth we now all know. And even at the time we might have known this much, that assurances of that kind from statesmen, though the public always receives them again with the same innocent trust, really contain no guarantee—literally none. The European situation shows no question in agitation—therefore peace is secure. What feeble logic! Questions may come into agitation any moment; it is not till we have prepared some means against such a contingency other than war, that we can ever be secure against war.

CHAPTER XVII.

We remain in Paris to get ready a new house.—The "question" between France and Prussia.—Candidature of Prince Hohenzollern for the crown of Spain.—The war rumours and the speeches in the Chamber become menacing.—The Hohenzollern candidature withdrawn.—Further demands of France.—Threatening debate in the French Chamber.—War declared.—Excitement and enthusiasm in Paris.—With which side should we sympathise?—The opposing manifestoes.—We linger in Paris.—Opinions about war of eminent French writers.—Proclamations of the two armies.—Secret history.

PARIS society again dispersed in all directions. We, however, remained behind on business. For an extraordinarily advantageous bargain had been offered to us. Through the sudden departure of an American a little, half-finished hotel, in the Avenue de l'Imperatrice, had had to be offered for sale, and at a price which did not amount to much more than the sum already expended on the decoration and furnishing of the thing itself. As we had already the intention of spending in future some months of each year in Paris, and as the purchase in question was also at the same time an excellent bargain, we closed with it. We wished to superintend the completion ourselves, and for this purpose stopped in Paris. The decoration of one's own nest is, besides, such a pleasurable task that we willingly endured the unpleasantness of staying in a city the whole summer. Besides, we had plenty of houses to which we could resort for company. The château of Princess Mathilde,

(380)

St. Gratien, then Château Mouchy, and next Baron Rothschild's place, Ferrières, and other summer residences besides of our acquaintance, were situated near Paris, and we arranged once or twice a week to pay a visit, now to one of them, now to another.

It was, I recollect, in the *salon* of Princess Mathilde that I first heard of "the question" that was soon to come into "agitation".

The company was sitting, after *déjeûner*, on the terrace, looking on to the park. Who were all the people there? I do not recollect them all now; only two of the persons present remain in my memory, Taine and Renan. The conversation was a very lively one, and I recollect that it was Renan chiefly who led the talk, sparkling with *esprit* and witticisms. The author of the *Vie de Jésus* is an example that a man may be incredibly ugly and yet exercise an incredible fascination.

Now the talk turned upon politics. A candidate had been sought for the crown of Spain. A prince of Hohenzollern was to receive the crown. I had scarcely been listening, for what could the throne of Spain or he who was to sit upon it have to do with me or all these nonchalant folks here? But then some one said :—

"A Hohenzollern? France would not permit that !"

The words cut me to the heart, for what did that "not permit" imply? When such an utterance comes from any country one sees with one's mind's eye the statue personifying that country as a gigantic virgin, her head thrown back in defiance, her hand on her sword.

The conversation, however, soon turned to another subject. How full of tremendous results this question of the Spanish throne would be none of us yet suspected. I, of course, did not either. Only, that arrogant "France would not permit that" stuck in my memory like a discord, and along with it the whole scenery did so in which it was spoken.

From that time the question of the Spanish throne became constantly more loud and more pressing. Every day the space became larger which it occupied in the newspapers and in conversations in the *salons*, and I know that it bored me in the highest degree, this Hohenzollern candidature : soon there was nothing else spoken of.   And it was spoken of in an offended tone, as if nothing more insulting to France could take place. Most people saw behind it a provocation to war on the part of Prussia.   But it was clear, so it was said, that "France could not permit such a thing, so, if the Hohenzollerns persist in it, that is a simple challenge".   I could not understand that ; but in other respects I was free from anxiety.   We received letters from Berlin, telling us from a well-instructed quarter that not the slightest importance was attached at court to the succession of a Hohenzollern to the Spanish crown.   And, therefore, we were much more occupied with the work at our house than with politics.

But gradually we became more attentive to the subject for all that.   As, before the storm, a certain rustling of leaves goes through the forest, so, before war, a rustle of certain voices goes through the world.   " Nous aurons la guerre—nous aurons la guerre," was what resounded in the air of Paris. Then an unspeakable anxiety possessed me.   Not for my own people—for we, as Austrians, were at first out of the game. On the contrary, we might possibly have some "satisfaction" offered to us—the well-known "revenge for Sadowa".   But we had untaught ourselves the habit of looking at war from a national point of view ; and what war is from the point of view of humanity—of the highest humanity—is surely notorious. That is expressed in the following words which I heard spoken by Guy de Maupassant :—

" Quand je songe seulement à ce mot 'la guerre' il me vient un effarement, comme si l'on me parlait de sorcellerie, d'inquisition, d'une chose lontaine, finie, abominable, contre nature".

When the news arrived that the crown had been offered by Prim to Prince Leopold, the Duke of Grammont made a speech in Parliament, which was received with great approbation, to the following effect :—

"We do not meddle with the affairs of foreign nations, but we do not believe that respect for the rights of a neighbouring state binds us to permit a foreign power, by seating one of its own princes on the throne of Charles V., to destroy, to our detriment, the equilibrium which exists between the states of Europe (Oh that equilibrium! What war-loving hypocrite invented that hollow phrase?), and so bring into danger the interests, the honour of France".

I know a tale of George Sand named *Gribouille.* This Gribouille has the peculiarity, when rain is threatened, of plunging into the river, for fear of getting wet. Whenever I hear that war is contemplated in order to avert threatened dangers, I can never help thinking of Gribouille. A whole branch of Hohenzollerns might very well have seated themselves on Charles V.'s throne, and many other thrones as well, without exposing the interests or the honour of France to one thousandth part of the damage that resulted to them from this bold "We cannot permit it".

"The case," the speaker continued, "will, as we most confidently believe, not occur. We reckon, in this regard, on the wisdom of the German and the friendship of the Spanish people. But if it should turn out otherwise, *then*, gentlemen, we, strong in your support and that of the nation, shall know how to do our duty, without vacillation and without weakness." (Loud applause.)

From that time began in the press the cry for war. It was Girardin in particular, who could not inflame his countrymen sufficiently to punish the unheard-of audacity contained in this candidature for the throne. It would be unworthy of the dignity of France not to interpose her veto upon it. Prussia, it is true, would not give in, for she is bent, mad as she is, on conjuring up war. Intoxicated by her success of 1866, she believes that she may extend her march of victory and robbery on the Rhine also; but, thank God, we are ready to baulk all these appetites of the Pickelhaubers. And so it went on, in the same key. Napoleon III., it is true, as we found out through persons who were about him, still wished, as before, for the preservation of peace ; but most of the people of his *entourage* now thought that a war was inevitable—that, since apart from all this there was discontent among the people with the Government, the best thing that could be done to secure the respect of the country, anxious as it was for glory, would be to carry out a successful war. " Il faut faire grand."

And now inquiries were made of all the European Cabinets about the situation. Each declared that they wished for peace. In Germany a manifesto was published, originating in popular articles signed by Liebknecht amongst others, wherein it was said " the mere thought of a war between Germany and France is a crime ".

Benedetti was sent with the charge of demanding from the King of Prussia that he would forbid Prince Leopold to assume the crown. King William was at that moment taking the waters at Ems. Benedetti went there, and got an audience on July 9.

What would the result be ? I waited for the news with trembling.

The answer of the king simply said that he could not forbid anything to a prince who had attained adult years.

This answer sent the war party into triumphant joy. " There —will you suffer that ? Do they want to provoke us to the utmost ? That the head of the house cannot command or forbid anything to one of its members ! Ridiculous ! It is clearly a made-up plot—the Hohenzollerns want to get a footing in Spain, and then fall upon our country from the east and south at once. And are we to wait for that ? Are we to be content to take with humility the utter disregard of our protest ? Surely not. We know what honour, what patriotism, commands us to do."

Ever louder and louder, ever more and more threatening sounded the storm-warnings. Then on July 12 came a piece of news which filled me with delight. Don Salusto Olozaga announced officially to the French Government that Prince

Leopold of Hohenzollern, in order not to give any pretext for war, refused to assume the crown offered to him.

Now, thank God, the entire "question" is thus simply put aside. The news was communicated to the Chamber at 12 at noon, and Ollivier declared that this put an end to the dispute. Yet, on the same day, troops and war material were forwarded to Metz (publicly said to be in pursuance of previous orders), and in the same sitting Clement Duvernois put the following question :—

"What securities have we that Prussia will not originate fresh complications, like this Spanish candidature? That should be provided against."

There Gribouille comes up again. It may happen, perhaps, at some time, that a trifling rain may threaten to wet us ; so let us jump into the river at once !

And so Benedetti was despatched again to Ems ; this time to demand of the King of Prussia that he would forbid Prince Leopold once for all, and for all future time, to revive his candidature. What could follow such an attempt at dictating a course of action, which the party on whom the demand is made is not competent to carry out, except an impatient shrug of the shoulders? Those who made the demand must have known as much.

There was another memorable sitting on July 15. Ollivier demanded a credit of 500,000,000 frs. for the war. *Thiers opposed it.* Ollivier replied. He took on himself to justify before the bar of history what had been done. The King of Prussia had refused to receive the French envoy, and had notified this to the Government in a letter. The Left wanted to see this letter. The majority forbade, by clamour and by a counter-vote, the production of the document, which probably had no existence. This majority supported any demand made by the Government in favour of the war. This patriotic readiness for sacrifice, which would accept even *ruin* without hesitation, was of course again applauded becomingly with the usual ready-made turns of sentence.

July 16. England made attempts to prevent the war. In vain. Ah! if there had been an arbitration court established how easily and simply might such a trivial dispute have been decided.

July 19. The French *chargé d'affaires* in Berlin handed the Prussian Government the declaration of war.

Declaration of war! Three words, which can be pronounced quite calmly. But what is connected with them? The beginning of an extra-political action, and thus, along with it, half-a-million sentences of death.

This document also I entered in the red volumes. It runs thus :—

The Government of His Majesty the Emperor of the French could not regard the design of raising a Prussian prince to the throne of Spain otherwise than as an attack on the territorial security of France, and has therefore found itself compelled to request from His Majesty the King of Prussia the assurance that such a combination should never again occur with his consent. As His Majesty refuses any such assurance, and has, on the contrary, declared to our ambassador that he must reserve to himself the possibility of such an event, and inquire into the circumstances, the Imperial Government cannot help recognising in this declaration of the king an *arrière-pensée*, which, for France and for the European equilibrium . . . (There it comes again—this famous equilibrium. Look at this shelf, and the precious china on it—it is tottering; the dishes may fall, so let us smash it down.) This declaration has assumed a still graver character from the communication which has been made to the Cabinet of the refusal to receive the emperor's ambassador, and to introduce, in common with him, a new method of solution. (So, by such things as these, by a more or less friendly conversation between rulers and diplomatists, the fate of nations may be decided.) In consequence of this the French Government has thought it its duty (!) without delay to think of the defence (Yes, yes, defence : never attack) of its outraged dignity and its outraged interests, and being determined to employ for that end all means which are offered by the position which has been imposed upon it, regards itself from this time forward as in a state of war with Prussia.

State of war! Does the man think who puts these words on paper, on the green cloth of his writing-table, that he is plunging his pen in flames, in tears of blood, in the poison of plague?

And so the storm is unchained, this time on account of a king being sought for a vacant throne, and as the consequence of a negotiation undertaken between two monarchs! Must Kant then be right in his first definitive condition for everlasting peace? "The civil constitution in every state should be republican." To be sure, the effect of this article would be to remove many causes of war; for history shows how many campaigns have been undertaken for dynastic questions, and the whole establishment of monarchical power rests assuredly on successful conduct of war—still republics also are warlike. It is the *spirit*, the old savage spirit which lights up hatred, lust of plunder, and ambition of conquest in peoples, whether governed in one form or another.

I recollect what an altogether peculiar humour seized me at this time, when the Franco-German war was in preparation and then broke out. The stormy sultriness before, the howling tempest after its declaration. The whole population was in a fever, and who can keep himself aloof from such an epidemic? Naturally, according to old custom, the beginning of the campaign was at once looked on as a triumphal procession—that is no more than patriotic duty. "A Berlin, à Berlin," was shouted through the streets and from the outside of the omnibusses—the Marseillaise at every street corner, "Le jour de gloire est arrivé". At every theatrical representation the first actress or singer, at the opera it was Marie Sass, had to come before the curtain in a Jeanne d'Arc costume, waving a flag, and sing this battle song, which was received by the audience standing, and in which they often joined. We also were among the spectators one evening, Frederick and I, and we also had to rise from our seats. I say "had to," not from any external pressure, for we could of course have withdrawn into the back of the box, but "had to," because we were *electrified*.

"Look, Martha," Frederick explained to me, "a spark like that which runs from one man to another and makes this whole mass rise to one united and excited heart-beat, that is *love*."

"What do you mean? It is surely a song of hatred : —

> That their unholy blood
> May sink into our furrows."

" That is no matter, united hatred also is one form of love. Wherever two or more unite in one common feeling, they love each other. Let but a higher conception than that of the nation, *i.e.*, of mankind and of humanity, once be seized as the general idea, and then ——"

" Ah," I sighed, " when will that be?"

"When? that is a very relative term. In regard to the duration of our life, never; in regard to that of our race, to-morrow."

. . . .

When war has broken out all the subjects of neutral states divide themselves into two camps, one takes the side of the one, the other of the opposite party; it is like a great fluctuating wager, in which every one has a share.

We too—Frederick and I—with which side should we sympathise, which wish to conquer? As Austrians we should have been fully justified, " patriotically," in wishing to see our victor in the former war vanquished in this one. Besides, it is again natural that one should give the greater sympathy to those in whose midst one is living, and with whose feelings one is involuntarily infected; and we were then surrounded by the French. Still, Frederick was of Prussian descent, and were we not more allied with the Germans, whose speech even was my own, than with their adversaries? Besides, had not the declaration of war proceeded from the French, on such trifling grounds—nay, not grounds, but pretexts? And must we not conclude from that that the Prussian cause was the more just one, and that they were going into battle only as defenders, and in obedience to compulsion? King William had spoken with much justice in his speech from the throne on July 19 :—

The German and the French nations, both enjoying equally the blessings of Christian training and increasing prosperity, have been called to a more holy strife than the bloody one of arms. The rulers of France, however, have contrived to make profit for their own personal interests and passions out of the justifiable but irritable self-consciousness of our great neighbour by means of deliberate deception.

The Emperor Napoleon, on his side, published the following proclamation :—

In view of the presumptuous pretensions of Prussia, we were obliged to make protests. These were treated with scorn. Transactions[1] followed which showed their contempt for us. Our country has been deeply irritated at this, and at present the cry for war resounds from one end of France to the other. There remains nothing possible for us except to trust our fate to the arbitrament of arms. We are not making war on Germany, whose independence we respect. It is the object of our best wishes that the people composing the great German nationality should dispose freely of their own fate. As far as concerns ourselves, we desire to set up a state of things which will guarantee our security and make our future safe. We wish to obtain a lasting peace, founded on the true interests of the peoples. We wish for the termination of this miserable situation, in which all the nations are expending their resources in arming on all sides against each other.

What a lesson! what a mighty lesson speaks from this writing, when compared with the events which ensued upon it! This campaign, then, was undertaken by France in order to

---

[1] These transactions were described eighteen years later as follows : General Boulanger writes in his work on the campaign of 1870 : "After having obtained a legitimate satisfaction we wanted to impose a humiliation on the King of Prussia ; and in doing so we went on to take a diplomatic attitude which was aggressive, nay, almost inconsistent. The formal renunciation of Prince Leopold of Hohenzollern had been gained by us, and we had, besides, the assent of the King of Prussia to this renunciation. The reparation was sufficient, for it covered the respective domains of the interests of France, the rights of France, and the obligations of the chief of the house of Hohenzollern. We ought to have stopped there. Our Government pushed on farther. It wanted a categorical engagement from King William for the future. By carrying our claims so high it changed the object and ground of the strife. It converted it into a direct challenge to the sovereign of Prussia."

attain security—to attain lasting peace? And what came of it? *L'année terrible* and lasting enmity—enmity which still prevails. No; as with coal you cannot white-wash, as with assafœtida you cannot diffuse a sweet perfume, so neither with war can you make peace secure. This "miserable situation," to which Napoleon alludes, how much has it not changed for the worse since then! The emperor was in earnest, thoroughly in earnest about the scheme for setting on foot a European disarmament. I have it quite certainly from his nearest relations; but the war party put pressure on him—coerced him—and he yielded. And yet he could not refrain, even in the war proclamation, from harping on his favourite idea. Its carrying out was only to be deferred. "After the campaign"—"after the victory," said he, to console himself. It turned out otherwise.

So, on which side were our sympathies? If one has got to the point of detesting all war in and for itself, as was the case with Frederick and me, the genuine, pure, "passionate attachment" to either side can exist no more. One's only feeling is "Oh that it had never begun—this campaign! Oh that it were only already over!"

I did not think that the existing war would last long, or have important consequences. Two or three battles won here and there, and then there would be parleys for certain, and the thing would be brought to an end. What were they really fighting for? Literally for nothing. The whole thing was more of an armed promenade, undertaken by the French from love of knightly adventure, by the Germans from brave feelings of defensive duty. A few sabre-cuts would be exchanged, and the adversaries would shake hands again. Fool that I was! As if the consequences of a war remained in any proportion to the causes which produced it. It is its *course* which determines its consequences.

We should have been glad to leave Paris, for all the enthusiasm which the whole population displayed produced the most painful effect on us. But the way eastward was barred for the present, and the business of our house-building detained us. In short, we stayed. We had hardly any society connections left. Everybody that could anyhow do so had fled from Paris; and even of those who remained, no one under present circumstances even thought of issuing invitations. A few, however, of our acquaintances among the literary circles, who were still in the city, we did frequently visit. Just at this phase of the commencing war, it interested Frederick to make himself acquainted with the judgments and views then entertained by the master spirits of the time. There was an author, then quite young, who later on attained much fame, Guy de Maupassant, some of whose utterances, which penetrated into my soul, I entered in the red volumes :—

War—if I only think of the word a horror comes over me, as if people were talking to me about witches, about the inquisition, about some far-away, overmastering, horrible, unnatural thing. War—to fight each other, strangle, cut each other to pieces! And we have amongst us at this day, in our times, with our culture, with such an extension of science, with so high a grade of development as we believe ourselves to have attained—we have schools, where people are taught to kill, to kill at a good distance, and a good round number at a time. What is wonderful is that the people do not rise up against it, that the whole of society does not revolt at the bare word—war!

Every man who governs is just as much bound to avoid war as a ship's captain is bound to avoid shipwreck. If a captain has lost a ship he is brought before a court and tried, so that it may be known whether he has been guilty of negligence. Why should not a Government be put on its trial whenever a war has been declared? If the people understood it, if they refused to allow themselves to be killed without cause, there would be an end of war.

I had also an opportunity of reading a letter, written by Gustave Flaubert to George Sand in the early days of July, just after the outbreak of the war. Here it is :—

I am in despair at the stupidity of my countrymen. The incorrigible barbarity of men fills me with deep grief. This enthusiasm, which is inspired by no idea, makes me wish to die in order to see no more of it. These good Frenchmen wish to fight (1) because they believe themselves challenged by Prussia, (2) because savagery is the natural state of men, (3) because war has an element of mystery in it which is alluring to men. Are we coming to indiscriminate fighting? I fear it, . . . The horrible battles which are in preparation have no pretext whatever for them. It is the love of fighting for fighting's sake. I lament for the bridges and tunnels blown up. All this human labour gone to ruin. You will have seen that a gentleman recommended in the Chamber the plundering of the Grand Duchy of Baden. Oh that I could be with the Bedouins!

"Oh," cried I, as I read this letter, "that we could have been born 500 years later! that would be even better than the Bedouins."

"Men will not want all that time to become reasonable," said Frederick confidently.

.   .   .   .

The period of proclamations and general orders was now come.

The old hum-drum tune again always, and always again the public carried away to give it support and enthusiasm! There was joy over the victories guaranteed in the manifestoes, just as if they had been gained already.

On July 28 Napoleon III. issued the following document from his headquarters at Metz. This also I entered in my book, not, indeed, because I shared in the admiration but from contempt for the everlasting sameness and hollowness of its phrase-mongering :—

We are defending the honour and the soil of our country. We shall conquer. Nothing is too much for the persevering exertions of the soldiers of Africa, the Crimea, China, Italy and Mexico. Once more you will show what a French army can do, which is on fire with the love of country. Whatever way we take out of our boundaries, we find there the glorious footsteps of our forefathers. We will show ourselves worthy of them. On our success depends the fate of Freedom and Civilisation. Soldiers! let every one do his duty, and the God of Battles will be with us.

Of course, "*le Dieu des Armées*" could not be left out. That the leaders of defeated armies have said the same thing a hundred times over does not prevent the others from saying the same words at the beginning of every new campaign and awakening the same confidence by doing so. Is there anything more short and more weak than the memory of the people?

On July 31 King William quitted Berlin and left the following writing :—

In going to-day to the army, to fight along with it for honour and for the preservation of our noblest possessions, I leave an amnesty for all political offenders. My people know as well as I that the breach of treaty and hostile proceedings are not on our side. But as we have been provoked, we are determined, like our fathers, and in firm reliance on God, to brave the battle for the deliverance of our fatherland.

Necessity of defence—necessity of defence—that is the only recognised way of killing, and so both parties cry out: "I am defending myself". Is not that a contradiction? Not altogether, for over both there presides a third power, the power of the conquering, ancient war-spirit. It is only against *him* that all should join in a defensive league.

Along with the above manifestoes, I find in my red volumes an entry, with the singular title written over it : " If Ollivier had married Meyerbeer's daughter would the war have broken out ?" This is how the matter stood. Amongst our Parisian acquaintance there was a literary man named Alexander Weill, and it was he who threw out the above question, while he told us the following story :—

"Meyerbeer was looking out for a man of talent for his second daughter, and his choice fell on my friend Emile Ollivier. Ollivier was a widower. He had married for his first wife the daughter of Liszt, whom the renowned pianist had by the Countess d'Agoult (Daniel Stern), with whom he long lived as his wife. The marriage was very happy, and Ollivier had the reputation of a virtuous husband. He possessed no fortune, but as a speaker and statesman he was already famous. Meyerbeer wanted to make his personal acquaintance, and to this end I gave, in April, 1864, a great ball, which was attended by most of the celebrities of art and science, and where, of course, Ollivier, who had been informed by me of Meyerbeer's purpose, played the first part. He pleased Meyerbeer. The matter was not easy to bring to a head. Meyerbeer knew the independent originality of his second daughter, who would never marry any other husband than one of her own choice. It was arranged that Ollivier should pay a visit to Baden, and there be introduced as if by chance to the young lady. When Meyerbeer died suddenly a fortnight after this ball, it was Ollivier, if you recollect, who pronounced his *éloge* and funeral oration at the Northern Railway Station. Now, I affirm, nay I am certain of it, that if Ollivier had married Meyerbeer's daughter, the war between France and Germany would not have broken out. Look how plausible my proofs are. In the first place, Meyerbeer, who hated the empire to the point of contempt, would never have permitted his daughter's husband to become a minister of the emperor. It is well known that, if Ollivier had threatened the Chamber to give in his resignation sooner than declare war, the Chamber would never have declared war. The present war is the work of three back-stairs confidants and secret ministers of the empress, named, Jérôme David, Paul de Cassagnac, and the Duc de Grammont. The empress, excited by the Pope, whose religious puppet she is, would have this war, as to the success of which she never doubted, in order to ensure her son's succession. She said: 'C'est ma guerre à moi et à mon fils,' and the three above-named papal 'anabaptists' were her secret tools to force the emperor, who did not want any war, and the Chamber into war by false and secret despatches from Germany."

" And this is what is called diplomacy !" I interrupted with a shudder.

" Listen further," pursued Alexander Weill. " Ollivier said to me on July 15, when I met him on the Place de la Concorde: ' Peace is assured, or I resign '. Whence came it then that this same man, a few days later, instead of resigning, declared war himself, ' *d'un cœur léger*,' as he said in the Chamber ? "

" With a light heart ! " I cried, shuddering again.

" There is a secret in this that I can throw light upon. The emperor, for whom money had never any other value than to purchase love or friendship with it (he believes, like Jugurtha in Rome, that all in France, men and women, have their price), has the custom, when he takes a minister who is not rich, of binding him more closely to himself by a present of a million francs. Daru alone, who told me this secret, declined this present—' Timeo Danaos et dona ferentes '. And he alone, being unfettered, sent in his resignation. As long as the emperor hesitated, Ollivier, being bound to his master by this chain of gold, declared himself neutral—rather inclined to peace. But as soon as the emperor had been overborne by his wife and her three ultramontane anabaptists, Ollivier declared for war, and gave it lively utterance, with light heart, ' and with full pockets '."[1]

.   .   '   .

[1] Briefe hervorragender Männer an Alexander Weill—Zürich.

CHAPTER XVIII.

First days of the war in Paris.—Constant reverses of the French arms.—Fall of Metz.—Paris turned into a fortress.— The Prussians expelled from Paris.—Surrender of the Emperor Napoleon and his army at Sedan.—Proclamation of the Republic.—Futile negotiations for peace.— We determine to quit Paris.—This is prevented by my illness.—When I recover the winter has set in, and Paris has long been beleaguered.—Fall of Strasbourg.—Paris bombarded.— The proclamation of the German Empire at Versailles.—Dreams of release and future happiness suddenly interrupted by the arrest and execution of my husband by the Communards.

"OH monsieur! Oh madame! What happiness! What great news!" With these words Frederick's valet rushed into our room one day, and the cook after him. It was the day of Wörth.

"What is it?"

"A telegram has been posted up at the Bourse. We have conquered. The King of Prussia's army is as good as annihilated. The city is adorning itself with tricolour flags. There will be an illumination to-night."

But in the course of the afternoon it turned out that the news was false—a Bourse trick. Ollivier made a speech to the crowd from his balcony. Well, so much the better; at least one would not be obliged to illuminate. These joyful tidings of "armies annihilated"—*i.e.*, of numberless lives torn asunder, and hearts broken—awoke again in me too the same wish as Flaubert's—"Oh that I were with the Bedouins!"

On August 7, news of a catastrophe. The emperor hastened from St. Cloud to the theatre of war. The enemy had penetrated into the country. The newspapers could not give expression hot enough to their rage at the "invasion". The cry "À Berlin," as it seemed to me, pointed to an intended invasion; but in that there was nothing to cause anger. But that these eastern barbarians should venture to make an incursion into beautiful, God-beloved France—that was sheer savagery and sin. That must be stopped, and quickly too.

The Minister of War *ad interim* published a decree that all citizens fit for service, from the age of thirty to forty, who did not belong to the National Guard, should be immediately enrolled in that body. A Ministry of the Defence of the Country was formed. The war loan of 500 millions, which had been voted, was raised to 1000. It is quite refreshing to see how freely people always offer up the money and the lives of others. A trifling financial unpleasantness, to be sure, was soon perceptible to the public. If one wanted to change bank notes one had to pay the money-changer ten per cent. There was not gold at hand to meet all the notes which the Bank of France was authorised to issue.

And now, victory after victory on the German side.

The physiognomy of the city of Paris and its inhabitants altered. Instead of its proud, magnificent, resplendent mood, came confusion and savage indignation. The feeling spread ever wider and wider that a horde of Vandals had descended on to the land—something terrible, unheard of, like some cloud of locusts, or some such natural portent. That they had themselves brought this plague on themselves by their declaration of war—that they had considered such a declaration indispensable, in order that no Hohenzollern, even in the distant future, should even conceive the idea of succeeding to the Spanish throne—all that they had forgotten. Hideous tales were circulated about the enemy. "The Uhlans! the Uhlans!" These words had a fantastically-demoniacal sound, as if one had said "the horde of savages". In the imagination

of the people this kind of troops assumed a demoniacal
shape. Wherever a bold stroke was executed by the German
cavalry, it was attributed to the Uhlans—a kind of half-men,
getting no pay, and therefore bound to live on their plunder.
Along with the rumours of terror arose rumours also of triumph.
To tell lies about successes is one of the duties of Chauvinism.
Of course, because courage must be kept up. The command,
to tell truth, like so many other commands, loses its obligation
in war time. Frederick dictated to me the following passage out
of the newspaper *Le Volontaire* for my red book :—

Up to the 16th of August, the Germans have lost already 144,000 men.
The rest are almost starving. The last reserves are coming up from
Germany—"la landwehr et la landsturm". Old men of sixty, with
flint muskets, with an enormous tobacco pouch on their right side and
a still larger schnaps-flask on their left, a long clay pipe in their mouth;
stooping under the weight of the knapsack (on the top of which there
must not be omitted the coffee mill and the elder tea inside), are crawling
along, coughing and blowing their noses, from the right to the left bank of
the Rhine, cursing those who have torn them from the embraces of their
grandchildren, to lead them on to certain death. "As to the news of
victory, brought from German sources," it was said in the French
newspapers, "they are the usual Prussian lies."

On August 20 Count Palikao announced in the Chamber
that three army corps which had coalesced against Bazaine
had been thrown into the quarries at Jaumont (Bravo! Bravo!).
It is true that no one knew what quarries these were, or where
they were ; nor did any one explain how they could contain
three army corps ; but the joyous message went round from
mouth to mouth. "Have you heard ? In the quarries ——"
"Oh yes ! Of Jaumont." No one uttered a doubt or question. It was as if everybody had been born at Jaumont, and
knew these army-swallowing quarries as well as his own pocket.
About this time the rumour also prevailed that the King of
Prussia had *gone mad* from despair at the condition of his
army.

Nothing but monstrous things were heard of. The excite-

ment, the fever, of the populace increased hourly. The war
"*là-bas*" had ceased to be regarded as an armed promenade.
It was felt that the forces which had been let loose were now
bringing something terrible on the world. Nothing was spoken
of but armies annihilated, princes driven mad, diabolical hordes,
war to the knife. I listened to it thundering and growling. It
was the storm of rage and despair that was rising. The battle
at Bazeilles near Metz was described, and it was stated
that inhuman cruelties had been committed there by the
Bavarians.

"Do you believe that?" I asked Frederick. "Do you
believe that of the gentle Bavarians?"

"It is quite possible. Bavarian or Turco, German, French,
or Indian, the warrior who is defending his own life, and lifting
up his arm to kill another, has ceased for the time to be
'human'. What has been awakened in him and stirred up
with all possible force is nothing else than bestiality."

. . . .

Metz fallen! The news resounded in the city like some
strange and overpowering cry of terror. To me the news of
the taking of a fortress was a message which brought rather a
relief; for I thought, "Well, that is decisive". And it was only
for this, that the bloody game might be over, it was for this,
only this that I longed. But no, there was nothing decisive
in it—more fortresses remained. After a defeat all that is to
be done is to pick yourself up again, and strike out again at
them twice as hard. The chance of arms may change at any
time. Ah yes! The advantage may be now on this side, now
on that. It is only woe that is certain—death that is certain—
to be on both.

Trochu felt himself called upon to arouse the spirit of the
populace by a new proclamation, and in it appealed to an
old motto of Bretagne, "With God's help for our fatherland".
That did not sound new to me. I had met with something
like it before in other proclamations. It did not fail to have

its effect. The people were inspirited. Now, the thing was to
turn Paris into a fortress.

Paris a fortress! I could not take in the idea. The city
which V. Hugo called "*la ville-lumière*," which is the point
of attraction for the whole world of civilisation, riches, the
pursuit of art, and the enjoyment of life—the point from
which radiate splendour, fashions, *esprit*—this city is now to
be "fortified"—*i.e.*, become the point at which hostile attacks
are to be aimed; the target for shot; to close itself against all
intercourse, and expose itself to the danger of being set in flames
by bombardment, or starved by famine! And that is done
by these people, *de gaieté de cœur*, in the spirit of self-
sacrifice, with joyous emulation, as if it was a question of
carrying out the most useful, the most noble work! The work
was proceeded with in feverish haste. Ramparts had to be
erected on which troops could be placed, and shot holes cut in
them; also trenches dug outside the gates, drawbridges
erected, covering works repaired, canals bridged over, and
protected by breastworks, powder magazines built, and a flotilla
of gunboats placed on the Seine. What a fever of activity!
What expenditure of exertion and industry! What gigantic
expense in labour and money! How exhilarating and
ennobling all that would have been, if it had been expended
on works of public utility; but for the purpose of working
mischief, of annihilation—a purpose which is not even one's
own, but only a move on the strategic chess-board—it is inconceivable!

In order to be able to stand a siege, which might possibly be
a long one, the city was provisioned. Up to the present time,
according to all experience, no such thing as an impregnable
fortification has been known, capitulation is always only a
question of time. And yet fortresses have always been erected
anew, and provisioned anew with necessaries, in spite of the
mathematical *impossibility* of protecting oneself against the
duration of a blockade.

The measures taken were on a great scale. Mills were

erected, and cattle parks laid out, and yet at last the moment *must* come when the corn will give out and the meat be consumed. But people do not carry their thoughts so far—by that time the enemy will be driven back over the frontier, or annihilated in the country. Now the whole people are joining the army of the fatherland. Every one offers himself for the service, or is pressed into it; and all the firemen in the country were called in to join the garrison of Paris. There might be fires in the provinces, but what of that? Such little accidents disappear when a national "disaster" is in question. On Aug. 17, 60,000 firemen had already been enrolled in the capital. The sailors too were called in, and new troops of soldiers were formed every day under various names—*volontaires, éclaireurs, franc-tireurs.*

. . . .

Events followed each other in ever-hastening movement. But now only military events. Everything else was suspended. Nothing else was any more thought of around us except "*mort aux Prussiens*". A storm of savage hatred collected: it had not yet broken out, but one heard it rumble. In all official proclamations, in all the street cries, in all public transactions, the conclusion was always "*mort aux Prussiens*". All these troops, regular and irregular, these munitions, these work-people pressing to the fortifications with their tools and barrows, these transports for weapons, everything that one sees and hears means, in its every form and tone, in all its lightning and bluster, in all its flame and rage, "*mort aux Prussiens*". Or in other words, and then indeed it sounds like a cry of love and warms even the softest hearts, it means "*pour la patrie*," but in essence it is the same.

I asked Frederick: "You are of Prussian extraction, how does all this unfriendly feeling, which is now finding loud expression, affect you?"

"You said the same to me before, in 1866, and I answered you then as I do to-day, that I suffer from these expressions of

26

hatred not as the subject of any country, but as a man. If I
judge of the opinions of the people here from a national point
of view I cannot but think them right, they call it *la haine
sacrée de l'ennemi*, and that motive forms an important element
in warlike patriotism.   They are now occupied with this one
thought, to liberate their country from a hostile invasion. That
it is themselves who provoked this invasion by declaring war,
they have forgotten.   Indeed it was not they who did it, but
their Government, which they believed on its word; and now
they lose no time over reproaches or reflections, as to who
called down this misfortune on them: it has come, and all their
force, all their enthusiasm must be spent on turning it aside
again, or else uniting with unthinking self-sacrifice in a common
ruin.   Trust me, there is much noble capacity for love in us
children of men, the pity only is that we lavish it on the old-
world tracks of hatred. . . . And on the other side, the hated
ones, the invaders, 'the red-haired eastern barbarians,' what are
they doing?   They were the challenged; and they are pressing
forward into the country of those who threatened to overrun
theirs— '*À Berlin, à Berlin*'.   Do not you recollect how this
cry kept pealing through the whole city, even down from the
roofs of omnibusses?"

   "And now these are marching '*Nach Paris*'.   Why do the
shouters of '*À Berlin*' attribute that as a crime to them?"

   "Because there cannot be any logic or justice in that national
sentiment whose foundation is the assumption that *we* are
ourselves, that is the first, and the others are barbarians.   And
this forward march of the Germans from victory to victory
strikes me with admiration.   I have been a soldier also, and I
know with what a magical power victory fastens on the mind,
what pride, what joy are contained in it.   It is in any case the
aim, the reward for all the sacrifices made, for the renunciation
of rest and happiness, for the risk of life."

   "But then why do not the conquered adversaries, since they
too are soldiers, and know what fame accompanies victory, why
do they not admire their conquerors?   Why is it never said in

an account of a battle by the losing party: 'The enemy has obtained a glorious victory' ? "

" I repeat, because the war spirit and patriotic egotism are the *denial of all justice.*"

So it came about—I can see it from all our conversations entered in the red books in those days—that we did not and could not think of anything at that time except the result of the present national duel.

Our happiness, our poor happiness, we had it, but we dared not enjoy it. Yes, we possessed everything that might have procured for us a heaven of delight on earth—boundless love, riches, rank, the charming, growing boy Rudolf, our heart's idol Sylvia, independence, ardent interest in the world of mind ; but before all this a curtain had fallen. How dared we, how could we taste of our joys while around us every one was suffering and trembling, shrieking and raving ? It was as if one should set oneself to enjoy oneself heartily on board a storm-tossed vessel.

" A theatrical fellow, this Trochu," Frederick told me—it was on August 25. " Such a *coup de théâtre* has been played off to-day ! You will never guess it."

" The women called out for military service ? " I guessed.

" Well, it does concern the women ; but they are not called out. On the contrary."

" Then are the sutlers discharged ? or the Sisters of Mercy ? "

" You have not guessed it yet, either. There is something of dismissal in it to be sure, and as to sutlers, too, in the sense that these ladies minister the cup of pleasure, and in a sense the ladies dismissed are merciful too ; but in short, without more riddles, the *demimonde* is exiled."

" And the Minister of War has taken that step ? What connection —— ? "

" I cannot see any either. But the people are in ecstasies over the regulation. In fact they are always glad when *any-thing* happens. From every new order they expect a change, like many sick folks who greet every medicine which is given them as possibly a panacea. When vice is driven out of the city—so think the pious—who knows whether Heaven, now evidently angry, will not again extend its protection over the ‘inhabitants? And now, when people are preparing for the serious time of the siege, with all its privations, what have these silly, wasteful women of pleasure to do here? And so most people, excluding those concerned, think the regulation a proper, moral, and besides, a patriotic one, since a great number of these women are foreigners, English, Southerners, nay even Germans, some of whom may perhaps be spies. No, no; there is only room in the city now for her own children, and only for her virtuous children!"

On August 28 occurred something still worse. Another banishment. *All Germans* had to quit Paris within three days. The poison, the deadly, long-abiding poison, which lay in this regulation those who wrote the decree possibly had not in any way suspected. *The hatred of Germans* was awakened by it. For how long a time even after the war, this misfortune was to go on bearing its terrible fruit, I know at this day. From that time forward, France and Germany, those two great, flourishing, magnificent countries, were no longer two nations whose armies had fought out a chivalrous conflict; hatred for the whole of the opposed nation pervaded the entire people. Enmity was erected into an institution which was not restricted to the duration of the war, but ensured its continuance as "hereditary enmity," even to future generations.

Exiled. Obliged to leave the city within three days. I had occasion to see how hardly, how inhumanly hardly, this command pressed on many worthy, harmless families. Among the business people who were supplying us with goods for the decoration of our house, several were Germans—one a carriage-builder, one an upholsterer, one an art-furniture manufacturer —settled from ten to twenty years in Paris, where they had got their domestic hearth, where they had allied themselves in marriage with Parisians, where they had the whole of their business connection ; and now they had to go out, out in three days—shut up their house, leave all that was dear and familiar to them, lose their fortune, their customers, their inheritance. The poor creatures came running to us in consternation, and told us of the misery that had fallen on them. Even the work which they were on the point of delivering to us had to be put aside, and the workshops closed. Wringing their hands and with tears in their eyes, they complained of their sufferings to us. " I have an old father an invalid," said one, " and my wife is looking for her confinement any day ; and now we must go in three days I" "I have not a sou in the house," another complained ; " all my customers who owe me money will be in no hurry to meet their obligations. A week hence I should have completed a large order which would have made me comfortably off, and now I must leave all in confusion I "

And why, *why* was all this misery brought on these poor people ? Because they belonged to a nation whose army did its duty successfully, or because (to go further back in the chain of causes) a Hohenzollern might possibly have allowed it to enter into his mind to assume the Spanish throne if offered to him ? No; this "because," too, has not arrived at the ultimate reason. All this is only the pretext—not the cause of that war.

. . . .

Sedan I "*The Emperor Napoleon has given up his sword.*"

The news overwhelmed us. Now there had really occurred a great, an historical catastrophe. The French army beaten, its leader checkmated. Then the game was over, won triumphantly by Germany. " Over I over I " I shouted. " If there were people who have the right to call themselves citizens of the world they might illuminate their windows to-day. If we had temples of Humanity yet, *Te Deums* would have to be sung in them on this occasion—the butchery is over I "

" Do not rejoice too soon, my darling," said Frederick in a warning tone. " This war has now for some time lost the character of a game fought out on the chess-board of the battle-field. The whole nation is joining in the fight. For *one* army annihilated ten others will start out of the earth."

" But would that be just? It is only German soldiers who have forced themselves into the country—not the German people—and so they ought only to oppose them with French soldiers."

" How you keep on appealing to justice and reason, you unreasonable creature, in dealing with a madman! France is mad with pain and rage; and from the point of view of loss of country, her pain is pious, her rage justifiable. Whatever desperate thing she may do now is inspired, not by personal self-seeking, but by the highest spirit of sacrifice. If only the time were come when the powers of virtue, which is the essential thing that binds men together, were diverted from the work of destruction and devoted to the work of felicity! But this unholy war has again thrown us back a long distance from that goal."

" No, no! I hope the war is over now."

" If it were so (and I despair of it) there would be sown the seeds of future wars, and it could only be the seed of hatred which is contained in this expulsion of the Germans. Such a thing as that has an effect far beyond the present generation."

September 4. Another act of violence, an outbreak of passion, and, at the same time, a remedy tried for the salvation of the country—the emperor is deposed. France proclaims herself a republic. Whatever Napoleon III. and his army may have done matters not. Mistakes, treachery, cowardice, all these faults have been committed by individuals, the emperor and his generals; but France has not committed them, she is not answerable for it. When the throne was overturned, the leaves in France's history, on which Metz and Sedan were inscribed, were simply torn out of the book. From this time the country itself would carry on the war, if, at least, Germany dared to continue this infamous invasion.

"But how if Napoleon had conquered?" I asked, when Frederick communicated this to me.

"Oh, then, France would have taken his victory and his glory as the country's victory and glory."

"Is that just?"

"Cannot you get out of the habit of putting that question?"

I had soon to see my hopes, that the catastrophe of Sedan would put an end to the campaign, vanish. All around us seemed as warlike as ever. The air was laden with savage rage and hot lust of vengeance. Rage against the enemy, and almost as much against the fallen dynasty. The scandalous talk, the pamphlets which now poured down against the emperor, the empress, and the unfortunate generals; the contempt, the slanders, the insults, the jests—it was disgusting. In this way the uncultured masses thought they could lay the whole burden of the defeats of the country on the shoulders of one or two persons, and, now that these persons were down, pelted them with dung and stones. And this was the beginning of the time when the country was to show that she was invincible!

The preparations for intrenching Paris were carried on zealously. The buildings in the fighting area of the chief *enceinte* were abandoned or taken down entirely. The suburbs became deserts. Troops of men kept coming from outside into the city with all their belongings. Oh, those sorrowful trains of carts and pack horses, and laden men, who were trailing the ruins of their desolated hearths through the streets! I had already seen the same thing once in Bohemia, when the poor country folk were flying from the enemy; and now I had to look on the same picture of wretchedness in the joyous, brilliant capital of the world. There were the same frightened, sorrowful visages, the same weariness and haste, the same woe.

At last, God be praised, once more a good piece of news! On the proposal of a mediation on the part of England, a

meeting was arranged at Ferrières between Jules Favre and
Bismarck. Now surely they would succeed in coming to an
agreement—in making peace!

On the contrary, it was not till now that the extent of the gulf
was seen. For so ne little time before this there had been
some talk in the German papers of the annexation of Alsace and
Lorraine. A desire was shown to incorporate once more the
land which had formerly been German. The historical argument for the claim on these provinces appearing only partially
sustainable, the *strategic* argument was brought forward to
support it—"indispensable as a fortress in future wars which may
be expected". And it is well known, of course, that the strategic
grounds are the weightiest, the most impregnable; and that in
comparison with them a moral ground can only reckon as
secondary. On the other hand, the war game had been lost
by France; was it not fair that the prize should fall to the
winners? In case *they* had won, would not the French have
seized the Rhine provinces? If the result of a war is not to
have for its consequence an extension of territory for one side
or the other, what good would it be to make war at all?

Meantime the victorious army made no halt in its onward
march. The Germans were already before the gates of Paris.
The cession of Alsace and Lorraine was officially demanded;
to which came the well-known reply: "Not an inch of our
territory, not a stone of our fortresses"—("Pas un pouce—pas
une pierre").

Yes, yes—thousands of lives, but not an inch of ground.
That is the rooted idea of the patriotic spirit. "They wish to
humble us," cried the French patriots. "No! sooner shall
exasperated Paris bury itself under its own ruins!"

Away! away! was now our resolution. Why should we
stay in a beleaguered foreign city without any necessity; why
live among people full of no other thoughts than those of hate
and vengeance, who looked at us with sidelong glances and
often with clenched fists, when they heard us talking German?
It is true, we could no longer leave Paris, or leave France,

without difficulty. One had in all directions to pass over war
districts, the railway traffic was frequently suspended for
private travellers. To leave our new building in the lurch was
unpleasant, but this was of no consequence, for our stay was
impossible. In fact we had already stayed far too long.
The events which I had experienced recently had shaken me so
much that my nerves had suffered grievously from it. I was
seized often with shivering, and once or twice also with crying
fits.

Our boxes were all ready packed, and everything prepared
for departure, when I had another attack, and this time so
violent that I had to be carried to bed. The physician who
was sent for said that either a nervous fever or even an inflam-
mation of the brain was commencing, and for the present it was
not to be thought of to expose me to the fatigues of travelling.

I lay in bed for long, long weeks. Only a very dreamy
recollection of that whole time remains with me. And strangely
enough, a pleasant recollection. I was, it is true, very ill, and
everything in the place where I resided was unceasingly mournful and terrible; and yet when I look back on it it was a
singularly joyful time. Yes, joy, perfectly intense joy, such as
children are in the habit of feeling. The cerebral affection
which I was suffering, and which brought with it an almost
continuous absence, or at least only half-presence of consciousness, caused all thoughts and judgments, all reflections and
deliberations, to vanish out of my head, and there remained
only a vague enjoyment of existence, just like that which
children experience, as I said just now, and especially those
children who are tenderly watched over. There was no want
of tender watching for me. My husband, thoughtful and
loving and untiring, was with me day and night. He brought
the children also often to my bedside. How much my Rudolf
had to tell me! For the most part I did not understand it,
but his beloved voice sounded to me like music, and the
babbling of our little Sylvia, our heart's idol, how sweetly that
began to charm me! Then there were a hundred little jokes

and intelligences between Frederick and me about the tricks of
our little daughter.   What these jokes were about I have quite
forgotten, but I know that I laughed and enjoyed myself quite
unrestrainedly.   Each one of the customary jests seemed to
me the height of wit, and the oftener repeated the more witty
and more precious ; and with what delight did I not swallow
the draughts given me—for every day at a given hour I took a
glass of lemonade.   Such nectar I have never tasted during
my whole life of health ; and how entirely refreshing was a
medicine with opium in it, whose softly soothing action,
putting me into a conscious slumber, sent a thrill of happy
calm through my soul.   I knew all the while that my beloved
husband was by my side, protecting me and watching over me
as his heart's dearest treasure. Of the war, which was raging at
my door, I had now hardly any cognisance ; and if, for all that,
some remembrance of it flashed on me sometimes, I looked on
it as something situated as far away and as completely without
any concern for me, as if it was being played out in China or
on another planet.   My world was here, in this sick-room, or
rather in this chamber of recovery ; for I felt myself getting
better, and all tended to happiness.

.   .   .   .

To happiness ? No. With recovery, understanding came
back too, and the perception of the horrors that surrounded
us.   We were in a beleaguered, famishing, freezing, miserable
city.   The war was still raging on.

The winter had come in the meantime—icy cold. I now,
for the first time, learned all that had taken place during my
long unconsciousness.   The capital of " the brotherland,"
Strasbourg — the "lovely," the " true German," the city
" German to its core," had been bombarded, its library
destroyed.   One hundred and ninety-three thousand seven
hundred and twenty-two shots had been poured into the town
—four or five a minute.

Strasbourg was taken.

The country fell into wild despair—such a despair as issues in raving madness. People began to hunt in *Nostradamus* to find prophecies for the present events, and new seers began to put out fresh predictions. Still worse, *possessed* folks came forward. It was like falling back into a ghost-night of the middle ages, lighted by the fire of hell. "Oh that I could be among the Bedouins!" cried Gustave Flaubert. "Oh that I could be back in the half-conscious dreamland of my illness," cried I, weeping. I was well again now, and had to hear and comprehend all the terrible things that were going on around us. Then began again the entries in the red books, and I have lit on the following notes :—

December 1. Trochu has established himself on the heights of Champigny.

December 2. Obstinate fight around Brie and Champigny.

December 5. The cold is becoming constantly more powerful. Oh ! the trembling, bleeding, wretched wights, who are lying out there in the snow, *and dying*. Even here in the city, there is terrible suffering from cold. Business has fallen to nothing. There is no firing to be had. What would not many an one give if there were only two little pieces of wood to be had—even the certainty of the throne of Spain !

December 21. Sortie out of Paris.

December 25. A small detachment of Prussian cavalry was saluted with musket shot (that is a patriotic duty) from the houses of the villages of Troo and Sougé. General Kraatz commanded the punishment of the villages (that is a commander's duty) and had them burnt. "Set them on fire," was the word of command, and the men, probably gentle, good-natured fellows, obeyed (that is the soldier's duty), and set fire to them. The flames burst up to heaven, and the poor homesteads fell crashing, on man, wife, and child—on flying, weeping, roaring, burning men and beasts.

What a joyous, happy, holy Christmas night !

.   .   .   .

Is Paris to be starved out, or bombarded as well ?

Against the last supposition the civilised conscience revolts. To bombard this *ville-lumière*, this point of attraction of all nations, this brilliant home of the arts—bombard it with

its irreplaceable riches and treasures, like the first fort that
comes to hand! It is not to be thought of. The whole neutral
press (as I found out afterwards) protested against it. On
the other hand, the press of the war party in Berlin was favourable to it: that would be the only way to bring the war to a
close—and to conquer the city on the Seine, what glory!
Besides, it was just these protests which determined certain
circles at Versailles to seize this strategic weapon; and, after all,
a bombardment is nothing. And so it came about that on
December 28 I was writing in shaking characters: "Here it is
—another heavy stroke—a pause—and again ——"

I wrote no further, but I well remember the feelings of that
day. In those words: "Here it is," there lay, along with the
terror, a kind of freedom, a relief, a cessation of the nervous
expectation that had by that time become well nigh insufferable.
What one had been for so long partly expecting and fearing,
partly thinking hardly humanly possible, is now come. We
were sitting at *déjeûner à la fourchette, i.e.,* we were taking
bread and coffee—food was getting scarce already—Frederick,
Rudolf, the tutor and I—when the first stroke resounded. All
of us raised our heads and exchanged glances. Is that it?
But no. It may have been a house door slamming, or something of that sort. Now all was quiet. We resumed the talk
that had been interrupted, without saying anything about the
thought which that sound had caused. Then, after two or
three minutes it came again. Frederick started up. "That
is the bombardment," he said, and hurried to the window.
I followed him. A hubbub came in from the street. Groups
had formed; the people were standing and listening, or were
exchanging excited words.

Now our *valet de chambre* came rushing into the room, and
at the same time a fresh salvo resounded.

"Oh monsieur et madame—c'est le bombardment."

And now all the other men and maids, down to the kitchen-
maid, came pushing into the room. In such catastrophies—in
the exigencies of war, fire, or water, all distinctions of society

fall away, and those threatened all cluster together. All feel equal before danger—much more than before the law—much more than before Death, which in its burial ceremonies knows so much of distinction of rank. " C'est le bombardment, c'est le bombardment." Every one who came into the room uttered the same cry.

It was horrible, and yet I recollect quite well what I felt—a sort of admiring shudder, a kind of satisfaction at such a mighty experience—to be present at a situation so freighted with destiny and not to fear the danger to my own life in it. My pulses beat, and I felt--what shall I call it?—the pride of courage.

.   .   .   .

The thing was on the whole less terrible than it had seemed at the first instant. No flaming buildings, no crowds shrieking with terror, no bombshells whizzing continually through the air ; but only always this heavy, far-off thunder, with long and still longer intervals between. One came after a time to get almost accustomed to it. The Parisians chose as objects for a walk those points where the cannon music was best heard. Here and there a bomb would fall in the street and burst ; but how rarely did it occur to any given person to happen to be near ? It is true that many shells did fall which carried death, but in the city of a million men these cases were heard of in the same scattered way in which at other times one is accustomed to see in one's newspaper various cases of accident, without its coming specially near to oneself. "A bricklayer fell from a scaffold four storeys high," or "A genteelly dressed female threw herself over the balustrades of the bridge into the river," and so forth. The real grief, the real terror of the populace, was not for the bombardment, but hunger, cold, and starvation. But *one* such account of the death-dealing shot gave me a deep shock. It came in the form of a black-bordered mourning-card sent to the house : —

Monsieur and Madame R—— inform you of the death of their two children, François aged eight, and Amélie aged four, who were struck by a bomb coming through the window. Your silent sympathy is requested.

Silent sympathy! I gave a loud shriek as I read the paper. A thought—a picture flashing before my inner eye with lightning clearness, showed me the whole of the woe which lay in this simple mourning-notice. I saw *our* two children, Rudolf and Sylvia—no! I could not pursue the thought!

The tidings which one got were scanty. All communication by post was, of course, cut off. It was by carrier pigeons and balloons only that we had intercourse with the world outside. The rumours that cropped up everywhere were of the most contradictory nature. Victorious sallies were announced, or the information was spread that the enemy was on the point of storming Paris, with a view of setting it on fire in all corners, and levelling it to the ground, or it was asseverated that sooner than allow one German to get within the walls, the commandants of the forts would blow up themselves and the whole of Paris into the air. It was related that the whole population of the country, especially of the south (*le midi se lève*), were falling on the besiegers' rear, in order to cut off their retreat, and annihilate them to the last man.

Along with the false news, some true intelligence also came to us—some whose truth was proved afterwards. Such as about a panic that broke out on the road of Grand Luce near Mans, in which horrible deeds took place—soldiers getting beyond control, throwing the wounded out of the railway carriages that were all standing ready, and taking their places themselves.

It became more difficult every day to get food. The supply of meat was exhausted; there had for a long time now been no longer any beeves or sheep in the cattle parks that had been formed; all the horses also were soon eaten up, and then the period began when the dogs and cats, the rats and mice, and finally the beasts in the Jardin des Plantes also, even the poor elephant, who was such a favourite, had to serve as food. Bread could now be hardly procured. The people had to stand in rows for hours after hours in front of the bakers' shops in order to get their little ration, and still most of them

had to go empty away.   Exhaustion and sickness made Death's
harvest a rich one.   Whilst ordinarily 1100 died in a week,
the death-list of Paris in these times rose to between 4000 and
5000 weekly.   That is, there were every day between 400 and
500 unnatural deaths—that is to say, *murders*.   For if the
murderer is not an individual man, but an impersonal thing,
vis., war, it is not any the less murder.   Whose is the responsibility?   Does it not lie on those parliamentary swaggerers,
who in their provocative speeches declared with proud self-
assumption—as that Girardin did in the sitting of July 15—
that they "took on themselves the responsibility for this war
in the face of history"?   Could, then, any man's shoulders be
sufficiently strong to bear such a load of guilt?   Surely not.
But no one thinks of taking such boasters at their word.

One day—it was about January 20—Frederick came into
my room, with an excited look, on his return from a walk in
the city.

"Take your diary in hand, my busy little historian," he
called out to me.   "To-day a mighty despatch has come."
And he threw himself into a chair.

"Which of my books?" I asked.   "*The Protocol of
Peace?*"

Frederick shook his head.

"Oh that will be out of use for long.   The war, which is
now being fought out, is of too powerful a nature not to
proceed to its end, and give rise to renewed war.   On the side
of the vanquished it has scattered such a plenty of the seeds of
hatred and revenge, that a future harvest of war must grow out
of them; and on the other side, it has brought such magnificent
and bewildering successes to the victors, that for them an
equally great seed-time of warlike pride must grow out of it."

"What, then, has happened of such importance?"

"King William has been proclaimed German Emperor in
Versailles.   There is now *one* Germany—one single empire—
and a mighty empire too.   That forms a new chapter in what
is called the history of the world.   And you may think for

yourself, how, from the birth of this empire, which is the product of war, that trade will be held high in honour. It is, therefore, from this time, the two continental states most advanced in civilisation which will chiefly nourish the war spirit—the one, in order to return the blow it has received, the other, in order to keep the position it has conquered amongst the powers—from hatred on that side, from love on this—on that side from lust of revenge, on this from gratitude —it comes to the same thing. Shut your *Protocol of Peace* —for a long time henceforth we shall abide under the blood-and-iron sign of Mars."

"German Emperor!" I cried, "that really is grand;" and I got him to tell me the particulars of this event.

"I cannot help, Frederick," I said, "being pleased at this news. The whole work of slaughter has not then been for nothing, if a great new empire has grown out of it."

"But from a French point of view it has been for less than nothing. And we two must have surely the right of looking at this war, not from one side—the German side—only. Not only as men, but even from the narrow national conception, we should have the right to bewail the successes of our enemies and conquerors in 1866. However I agree with you that the union of dismembered Germany, which has now been attained, is a *fine* thing—that this agreement of the rest of the German princes to give the Imperial Crown to the old victor, has something inspiring, something admirable about it. The only pity is that this union did not arise from a peaceful, but from a warlike exploit. How was it then that there was not enough love of country, enough popular power in Germany, even though Napoleon III. had never sent the challenge of July 19, to form, of their own will, that entity on which their national pride is now to rest—'one single people of brothers'? Now they will be jubilant—the poet's wish is fulfilled. That only four short years ago all were at daggers drawn with each other, that for Hanoverians, Saxons, Frankforters, Nassauers, there was no name more hateful than 'Prussians,' will luckily be forgotten. In place of this, however, the hatred of Germans in this country, how it will ripen from this time!"

I shuddered. "The mere word, hatred ——" I began.

"Is hateful to you? You are right. As long as this feeling is not banished and outlawed, so long is there no humane humanity. Religious hatred is conquered, but national hatred forms still part of civil education. And yet there is only one ennobling, cheering feeling on this earth, and that is Love. We could say something about that, Martha, could we not?" I leaned my head on his shoulder, and looked up at him, while he tenderly stroked the hair off my forehead.

"We know," he went on, "how sweet it is that so much love should reside in our hearts for our little ones, for all the brothers and sisters of the Great Family of Man, whom one would so gladly—aye, so gladly—spare the pain that threatens them. But they will not ——"

"No, no, Frederick. My heart is not yet so comprehensive. I cannot love all the haters."

"You can, however, pity them?"

And so we talked on a long while in this strain. I still know it all so exactly, because at that time I often—along with the events of the war—entered also fragments of our conversation which bore upon them into the red volumes. On that day we talked again once more about the future; Paris would now capitulate, the war would be over, and then we could be happy with a safe conscience. Then we recapitulated all the guarantees of our happiness. During the eight years of our married life there had never been a harsh or unfriendly word between us—we had passed through so many sorrows and joys together—and so our love, our unity, was of such a solid kind, that no diminution of it was any longer to be feared. On the contrary, we should only be ever more intimately joined together, every new experience in common would at the same time result in a new tie. When we had become a pair of white-haired old folks, with what joy should we look back on the untroubled past, and what a softly glowing evening of

27

life would then lie before us ! This picture of the happy old
couple, into which we should then have turned, I had set
before myself so often and so livelily, that it became quite
clearly stamped on my mind, and even reproduced itself in
dreams, as if it had really happened, with various details—
Frederick in a velvet skull-cap, and with a pair of gardening
shears—I have no notion why, for he had never shown any
love for gardening, and there had yet been no talk of any
skull-cap—I with a very coquettishly arranged black lace
mantilla over my silvery hair, and as a surrounding for
all this a corner of the park warmly lighted by the setting
summer sun ; and friendly looks and words smilingly exchanged
the while. " Do you know now ——" " Do you recollect that
time when ——"

.   .   .   .

Many of the previous pages have I written with shuddering
and with self-compulsion. It was not without inward horror
that I could describe the scenes through which I passed in my
journey to Bohemia, and the cholera week at Grumitz. I have
done it in order to obey my sense of duty. Beloved lips once
gave me the solemn command: "In case I die before you,
you must take my task in hand and labour for the work of
Peace". If this binding injunction had not been laid on me,
I could never have so far prevailed over myself as to tear open
the agonised wounds of my reminiscences so unsparingly.

Now, however, I have come to an event, which I will relate,
but which I will not, nor can I describe.

No—I cannot, I cannot !

I have tried —ten half-written torn pages are lying on the
floor by the side of my writing-table—but a heart-pang seized
me ; my thoughts froze up, or got into wild entanglement in
my brain, and I had to throw the pen aside and weep, bitter
hot tears, with cries like a child.

Now a few hours afterwards I resume my pen. But as to
describing the particulars of the next event, as to relating

what I felt when it happened, I must give that up—the thing itself is sufficient.

Frederick—my own one—was, in consequence of a letter from Berlin that was found in his house, suspected of espionage—was surrounded by a mob of fanatics, crying: "*A mort—à mort le Prussien*"—dragged before a tribunal of patriots, and on February 1, 1871, shot by order of a court-martial.

CHAPTER XIX.

Serious mental illness, consequent on my husband's death.—This recurs occasionally.—Conclusion of my diary.—Additions to "The Protocol of Peace".—Progress of the Peace movement. —Mr. Hodgson Pratt's letter.—The Emperor Frederick's manifesto.—I write the last word of my autobiography.— My grandson's christening.—My daughter's engagement.— Rudolf's speech at the christening.—" Hail to the Future !" —Finis.

WHEN for the first time I came to myself again peace had been concluded and the Commune was over. I had been in bed for a month ill, nursed by my faithful Mrs. Anna, without any consciousness of being alive. And what the illness was I know not to the present day. The people about me called it considerately "typhus," but I believe that it was simply—madness.

So much I darkly recall, that the last interval had been filled with imaginations of crackling shots and blazing conflagrations; probably the events which were spoken of in my presence mingled in my phantasy with the truth, the battles, that is, between the Versaillese and the Communards, and the incendiary fires of the Petroleuses. That, when I recovered my reason and with it the knowledge of my deep misery, I did not do myself some harm, or the pang did not kill me, probably was due to my possession of my children. Through them I could, for them I was forced, to live. Even before my illness, on the very day when that terrible thing broke over me, Rudolf kept me alive. I was shrieking aloud, on my knees, while I repeated : " Die ! Die ! I must die !" Then two arms

(420)

embraced me, and a praying, painfully solemn, lovely boy's face
was looking at me—" Mother ! "

Up to that time I had never been called by my boy anything
but " Mamma ". His using at this moment, for the first time,
the word " Mother " said to me, in those two syllables : " You
are not alone ; you have a son who shares your pain, who loves
and honours you above all things, who has no one in this world
except you. Do not abandon your child, Mother ! "

I pressed the dear creature to my heart, and to show him
that I had understood him, I too faltered out : " My son, my
son ! "

At the same time I recollected my girl, *his* girl, and my
resolution to live was fixed. But the pain was too intolerable.
I fell into intellectual darkness ; and not at this time only. For
the space of years, at ever-increasing intervals, I remained
subject to recurring attacks of abstraction, of which afterwards
in the state of health absolutely no recollection remained to
me. Now for several years I have been free from them. Free,
that is, from the insensibility of my spirit pangs, but not from
conscious attacks of the bitterest pain of soul. Eighteen years
have gone since the 1st of February, 1871, but the deep
resentment and the deep mourning, which the tragedy of that
day awoke in me, no time can remove, even should I live a
hundred years. Even though in these later times the days
come ever more frequently in which I, absorbed in the events
of the present, do not think about the misery of the past, in
which I even sympathise so livelily with the joy of my children
as to feel myself also filled with something like joy in my life,
yet no night passes, *no, not one*, in which my wretchedness
does not seize on me. That is something quite peculiar, something I can hardly describe, and which only those will understand who have experienced something similar themselves. It
appears to me like a kind of double life of the soul. Although
the *single* consciousness in the waking condition can sometimes be so taken possession of by the things of the outer
world that it from time to time forgets, yet in the depths of my

personality there is a *second* consciousness still which always retains that awful recollection with the same true pain; and that self, when the other has gone to sleep, asserts itself, and rouses the other up, as it were, to share its pain with it. Every night, and it must be at the same hour, I wake with an indescribable feeling of pain. My heart contracts painfully, and I feel as if forced to weep bitter tears and utter sighs of agony. This lasts a few seconds, without my awakened self quite knowing why the other unhappy self is so unhappy. The next stage after this is a compassion embracing the whole world, and a sigh, full of the most painful pity: "Oh you poor, poor men!" And then I see next shrieking shapes which are being torn to pieces by a rain of murderous shot, and then I recollect that my dearest love too was so torn in pieces.

But in my dreams, wonderful to relate, I never knew anything of my loss. Thus it happened often that I was speaking to Frederick and conversing with him as during his life. Whole scenes from the past were represented, but never any sad ones, our meeting again after Schleswig-Holstein, our jokes over Sylvia's cradle, our walking tours in Switzerland, our hours of study over favourite books, and occasionally that same picture in the evening light, where my white-haired husband with his garden-shears was pruning the rose-branches, and was saying with a smile to me: "Are we not a happy old couple?"

I have never put off my mourning, not even at my son's wedding. When any one has loved, possessed, and lost such a husband, and lost him as I did, her love "must be stronger than death," her passion for vengeance can never cool. But whom does this anger threaten? On whom would I execute vengeance? The men who did the deed were not in fault. The only guilty party is the *spirit of war*, and it is on this that my work of persecution, all too weak as it is, must be exercised.

My son Rudolf agrees with my views, though this of course does not prevent him from going through his military exercises every year, and could not prevent him, either, from marching to

the frontier, if the European war, which is always hanging over
our heads, should break out. And then, perhaps, I shall have
once more to see how all that is dearest to me in the world has
to be sacrificed on the altar of Moloch, how a hearth blessed
with love, and which is the sign to my old age of all its rest and
peace, has to be laid in ruins. Shall I have to see all this once
more, and then once more to fall into irrecoverable madness,
or shall I yet behold the triumph of justice and humanity,
which now, at this very moment, is striving for accomplish-
ment in widely extended associations and in all strata of
society?

The red volumes, my diary, contain no further entries.
Under the date February 1, 1871, I marked a great cross, and
so closed the history of my life also. Only the so-called
Protocol, a blue volume which Frederick began along with me
and in which we described the phases of the idea of peace,
has been since that time enriched with a few notes.

In the first years which succeeded the Franco-German war, I
had few opportunities, even apart from my diseased condition
of mind, for marking any tidings of peace. The two most
influential nations on the Continent were revelling in thoughts
of war; the one proudly looking back on the victories she had
gained, the other longingly expecting her impending revenge.
The current of these feelings gradually began to subside. On
this side of the Rhine the statues of Germania were a little less
shouted over, and on that side those of Strasbourg decked with
fewer mourning-wreaths. Then, after ten years, the voice of
the servants of peace might again be heard. It was Bluntschli,
the great professor of international law, the same with whom
my lost one had put himself in communication, who set to
work to obtain the views of various dignitaries and Governments on the subject of national peace. And then the silent
"thinker-out of battles" let fall the well-known expression:
"Everlasting peace is a dream, and not a pretty dream
either".

"Oh, of course," I wrote at the time in my blue book, beside

Moltke's words, "if Luther had asked the Pope what he thought
of the revolt from Rome, the answer he would have received
would not have been very favourable to the Reformation."
To-day there is hardly any one left who has not dreamed
this dream, or who would not confess its beauty. And there
are watchers too; watchers conspicuous enough, who are
longing to awake mankind out of the long sleep of savagery,
and energetically and with a single eye to their object collecting
themselves for the purpose of planting the white flag. Their
battle-cry is, "War on War," their watchword, the only word
which can have power to deliver from ruin Europe armed against
herself is, "Lay down your arms". In all places, in England and
France, in Italy, in the northern countries, in Germany, in
Switzerland, in America, associations have been formed, whose
object is, through the compulsion of public opinion, through
the commanding pressure of the people's will, to move the
Governments to submit their differences in future to an
Arbitration Court, appointed by themselves, and so once for all
to enthrone justice in place of brute force. That this is no
dream, no "enthusiasm," is proved by the facts that the
questions of the Alabama, the Caroline Islands, and several
others have already been settled in this manner. And it is not
only people without power or position, like the poor blacksmith of a former time, who are now co-operating in this work of
peace; no, members of parliament, bishops, professors, senators,
ministers are inscribed on the lists. I know all this (which is
unknown to most people), because I have kept in communication with all those persons, with whom Frederick established
relations in the pursuit of his noble aim. What I found out,
by means of these persons, about the successes and the designs
of the peace societies has been duly entered in *The Protocol of
Peace.* The last of these entries is the following letter which
the president of the International Arbitration and Peace
Association, having its headquarters in London, wrote me in
answer to an inquiry bearing on this subject :—

"INTERNATIONAL ARBITRATION AND PEACE ASSOCIATION,
"LONDON, 41 OUTER TEMPLE, *July*, 1889.

"Madam,—You have honoured me by inquiring as to the
actual position of the great question to which you have devoted
your life. Here is my answer: At no time, perhaps, in the
history of the world has the cause of peace and good-will been
more hopeful. It seems that, at last, the long night of death
and destruction will pass away; and we who are on the moun-
tain-top of humanity think that we see the first streaks of the
dawn of the kingdom of Heaven upon earth. It may seem
strange that we should say this at a moment when the world
has never seen so many armed men and such frightful engines
of destruction ready for their accursed work; but when things
are at their worst they begin to mend. Indeed, the very
ruin which these armies are bringing in their train produces
universal consternation; and soon the oppressed peoples must
rise and with one voice say to their rulers: 'Save us, and save
our children from the famine which awaits us, if these things
continue; save civilisation and all the triumphs which the
efforts of wise and great men have accomplished in its name;
save the world from a return to barbarism, rapine and terror!'

"'What indications,' do you ask, 'are there of such a dawn
of a better day?' Well, let me ask in reply, is not the recent
meeting at Paris of the representatives of one hundred
societies for the declaration of international concord, for the
substitution of a state of law and justice for that of force and
wrong, an event unparalleled in history? Have we not seen
men of many nations assembled on this occasion and
elaborating, with enthusiasm and unanimity, practical schemes
for this great end? Have we not seen, for the first time in
history, a Congress of Representatives of the parliaments of
free nations declaring in favour of treaties being signed by all
civilised states, whereby they shall bind themselves to defer
their differences to the arbitrament of equity, pronounced by an
authorised tribunal instead of a resort to wholesale murder?

" Moreover, these representatives have pledged themselves to meet every year in some city of Europe, in order to consider every case of misunderstanding or conflict, and to exercise their influence upon Governments in the cause of just and pacific settlements. Surely, the most hopeless pessimist must admit that these are signs of a future when war shall be regarded as the most foolish and most criminal blot upon man's record?

"Dear madam, accept the expression of my profound esteem.

" Yours truly,

" HODGSON PRATT."

There is also to be found in the blue book the manifesto of a prince, dated March, 1888, a manifesto from which at last, breaking with old usage, instead of a warlike a peaceful spirit shines forth. But the noble one, who left these words to his people, the dying one, who with the last effort of his strength grasped the sceptre which he would have swayed as if it had been a palm branch, remained helplessly chained to his bed of pain, and after a short interval all was over.

. . . .

" Mother, will you not put your mourning off for the day after to-morrow?"

Rudolf came into my room with these words to-day. For the christening of his first-born son is fixed for the day after to-morrow.

"No, my dear," I replied.

" But think ; at such a festival you surely will not be mournful. Why then keep the outer signs of mourning?"

" And you will not be superstitious, and fear that the black dress of the grandmother will bring bad luck to the child ?"

"Oh no; but it does not harmonise with the surrounding gaiety. Have you then sworn an oath?"

" No ; it is only a firm resolution. But a resolution linked to such a memory—you know my meaning—that it partakes of the inviolability of an oath."

My son bowed his head, and did not urge me further.

"I have interrupted you in what you were about—you were writing?"

"Yes—my autobiography. God be praised, it is at an end. That was the last chapter."

"But how can you bring your history to an end? For you are still alive, and will live many years yet—many happy years —amongst us, mother. Surely with the birth of my little Frederick, whom I will bring up to adore his grandmamma, a new chapter must be opening for you."

"You are a good child, dear Rudolf. I should be un-thankful if I did not take pride and joy in you; and just as much joy does my—and *his*—beautiful Sylvia give me. Oh yes! I am reserved for a blessed old age. A quiet evening! But still, the history of the day is over when the sun has set, is it not?"

He concurred with a silent look of compassion.

"Yes, the word 'Finis' at the end of my biography is correct. When I made the resolve to write it, I also deter-mined to break off at February 1, 1871. Only in the case of your being torn from me also by war, which might indeed so easily have happened; but by good luck you were not of age for service at the time of the Bosnian campaign—only in that case would I have been forced to prolong my book. Still, even as it is, it was pain enough to write it."

"And possibly, too, it may be painful to read it," remarked Rudolf, turning over the leaves of the MS.

"I hope so. If that pain should only awake in a few hearts an energetic hatred against the source of all the misery here described, I shall not have put myself to the torture in vain."

"Do you not fear one thing? Its purpose may be seen, and people so be put out of humour with it."

"That can only happen with a purpose which is perceived, but which the author has tried cunningly to conceal. Mine, however, lies exposed to the light—it is announced in plain words at the first glance on the title-page."

July, 1889. The christening came off yesterday. It was turned into a festival promising twofold happiness : for my daughter Sylvia, the godmother of her little nephew, and his godfather, whom we had long cherished secretly in our hearts—Count Anton Delnitzky—took this opportunity to announce their engagement.

And thus I am surrounded on all hands with happy relations, by means of my children. Rudolf, who has six years since come into possession of the Dotzky estate, and has been for four years married to Beatrix *née* Griesbach, who had been intended for him since childhood—the most lovely creature that can be imagined—sees now his most ardent wish fulfilled by the birth of an heir. In short, an enviable, brilliant destiny.

The christening guests assembled at a dinner in the summer-house. The glass doors were left open, and the air of the summer noon streamed in, laden with the scent of the roses.

Next me, in our circle, sat Countess Lori Griesbach, Beatrix's mother. She was now a widow. Her husband fell in the Bosnian expedition. She did not take her loss very deeply to heart. In no case would *she* wear continual mourning. On the contrary, this time she had put on garnet-red brocade, with brilliant jewels. She had remained just as superficial as she was in her youth. Questions of toilette, one or two fashionable French or English romances, and society chatter—that was always sufficient to fill her horizon. Even coquetting she had not entirely given up. She no longer had designs on young folks, but older personages endowed with high rank or high position were not safe from her appetite for conquest. At this time, as it seemed to me, Minister To-be-sure was her mark. The latter had, besides, changed his name—and so we called him now Minister T'other-side, from his new catch-word.

"I must make a confession to you," Lori said to me as I clinked my glass with hers to the health of the baby. "On this solemn occasion when we have been christening the grandson of each of us, I must unburden my conscience before you. I was quite seriously in love with your husband."

"*That* you have often confessed to me, dear Lori."

"But he always remained quite indifferent."

"That, too, I knew."

"Well, you had a husband true as steel, Martha. I could not say as much for mine. But none the less for that, I was very sorry about Griesbach. Well, he died a glorious death; that is one comfort. A widow's life is truly a tedious one; especially as one grows older. As long as there are treats, and people to pay court to you, widowhood is not devoid of . . . but now I assure you, one is quite melancholy all alone. With you the case is rather different. You live with your son; but I am not at all anxious to live with Beatrix. And she, too, is not anxious for it. The mother-in-law in the house does not do well; for after all one likes to be mistress at home. Servants certainly are a plague—that is very true—still one can at least give them their orders. You will hardly believe me, but I should not feel very much averse to marrying again. A marriage of reason, of course, and with some sedate ——"

"Minister, or something of that sort," I interposed smiling.

"Oh, you sly creature! You have seen through me again! But just look there! Do you not notice how Toni Delnitzky is talking to your Sylvia? It is really quite compromising."

"Don't trouble yourself. Godfather and godmother made it up between them on their way from church. Sylvia has confided it to me. To-morrow the young man will come to me to ask her hand."

"What do you say? Well, you *are* to be congratulated. The handsome Toni may no doubt have been a little gay from time to time; but they are all that—that cannot be otherwise —and when one thinks what a good match ——"

"My Sylvia has never thought of that. She loves him."

"Well, so much the better; that is a fine addition to a wedding."

" An addition ?   It is all in all."

One of the guests—an imperial and royal colonel on the
retired list—tapped his glass and : " Oh dear, a toast," most
of them probably thought, as they broke off their separate talk,
and, sighing, set themselves to listen to the speaker ; and it
was something to sigh for.   The unhappy man stuck in his
speech three times, and his choice of a wish to offer to us was
not less unfortunate.   The infant was congratulated on being
born at a time when the country was about soon to employ the
services of her sons, and : " May he one day use his sword
gloriously, as his maternal great-grandfather and as his paternal
grandfather did ; and may he himself bring up many sons who
in their turn may do honour to their father and their ancestors,
and like so many of those who have fallen—their ancestors—
ancestors—for the honour of the land of their ancestors—their
ancestors and the ancestors of their ancestors—conquer or ——
In a word, the health of Frederick Dotzky !"

The glasses clinked, but the speech had not warmed us.
That this being, only just come into life, should already be
entered on the death-roll of future battles did not make a
pleasant impression on us.

To drive away this painful picture, one of those present felt
prompted to hazard the comforting remark that present
conjunctures guaranteed a long peace — that the triple
alliance ——

On this the general conversation was luckily brought back
to the domain of politics, and Minister T'other-side took the
word.

" In reality " (Lori Griesbach was hanging on his words), " it
is clear that the defensive power which we have attained is
something tremendous, and must deter all peace-breakers.   The
law of the Landsturm, which binds all citizens fit for service
from nineteen to forty-two years of age, and those who have been
officers even up to sixty years, to military service, enables us at
the first summons to put 4,800,000 soldiers in the field at once.
On the other side, it is not to be denied that the increased

demands which are contemplated by the war-ministry press heavily on the people, and that the measures necessitated by these demands, to secure the necessary readiness of the country for war, act in the opposite way on the regulation of the finances; but, on the other side, it is exhilarating to see with what joyful, self-sacrificing patriotism the representatives of the people always and in all places vote the increased burdens which the ministry of war demands. They recognise the necessity admitted by all enlightened politicians, and conditioned by the increase in the defensive forces of the neighbouring states, and by the political situation, for subordinating all other considerations to the iron compulsion of military development."

" A live leading article," said some one half aloud.

"T'other-side," however, went on :—

" And all the more, because it is in this way that a security will undoubtedly be taken for the maintenance of peace. For while we, in obedience to traditional patriotism, emulate the :teady increase of the defensive power of our neighbours, in order to secure our own borders, we are fulfilling an exalted duty, and are in hopes to banish also far away all the dangers which may threaten us from any side ; and therefore I raise my glass in honour of that principle which, as I know, is so dear to the heart of our friend, the Baroness Martha—a principle which the signatories of the League of Peace of Central Europe also prize highly—and I ask you to join with me in drinking : ' Long live peace I and may its blessings be right long preserved to us I ' "

" I will not drink to that," I said. " An armed peace is *no* benefit ; and war ought to be avoided, not for a long time, but for *ever*. If one were making a sea voyage, the assurance would not suffice that it would be ' right long ' before the ship struck on a rock. The honourable captain should aim at *this*—that the *whole* voyage shall be got over prosperously."

Dr. Bresser, who was still our best home friend, came to my aid.

"In reality, your excellence, can you trust to the honest and sincere desire for peace of men who are soldiers from passionate enthusiasm? who will not hear of anything which endangers war—*viz.*, disarmaments, leagues of states, arbitration courts? And could the delight in arsenals and fortresses and manœuvres and so forth persist, if these things were looked on merely as what they are held out as being—mere scarecrows? So that the whole money expended on their erection is spent only in order that they may never be used? The peoples are to be obliged to give up all their money to make fortifications on their frontiers with a view of kissing hands to each other across those frontiers? The army is thus to be brought down to the level of a mere *gendarmerie* for the maintenance of peace, and 'the most exalted War-lord' is to preside merely over a crowd of perpetual shunners of war? No; behind this mask, the *si vis pacem* mask, glances of understanding wink at each other, and the deputies who vote every war-budget wink at the same time."

"The representatives of the people?" broke in the Minister. "Surely the spirit of sacrifice is worthy of nothing but praise, which in threatening seasons they never fail to show, and which finds cheering expression in the unanimous acceptance of the appropriate laws."

"Forgive me, your excellence. I should like to call out to those unanimous voters, one after the other, 'Your "Yes" will rob that mother of her only child. Yours will put that poor fellow's eyes out. Yours will set fire to a collection of books which cannot be replaced. Yours will dash out the brains of a poet who would have been the glory of your country. But you have all voted "yes" to this, just in order not to appear cowards, as if the only thing one had to fear in giving assent was what regards *oneself*. Is then human egotism so great that this is the only motive which can be suggested for opposing war? Well, I grant you egotism is great: for each one of you prefers to hound on a hundred thousand men to destruction rather than that you should expose your dear self

even to the suspicion of having ever experienced one single
paroxysm of fear.' "

" I hope, my good doctor," said the colonel dryly, " that
you may never become a deputy ; the whole house would hiss
you down."

" Well, to expose myself to the risk of that would suffice for
a proof that I am not a coward. It is swimming *against* the
stream which requires the strength of steel."

" But suppose the moment of danger should come, and we
should be found unprepared ?"

" Let such a condition of justice be instituted as would
make the occurrence of 'the moment of danger' an impossibility. For what such a moment might be, colonel, no one
can at present form any clear conception. With the dreadful-
ness of the science of warlike implements which we have already
attained, and which is constantly advancing, with the enormous
proportions of the powers engaged in the contest, the next war
will in reality be no mere 'moment of danger'. But there is really
no word for it. A time of gigantic misery—aid and nursing
out of the question—sanitary reforms and the arrangements for
provisioning will appear as mere irony in face of the demands
upon them. The next war, about which people talk so glibly
and so indifferently, will not be a gain for one side and loss
for the other, but *ruin* for *all*. Who amongst us here votes
for this ' moment of danger ' ? "

" Not I, to be sure," said the Minister, " and not you either,
dear doctor ; but men in general, and not our Government—
I will be surety for them--but the other states."

" What right have you to think other men worse and
more unreasonable than you or I ? Now I will tell you
a little story :—

" Before the closed gate of a beautiful garden stood a crowd
of men, one thousand and one in number, looking in very
longingly. The gatekeeper had orders to let the people in, in
case the majority among them wished for admission. He
called one of them to him, 'Tell me—only speak honestly—
28

do you wish to come in?'   'Oh yes, to be sure I do; but the other thousand, I am certain, do not.' The careful gate-keeper wrote this answer in his notebook.   Then he called up a second.   He said the same.   Again the other entered in the 'Yes' column the number 1, and in the 'No' column the number 1000.   And so it went on up to the last man.   Then he added up the figures.   The result was—one thousand and one 'Yes'; over a million 'No'.   So the gate remained shut, for the 'Noes' had a crushing majority; and that proceeded from the fact that every one considered himself obliged to answer for the others too, instead of for himself only."

"To be sure," began the Minister thoughtfully; and again Lori Griesbach turned her eyes on him with admiration.   "To be sure, it would be a fine thing if a unanimous vote in favour of laying down one's arms could be brought about; but, on the other side, what Government would dare to make the beginning? To be sure, there is nothing so desirable as concord; but, on the other side, how can lasting concord be thought possible so long as human passions, separate interests, and so forth, still continue?"

"I beg your pardon," said my son Rudolf, now taking the word.   "Forty millions of inhabitants in a state form one whole.   Then why not several hundred millions? Can this be susceptible of logical and mathematical proof, that so long as human passions, separate interests, and so forth, still continue, it is indeed possible for forty millions of people to renounce the right to go to war with each other about them; nay, three states, like the present triple alliance, may ally themselves together, and form a 'League of Peace'; but five states cannot do it, and must not do it.   Truly, truly, our world of to-day gives itself out as wondrous wise, and laughs at the savages; and yet in many things we also cannot count up to five."

Some voices made themselves heard: "What?"   "Savages?" "That about us, with our over-refined culture?"   "At the end of the nineteenth century?"

Rudolf stood up.

"Yes; savages. I will not recall the word. And so long as we cling to the past we shall remain savages. But we are already standing at the gate of a new period. Glances are directed forwards. All are pressing on strongly towards another, a higher form. Savagery, with its idols and its weapons—there are many who are already edging away gradually from it. If even we may be nearer to barbarism than most people believe, we are also perhaps nearer to our ennoblement than most people hope. *The prince or statesman is perhaps already alive* who is to bring to perfection the exploit which will live in all future history as the most glorious and most enlightened of all exploits—that which will carry universal disarmament. We have placed our feet already on the threshold of an age in which manhood is to raise itself into humanity—to the nobility of humanity, as Frederick Tilling used to say. Mother, I drink this glass now to the memory of your unforgotten, loved, and trusted one, to whom I too owe everything, all I think and all I am ; and from that glass (and he threw it against the wall, where it shattered to pieces) shall no other drop ever be drunk again ; and to-day, at my new-born child's christening, shall no other toast be proposed than *this*—' Hail to the future !' To fulfil its tasks shall we clothe ourselves in steel ? No. Shall we endeavour to show ourselves worthy of our fathers' fathers, as the old phrase goes ? No. But of our grandsons' grandsons. Mother," said he, breaking off, " you are weeping. What is the matter with you ? What do you see there ?"

My gaze had been directed to the open glass door. The rays of the setting sun had thrown a halo of tremulous gold round a rose-bush, and from this, rising up in life-like clearness, was my dream-picture. I saw the garden-shears glitter, the white hair shine. He smiled at me as he said, " Are we not a happy old couple ?"

Ah, woe is me !

FINIS.

www.ingramcontent.com/pod-product-compliance
Lightning Source LLC
Chambersburg PA
CBHW030944110726
47900CB00004B/1119